AF823942

## Select praise for internationally bestselling author Rachel Reid

"Rachel Reid puts the biscuit in the basket. This is the sequel we've all been waiting for!"

**—Sarina Bowen, *USA TODAY* bestselling author of *Roommate***

"This is another success in a fabulous series . . . Reid's characters—including many familiar faces for series fans—are all charming and sexy, and she mixes humor, hockey, and positive messaging with aplomb."

**—*Publishers Weekly*, starred review**

"Sexy, hot, funny and sweet, *Heated Rivalry* is a game changer in sexy sports romance."

***—All About Romance on Heated Rivalry***

"It's enemies-to-lovers with loads (and loads, literally) of sizzling hot hate sex and hot hockey action and it's all tied up in a helluva sweet slow-burn love story."

***—Gay Book Reviews on Heated Rivalry***

**Also available from Rachel Reid**

*Time to Shine*
*The Shots You Take*

**The Game Changers Series**

*Game Changer*
*Heated Rivalry*
*Tough Guy*
*Common Goal*
*Role Model*
*The Long Game*
*Unrivaled*

# THE LONG GAME

RACHEL REID

HARLEQUIN

HARLEQUIN®

Recycling programs
for this product may
not exist in your area.

ISBN-13: 978-1-335-00413-0

The Long Game

First published in 2022. This edition published in 2026.



Illustration by Monika Roe (Loon).

Stock Images: © top dog/stock.adobe.com (Diamond); © FARBAI/stock.adobe.com (Sandwich); © drawing lines/stock.adobe.com (Soda can); © Digital Bazaar/stockadobe.com (Cocktail); © Menthol/stock.adobe.com (Quote bubble); © PURE VECTOR WORK/stock.adobe.com (Loon)



For questions and comments about the quality of this book, please contact us at CustomerService@Harlequin.com.



Harlequin Enterprises ULC
22 Adelaide St. West, 41st Floor
Toronto, Ontario M5H 4E3, Canada
www.Harlequin.com

HarperCollins Publishers
Macken House, 39/40 Mayor Street Upper,
Dublin 1, D01 C9W8, Ireland
www.HarperCollins.com

**Printed in the United Kingdom**

**26 27 27 28 29 CPI 10 9 8 7 6 5 4 3**

*The Long Game* includes mentions and descriptions of suicide and depression.

This book is for the Shane and Ilya fans.
Thanks for making this happen.

Dear Reader,

My only hope when *Game Changer* was first published in October 2018 was for at least one person to read my book and love my characters.

It was the very beginning of what would become an amazing adventure. With each book that was published in the Game Changers series, I received more love from readers. When the *Heated Rivalry* television series based on those books debuted in November 2025, my characters received more love than I could have ever thought possible. I am truly, enormously blessed and grateful for that love and for my readers.

I wrote these books as a lifelong hockey fan, and as someone who wants the culture of the sport I love to be better. The series is based on an idea: that the bravery of one person could create a ripple effect that benefits others and eventually leads to real change. Each book focuses on at least one hockey player, and the man who makes him braver. Stoic New York captain Scott Hunter is charmed by cute and clever history student Kip Grady. Weary Toronto defenseman Ryan Price reunites with bold and beautiful musician Fabian Salah. Distinguished New York goaltender Eric Bennett falls for witty young bartender Kyle Swift. Miserable Ottawa forward Troy Barrett learns how to smile with adorable social media manager Harris Drover. And, of course, despite their best efforts, Shane Hollander and Ilya Rozanov couldn't stop themselves from falling in love with each other.

I love each and every one of these characters, and as I write this letter in February 2026, it feels like the whole world loves them too. It's an incredible feeling, and I'm very aware that none of what I'm experiencing now would have happened without the enthusiastic support from the early fans of my books. The success of the Game Changers series was largely driven simply by readers recommending the books to their friends and online followers. It was driven by booksellers and librarians, by reviewers and bloggers, and by BookTokers and Bookstagrammers. I will always remember and appreciate that support.

Thank you for the love, and I hope you enjoy having these beautiful special editions on your shelves.

Love,
*Rachel*

# THE LONG GAME

# CHAPTER ONE

*July*

Shane had never wanted anything so badly in his life. His goal was right in front of him, and nothing would stop him from reaching it.

"You wish, Hollander," called a hoarse voice behind him.

Shane felt like his chest was going to explode, but he huffed and pushed himself harder, refusing to give up. The pounding of sneakers on the trail and of Shane's own heartbeat almost drowned out the laughter behind him. Shane tried to ignore it all as he focused on the trail exit just ahead.

Suddenly, Ilya was right beside him, drenched in sweat, T-shirt balled up in one fist. Ilya winked at him before speeding past him like a cartoon character. Shane grunted in frustration and tried to catch up, but Ilya's long legs and seemingly superhuman stamina were making it impossible.

Ilya reached the end of the trail first, arms raised in victory. Then he collapsed on a grassy patch at the edge of the small parking lot.

Shane stumbled over to him, gasping and swearing. He put

his hands on his knees as he waited for breathing to stop being painful.

"Fuck," he wheezed, "you."

Ilya flopped onto his back, shaking with laughter. He mopped at his forehead with the damp shirt he was holding. "I almost let you win."

"Liar."

"The view was not bad. From behind. Almost worth staying there."

Shane didn't know how his boyfriend was able to speak in full sentences. "Shut up."

"I like those little shorts."

Shane laughed, but it sounded more like a steam engine puffing. "Thanks."

Ilya pulled himself up to rest on his elbows. He closed his eyes and tilted his head back, rolling it gently from side to side. His hair was soaked, curls sticking to his face and neck, and his chest glistened with sweat. The crucifix he always wore around his neck was resting on his shoulder.

Shane dropped to his knees beside him. "I hate that you can outrun me like that. It doesn't make sense."

Ilya opened one eye. "Maybe you should eat carbs."

"I eat *healthy* carbs."

"You eat nothing."

"You *smoke*."

"Almost never."

"You had a cigarette *last night*."

"How do you know?"

"I have a nose."

Ilya booped the tip of Shane's nose. "A cute one."

Shane tried to glare at him, but he couldn't keep it up. Not when Ilya was smiling at him like that. Instead, he gently adjusted Ilya's crucifix, moving it to rest in the middle of his chest.

"So you like the shorts, huh?" They were a shorter style than the basketball ones he usually wore to work out in. Something new Shane was trying. His hair was longer than it had ever been too. He'd grown it out during the playoffs, and Ilya had protested when Shane had suggested it was time to get it cut. He'd let Shane shave his terrible, patchy excuse for a playoff beard, though.

Ilya traced the hem of one leg of the shorts where it was pulled tight against Shane's thigh. "I think your dick would rip right through these if you got hard."

Oh wow. Yikes. Shane glanced around. They were the only ones in the parking lot, which was secluded by thick trees on all sides, but they were still in public. "Let's not test that here."

Without warning, Ilya grabbed him and rolled them both until Shane was on his back, Ilya stretched out on top of him, grinning down at him.

Shane shoved at his sweaty chest. "You're disgusting."

"We are both disgusting." Ilya dipped his head and kissed him, quickly.

"Enough," Shane said, though he didn't sound like he meant it. "We should go home. Shower."

"Fine." Ilya sprang off of him, then offered a hand to help Shane up.

"You're just full of energy," Shane grumbled, taking his hand and allowing himself to be hauled up.

"I can think of ways to use it up," Ilya said.

God, Shane wished. "We have that call with Farah soon." He started walking toward the car.

Ilya sighed heavily behind him. "Why do we need this call?"

"Because she's our agent and it's her job to, like, check in on us."

Ilya had signed with Shane's agent last year, after parting ways with the Russian agent he'd had since he'd been a teenager.

He'd wanted a Canadian agent, and Shane couldn't recommend Farah Jalali highly enough. On top of being a great agent, she'd been nothing but supportive when Shane had told her he was gay two years ago.

"We could tell her, maybe," Ilya said.

"Tell her what?"

"About us."

"What? Today? *Now?*" Despite the summer heat, and his blood still churned up from the run, Shane suddenly felt icy cold.

Ilya shrugged easily. "She probably knows already."

The panic alarm that lived inside Shane started blaring. "Why would she?"

"We are together at your cottage. You are gay. I am hot."

"It's a bit . . . soon. We should talk about it more. Figure out how to word it and—"

Ilya was gazing at him with a mixture of fondness and exasperation. "Is not complicated. And if she does not support us, then she should not be our agent."

Shane chewed his lip, considering the undeniable truth of that. "She'll support us."

"I know. So we tell her."

The shower they'd taken together had lasted longer than was strictly necessary. As a result, Shane was still struggling into his T-shirt when Farah's FaceTime request lit up his phone. Ilya was only wearing underwear.

"Should I answer?" Ilya asked, picking up Shane's phone from the dresser.

"No! Get dressed!" Shane snatched the phone and accepted Farah's request. Her face filled the screen, elegantly put together as always.

"Hi, guys," she said cheerfully. "Or, hi, Shane, anyway."

"Ilya's here. He's just . . ." Shane trailed off, momentarily distracted by Ilya's low-slung shorts and bare torso.

"Hi, Farah," Ilya called out.

Farah smiled, probably used to dealing with idiot hockey players by now. She was only about ten years older than Ilya and Shane, but seemed twice as mature as they'd ever be. "Hi, Ilya. Are you guys having a nice summer?"

"Great. Yeah," Shane said, probably a little too enthusiastically. He was nervous. And he'd just realized that they were doing this video call from his bedroom, which was probably a bit weird. He sat on the edge of his bed, holding the phone at eye level. "How's your summer going?"

"Busy."

Ilya joined Shane on the bed, still tugging his T-shirt into place. Farah glanced between them, probably noticing that they both had wet hair.

Fuck. This was ridiculous.

"Before we talk about . . . other stuff," Shane said. "We have something we want to tell you."

"I'm all ears."

Shane met Ilya's gaze. Ilya rested a hand on Shane's knee and squeezed.

"So," Shane said slowly, "you know that I'm gay."

"Of course. You told me."

"Yeah. So here's the thing . . ."

"I am bisexual," Ilya blurted out.

Farah's lips curved up. "I think I can see where this is going," she said calmly.

Well, now they knew how easy it would be for someone to put two and two together if they knew the truth about Ilya's sexuality.

"Yeah," Shane said. "I think you do."

"We are together," Ilya said, in case she didn't.

"Sorry," Shane said. "I know this is going to be complicated for you."

"Don't apologize. I love you guys, and I'm happy for you." She laughed. "Can't say I predicted this when I woke up this morning. May I ask how long you've been together?"

Shane and Ilya shared a smile, then Ilya said, "A long time. Years."

"So it isn't brand-new," Farah said, more to herself than to them, Shane suspected. "Not to ask a stupid question, but it's serious?"

"Very," Ilya said. Shane's heart flipped the way it always did when Ilya made it clear how much Shane meant to him.

"Do you want to tell people?" Farah asked.

"No," Shane said quickly, at the same time Ilya said, "Not yet."

"We just wanted you to know," Shane clarified. "Not many people do, but we thought you should."

Farah nodded. "I'm on your side. So whatever you need from me, you've got it. There's no precedent for NHL rivals being romantically involved, obviously, so we're in uncharted waters here. Whatever happens, it definitely won't be boring!"

"I wouldn't mind boring," Shane mumbled.

"Shane loves boring," Ilya said.

Farah laughed. "Well, good, because I have a whole list of boring stuff to go over with both of you."

They talked about endorsement opportunities, about the scheduled air date for a documentary ESPN had made about their rivalry, about Shane's impending free agency at the end of this upcoming season, about the charity hockey camps that started next week. None of it, as far as Shane was concerned, was boring.

"I'm looking forward to seeing the documentary," Farah said. "Their Scott Hunter doc was fantastic."

"Did not see it," Ilya said flatly.

"I guess they didn't quite capture the *real* story about you guys, though."

No. Ilya and Shane had both been very careful not to give *that* away. Not that they'd had a lot of direct involvement in the documentary. They'd sat for separate interviews, and had endured a bit of the film crew following them around for a couple of days last season—again, separately—but as far as Shane knew the doc was mostly going to consist of existing game footage and interviews with other people.

As soon as their call with Farah ended, Ilya pinned Shane on the mattress, holding his wrists and kissing him breathless.

"That went okay," Shane said between kisses.

"Was great. I told you."

Shane loved Ilya so much it physically hurt to contain it some days. He didn't want to be a gay icon, or deal with any of the attention they would get from the hockey world—both good and bad—if they ever disclosed their relationship, but he wished he could love Ilya openly without dealing with any of that.

Maybe one day. After they were both retired. Shane knew some retired NHL stars and they'd been able to easily fade into the background if they'd wanted to. Sometimes even if they didn't want to. Eventually, the world just stopped caring about them.

At the moment, Shane and Ilya were both in their prime at twenty-nine years old. Shane had just led his team to his third Stanley Cup victory, and while Ilya was the captain of a much worse team, he was still putting up big numbers in Ottawa. They were both superstars, and they both had a lot of hockey left in them. Shane had every intention of playing another decade at least, and he expected Ilya to do the same.

Which meant another decade of hiding, probably. But Shane

would do it. He would do anything for Ilya. He'd told him, once, that he was willing to play the long game when it came to their relationship and he'd meant it.

"Why are you getting sad?" Ilya asked.

Shane blinked at him. "Sorry. Nothing." He kissed him quickly. "I love you."

Ilya gave him one of his crooked, sexy smiles. "Of course. Why wouldn't you?"

# CHAPTER TWO

Ilya was dreaming of his mother.

He knew, somehow, that he was dreaming, but his stomach still twisted with dread as he slowly crossed the familiar lawn behind Shane's cottage to where he could see a pale arm hanging limply from the hammock. The same way it had hung from her bed once, when he'd been twelve years old.

Then, in the dream, her hand moved. Her wrist twisted, and her fingers danced, as if she was moving them to music. Ilya smiled, and walked faster.

"Mom," he said when he reached her, in English, for some reason. Irina Rozanova smiled at him from her hammock—the one that he and Shane had installed together last summer—looking young and beautiful and perfectly relaxed. She didn't speak, only smiled and took his hand.

"Shane is in the house," Ilya told her. "I want you to meet him."

Her smile grew wider, but she stayed silent. Ilya looked toward the house, where he could see his boyfriend's silhouette in the kitchen window. Ilya waved to him, and Shane moved away from the window. Good. He would be here soon, then.

Ilya gazed at his mother while he waited, knowing that this wouldn't last. He would wake up, she would disappear. But still he wanted her to meet Shane.

Shane was taking his fucking time. There was no sign of him when Ilya looked back at the house, and he began to panic.

Irina patted his hand. She was still smiling, but it looked pained. Her skin was tinged with gray.

"No," Ilya said. "Wait. He will be here."

An annoying bird started chirping loudly nearby, and Ilya gripped his mother's hand more tightly. "Just . . . wait. Don't go."

Everything dissolved. The bird turned into Ilya's alarm, and Ilya found himself in Shane's bed in Montreal.

He snarled at his phone as he turned off the alarm, then scrunched his eyes closed, trying to get the dream back.

It was gone.

He stretched out one hand, searching for Shane, but found his half of the bed empty. And cold.

Jesus, how long had Shane been awake?

It was the first day of that summer's charity hockey camps, so Ilya shouldn't be surprised Shane had gotten an early start. He supposed he should get out of bed and find him.

He rolled to his back and exhaled loudly, trying to release the vortex of feelings that the dreams always churned up inside him. The joy of seeing his mother again, the heartbreak of realizing it wasn't real, and the frustration of Shane not moving fast enough. Of not caring enough. It was this last emotion that Ilya needed to shake off most of all, because it was ridiculous. Shane cared. Shane cared enough that he'd suggested naming their charity after Ilya's mother.

He threw on a pair of sweatpants and headed to the kitchen. He found Shane sitting at the kitchen table, already wearing a camp-branded polo shirt, studying his laptop screen through his glasses.

"Good morning," Ilya said.

"Hey," Shane said without looking away from the screen. "Just going over the medical forms for the kids. There are so many different things. A couple of the kids are allergic to eggs."

"Then we won't throw eggs at them."

"It's serious! What if something goes wrong?"

"Nothing did last year."

"I know, but it still could."

Ilya crossed the room and stopped directly behind him. He put his hands on Shane's shoulders and squeezed gently. "It will probably happen, someone getting sick or hurt. But it will be okay. Is hockey. And kids."

He combed his fingers through the long strands at the back of Shane's head. Ilya liked it long; he'd liked the way it matched Shane's transformation when they were alone together by the lake, relaxed and even a bit silly.

Shane rubbed his eyes under his glasses. "I don't want this week to be a disaster."

"You are worrying too much."

"Easy for you to say," Shane grumbled. "*Your* mom hasn't been texting all week with stressful details about this damn camp."

Ilya's hands dropped to his sides. "No," he said quietly. "She has not."

It was early, and Shane had probably barely slept and was tied into even more knots than usual, so Ilya decided to let the insensitive comment go. He knew Shane hadn't meant anything by it. Just like he knew he couldn't be mad at him for never rushing outside to meet Ilya's mother in his recurring dreams.

Instead, Ilya made coffee, because it seemed Shane hadn't done that yet.

"Where is Yuna?" Ilya asked, suddenly realizing she wasn't in the kitchen. She was staying with them for the week of the camp. Shane's dad, David, was back home in Ottawa, working.

Shane huffed. "She left for the rink like forty minutes ago."

As Ilya had gotten to know Shane's parents better, he'd been surprised to learn that Shane—the most determined overachiever Ilya had ever met—was the slacker in the family. "And how many times has she texted you since?"

"Too many. There's a local news crew coming this afternoon, I guess. It's French, so I'll talk to them."

"Okay."

"I know it's annoying to have them come on the first day, but . . ."

"Is fine."

Shane turned in his chair to face Ilya. "Do you think we're ready?"

"I don't know," Ilya said mildly. "We only have eight pro hockey players coaching this thing. Do you think that is enough to teach some kids how to play hockey?"

"I'm just . . ." Whatever Shane was going to say dissolved into a frustrated sigh.

Ilya grabbed the back of Shane's chair and pulled him away from the table and his laptop. He crouched in front of him, resting his folded arms on Shane's knees. "You are just being you."

Ilya was excited about the camps—he'd enjoyed them last year—but he didn't like how quickly Shane had reverted to his usual, uptight self. These weeks could have been spent at the cottage, laughing together in the kitchen, dunking each other underwater in the lake, and enjoying unhurried, indulgent sex in a place where they were safe and alone. Ilya could be sitting on the dock there right now, his feet dangling in the cool water with Shane's head in his lap.

But these camps were important to both of them. They would raise money for organizations and initiatives that helped people who struggled with mental illness. People who struggled the way Ilya's mother had struggled.

The worry didn't leave Shane's eyes, but his voice was soft when he said, "What if someone figures us out?"

"We are good at protecting this thing," Ilya said. "We have been doing it for years. And we did it last year."

"Barely! Ryan Price fucking walked in on us kissing! What if that happens again?"

Ilya grinned. "Am I so impossible to resist?"

Shane lightly kicked Ilya's ankle. "As if. It's *you* I'm worried about."

"I will try to control myself."

Shane played with a curl of hair near Ilya's ear. "No kissing," he said sternly. "Not even behind closed doors, okay? Not until we get home."

"Yes, no problem. I barely even like you." Ilya's words were undermined by the way he was pressing his cheek into Shane's palm.

"I'm worried about Hayden too," Shane said.

"Kissing you?"

"No! Giving us away, I mean."

Ilya huffed. "Is possible. He is not smart."

Hayden Pike was Shane's teammate, and, for reasons Ilya still couldn't understand, was also one of the very few people on earth who knew the truth about Shane and Ilya's relationship. And he was one of the coaches at their camp, despite Ilya's protests that he wasn't coach material.

Shane tugged hard on the curl he'd been gently twisting. "He's my best friend."

"I thought I was your best friend."

"Hayden's my best friend that I don't kiss," Shane clarified.

"Too bad for Hayden." Ilya stood, stopping halfway to give

Shane a quick kiss, then went to the coffeemaker. He filled two mugs with black coffee, placed one on the table beside Shane's laptop, then began adding cream and sugar to his own mug. Shane was doing a strict performance diet thing, so any dairy products or sugar in the house were Ilya's.

"Thanks," Shane mumbled, about a minute after Ilya gave him his coffee. He was looking at his phone now.

"Yuna again?"

"Yeah."

"Should we go?"

"No. It's okay. Enjoy your coffee." Shane stood and turned to face Ilya. "How'd you sleep?"

"Fine," Ilya lied. "Better than you, probably."

"Probably." Shane removed his reading glasses, then raked his gaze over Ilya's body. "You're unfairly handsome in the mornings, you know that?"

Ilya grinned. "Tell me in Russian."

Shane's nose scrunched up in concentration. "Um . . . ty ochen' krasiv?"

Ilya's heart fluttered the way it always did when Shane attempted Russian. "Close enough."

"No. Tell me how I could have said it better," Shane insisted.

Instead, Ilya kissed him, slow and lazy with Shane's palms gliding over Ilya's bare chest.

"You need to get dressed," Shane murmured. "And eat something."

"I will get McDonald's breakfast on the way."

"Gross." Shane stepped back and retrieved his coffee from the table. "I'm serious about the no kissing today. And don't, like, be sexy."

"Impossible."

"You know what I mean. No innuendo."

"Innu-what? Is this a sex thing?"

"No flirting. No, y'know, trying to get me all turned on or whatever. Be professional."

Ilya stepped close to him. "I do not have to *try* to get you all turned on, moy lyubimyy."

Shane's lips parted and he shifted his stance, just slightly. Then he blinked and said, "That. Exactly that. Don't do anything like it today."

Ilya trailed a fingertip down Shane's cheek. "Why? Are you *all turned on*?"

"No. And as soon as I see you eating one of those disgusting breakfast sandwiches I'll never want to kiss you again."

Ilya laughed. "I'd better eat two, then. To be safe."

"Welcome to Camp Rozanov," Ilya announced.

"Boooo," said Wyatt Hayes, and the kids laughed.

"Is that not the name?" Ilya asked innocently. "I thought we had agreed."

Shane could only shake his head, pressing his lips tight together to suppress his grin.

"It's the Game Changers Hockey Camp!" one of the kids yelled out.

"Ugh. Bad. Camp Rozanov is better. I am Ilya, and this is my friend Shane."

"Hi," Shane said.

"Everyone knows that me and Shane like each other a lot and always get along," Ilya said. The kids laughed more. Some called out protests. "But in case we . . . *disagree* . . . we have brought more friends to help. For the goalies, your coaches will be Wyatt Hayes, who plays with me for your favorite team, the Ottawa Centaurs."

Some of the kids were brave enough to boo.

"We're all on the same team this week," Wyatt said, grinning. "Save the booing for the winter."

"And also, Leah Campbell, who has more medals and awards than anyone else here, I think."

"By two," Leah said cheerfully. "Not that anyone's counting."

Ilya tapped his stick on the ice as applause, and the kids and other coaches all did the same. "For defense players, the coaches will be Ryan Price, who is the very tall and handsome man over there . . ."

"Uh, hi," Ryan said quietly as he shuffled his skates.

". . . and J.J. Boiziau, the tall and sort of handsome man next to him."

"Watch it, Rozanov," J.J. said, and Shane knew he was only partly kidding. J.J., one of Shane's alternate captains and closest friends, had not been impressed when he'd first learned that Shane and Ilya were friends. He'd mostly gotten over it but, like Hayden, had never quite warmed to Ilya. Shane certainly wasn't ready to tell J.J. that he and Ilya were *more than friends*. Not yet.

Despite Ilya's teasing assessment, J.J. was undeniably handsome, though he and Ryan Price couldn't look or *be* more different from each other. Ryan was pale with nervous hazel eyes, red hair, and a beard that, at the moment, was more trimmed than when Shane had seen him in the past. He also suffered from anxiety, which was one of the reasons he had retired early at age thirty-one. J.J., at six-six, was nearly as tall as Ryan, and just as broad, but he had dark skin, short hair, a Quebecois accent with a bit of a Haitian Creole lilt from his parents, and all the confidence in the world.

The other major difference between them was that Ryan Price *did* know Shane and Ilya's secret. He'd walked in on them kissing last year at the end of the first day of camp. Shane still barely knew the guy because he was too embarrassed to even look Ryan in the eye. But Ryan was gay himself, and he wasn't much of a talker. He'd kept their secret, as far as Shane could tell.

"And for the forwards," Ilya continued after the kids had stopped scolding him. "We have me and Shane, and also Max Riley, who you know from Team Canada. And from being Leah's husband."

Shane was pleased by the enthusiastic stick tapping for Max. Ilya had suggested inviting him to be a coach, and Shane had quickly agreed. Max had been in the media spotlight quite a bit over the past couple of years after coming out as a trans man. He'd played with his wife for Team Canada for years, including in two Olympics but, since coming out, had been without a team. He was a vocal advocate for trans rights in sports, and Shane was glad both he and Leah were part of their staff. Not only because they were activists, but because they were both incredible hockey players.

"And also Hayden Pike," Ilya said quickly. "Okay! Let's get started."

Shane was, Ilya had to admit, a pretty terrible coach. But in an adorable way.

"Okay," Shane mumbled to a group of forty young hockey players. "So, you start at the goal line, and you receive a pass when you hit the blue line. I mean, there'll be a whistle and then you go. And the puck is coming from the next person in line. No. Wait. It's coming from the next person in line, but the opposite corner. Um . . . there's two groups. One in each corner, and, uh . . ."

Ilya felt like he'd somehow walked into one of Shane's nightmares. Like he was being forced to present a lecture on a topic he knew nothing about.

Likely also noticing the confusion and panic on the kids'

faces, J.J. took over. As he explained the fairly simple drill with his cheerful, booming voice, Shane retreated to stand next to Ilya.

"Very good job, Coach Shane," Ilya teased.

"I suck at this," Shane said.

"Yes, but the rest of us are good, so no problem."

It was true. Even Ryan Price, who was one of the shyest and most socially awkward people Ilya had ever met, was remarkably good with kids.

"I'm supposed to be in charge, though," Shane said unhappily.

"You're supposed to be in charge of your team too, but we all know J.J. is the real Montreal captain."

Shane nudged him in the ribs with the butt end of his stick. "I'm a great captain."

"I know, sweetheart."

Shane jabbed him again, harder this time. "Knock it off."

The drill began, and Ilya watched as the kids took passes and skated around pylons with the puck. Everyone seemed to understand what to do, so J.J. had done a good job. Ilya glanced at the far end of the rink, where Wyatt Hayes and Leah Campbell were working with six young goaltenders. Max was also assisting by taking careful shots on the goalies. There was a lot of laughter and whooping coming from that end of the ice.

"This is going well," Ilya said.

"You think so?"

"Yes. The kids are having fun. The coaches are good. And I think Number Twenty-Two has a crush on me." He nodded in the direction of a girl whose eyes went wide behind her mask, and she quickly looked away.

Shane scoffed. "Who *doesn't* have a crush on you?"

"Hayden." Ilya paused, as if deep in thought. "Unless . . ."

"Hold on a sec," Shane said. Then he skated toward a boy

who had just finished the drill. He bent at the waist to talk to the kid, then began showing him something to do with the angle of the boy's stick blade. Ilya felt a lot of things at once, both from the way Shane's track pants pulled tight against his thigh muscles, and from the warmth that bloomed in Ilya's chest whenever he watched Shane interact with children.

"Are you actually going to do some coaching, or are you just here to shoot heart eyes at Shane?"

Ilya blinked and turned his gaze away from his boyfriend to look way down at Hayden Pike. "Are you here for any reason at all?"

Hayden tapped the brim of his Montreal Voyageurs Stanley Cup Champions ball cap. "Here to represent the winning team, buddy."

Well. Ilya couldn't argue with that. His own team wasn't going to be winning cups anytime soon. He made a mental note to wear Shane's identical ball cap tomorrow, because it would make Hayden furious, and said, "You lead the next passing drill. You are good at passing."

Hayden's eyes narrowed, as if he was analyzing Ilya's words, searching for the insult. Finally, cautiously, he said, "I *am* good at passing. I lead Montreal in assists."

"I know. That is why I said it."

"Okay then."

"Okay."

Hayden studied him another moment, then nodded and skated away. Ilya hadn't realized how much fun it would be to confuse Hayden with compliments. He would have to do it more often.

Ilya couldn't help but notice that the reporter guy Shane was talking to was very . . . attractive. Ilya tried to keep his focus on the kids he was coaching, but his gaze kept drifting back to where Shane was standing just behind the glass in one corner. Even from here, Ilya could see the flirtatious smiles the man was giving Shane.

Or maybe they were just regular smiles and Ilya was being ridiculous.

"Mr. Rozanov?"

He dragged his attention away from his boyfriend and the handsome stranger and looked down at the girl in front of him.

"Ilya," he corrected her, warmly. "Is something wrong, Chloe?"

"No. I just, um . . ." She glanced down at her skates, which she was shuffling nervously.

Ilya crouched down. "Yes?"

"I keep missing backhand passes. Not just in the drill, but, like, all the time. Do you know what I'm doing wrong?"

Ilya smiled. "We will try some and see what the problem is."

He spent the next fifteen minutes sending passes to Chloe, and correcting her stick placement when she was receiving them. By the end of it, she was beaming with pride as she easily accepted a bunch of consecutive passes from him, and Ilya had barely glanced in Shane's direction.

As Chloe joined the group that J.J. had called to center ice, Ilya took a peek and saw the handsome man laughing with Shane about something. And then the fucker placed a hand on Shane's arm.

There was no *good* reason for Ilya to skate down the ice with one of the pucks and fire it at the glass behind Shane's head, but he did it anyway. He could hear Shane scream, and Ilya laughed when he whipped around, eyes flashing with fury.

"Asshole!" Shane yelled.

Ilya gestured with his stick toward the children on the ice and shook his head. "Language, Hollander."

Things were tense between them for the rest of the day. Ilya couldn't even apologize because Shane wouldn't talk to him. Not that he felt like apologizing; he just wanted Shane to stop being mad about it.

And Ilya wanted to stop feeling embarrassed about doing it. It had been immature and petty and unprofessional. He still didn't want to apologize, though.

They had a debriefing, of sorts, at the end of the day with Yuna in the room they all used as an office. Shane didn't even look at Ilya for the entire conversation. When Yuna left, Ilya braced himself for Shane's fury.

The storm started with Shane loudly shuffling papers for no reason. Then he crossed his arms, huffed, and stared at the wall opposite Ilya.

Ilya couldn't stand it. He'd rather Shane unleash whatever anger he had inside him so they could move on. Fortunately, he was an expert when it came to making Shane unleash his anger.

"What is the problem?" Ilya asked.

Shane spun to face him, eyes glinting. "The *problem* is that I'm trying to run a camp with a fucking *toddler*."

"Is this about the puck thing?" Ilya asked innocently.

"It's about *you* having to always make me look like an idiot!"

"Come on."

"Why'd you do it? Because Laurent's handsome?"

*"Laurent."* Ilya took a triumphant step toward him. "So you *are* attracted to him."

"What? No. I mean, yes. He's nice to look at but—"

"And he liked looking at you."

Shane paused at that, and his cheeks pinked in a way that Ilya normally loved. He was not so into it now. "As if," Shane said. "You weren't even there."

"I could tell."

Shane was only inches away from him now, his head tilted back so he could glare directly at Ilya despite their height difference. "You almost gave me a heart attack with that stupid puck, and why? Because you thought I was *flirting*?"

Ilya huffed. "You do not know how to flirt."

Shane's eyes narrowed dangerously. "Ilya."

Ilya looked away. "I was jealous, maybe."

"Keep going."

"I . . . It was stupid, okay? I am not proud."

When he turned his gaze back to Shane, he found him smiling at him, but not in a nice way. More in a victorious, smug way. "What did you really think was going to happen?"

Ilya shrugged. "Maybe you would think he was nice. Hot. Not a rival hockey player." He was terrified that one day Shane would realize he could be with someone who wasn't a dark secret. That it could be easy to love someone.

Shane exhaled loudly, his exasperation clear. "I have spent the *whole day* trying not to—" His eyes darted to the door, which was ajar, likely realizing how loudly he was talking. He dropped his voice to a near whisper. "Trying not to be obvious about how fucking in love with you I am."

"Shane—"

"No. Shut up. If you really don't get that I'm not going to leave you for the first cute guy who smiles at me, then I don't know what we're even doing, Ilya."

"I'm sorry," Ilya said, because suddenly he really was. "Was a weird day. I was maybe just . . ." He sighed. "I'm sorry."

Shane rested a hand on Ilya's chest. "I'm yours. You know that."

"I know." Ilya found himself leaning in for a kiss, completely forgetting where they were.

He remembered slightly too late.

"Oh god," said a voice from the doorway. "Not again."

Ryan Price was filling the doorway with his massive body, looking mortified.

"We weren't!" Shane said quickly. "We were just talking."

Ryan glanced between them, which wasn't hard to do because they were practically stuck together. "Okay."

Ilya took a step back, and very calmly said, "Can we help you with something?"

"The, uh, news guys are packing up and wanted to talk to you. I ran into them on my way out."

"Thanks." Shane sounded like he wanted to die. "We'll be right there."

Ryan nodded again. "Okay. Well. See you tomorrow." He darted away before either Shane or Ilya could respond.

"I like that guy," Ilya said.

"Me too. And I like that he can keep a secret."

"Yes. Maybe we can go out this week with him and his Fabian."

"What, like a double date?"

"Sure. Why not?" They'd had Hayden Pike and his wife, Jackie, over to Shane's house a few times. And they'd gone to the Pikes' house once, which had been fun because Ilya had been able to play with their four awesome kids and ignore Hayden. But they'd never hung out together with another queer couple. Not one that knew about their relationship. Ilya thought it might be . . . neat.

Shane's face scrunched up in an adorable way and Ilya knew he was trying to find a reason to protest, but in the end he smiled and said, "Wow. We could really do that, couldn't we?"

Ilya smiled back. "We could."

Shane blew out a breath. "Okay. I'm going to go talk to Laurent."

"Is he invited on our date too? Are we breaking your no threesomes rule?"

Shane was already walking out the door, flipping Ilya off with a hand behind his back.

"What's Shane's problem?" Yuna asked.

Ilya glanced at the kitchen table, where Shane was staring miserably into the middle distance, the lower part of his face covered by his folded hands.

"Looks normal to me," Ilya said dryly. He sprinkled some blueberries over the salad he'd made to go with the chicken Yuna had baked for dinner.

"Shane, what's wrong?" Yuna asked.

Shane exhaled slowly, lowered his hands, and said, "Nothing. Just, y'know, replaying the entire day in my head. I can't believe Ryan walked in on us again."

Yuna turned away from the chicken breasts she'd been checking. "Seriously, guys?"

"We weren't doing anything!" Shane clarified.

"Shane was about to," Ilya said.

"I was not."

"You were going to kiss me."

"*You* were going to kiss *me*."

"Okay. Enough," Yuna said. "It's not such a big deal, right? Ryan's gay, so he must be . . ." She rotated one hand in the air, searching for the right words. "Cool with it."

"He looked horrified," Shane said.

"Is fine," Ilya said easily. "He has known for a year and has not told anyone. Where is the goat cheese?"

"I know, but it's embarrassing. And unprofessional. And we've burdened the poor guy with a pretty huge secret," Shane said. "Leave the cheese off my salad, okay?"

"I *know*."

"I like Ryan," Yuna said. "He's a big sweetie."

"Yes," Ilya agreed. "We are going to ask about a double date with him and his boyfriend, maybe."

Yuna placed her hands on Ilya's shoulders and squeezed, once. "I love that idea."

Ilya bit his lip to contain his smile. He really liked Shane's family.

"You don't think you could tell the rest of the staff about your relationship?" Yuna asked, returning to the chicken. It was a question Ilya had been asking himself a lot. He focused on getting the goat cheese out of the fridge and let Shane answer.

"Not yet," Shane said. "Leah and Max would be safe, I think. But we don't know them that well, so I don't really see the point in telling them, y'know?"

"We could tell Wyatt, maybe," Ilya said.

"You think?" Shane asked. Then he shook his head. "I don't want your goalie to know. Too weird."

"Hayden knows," Yuna pointed out. "Why can't Ilya's teammate know?"

"Hayden is my best friend, and the only one of my teammates who knows. I'm sure as hell not telling J.J."

"Can I tell him?" Ilya asked.

"Don't even joke about that." Shane sighed. "I love J.J., and he's been really supportive of me being gay, but he's not ready to hear about us. Trust me."

"Well, neither was I," Yuna said. "But I got over it."

"J.J. isn't my mom."

"No," Yuna said. "Your *mom* is the one making dinner at the end of a long day while you sit on your butt and mope. Come help."

"*I'm* helping," Ilya couldn't resist pointing out.

"I know you are." Yuna patted his cheek. "That's why you're my favorite son."

Ilya grinned at Shane, who tried to look annoyed but mostly failed because his eyes had gone soft.

Later, they sat around the table and toasted their successful first day of camp with glasses of water. They ate their healthy, Shane-approved dinner and talked about hockey, and the charity, and decor ideas for Shane's house, and plans for the rest of the summer. It felt, as it always did to Ilya, wonderful and surreal at the same time. He'd never expected to have this domestic comfort in his life. Not with anyone. He'd never expected to be part of a family, and have parents again.

He would do absolutely everything to protect this, and he was constantly terrified that, when it came to it, he wouldn't be able to. Because the day *would* come.

Shane offered to clean up after dinner to make up for slacking off during the preparation. Yuna insisted on helping, which probably meant she wanted to talk to Shane, so Ilya headed outside to the back deck.

He leaned on the railing and stared up at the sky where the stars were barely visible from all of the city lights. Nothing like at Shane's cottage.

"I think you'd like what we did today." Ilya spoke quietly, in Russian, to the sky. "I hope you are proud."

He only ever spoke to one of his parents, though both were dead now. His mother's death had been sudden and devastating. His father had faded away gradually from Alzheimer's, and Ilya still hadn't sorted out his feelings about losing the man who'd never had a nice word to say to him. Or to Ilya's wonderful mother.

Ilya's friend Harris, back in Ottawa, swore there was a ghost living in his parents' house. A great-uncle or something. Ilya didn't think he believed in ghosts, but he clung to the idea that his mother's spirit was with him, somehow. He needed her to be.

"Hey," Shane said in a hushed voice behind him. "Mom's gone to bed."

Ilya turned to face him. He'd changed, when they'd gotten home, into sweat shorts and a Voyageurs T-shirt. His feet were bare and his shaggy hair was rumpled. Ilya immediately opened his arms and Shane practically fell into them, resting his forehead on Ilya's shoulder and exhaling loudly.

"I'm exhausted," Shane said. "Let's go to bed, okay?"

"Sure."

But Shane didn't move. He wrapped his strong arms around Ilya's waist and held him, breathing slowly against Ilya's neck. Ilya rocked them a bit, gently, from side to side, and enjoyed the quiet. He closed his eyes and focused on how good it felt to be with Shane, alone in the dark, and tried not to wish it could be the same in the light.

# CHAPTER THREE

Shane asked Ryan to help him get some gear out of storage at the rink the next morning. Ryan, understandably, looked uneasy about it.

"I haven't told anyone," Ryan blurted out as soon as they were alone in the equipment room.

"I know. I'm not worried about that," Shane assured him.

"Oh." Ryan's massive shoulders dropped away from his ears. "So what equipment do we need?"

"The mini-nets and some of those, um, things for, like, stickhandling practice. Y'know. The little . . . things?"

"Things," Ryan repeated slowly, glancing around like maybe the *things* would reveal themselves.

"Listen, um," Shane said.

Ryan's attention snapped back to Shane.

"Your boyfriend's in town with you, right? Fabian?"

"Yes," Ryan said suspiciously.

"Cool. We were thinking—I mean, Ilya and I were thinking—that you guys might like to go out tonight. Get some dinner, maybe? With us?"

Ryan's brow furrowed. "Like a double date?"

"Yeah, I guess. Sort of. Or, y'know. Yes." Shane exhaled and tried to pull himself together. "We've never been out with another couple. Like, a gay couple. As a couple."

"Um."

Shane felt like a dam had burst inside him, and he unleashed a tidal wave of excited babbling on poor Ryan. "No one knows about us, I mean, almost no one, so it would be cool to, like, not have to hide. Well, we'd still have to hide if we're at a restaurant or whatever. We wouldn't, like, be obvious about being . . . anyway, it would be nice to spend an evening with people who won't judge us. Unless you *are* judging us. Maybe you think what we're doing is fucked up, because I guess it *is* kind of fucked up, but—"

"Other people know?" Ryan interrupted.

"What?"

"I'm not the only one who knows. Other people know?"

"Yeah. Sure. A few people. My parents. Hayden and his wife. My teammates know I'm gay, but they don't know about Ilya. Except Hayden. But I just said that, so—"

Ryan closed his eyes and exhaled loudly. "Thank fuck. I thought I was the only one who knew or something."

"It's not just you. Sorry if we let you think that."

"It's okay. I should have figured." He sighed. "Fabian was talking about a pizza place he wanted to go to tonight. You guys could come too, I guess."

Shane's current diet meant he could eat basically nothing at a pizza restaurant, but he nodded enthusiastically. "Sounds great. Let's do it."

"Okay." Ryan turned to look at one of the piles of equipment along a wall. "So . . . can we get whatever we need and get out of here now?"

Shane realized that he'd basically trapped Ryan in a small space and unloaded a bunch of weirdness on him, which probably wasn't an ideal situation for someone with clinical anxiety. "Yes. Sorry. Shit, Ryan. I'm being super fucking weird. I'm just . . ."

"Nervous?" Ryan guessed.

"Yeah. But excited too." Shane laughed shakily. "I'm sort of glad you walked in on us last year."

Ryan's face told him that he was *not* glad that he'd walked in on them.

"And I'm really looking forward to meeting your boyfriend," Shane said. "I didn't get the chance to last year."

Ryan finally smiled at that. "He's nothing like me. No one can believe we're together."

"I know the feeling."

The pizza place turned out to be more of a bar that served pizza. A *gay bar* that served pizza.

Shane hesitated as they approached the entrance. Ilya noticed.

"Problem?" Ilya asked.

Shane attempted to school his features into the face of someone who was chill and up for whatever. "Nope." He walked confidently through the door.

He was on a date. With his boyfriend. In Montreal. No big deal.

His boyfriend who, incidentally, looked super fucking hot. Ilya was wearing a teal tank top with a faded floral print that showed off his muscular arms, as well as the loon tattoo near his left shoulder that Shane still couldn't believe Ilya had gotten. He'd surprised Shane with it a couple of months ago and had blamed being bored while Shane was in the playoffs, but Shane knew it wasn't something Ilya had gotten out of boredom. The tattoo meant something, to both of them. It represented their time together in the summers, at their home on the lake.

Ilya was also wearing loose-fitting gray shorts and black slip-on sneakers, and looked so relaxed and summery that

Shane was tempted to drive them both directly to the cottage and make love to him on the grassy shore.

"Over there," Ilya said, breaking Shane's fantasy. He was pointing to a table against a wall where Ryan Price was sitting beside a much smaller man.

When they reached the table, Ilya immediately took charge. "I like that shirt, Price. Purple is good on you."

"Oh. Uh. Thanks."

"And you are Fabian, yes?"

"The one and only."

Shane hadn't really put any effort into imagining Ryan's boyfriend, but he never would have pictured him looking like *this*. Fabian Salah was *pretty*. He had warm, golden skin and silky dark hair that was cut short on the sides, but long enough on top to fall into his dark eyes, which were decorated with makeup. He was wearing a black lace tank top that fit close to his slim torso, and had a heart-shaped diamond pendant hanging from his elegant neck.

He was, like, really blatantly not straight in a way that Shane wasn't used to. The kind of man who, when Shane had been younger and still figuring himself out, he would look at and think "I'm not gay because I'm not like *him*." It wasn't a good way to think about anything, but even as a gay man who was in love with another man who he had gay sex with, Shane couldn't help the knee-jerk reaction of uneasiness in Fabian's presence.

Which just proved that Shane needed to spend more time around other queer people. Particularly, queer people who didn't play hockey.

"I am Ilya. This is my . . . Shane."

Shane tried to ignore how cute that was because otherwise Fabian's first impression of him was going to involve a big, goofy grin. "Hi, Fabian," Shane said, shaking his hand as he sat in the chair opposite him. Fabian's fingernails were painted periwinkle blue. "Nice to meet you."

"Same." The single word did something funny to Shane's insides. Fabian radiated an effortless sensuality that was distracting, to say the least.

"I like your hair," Shane tried, because it was true. Fabian's hair was cool.

Fabian's lips curved into a smile that was warm and teasing at the same time, not unlike the way Ilya often smiled. "Thank you. I like your glasses."

"Oh. Thanks."

"He thinks they are a disguise," Ilya quipped. "Like Superman."

"Well!" Shane protested. "They can't hurt. Also, I can't read a menu without them. So shut up."

Ilya lightly tapped his sneaker against Shane's ankle under the table, which made Shane realize his leg had been bouncing nervously. He stilled, but Ilya kept his foot pressed against Shane's.

"Ryan has told me all about your camps and your charity," Fabian said. "It's wonderful. I play fundraisers for youth shelters and mental health initiatives in Toronto as often as I can."

"You're a musician, right?" Shane asked. "Sorry, I know almost nothing about music."

"He's amazing," Ryan said earnestly. "You should see him perform. He's playing a show on Friday night here in town if you—um. I mean."

"I can put you on the guest list," Fabian said easily. "Don't worry about it if you choose not to go."

"I already bought tickets," Ilya said. "For us both."

*The hell?* "You did? You didn't tell me."

"Surprise."

Shane wasn't sure how to feel about this. He and Ilya never

went anywhere together, and this particular outing seemed pretty far outside Shane's comfort zone.

"What kind of venue is the show at?" Shane asked as casually as he could. "Like, a club, or . . ."

"He wants to know if it is a gay club," Ilya said helpfully.

Shane stepped on Ilya's foot. *"No."*

"It's just a bar. Club. Whatever," Fabian said with a wave of his elegant hand. Then he leaned in and, with a mischievous grin, said, "But it will be gay by the time I'm done playing."

Ilya laughed loudly at that while Ryan huffed and shook his head, smiling at his boyfriend with a palpable amount of love in his eyes.

"Sounds fun," Shane said, mostly meaning it. He'd never been one for live music, but he was curious to see Fabian do his thing. And he was a bit charmed by the fact that Ilya had planned a surprise date, of sorts, for the two of them.

They made small talk about Montreal until their server came to take their drink order. The young man introduced himself as Leo, and then his eyes went wide as if he'd just recognized who was at his table. Shane braced himself for a selfie request, but Leo surprised him.

"Are you Fabian Salah?" he asked in a hushed voice.

Fabian only answered with a sly smile.

"Holy shit," Leo said. "I am such a huge fan." He pressed a hand briefly over his mouth, then removed it just as quickly. "Sorry. I'm going to your show on Friday. I booked the night off weeks ago."

"That's lovely," Fabian said. "Thank you. I'll try to make it worth it."

"Everything you do is incredible. I saw you play in Toronto once and I am just so . . . wow. Sorry. Okay, I'm cool. What can I get you to drink?"

Shane heard Ilya snicker beside him. Across the table, Ryan was beaming with pride.

"I'd love one of your mojitos," Fabian said. "I see other tables with them and I'm jealous."

"Of course," Leo said, smiling dopily as if Fabian had him in a trance.

"I will have this one," Ilya said, pointing to a card on the table advertising a local brewery's products. "The pilsner."

"Right! Yes," Leo said, snapping back to attention. "Good choice."

"I'll have the same," Ryan said quietly.

"Do you have unsweetened iced tea?" Shane asked. He saw the panic creep into Leo's face right away. "Never mind. I'll just have a sparkling water with lime. Or lemon. Whichever."

Leo gave Fabian one last nervous, giddy smile, then darted off to get their drinks. Ilya poked Ryan's forearm, which was resting on the table. "Leo is in love with your boyfriend."

Ryan smiled. "I'm used to that sort of thing happening. Still nice, though."

"Ryan gets plenty of attention too," Fabian said. "But we rarely get recognized by the same people."

"Very different fan bases," Ryan agreed.

"Except the queer hockey fans who think it's, like, the best that we're a couple."

"Oh yeah?" Shane asked, suddenly very interested in the conversation. "What do they say?"

"They're happy for me," Ryan said quietly.

"And jealous of me, I'm sure," Fabian said.

"As if," Ryan huffed.

"Do you ever get the other side of it?" Shane asked. "From hockey fans?"

"Maybe," Ryan said. "I stay offline and I don't play hockey anymore, so I guess I don't hear it if it's out there."

Well. Shane *did* play hockey still, and while he wasn't very active online, he'd been doing more with his Instagram account since he and Ilya had started the charity. And also he was, y'know, in a committed relationship with his archrival. That was a bit different from Ryan's situation.

Leo returned with their drinks. He gave Fabian his mojito first, which was packed with mint leaves and looked very refreshing.

"You're a lifesaver, darling," Fabian told him. "This is exactly what I need."

Leo smiled widely as he handed out the rest of the drinks. He placed a tall glass of sparkling water in front of Shane with both lime and lemon wedges decorating the rim. "Have you decided what you want to eat?"

Shane hadn't even looked at the menu. Fabian ordered a fancy-sounding pizza for him and Ryan to share, Ilya ordered a less fancy pizza to eat by himself, and Shane frantically read the menu's salad selection.

"Um."

"Look," Ilya said, pointing to something lower down the menu. Shane quickly read the description of the grilled salmon with sauteed vegetables and roasted potato and almost kissed him.

"I'll have the salmon with no sauce, and could I get the vegetables with no butter? If that's a problem, maybe a side garden salad instead of the vegetables?"

"Sure, uh. That shouldn't be a problem." Leo sounded uncertain as he wrote everything down. "If it's a salad, which dressing would you like?"

"Just a bit of olive oil and red wine vinegar, if it's not too much trouble. Or a lemon wedge."

"He is *very* fun to go to restaurants with," Ilya teased. Everyone laughed except Shane, who irritably bumped his knee against Ilya's.

"I'm on a strict performance diet," Shane explained defensively after Leo left. "It's normal for professional athletes and *recommended*." He aimed this last word at Ilya, who ate like a thirteen-year-old most of the time.

"Shane thinks he is getting old," Ilya said. "He fears death."

"That's not it at all! I fear not living up to the expectations of the Montreal Voyageurs organization and our fans."

"Would be easier to cheat death," Ilya said, "than to meet Montreal's hockey expectations."

He wasn't wrong.

"Do you both play for Montreal?" Fabian asked.

"No. Just me. Ilya plays for Ottawa."

"So it's not a super-long-distance relationship," Fabian observed.

Shane squirmed because this was the first time anyone at the table had directly acknowledged the fact that Ilya and Shane were a couple. "It's, um. It's not a huge distance, but—"

"Feels farther," Ilya said. "We are so busy, during the season. Not much time together."

"That must be hard. And this—" Fabian waved a hand between them "—is a secret, right?"

"A big one," Ryan said.

"That makes it harder," Fabian said sympathetically. He leaned in so he could lower his voice. "Why is it a secret? You wouldn't be the only gay hockey players. Or queer. Sorry, I shouldn't assume."

"I am bisexual," Ilya said, nodding. "Shane is super gay."

"I'm *regular* gay," Shane argued. "And, no, we aren't the only queer NHL players. But our situation is complicated."

"Because you're on different teams?"

"Mostly, yes. It's a little bigger than that, though."

"The league has built up this huge rivalry between them," Ryan explained. "Been going on since their rookie seasons."

"Before that, even," Shane said.

"Oh wow. That's kind of fascinating," Fabian said. "But everyone knows you're friends, obviously. You have this charity together. What difference does it make if you also kiss?"

Shane opened his mouth to explain the difference, but couldn't quite find the words. The way Fabian said it made the distinction sound so unimportant. It really *shouldn't* make a difference. But it did.

"It would make things very . . . hard for us," Ilya said. "Distracting."

"It would be a fucking shitshow," Shane agreed. "I think we'd both rather focus on hockey for now."

Fabian hummed, then said, "For now. How long have you been together?"

Shane and Ilya looked at each other, which made Shane blush for some reason.

"Not an easy question," Ilya said.

"Over ten years, though," Shane clarified, "depending on your definition of 'together.'"

"That's a long time to keep a secret," Fabian said thoughtfully. "Isn't that a distraction too? Having to hide?"

Shane wasn't sure how to answer that, and, judging by Ilya's expression, Ilya wasn't sure either.

"Sorry," Fabian said quickly. "I'm super nosy. It's none of my business."

"No, it's fine," Shane said. "It's just, you know, a lot to think about."

"Yes," Ilya agreed quietly.

Their food arrived and the conversation turned to the best pizza in various cities. Shane was dying for a slice of Ilya's greasy, sausage-covered dinner, but he dutifully ate his salmon and garden salad. He'd started this diet in February and he didn't care what Ilya said—Shane felt better. And he'd just won the Stanley Cup *and* the Conn Smythe Trophy. So there.

As he chewed his salmon, Shane thought about the questions Fabian had asked. He'd always imagined that the hockey world's reaction if he and Ilya were ever found out would be the biggest nightmare to deal with, but maybe the bigger challenge was hiding. Maybe keeping how he felt about Ilya a secret was more draining than facing the backlash.

It was possible he was on a bit of a high from the past two weeks together at the cottage, followed by a successful start to their camp, and now being on their first ever double date. He may not be thinking clearly.

When they'd all finished eating, Ryan left to go to the bathroom. As soon as he was out of earshot, Fabian said, "I want to thank you both for inviting Ryan to be a part of these camps. It's meant so much to him. He absolutely loves working with kids and I think it's been healing for him."

"Healing?" Shane asked.

Fabian nodded. "He had a bad breakup with hockey, you know? I don't think he's ever regretted retiring, but he misses how hockey used to make him feel. Before it made him feel bad all the time."

"Oh." Shane couldn't imagine hockey ever making him feel bad, but Ryan had a very different career from his own. "Well, I'm glad if we helped him gain back some of that love for the game."

"You did." Fabian smiled. "And he's so proud, being a part of this initiative of yours. I think he's still a bit intimidated by the other coaches. He told me they're all superstars, and he feels out of place."

"Not all superstars," Ilya said. "Hayden is there."

Shane flicked Ilya's thigh. "We're happy to have Ryan as part of the team. We're glad he can do both weeks this year."

"He is a great coach," Ilya agreed. "The kids love him."

Fabian beamed, which made him look younger and less intimidatingly sexy. When Ryan returned to the table, Fabian smiled up at him with unguarded adoration in his eyes.

"What?" Ryan asked suspiciously.

"Nothing, darling. We were just talking about hockey."

Ryan scoffed. "If you say so."

Fabian stretched his neck and kissed him, quickly, on the mouth. Ryan grinned, then tried to hide his grin as he glanced sideways at Ilya and Shane. He didn't quite manage.

"Fabian really loves him, huh?" Shane asked, later, as Ilya was driving them back home over the Champlain Bridge to Brossard. They were in one of Ilya's "summer cars," a bright orange Porsche something-or-other.

"Yes. Too bad for you."

Shane turned in his seat to face him. "The hell is that supposed to mean?"

Ilya's lips quirked up, but he kept his gaze fixed on the road. "You were checking him out."

"I wasn't!"

"Okay."

"If I *was* it was only because, like, I'd never seen anyone who was so . . ."

"Beautiful?" Ilya suggested.

"No! Shut up."

"He *is* beautiful," Ilya said plainly. "And, like, sexy. You know what I mean."

"I guess," Shane said, as if he didn't know exactly what Ilya was talking about. "But if I was staring at him it was only because I couldn't figure out how he and Ryan are together."

"Ryan is not ugly."

"No," Shane agreed. "Especially now that his hair and beard are all trimmed up. But I spent so many years being terrified of the guy, it's still hard to see him as handsome, y'know?"

"He is a sweetheart. I am glad Fabian loves him."

"How did they even meet?"

"Ryan lived with Fabian's family when he played junior hockey."

"*What?* Fabian's parents billeted hockey players?"

"Yes. Big hockey family, I guess. Ryan told me he and Fabian, um . . . met again?"

"Reunited?"

"Yes. In Toronto when Ryan played there. Cute, right?"

It was really fucking cute. "Wow. So it was, like, destiny."

"Maybe."

Shane still couldn't get over how *different* Ryan and Fabian were. Ryan was so huge and shy, often hunched to make himself appear smaller. Fabian was possibly a full foot shorter than him, but made himself impossible to ignore with his beauty and the unapologetic way he decorated himself with makeup, feminine clothing, and sparkly jewelry. "I'll bet their sex life is wild."

Ilya grinned. "Pervert."

"As if you've never thought about it." Shane waited for Ilya to merge from the off-ramp before he asked, "Do you think we looked like that to them?"

"What, sexy? I probably did."

"No, like . . . in love?"

Ilya seemed to consider the question before answering. "We are very good at pretending to not be in love. Maybe we are bad at showing it when we are allowed."

Ilya's words felt like a lead vest. Shane slid down in his seat and stared out the window, frowning. Neither man said a word for the rest of the drive.

# CHAPTER FOUR

"I fucking love hockey," Max said with a big grin. He tossed his camp-issued bagged lunch on the coaches' table and slid energetically into the seat opposite Ilya.

"It shows," Ilya said, because Max had absolutely thrown himself into coaching this camp.

"I just—" Max glanced at the tables of kids all around them. "This is seriously the best. I've been mad at the game for a while, and I needed this."

"I get that," Ryan said quietly. "I mean, not for the same reason. Your situation is unfair and awful, but I kind of hated hockey until I, y'know, quit."

Unlike Ryan, Max always spoke loudly and confidently. He pointed a finger at Ryan and said, "The NHL did you dirty, Ryan. I never liked how you were treated, and I like it even less now that I've met you and know what a sweetheart you are."

Leah dropped into the seat next to her husband. "Are we talking about how much we love Ryan?"

"No," Ryan mumbled to his sandwich.

"We're talking about how fucked up hockey is. And how we love it anyway," Max said.

Leah smiled. "Yep. That's the problem right there."

Ilya glanced at the end of the table, where Shane was sitting. As Ilya had suspected, Shane looked confused and uncomfortable. Hockey had never made Shane sad for a minute of his life.

Ilya couldn't pretend to know how it felt to be let down by the game he loved—not in the way Max or Ryan had been—but he was more aware of hockey's flaws than Shane was. He'd been paying more attention, over the past few years, to the darker side of his sport.

"Hey," Max said to Ilya, "what do you think of your new coach?"

Ilya shrugged. "Haven't met him yet."

"Yeah, but it's a pretty interesting hire, right? I mean, how old is Brandon Wiebe these days? He must be in his thirties still."

"He's forty-one," Shane said, because of course he knew. Brandon Wiebe had been a forward in the NHL for eleven seasons, before he'd retired nearly a decade ago. He'd never been a star, and had earned himself a reputation as a "difficult" player to manage, though Ilya had never known why. Wiebe had still been playing when Ilya had started his own NHL career, but Ilya had never interacted with him.

"He's cute," Leah said. "Like, I watched him being interviewed on TSN. He's aged well."

Max placed a hand dramatically over his heart. "I can't believe you'd say that right in front of me."

Leah laughed. "Well, he *is*. Ryan will back me up on this, right, buddy?"

"Nope," Ryan said. "No comment."

"There is no way Wiebe is hot enough for Ryan," Ilya said. "Have you *seen* his boyfriend?"

"Uh, yeah," Max said. "Leah and I Googled him last night. What the heck, dude? He's, like, an actual angel or something."

Ryan crumpled his empty lunch bag in one giant hand. "You guys are weird." He stood to leave, but paused and said, with a small smile, "But yeah. My boyfriend is super hot."

Max slapped the table. "Love it. Be proud of your hot man, Ryan."

Ryan walked away, shaking his head but probably smiling.

"So besides being *cute*," Shane said in a somewhat clipped tone, "what makes Wiebe a good coach?"

"He played in the NHL," Ilya said. "Might make him good."

"No offense," J.J. called from his end of the table, "but Ottawa probably didn't have a lot of coaches to choose from, y'know?"

"Hey," Wyatt protested. "Just because we're bad, and in a city that no one wants to play in, and we have no fans . . ."

J.J. laughed loudly at that. "See? Your goalie gets it."

"Just wait," Ilya warned. "We are turning it around this year. You will see."

"Sure," J.J. said. "I believe in you. One hundred percent."

Ilya was going to say something snarky back, but at that moment Hayden rushed up to the table clutching his own bagged lunch. "Sorry if I missed anything," he said. "Had to deal with a family emergency."

"Did your wife have another baby?" Ilya asked dryly.

"Is everything okay?" Shane asked with far more concern.

Hayden waved a hand. "Yeah, yeah. No big deal. Just a missing stuffed alligator."

"Wow," Ilya said. "Did you call the police?"

Hayden sat across from him and glared at him. "I know you don't, like, care about other people, but Arthur fucking loses his shit without Chompy."

"Did you find it?" Leah asked.

"Uh. Yeah. In the back seat of my car. Here at the rink. So I had to, like, do a FaceTime call so Arthur could see him and, y'know. Talk to him."

Ilya grinned. "What does Chompy sound like?"

Hayden ignored him. "Anyway. Crisis averted. But I'll have to check my back seat before I leave from now on."

"You're a good dad," J.J. said.

Hayden sighed as he poked a straw into his juice box. "Sometimes. I barely know what I'm doing most days, but I love them and would do literally anything for them, so that's something, I guess."

Ilya glanced down at the remains of his own sandwich. He made fun of Hayden a lot—for a million different reasons—but he secretly admired his ability to parent four young children. He *was* a good dad, as far as Ilya could tell. His kids were great; his wife, Jackie, was awesome. Ilya probably envied him, but he would never admit it.

"I'm pumped for this afternoon," Max said. He pointed at Shane. "Our team is gonna destroy you guys."

Shane smiled. "We'll see, pal."

The kids were being divided into four mini-teams, each led by two of the coaches. Shane and J.J. had one team, Ilya and Max had another, Ryan and Wyatt had one, and Leah and Hayden had the last group. They would be playing half-rink scrimmages, and, while officially the coaches weren't supposed to play, they probably all would. Ilya was looking forward to it.

"Hey," Max said, leaning over the table and dropping his voice. "Do you think it's a good idea, putting Glencross and Tremblay on the same team?"

Jordan Glencross and Ben Tremblay had been clashing with each other all week. There always seemed to be two kids who had a history at these camps.

"Sure," Ilya said easily. "It will bring them together."

Max put his hands up. "All right. I'm just saying, those two kids are ready to choose violence."

"Will be fine."

It wasn't fine. Less than halfway through the game against Ryan and Wyatt's team, Jordan had Ben pinned on the ice, and was punching his facemask with his gloved hand.

"Seriously?" Ilya said.

Max reacted more quickly, and usefully, by calling out, "Hey!" and hauling Jordan off the other boy.

"He started it!" Jordan protested.

"You're such a lying little bitch," Ben spat back.

"Yo!" Max said. "We don't use that language *at all*." He glanced at Ilya. "Want me to take them to the locker room, maybe?"

"I'll do it," Ilya said. "Come on, ding-dongs."

He heard Max calling out instructions to the remaining kids as Ilya left the ice, shifting their attention from Jordan and Ben being disciplined. Ilya kept his body between the two boys as they walked to the closest locker room. Once they were inside, he made them sit on opposite sides of the room, facing each other.

"What is going on?" Ilya asked.

"He's mad because I made the A team and he didn't," Jordan said.

"No I'm not!" Ben protested. "I'm mad because your dad fixed it so you'd get my spot."

"He did not! You weren't good enough!"

"I'm way better than you."

Good god. What had Ilya gotten himself into? He knew he should assure the boys that nothing unfair had taken place and maybe talk to Ben about being a sore loser, but he was curious. "What does your dad do, Jordan?"

Ben snorted. Jordan mumbled something that Ilya didn't catch.

"Sorry?" Ilya asked.

"He's the coach."

Ilya laughed. He couldn't help it. With this new information, he started to suspect that Ben might have a valid argument.

Jordan stood. "I'm on the team because I *earned my spot*."

Ben snorted. "As if."

"Okay," Ilya said, calmly, "there is only one way to decide this."

Both boys looked at him with wide eyes, as if they'd forgotten the NHL superstar in the room.

Ilya somehow managed to keep a straight face when he said, very seriously, "Both of you balance on one foot. Whoever does it longer is the best hockey player."

"What?" said Ben.

"That's stupid," said Jordan.

Ilya folded his arms. "Three, two, one . . . go."

Both boys immediately stood straight up, and lifted one foot each. Jordan wobbled slightly at first, but they both remained balanced. After a few minutes of the boys glaring at each other from across the room, Ilya said, "Hmm. You are both good at this. Maybe try hopping."

It took even less time than Ilya had expected for the boys to start laughing. Ben broke first, and Jordan quickly followed, grinning broadly and snickering as they hopped.

Finally, Jordan stumbled and had to put his second foot down.

"Wow," Ilya said. "I thought a coach's son would be a better hockey player, but okay."

Shane entered the room when everyone was laughing. He looked confused. "I saw you guys leave the ice," he said. "Is everything okay?"

"Fine," Ilya said. "We are heading back now."

The boys left first, shoving each other, but in a playful way, not an aggressive way. They were both still laughing.

"What the hell?" Shane asked, when he and Ilya were alone.

"They are rivals," Ilya said, grinning. "Jordan made the A team. Ben did not."

Shane wrinkled his nose. "Then Ben needs to be a better loser."

"Ah, but listen. Jordan's dad is the coach. So maybe skill was not the only thing that helped Jordan."

Shane shrugged. "Anyway. We need to get back out there."

"Did everyone see the fight?"

"Probably. But we'll get everyone focused on the right thing. This isn't Camp Ben and Jordan."

"Not yet," Ilya said, nudging Shane. "But maybe they will be the new us, one day."

"Then I'd better warn Jordan not to fall for Ben."

"Oh, are you Jordan?"

"Obviously. He made the A team."

They smiled at each other, and Ilya leaned in a bit. He couldn't help it. They hadn't had sex all week because Shane didn't want his mom to hear, and Ilya was crawling out of his skin.

Shane dodged him. "No way. We're not making that mistake again."

"I like making mistakes with you."

"You can make mistakes on the ice. As usual."

"Damn, that was a fun week," Max said to Shane on Friday afternoon. "Thanks again for inviting us."

The Montreal camp was over, the kids were gone, and it had been, Shane was pretty sure, a success. "Of course. Thanks for coaching. You ready to do it again next week in Ottawa?"

"For sure. I had a blast. That surprise appearance by the Stanley Cup was great."

"That was all J.J., just in case he hasn't made that *extremely* clear." Shane was teasing, but he was touched that J.J. had used his day with the cup to share it with the camp kids. Shane was using his own day next week at the Ottawa camp, and he was grateful that the Montreal kids hadn't been left out.

Max laughed. "He mentioned it. Invited us to a party tonight too."

"You gonna go?"

"Sure. How often do you get invited to a Haitian street party with the Stanley Cup?"

"Every time J.J. wins one."

"Are you going to be there?"

"Um." Shane glanced to his left and saw Ilya approaching. "Maybe. I have other plans but I'm going to try to do both," he lied.

"Are you talking about J.J.'s party?" Ilya asked.

"Yeah. You wanna go?" Shane hoped not.

"And celebrate Montreal's cup win? Yuck. No."

Shane made a show of rolling his eyes, which made Max laugh.

"You guys are kind of adorable," Max said.

Ilya waggled his eyebrows at Shane. "Adorable."

Shane's cheeks heated. Had they been *too* adorable? Maybe they should tone it down.

He took what he hoped was a subtle step away from Ilya and said, "Have a good night, Max. We'll see you and Leah in Ottawa."

As if summoned by her name, Leah appeared at the end of the hallway with Ryan. When she reached her husband, she kissed him on the cheek and said, "Ready to roll, babe?"

"Yeah. Let's get a nap in so we can party all night, okay?"

Leah rested her forehead on Max's shoulder. "I am way too old to party all night."

"Until midnight, then."

"Deal."

They smiled at each other lovingly, and Shane felt a hot flash of jealousy, followed by the urge to kiss Ilya in front of everyone. Would anyone here even care? Ryan already knew . . .

"Your mom is looking for you," Ryan said. "She's in the office."

"Right," Shane said, shaking off the absurd ideas that had momentarily clouded his brain. He turned and walked quickly toward the office. He was surprised when Ilya caught up with him a few seconds later.

"Okay?" Ilya asked.

"Yep," Shane said tightly.

Ilya hummed softly, then, as soon as they were around a corner, grabbed his wrist and tugged him toward an open door. It was one of the locker rooms, dingy and kind of gross and a whole lot like the one they'd first made eyes at each other in, over a decade ago when they'd filmed a commercial together.

Ilya closed and locked the door, then pressed Shane against it.

"Oh," Shane said, and then Ilya was kissing him, hard and with purpose, as if this was a form of physical therapy.

"Better?" Ilya asked, when they finally pulled apart. Both men were breathing unsteadily. Shane's fingers were digging into Ilya's hip and his shoulder, and Ilya had one hand tangled up in Shane's hair.

"Yeah," Shane whispered. "Fuck, I want you so bad."

"It has been a long week," Ilya agreed.

"Mom's going back to Ottawa now. We'll have the house to ourselves."

Ilya kissed him again, this time in that filthy way that made Shane's toes curl.

Jesus, what were they doing? He broke the kiss and said, "Later. Not here."

"Okay." Ilya stepped back and began to smooth out Shane's camp polo.

"This room remind you of anything?" Shane asked as he traced a finger along Ilya's forearm.

Ilya's lips curved up. "When you were very unprofessional, making that commercial with me."

"*Me?* You were the one who propositioned me."

"After you pointed your boner at me."

Shane's mouth fell open. He closed it. Then opened it again. "You were showing off."

"Showing off?"

"Yeah. With all your naked muscles and ass . . . flexing."

Ilya laughed. "What?"

"You knew what you were doing."

Ilya kissed his forehead. "Maybe."

Shane rested his head on Ilya's shoulder, breathing him in and trying not to wonder how things would be different if Shane hadn't been unable to control his dick that day in the showers. Would Ilya be holding him now, more than a decade later, with a tattoo of a loon on his arm?

"I'm glad you're such a show-off," Shane said.

Ilya patted his back. "I am glad you get hard so easily."

"Shut up," Shane said, but smiled into Ilya's neck, relieved that they were both thinking the same thing.

# CHAPTER FIVE

"What am I even supposed to wear to this thing?" Shane called from his walk-in closet.

"Do you have a leather, um. What is it? Like, for a horse . . . ?"

"A harness. And shut up."

Ilya laughed quietly to himself. He honestly couldn't wait to see what kind of outfit Shane put together for Fabian's show.

"Just wear a jock," Ilya suggested. "And sunglasses."

Shane poked his head out of the closet. "What are you wearing?"

Ilya was in the process of tugging his tight-fitting pale pink T-shirt into place. It was a recent purchase, and he looked amazing in it.

"Jesus," Shane said.

"Nice, right?"

"They didn't have it in your size?"

Ilya grinned. Shane was full of shit, and the heat in his gaze was telling on him. "Wear something light. It will be hot in the club."

"Okay. Um." Shane disappeared back into the closet. He emerged a minute later in stylish black pants that tapered at the ankle and a light gray linen shirt that he'd left open at the collar.

"Good," Ilya said, which was a massive understatement. The shirt stretched tight across Shane's wide shoulders, and the cuffs of the short sleeves accentuated the bulge of his biceps.

"Yeah?" Shane asked.

"Mm." Ilya pulled Shane in for a kiss. "You look hot," he murmured against his lips. "I will be thinking all night of what I want to do to you later."

"Shit, let's at least get to the club before you start making me want to leave."

Ilya smiled and kissed him again. "You will love the show. I have heard Fabian is very good."

"Oh yeah? Who told you that?"

"Harris. You know, the—"

"The social media guy who I haven't met but you can't stop talking about? The adorable gay one? You did say he was adorable, right?"

Ilya laughed softly and dipped his head to kiss the hinge of Shane's jaw. "He invited me to Fabian's show in Ottawa last year. But I had to rest an injury."

"So you're being invited on dates with adorable gay guys, are you?" Shane was probably trying to sound angry, but his voice was a bit strained and he was tilting his head to give Ilya better access to his neck. "To sexy music shows?"

"Yes. All the time."

"Is Harris going to be there tonight? Am I going to be in your way?"

"I don't know. Do you want me to text him?"

Shane was remarkably skilled at glaring and smiling at the same time. "Come on. Let's get going."

Fabian's show was every bit as sexy and mesmerizing as Harris had described it, and every aspect of it felt dialed up, because Ilya had Shane standing next to him.

Not as close as Ilya would have liked, but still. Next to him.

Ideally Ilya would be behind Shane with his arms wrapped around him, holding him close against his chest. Ilya would rest his chin on Shane's head, and kiss his hair whenever he felt the urge.

Instead, Ilya was standing between Shane and Ryan Price, at the back of the crowded bar. Ryan had explained that he always watched from the back, because of his size. Ilya and Shane had decided to keep him company.

Onstage, Fabian was holding his audience captive. Despite the enormous number of people there, the room was almost silent except for his ethereal voice, and the music he was making alone using a keyboard, a laptop, an assortment of pedals, and his violin. He was wearing billowy white pants, sheer enough that the stage lights shone through them. He was bare chested, but wore several sparkling chains around his neck, and a few more around his narrow waist. Gold armbands snaked around his biceps, and even from the back of the room, Ilya could see he was wearing a lot of makeup. He looked magical and sensual. A prize for sure. Ilya couldn't be happier that Ryan was the one who'd won him.

"He is beautiful," Ilya told Ryan, when Fabian finished his song.

"I know," Ryan said, without taking his eyes off the stage. He was wearing a simple black T-shirt and black jeans, and was probably going to be mistaken for a bouncer a few times tonight. Though, Ilya supposed, Ryan basically *was* a bouncer because he would definitely be the first one to intervene if anyone did anything even slightly threatening to his boyfriend. Fabian couldn't have had a better protector.

"It must feel powerful," Ilya said. "Knowing everyone in the room wants your boyfriend."

The smile that curved Ryan's lips was the most sexually

charged expression Ilya had ever seen on the shy man's face. "It does."

Yeah, Ilya could see how going to these shows would be some heady fucking foreplay for Ryan.

He glanced at his own boyfriend, who was watching Fabian intently with his arms folded. He may not be onstage, looking like a glittering diamond, but he was achingly beautiful. The sharp line of his jaw and straight slope of his nose in profile were more fascinating to Ilya than anything else in the room.

He took a step closer to him, and brushed his arm against Shane's elbow. Shane moved away, arms falling to his sides, and said, "He's really good."

"I know."

"And, like, captivating. You can't look away from him, y'know?"

"Yes," Ilya said, without glancing away from Shane's face. He wanted so desperately to touch him.

Sometimes Ilya was so starved for touch he felt like screaming. He felt it most when Shane was close, like he was now, but off-limits. Ilya used to go to clubs like this one all the time, in just about every NHL city. He'd find someone he liked, make out with them, then go home with them. Sometimes he would skip the club and just text one of his regulars, depending on where he was.

He didn't *miss* that. Not really. He was devoted to Shane, wholeheartedly, and their sex life was beyond anything he had experienced with another person. But he missed being *touched.* He missed the endorphin rush he used to get from hooking up with people, and how relaxed he'd felt after. He missed meeting new people, talking to them, charming them.

Most of all, though, he missed the comfort he got from human touch. Right now, in this club in Montreal, he wanted that comfort from the man he was in love with.

He took another step toward Shane, closing the slim gap between them again. This time he trailed a fingertip down Shane's arm from his elbow to his wrist. Shane flinched, and stared at him with wide, questioning eyes.

"What?" he asked.

*Kiss me*, Ilya wanted to say. *Kiss me and hold me in front of all these people. Pull me onstage and do it. I don't care anymore. Please. I'm dying.*

"Nothing," Ilya said, and stepped away. "Nothing."

Shane was so turned on he felt like he would burst into flames.

The sensuality of Fabian's performance—his whole *deal*—combined with having Ilya so close had created electricity that coursed through Shane's body. He wished he could grab Ilya and pull him closer, kiss him against the back wall of the club until they were both panting. But he didn't mind waiting. The forbidden aspect of their relationship—the discipline it took to hide how hot they were for each other—still did it for Shane. It was sexy.

Here, in public, Shane didn't mind pretending that they were two bros, hanging out with their retired NHL player friend. He didn't mind keeping his hands to himself, because he knew as soon as they were alone they would thoroughly take each other apart and it would be perfect. Their reward for a job well done. Shane thrived on that sort of thing.

But, fuck, Ilya looked hot tonight. That tight pink T-shirt was just barely holding itself together, stretched tight across Ilya's muscular chest and shoulders. That fucking loon tattoo staring Shane in the face, practically a brand on Ilya's skin.

*Mine*, Shane thought. *The world doesn't need to know, because I know.*

He wondered if Ilya was as horny as he was at that moment.

He kept glancing at Shane sideways, so probably. Also, it had been nearly a week since they'd last been able to have sex, and if the drought was affecting Shane this much, it must actually be killing Ilya.

Shane remembered the last time they'd been in any kind of club together. It had been years ago, before they'd admitted their feelings for each other. Shane had been with Rose at the time, had been out with her and her friends that night, and Ilya had happened to be at the same Montreal nightclub with some of his teammates. Shane had abandoned Rose on the dance floor, drawn to Ilya like a moth to a flame, and had helplessly watched Ilya make out with a beautiful woman.

There'd been a brief, terrifying moment when his and Ilya's eyes had met. When Ilya had *discovered* him. Then Shane had fled, embarrassed that he'd been caught watching, and horrified by how jealous he'd felt.

He'd needed to pull over while driving home that night because he hadn't been able to see the road through his tears. He'd been so confused and scared and devastated. He should have been going home with Rose, his gorgeous movie star girlfriend, not crying on the side of the road, alone in his car, over an obnoxious Russian hockey player.

He'd been in love with him, though he'd refused to even consider it at the time.

Now, he felt the light brush of a fingertip at his elbow, and tensed as the finger trailed down to his wrist. Ilya shouldn't be touching him like this.

"What?" Shane asked, because there had to be a reason why Ilya would break their most important rule.

For the briefest moment, Ilya's eyes looked sad, and even a bit scared. Then he blinked, and schooled his expression into something more neutral.

"Nothing," Ilya said as he stepped away. "Nothing."

Ilya turned his gaze back to the stage, but Shane kept watching Ilya. His shoulders were slumped, and his jaw was tense. He looked . . . defeated.

Shane glanced around. The room was dark. It was crowded, but everyone's attention was locked on Fabian, and he and Ilya were at the very back anyway. Shane chewed his lip, and made a quick decision before he started overthinking things.

He took a sideways step so his hip brushed against Ilya's, then placed a hand on the small of his back. It wasn't much, but Ilya's whole body relaxed as he leaned back into the touch. He glanced down at Shane and gave him a small, grateful smile.

Shane smiled back, and traced a little heart on Ilya's back with his finger. Ilya raised one hand toward Shane, and it hovered in the air for a moment before Ilya pulled it back to rest over his own heart. He nodded at Shane, then turned his gaze back to the stage.

Shane kept his hand on Ilya's back for the rest of the show, removing it only briefly to applaud after each song. He felt like he was getting away with something, the way his palm pressed into the heat of Ilya's sweat-soaked back. The way each of Ilya's silent breaths felt loud against Shane's fingers.

The song Fabian was performing had sex-drenched, murmured lyrics and sudden, unexpected acapella breaks where he would sigh out lyrics that sent actual shivers through Shane. Everything felt and sounded and smelled like the promise of sex, and Shane was losing his mind a little. How was Ryan not rushing the stage right now? *Shane* almost wanted to, but not as much as he wanted to grab Ilya's sweaty T-shirt and pull him into him. Shane wasn't the kind of guy who would ever fuck someone in a public place, but this was the most he'd *thought about it*.

Maybe ending a week of celibacy with a concert by Ryan's sex sorcerer boyfriend hadn't been the best idea. Shane hoped no one noticed as he carefully adjusted his erection so it wouldn't be quite so obvious against the tight fabric of his pants.

Ilya, of course, noticed. His smile sent a fresh shiver through Shane, and he bit his bottom lip, gaze locked with Ilya's.

*Soon*, Ilya mouthed.

Shane was far too distracted to be driving right now. He was so horny he felt drunk.

He'd insisted on driving tonight, because he'd had enough of putting his life in Ilya's hands, but now he doubted his decision. His body pulsed with the need to press his skin against Ilya's. To taste him and take him apart and show him everything he'd been thinking while Ilya had been standing so close to him in that stupidly tight T-shirt, his skin hot and glistening with sweat.

Also, Ilya was massaging Shane's dick through his pants as he drove.

"D-don't," Shane said weakly. "It's not—*fuck*—not safe."

Ilya chuckled and removed his hand. Shane bit back a whimper from the loss. He took a slow breath, steadying himself, and focused on the road.

"You're so hard," Ilya observed.

"I'm also *driving*."

"*I'm* not."

Shane glanced over and saw that Ilya had cupped his own dick through his shorts.

"Don't do that either," Shane said, forcing himself to look away.

A soft moan floated over from the passenger seat. Ilya's eyes were closed, head tipped back, lips parted.

Fuck. Shane was ignoring the road again.

"Stop it," Shane said. "Seriously. We'll be home soon."

"Mm. Not the way you drive."

Shane's jaw tightened. "I'm not turning this into a game." He did his best to ignore how hot the idea of trying to get home before Ilya came was. "I'll get us home safe and then you can touch all the dicks you want."

Ilya laughed and held up both of his hands so Shane could see he'd obeyed him. "Fine."

Shane blew out a breath. "Almost home," he said, mostly to himself.

"How many dicks will be there? Did you invite some people?"

"You wish."

"I think you would like it," Ilya said. "Having an audience."

Shane wriggled against the leather seat. He really wouldn't like to be watched, but as a purely imaginary scenario, it fucking did something to him.

"Would you show me off?" Shane asked quietly.

He could feel the heat of Ilya's gaze even without looking. "I would never stop showing you off," Ilya said. "If I could."

"Fucking hell," Shane muttered.

They made it home, and even got through the door before they crashed into each other, kissing and grabbing, trying to get closer while they struggled to get each other's clothes off. Ilya won that race, getting Shane naked and pressed against a wall with his hands pinned over his head. Ilya kissed him forcefully while Shane arched toward him, aching for more.

"Want," Shane murmured mindlessly as Ilya kissed his neck.

"You will get it," Ilya said in a delicious, low rumble. He was still wearing his shorts, though they were unzipped and barely clinging to his hips. "Was fucking dying in that club."

"Me too."

"All fucking week I have been dying."

Shane's body rippled against Ilya's. "Show me."

Ilya nipped at Shane's jaw. "Tell me what to do."

It was a power move for Ilya because he knew how awkward Shane got when he had to ask for things in bed. He was absolutely aware of the battle raging in Shane's head right now, as Shane tried to ignore his embarrassment in favor of bossing Ilya around.

"Suck me," Shane tried.

"Like this?" Ilya sucked at the pulse point under Shane's jaw, making Shane squirm.

"Don't," Shane panted, "be an ass."

Ilya laughed, released Shane's wrists, then took a step back. He quickly removed his own shorts and underwear, then went to his knees. He ran his hands over Shane's waist, hips and thighs as he gazed up at him in a blatantly admiring way that made Shane preen.

"So beautiful," Ilya said. He leaned in and kissed the tip of Shane's cock before parting his lips to suck the head in.

Shane let out a long, low moan, his head bumping back against the wall behind him. "Fuck, Ilya."

Ilya took his time, tracing and teasing him with his tongue, lighting Shane up. Shane dropped a hand to the back of Ilya's head and threaded his fingers into his slightly damp curls.

"You're so fucking good at that," Shane said breathlessly. He rolled his hips, just slightly, hoping Ilya would take the hint.

Ilya grunted and slid his hands up the backs of Shane's thighs, up to his ass, where he dug his fingers into the muscles there, pulling Shane closer, deeper. His throat muscles flexed around the head of Shane's cock, and Shane's fingers tightened in Ilya's hair, pulling slightly.

"Holy shit," Shane gasped. He squeezed his eyes shut and forced himself to breathe as Ilya swallowed around him.

Ilya stayed like that for another couple of seconds, then

pulled back slowly, dragging his tongue along Shane's length, until he reached the end and let Shane fall out of his mouth.

"I could make you come right now," Ilya said.

"Don't," Shane said, almost meaning it.

"Bedroom?"

God, that seemed far away. Shane glanced at the stairs mournfully, but then nodded. "Yeah. Hurry."

They scrambled up the stairs, naked and laughing and holding hands. They probably looked ridiculous, but Shane didn't care. He shoved Ilya against the wall at the top of the stairs and kissed him.

"Fucking love you," Shane murmured against his lips. "Want you in me."

Ilya growled and slapped Shane's ass hard, once, the sharp sound reverberating in the empty hallway. "Come to bed, then."

Shane backed Ilya into the bedroom, kissing him and practically trying to climb him. Ilya sat on the end of the bed when he reached it, pulling Shane into his lap and kissing him fiercely until they both fell to the mattress in a squirming tangle of limbs.

Ilya laughed into Shane's mouth and kept kissing him. Shane wondered if Ilya was as dizzy with happiness as he was. Some times he still couldn't believe they were actually together. That Shane could have this.

Shane crawled on top of him. He spread his thighs wide, straddling Ilya's hips, still kissing. Ilya's strong hands glided up Shane's back to his shoulders, then back down to his ass.

Lube. They needed lube immediately.

Shane stretched across the bed and opened his nightstand drawer. He felt around for one of the bottles of lube they stored in there among their growing collection of sex toys and pulled it out.

Ilya took the bottle and got to work. Shane groaned with relief at the first brush of Ilya's slick finger against his opening.

"Hurry," Shane said.

"So impatient."

"Yeah, I'm fucking impatient. It's been a *week*." He knew, once the summer was over, he'd have to go far longer without sex. But those weeks wouldn't be full of being close enough to Ilya to smell him. Wouldn't be full of hearing Ilya's unguarded laughter when he was playing with kids, or of seeing the way Ilya's eyes smoldered sometimes when he looked at Shane. When Ilya thought no one would notice. When he couldn't help it.

Those weeks he wouldn't be sharing a bed with Ilya, listening to him breathe in the dark, and sometimes hearing him whimper. He wouldn't be able to press himself against Ilya and kiss the back of his neck and whisper that he loved him. When he thought Ilya wouldn't notice. When he couldn't help it.

Those would be different weeks. Right now, Shane needed everything he could get from Ilya.

Ilya took his time, opening him with careful fingers as he watched Shane's face. He reached his free hand up and caressed Shane's cheek.

"My beloved," Ilya murmured, in Russian. "So beautiful."

Shane let his eyes close for a moment, letting Ilya know he understood. Ilya couldn't hide behind his native tongue anymore when he wanted to be sweet and soft. It was something Shane had worked for; while Shane's teammates were playing poker or games on their phones on the plane, Shane was studying Russian.

"Enough," Shane said, also in Russian. "I'm ready."

Ilya hummed and continued his slow penetration with two fingers. "I like this," Ilya said, switching back to English. "Let me watch you a bit longer."

Shane huffed and clenched around Ilya's fingers. It wasn't

enough. In frustration, he wrapped his hand around his own rigid cock and stroked.

"Even better," Ilya said, smiling. "Here." He hovered the bottle over Shane's dick and drizzled some lube on him. Because Ilya was full of good ideas.

"Oh shit," Shane gasped. Ilya started stroking Shane's prostate in time with the glide of Shane's hand over his cock. Heat flared low in Shane's belly, burning up the last of his control. "Ilya. Please."

Ilya withdrew his fingers. A moment later, Shane felt the head of Ilya's cock tapping against his hole. "This?" Ilya asked.

Shane didn't answer. He just shifted his weight and sank down onto Ilya's slick cock. He went slowly because they didn't do it this way very often, and because he wanted to draw out Ilya's delicious groan.

"Shit, Hollander," Ilya rasped.

God, Shane loved it when Ilya used his last name, the way he'd used to, before. Back when they'd used to fuck but before they were . . . this.

Shane lifted a bit and sank back down, earning another groan. He grinned at the man he loved and said, "Hold on to something, Rozanov."

Ilya gripped Shane's hips, digging his fingers in hard while Shane rode him. It was exciting to watch Ilya like this, sprawled out beneath him, chest heaving as he struggled to keep his eyes open.

"Love your dick," Shane panted. He had one hand planted on Ilya's chest, the other gripping the back of Ilya's left thigh. "Love taking you like this."

"You just love," Ilya gritted out, "exercise."

Shane let out a shaky laugh, adjusted his angle, and rode him harder.

Ilya was falling apart beneath him, murmuring in Russian so garbled Shane couldn't translate it. He didn't need to. "You gonna come for me?"

Ilya sucked in a breath. "Too soon. Fuck."

Shane stopped his ruthless bouncing and switched to a slow grind.

"Ah," Ilya cried out. "Fucking . . . *fuck*!"

Shane smirked, loving the power he held. Loving how much he could make Ilya *feel.* Loving what he could reduce him to.

"Too slow?" Shane asked, his voice surprisingly steady considering how close to the edge he was himself.

"Yes," Ilya said. "No. Fuck, you are perfect."

"Yeah?" Shane rolled his hips, careful and controlled. "This all you need?"

Ilya huffed and reached for Shane's dick. He wrapped his fingers lightly around him and just held him for a moment, his gaze locked with Shane's.

"Is this enough?" Ilya asked as he gently grazed his hand over Shane's cock, barely touching.

Fuck, it almost *was* enough. Shane arched and clenched around Ilya's dick involuntarily as he tried to thrust into Ilya's hand.

Ilya laughed and pulled his hand away. Shane whined in protest.

Ilya placed his hand on the back of Shane's neck and pulled him down until Ilya's lips were against his ear. "I think," he said, in Russian, "you need to be fucked properly."

Shane gasped and nodded, and seconds later he was flat on his stomach, face pressing into a pillow. Ilya grabbed his thighs and hauled his ass into the air, then thrust inside.

"Is this what you need?" Ilya asked in a low, rough voice.

"Yes," Shane said breathlessly. "Hard."

"Stroke yourself."

It didn't take long after that. Not with Shane ruthlessly jerking himself while Ilya pounded into him, making the headboard slam against the wall with every thrust.

"Now," Shane panted. "Fuck, I'm coming." His whole body shuddered as he began to spurt over his hand and onto the sheets.

Behind him, Ilya only said, "Hollander," before he stilled and pulsed inside him.

Ilya didn't pull out immediately. He carefully lowered himself until he was almost resting his full weight on Shane's back, breathing hard against Shane's neck. For several long moments, they just breathed together.

Eventually, Ilya began peppering Shane's shoulders with gentle kisses, and his softened dick slipped out of Shane's body. He kissed down Shane's spine in an adoring way that made Shane sigh happily.

"Love you," Shane murmured into his pillow. He reached a hand back, clumsily searching, and Ilya took it in his own.

"I will be back," Ilya said. He squeezed Shane's hand, then released it and shuffled off the bed. Shane heard footsteps, and then the bathroom door closing.

He was dimly aware that he needed to get up himself and get cleaned. The bed sheets should be changed too. But Shane was so loose and sleepy that he wondered how important any of that was.

Ilya seemed to take longer than usual in the bathroom. Eventually, he returned and tapped Shane on the shoulder. "Your turn."

"Mmpf."

Ilya laughed quietly and rumpled Shane's hair. "Come on. You hate to be dirty."

Shane couldn't argue that. He dragged himself to the bathroom.

When he returned he noticed that Ilya had already changed the sheets and was sitting on one side of the bed, staring at the wall.

"You okay?" Shane asked.

"Yes," Ilya said. He sounded distracted.

Shane got into bed, enjoying the crisp slide of clean sheets against his skin. "I'm zonked."

Ilya hummed in agreement and got under the covers beside him. He curled against Shane, wrapping an arm around him and holding him close. Shane fell asleep in minutes.

He woke some time later, blinking at the darkness as he felt Ilya crawl back into bed beside him. He had no idea what time it was or how long Ilya had been gone, but he smelled the sharp aroma of cigarette smoke.

"You were smoking," he complained sleepily.

"No."

"I can smell it."

Ilya kissed his shoulder. "Maybe your house is on fire."

Shane huffed and fell back asleep.

# CHAPTER SIX

*October*

"How many men have you been with?"

Ilya glanced up with interest from the coffee mug he'd been spooning sugar into. Shane had blurted the question out and was now staring fixedly at his poached eggs. His ears were bright pink.

"This week, you mean?" Ilya asked calmly.

Shane turned his gaze up, his annoyance radiating across the breakfast table in grumpy waves. "No, asshole. I mean ever."

Ilya took a long sip of coffee, his eyes locked on Shane's over the rim of his Ottawa Centaurs mug. He very slowly lowered the mug back to the table, leaned back in his chair, and said, "Why?"

"Because you've never told me."

"Maybe I don't keep track."

Shane glared at him, then turned his attention back to his eggs. "Never mind."

Ilya's mouth quirked up. He let a silence hang between

them, just long enough for Shane to perhaps believe that Ilya was going to let this go.

He wasn't.

"How many are you hoping it will be?"

Shane shook his head. "Forget it. I don't care anymore."

"Bullshit."

It was clear from the tightness in Shane's jaw when he looked back up at Ilya that he cared a lot. "You said there was one guy in Moscow. The, um . . ."

"My coach's son. Yes. He was one."

"The first one?"

"I said he was. Yes."

"You never said that. I mean, it was implied, I guess, but—"

"He was the first." Ilya bit the inside of his cheek, then added, "Possibly the best too."

"You're such a giant dick."

"You know who had a giant dick?" Ilya asked wistfully.

Shane's chair screeched across the kitchen floor as he stood up. He snatched his plate off the table and stormed off toward the sink. Ilya continued eating his breakfast.

"Was I the second?" Shane asked, after he had finished rinsing his plate.

"Biggest dick?"

"Stop it."

Ilya made a show of picking up a point of toast, chewing thoughtfully as if he couldn't quite recall how many men he'd bedded before Shane. "Maybe."

Shane folded his arms. "I didn't think this would be such a difficult question to answer."

"Can you remember every goal you have ever scored?"

"Oh, is it a similar number?" Shane had scored over five hundred goals in the NHL alone.

"Give or take."

Shane left the kitchen.

Ilya gave him a one-minute head start, then sauntered off after him. He found him near the front door, already wearing his jacket. "Where are you going?"

"Home."

Ilya leaned back against the wall. "So soon?" Shane did have to drive back to Montreal that morning, but Ilya certainly wasn't going to let him go like this.

"I told you *my* number," Shane said.

As if Ilya had ever forgotten. "Yes. Two men besides me. Both terrible."

"Not *terrible*. Just not . . ."

Ilya waggled his eyebrows.

"I'm leaving." Shane put his hand on the doorknob. Ilya put his hand on Shane's shoulder.

"You were the second."

Shane didn't turn around. "And after me?"

"Is there a wrong answer to this question?"

Shane exhaled, his shoulders slumping. "No."

"A few. Not many. Was dangerous, right? A rare treat."

"Yuck."

Ilya let his hand slide off Shane's shoulder and down his chest. Shane took a small step backward, and almost relaxed against him. Ilya dipped his head and kissed Shane's neck, and Shane relaxed more. "None of them matter. Not anymore."

Shane sighed. "I know."

"Then why ask?"

Shane turned. Ilya kept his arm draped over him, his hand now resting on Shane's back. "I don't know." He thunked his forehead against Ilya's chest. "Sorry."

Ilya wrapped his other arm around him and held him close as he nuzzled Shane's dark, glossy hair. It smelled like expensive shampoo. "I will miss you."

Shane exhaled loudly. "Are you ready to do another season of this?"

Ilya's heart stuttered. What did that question mean? "Another season of what?"

Shane pulled back enough to look him in the eye. "Hiding."

It would be, altogether, their eleventh NHL season of hiding. Seven seasons of secret hookups, and three seasons of being in a mostly secret committed relationship. It had been a *lot* of hiding.

"Sure," Ilya said.

"I hate it."

"I know. Me too."

"I can't believe no one has figured it out yet."

"Well," Ilya said, brushing a thumb over Shane's cheek. "I am way out of your league."

"Right."

"Who would believe you if you told them?"

Shane punched his arm, then captured Ilya's lips in a sweet kiss. He tasted like coffee and home, and Ilya really wished he didn't need to leave.

"You should quit hockey," Ilya murmured. "Send them a text. Say you quit. Stay here with me."

"I'm not ending my career via text."

"Email, then."

"I have to go."

Another long kiss, this one a little less sweet. A little more urgent. By the time they broke apart, Shane was pressed against a wall, and Ilya's T-shirt was rucked up to his chest. Both men were breathing heavily, with flushed skin and semi-hard dicks.

"I have to—" Shane said again.

"Go. Yes."

"Three weeks and you'll be in Montreal, right?"

"Three weeks."

"Not so bad." Shane smiled sadly at him. Three weeks wasn't

such a long time, but Ilya was so goddamned tired of having their relationship sliced up into single nights with weeks between them. Two nights in a row if they were lucky.

Except the summers, when they were together almost every day, and Ilya's soul lightened as he soaked up Shane's proximity the same way his golden-brown hair lightened in the sun. Ilya loved hockey, but he lived for the summers now.

Summer was over. The NHL regular season officially started in two days. His soul would have to live on sun-drenched memories and the anticipation of stolen nights of explosive sex and tender kisses.

"I love you," Ilya said between the deep breaths he was taking in an attempt to cool his blood.

Shane slipped out from between Ilya and the wall and squeezed his arm. "Love you too." Shane exhaled, and Ilya politely ignored the tremor in it. "Okay. Three weeks."

"Three weeks. Text me when you get home."

"Of course." Shane kissed him one more time, and then he was gone.

# CHAPTER SEVEN

*Dynasty.*

That was the word going through Shane's head—the word that had been repeated again and again in Montreal lately—as he watched the Stanley Cup Champions banner rise to the rafters.

It was his third banner ceremony. His third Stanley Cup win. After so many years of barely making the playoffs, Montreal had a dynasty hockey team again. And there was no reason to be modest—it had started with him.

"Doesn't get boring, does it?" J.J. said.

They were standing together on the ice, the whole team gathered around the trophies they'd won last season, including the Stanley Cup. The crowd—a packed house, as always—was roaring with pride as the banner ascended.

"Nope," Shane said.

He *loved* being a Montreal Voyageur. He loved what he and his teammates had accomplished here, and he wanted to keep doing it for the rest of his career. He was an unrestricted free agent at the end of this season, but he fully expected to sign with Montreal again. He didn't even want to look at options. This was his team. These were his fans.

And those were his three fucking Stanley Cup banners.

Someday his number would hang from the rafters too. He had no doubt that it would be retired here. He'd earned that. Even if he quit right now, he'd done enough to earn that.

"You know what's even better than three Stanley Cups?" J.J. asked.

Shane smiled. "Four Stanley Cups."

"Fucking right. Let's get it."

"Let's get it," Shane agreed.

Home openers in Ottawa always felt a bit ridiculous.

Like all NHL teams, there was a lot of fanfare: videos projected on the ice, a whole light show, lots of dry ice and loud exciting music. Each player was announced individually as they stepped off a red carpet and onto the ice.

When Ilya had played for Boston, the energy in the building had crackled with pride and possibility. The team had been making a promise to the fans to do everything they could to win for them. The fans in Boston had expectations; they wanted champions.

Ottawa's home openers were more like a pre-emptive apology. There were no promises being made here tonight, just a lot of fancy lights to distract from the fact that the team was truly terrible and would almost certainly lose this game. And the next one.

Ilya hated it. The worst part was that it didn't even make sense to him. Ottawa had the elements of a great team, himself included. Their new coach, Brandon Wiebe, was untested and very young, but Ilya liked him already. Wyatt was a great goalie, and was regularly stopping forty shots or more to keep them from losing too badly. Ilya was still scoring plenty of goals, but it wasn't enough. He couldn't be a whole team.

As the captain, Ilya's name was called last. He stepped onto the ice, and the fans went wild. They truly did love him here in Ottawa. It was nice.

He took his place, completing the circle his teammates had made around the logo at center ice. The Centaurs logo was one of many baffling things about the team: a cartoon drawing of a centaur playing hockey. Ilya wasn't sure how exactly that would work. It was sort of the perfect representation of Ottawa's team, though: a bunch of things mashed together that had no hope of winning hockey games.

"These poor bastards," muttered Ilya's linemate, Zane Boodram, as he gazed at the crowd through the dry ice and the dim lighting.

"Maybe we will win," Ilya said.

"Sure. Maybe this will be the season we finally decorate the ceiling of this dump."

Ilya glanced up at the rafters, where exactly zero Stanley Cup Champions banners hung.

"Maybe."

"This was one fucking game," Coach Theriault said in his usual gruff, humorless tone. "We've got a long season ahead of us, so let's not start jerking each other off just yet."

There were murmurs of solemn agreement from the players in the locker room. Shane nodded along with them, agreeing with his coach but wishing he could have used less homophobic wording. After nearly thirty years of a life in hockey, though, Shane barely knew what counted as homophobic anymore.

It had been a good game. Montreal had dominated from the very first minute, and their goalie, Patrice Drapeau, had only let in one goal. Nearly perfect, really.

"Tomorrow," Coach said, "we're going to talk about the power play because it was a fucking mess tonight. Video meeting before practice. Nine a.m."

There were mutters of "Yes, coach." Shane honestly wasn't sure what the power play problem was, since they'd only had three power plays and had scored on one of them, but he supposed he'd find out. This team strove for perfection, always. It wasn't easy being a Voyageur, but at least the hard work and sacrifice paid off. Only one team in the league had raised a banner tonight.

He couldn't imagine being on a team like Ottawa. Ilya rarely complained about it, but Shane wouldn't be able to cope with the embarrassment of losing that often. It was a bit disappointing, if he was being honest, that Ilya didn't care more. He missed actually *competing* against Ilya. These days there wasn't much challenge.

"Coach didn't cheer up any over the summer, huh?" Hayden said to Shane after Theriault left the room.

"He's our coach, not our friend," Shane said, somewhat automatically.

Hayden nudged him. "*You* didn't cheer up any over the summer either."

Shane scoffed, which didn't make him sound any more cheerful.

Hayden laughed and threw an arm around Shane's shoulders. "Love you, pal. Wanna get lunch tomorrow after practice?"

Shane ducked out from under Hayden's sweaty arm. "I have my meals pre-planned for the week."

Hayden shot him a withering look. "Can I get takeout and eat at your house? I just want to hang out, you fucking doofus."

"Oh." Shit. Was Shane a terrible friend? Probably. "Sure. Of course."

"Yeah?" Hayden asked. "You sure you're not busy with . . . you know."

"Nope," Shane said quickly. "We won't see each other for a while."

Hayden didn't look too sad about that. "Do you think Ottawa won tonight?" He stood and grabbed his phone off the shelf. "Let's see."

God, Shane hoped so.

Ottawa lost, of course. But Luca Haas scored his first ever NHL goal in his first ever NHL game, so there was reason to celebrate.

"Not the result we were hoping for," Coach Wiebe said. His tone was almost apologetic, as if it was his fault they'd lost. As if this team hadn't been losing all the time for basically its entire existence. "But I saw a lot that I liked out there tonight. Wyatt, amazing game. Ilya, can I just say, it's a pleasure to watch you up close. Incredible. And where's Luca?"

Across the room from Ilya, Luca shyly raised his hand.

"The fucking future right here," Bood announced loudly, ruffling Luca's short, sweaty hair. He handed Luca the goal puck and everyone cheered.

Not for the first time, Ilya wondered why the hell Bood wasn't the team captain. He was basically the team's social director, head cheerleader, and he'd been a Centaur since his first NHL game six seasons ago.

Ilya was a shit captain these days. He barely went out with his teammates, and hadn't gotten to know any of the younger players. He felt like ripping the C right off his own jersey and handing it to Bood right now.

Ilya watched his teammates laughing and chirping each other as he began to remove his gear, feeling a million miles away. He used to be the center of this sort of thing, dancing in the middle of the room to make his teammates laugh. Now he only felt a bone-deep exhaustion that couldn't entirely be blamed on the game he'd just played.

The press entered the room, and Ilya managed a few basic

statements for them. Yes, the loss was disappointing, but he believed in this team and was confident they would turn it around this season.

Mostly the reporters wanted to talk to Luca, which was a relief. Once they'd left Ilya, he happily pulled his sweat-soaked shirt off and tossed it into one of the laundry hampers.

"Howdy," said a cheerful voice.

"Harris," Ilya said, acknowledging the team's social media manager. "You need a shirtless picture of me for Instagram?"

Harris laughed. "I mean, it would get a few likes, I'm not gonna lie."

Ilya did a couple of silly muscleman flex poses, showing off his biceps. Harris jokingly fanned himself. "Jesus, I need to sit down," Harris said, plunking himself in the stall next to Ilya's. "I'm about to swoon."

Ilya grinned at him. If anyone could improve his mood in a hurry, it was Harris. Everyone on the team loved Harris, which Ilya appreciated because Harris was openly gay. He wasn't sure Harris would have been as warmly accepted in Boston. He wouldn't have been invited to team outings, that was for sure.

"Everyone's going to Monk's after," Harris said. "You coming?"

"I don't know," he said. "Maybe."

Harris smiled in a way that let Ilya know that he knew he wouldn't be there. He stood and patted Ilya's shoulder, which was a bit of a reach for him. He was even shorter than Shane. "I'd better get out of here before you take your shorts off and I actually combust."

Ilya's lips quirked up. "Do you even work for this team, or do you just hang out in the locker room?"

Harris winked at him. "Don't tell anyone."

He crossed the room to talk to Wyatt, and Ilya removed the rest of his gear and headed for the showers.

Ten minutes later he returned to the locker room, which was quieter than it had been when he'd left. He spotted Haas sitting in his stall, still wearing most of his gear, smiling at his puck. Ilya secured the towel around his waist and walked over to him.

"We can get that, um . . ." Ilya couldn't remember the right word. "Made like a trophy."

Luca quickly set the puck on the bench beside him, as if he were embarrassed about it. "It is just one goal," he said.

Ilya sat next to him. "I have mine still, in my trophy room at home."

"That room must be very full," Luca said earnestly.

Ilya grinned. "Very. But the first goal puck is my favorite."

Luca's cheeks pinked, making him look even younger than he was. "Really?"

"Yes. Because it was the beginning, you know? Soon you will have a room full of NHL pucks and trophies, but—" Ilya picked up the puck "—it all started with this one."

Luca ducked his head. "I wish we had won the game."

Ilya almost made a joke about how Luca would get used to losing soon, but that wasn't the message he wanted to send to his rookie. "Me too." He poked Luca's arm. "Are you going to Monk's?"

Luca's eyes went wide. "Are *you*?"

It hurt Ilya's heart how badly this kid wanted him to come out with the team. How much it would mean to him. He knew Luca had idolized him growing up; he'd read the interviews.

But Ilya just . . . couldn't. Not tonight. He didn't have the energy to even fake it tonight.

"Next time," he said with a weak attempt at a smile.

Later, in bed, Ilya couldn't get his brain to shut up. It was unfortunate because his brain had nothing nice to say about him.

He knew, rationally, that he wasn't worthless. He was an

NHL all-star, the captain of his team, and was beloved by fans. He had a wonderful boyfriend who loved him so much he was willing to endure a lot of stress and sneaking around just to be with him. He was *loved*.

But he wasn't sure he deserved to be. He couldn't make himself believe that. Not right now.

He wished Shane was with him. They'd only been apart for two days, but Ilya would give anything to have Shane in his arms right now.

*Weak*. His brain said it in his father's voice. Disgusted and cruel.

Ilya grabbed his phone off the nightstand. Maybe he *was* weak, but he needed whatever he could get from Shane right now. A sleepy selfie. A good-night text. A heart emoji. Anything.

Early the next morning, Shane woke to find a missed text on his phone, sent after one a.m.

**ILYA:**

Are you awake?

Shane huffed and shook his head. Was Ilya *ever* not horny?

# CHAPTER EIGHT

Ilya had a decision to make.

He could play it safe and take the sure thing, or he could risk it all for a shot at glory.

No decision at all, really. He rolled the dice.

"But that was a full house," Yuna pointed out.

Ilya rolled two dice onto the table. "And now it is four threes." He picked up the one nonconforming die and kissed it before rolling it.

"No!" said David as soon as the die came to a stop.

"Shit," said Yuna.

"Yahtzee!" Ilya yelled. He raised his arms in triumph.

"I don't know why we invite you over," Yuna grumbled.

"Because I bring hand pies." Ilya had learned from Harris about a bakery outside the city that sold the best hand pies Ilya had ever eaten. He especially liked the cherry ones.

"He has a point there," David said.

Ilya's phone rang then. When he saw who was calling, he grinned and stood up from the Hollanders' kitchen table.

"Let me guess who *that* is," Yuna teased.

Ilya winked at her as he walked into the living room and answered the call. "Hi."

"Hey," said Shane. "How's it going?"

"Good. I am at your parents' house."

"Oh yeah? What are you doing there?"

"Destroying them at Yahtzee."

Shane laughed. "Mom won't like that."

"She loves me." Ilya strolled over to the mantel, which was covered in framed photos of Shane at various ages, mostly in hockey gear. He'd been a truly adorable kid. "Ready for the game?"

"Sure. It's just Boston."

Ilya huffed. His own team hadn't won against Boston in ages. "Cocky."

"Usually. But you like it."

Ilya's lips curved up. "Yes."

"You're gonna watch, right?"

"Maybe." Ilya traced a finger over a photo of Shane in his junior hockey uniform. He looked about seventeen—the age he'd been when Ilya had first met him. "Maybe we will watch a movie instead."

"Dick," Shane said affectionately.

"But you like it."

"I do. But I also like the rest of you." His voice dipped into a more seductive tone. "I've been fucking dying to have you inside me, though."

Ilya grinned. "You are on speaker phone by the way."

*"What?"*

"I am kidding."

"Jesus." Shane exhaled. "Not funny."

"If you say so."

"I should probably go. We're leaving for the arena soon."

"Okay."

There was a long pause—the same long pause that made an appearance at the end of most of their phone conversations. Both men needing to end the call, neither one wanting to.

"Good luck tonight," Ilya said finally. "Try not to embarrass yourself too much."

Shane snorted. "Sure."

"Call me later, yes?"

"Of course."

Ilya smiled at the photo of teenage Shane. "Ya lyublyu tebya."

"Ya vsegda budu tebya lubit," Shane replied.

"Show-off."

They ended the call, and Ilya returned to the kitchen, shaking his head at how gross he and Shane had become.

"He looks good tonight," Yuna said.

Ilya murmured his agreement from his end of the couch. Shane looked good every night. He was a great player on a great team. Ilya was a great player on a terrible team, and he felt less great with each passing week.

"Is it weird to watch Boston play?" David asked.

It had been once, but not anymore. Their roster had changed quite a bit in the two seasons since Ilya had played for Boston. "I have a better team now," Ilya said. "Well, better for me. The team is bad."

"You don't regret it?" Yuna asked. "Leaving?"

"Never." It was mostly the truth. He might have led Boston to another Stanley Cup if he'd played for them last season. They'd gotten close, even without him.

But being in Canada, near Montreal, made it easier to be with Shane. Ilya could build a life here, in Shane's hometown of Ottawa. Eventually he could become a Canadian citizen, and retire, and start a new adventure with Shane.

"Do you need another Coke?" David asked during a commercial break.

"No, no, I am good. Full from the delicious dinner," Ilya said with a small smile. David had made chicken parmesan, one of Ilya's favorites. Ilya had eaten more than he'd needed to. Especially after eating two hand pies.

"There's ice cream," Yuna said. "If you want some."

"No, thank you," Ilya said. Then, "What kind?"

Yuna smiled. "Cookies and cream."

Ilya put his hand over his heart. "Impossible to resist."

A few minutes later, Ilya was tucked under a blanket on the couch, eating ice cream out of a little bowl. He felt like a child, and he kind of loved it.

They were showing Shane on the television, a close-up as he got ready for the face-off. His cheeks were flushed, his skin glistening with sweat. His dark hair stuck out from under his helmet the way it never had for most of his career.

"His hair is too long," Yuna complained.

"No," Ilya said quietly. "It is perfect."

In the second period, Shane took a long pass from J.J. that resulted in a breakaway. Shane raced through the Boston zone, using his incredible speed to make sure no one caught him. When he reached the net, he switched to his backhand, and in the split second before he took the shot, Ilya realized what he was doing. Shane had left the puck where it was, faking the backhand shot and forcing the goalie to move. Then, lightning-fast, Shane fired a forehand wrist shot over the goalie's shoulder.

And then, Shane winked at the camera. *Winked.* And Ilya knew it was meant for him.

"That's my move!" Ilya said. The blanket he'd been wrapped in fell to the floor as he stood, one hand waving at the television, the other cradling his ice cream bowl protectively to his chest. "He did *my move*!"

David and Yuna were laughing. Ilya wasn't.

"When did he learn that?" Ilya demanded. "I did not teach him."

"You know Shane," Yuna said. "He studied it, learned it, and, I would say, perfected it."

"That move is called the Rozanov!" Ilya exclaimed. "He cannot do it."

"He just did," David pointed out.

Ilya dropped back onto the couch with a huff. "Is bullshit."

"You should be honored," Yuna said. "It's a show of respect."

"Is a show of being a thief."

"You think kids aren't practicing that move all over the hockey-playing world?" David asked. "I'll bet half the NHL has practiced it, but no one can pull it off except you and Shane."

Well. That was nice to think about, not that Ilya would admit it.

"I can do it faster," he grumbled instead.

Shane was on the bench now, grinning and looking way too fucking proud of himself. Ilya shoved a spoonful of ice cream into his mouth to stop himself from smiling back.

"You little shit."

Shane laughed in face of his boyfriend's fury. "Did you like that?"

"How did you learn it?"

"Like it's hard," Shane said dismissively, as if he hadn't practiced it in secret for hours, visualizing this moment. Hoping for this exact expression on Ilya's face.

On Shane's phone, Ilya was scowling, but his eyes were glinting with the mixture of anger and desire that always made Shane's knees weak. He was shirtless, and Shane could see the top of the grizzly bear head tattoo on his left pec, and part of the loon tattoo near his left shoulder.

"Were you trying to make me angry?" Ilya's voice was low and dangerous, and it made Shane shiver.

"Did it work?"

"Are you alone?"

Shane moved the phone around to show his empty hotel room. "Yes."

"Take that shirt off. Get on the bed."

Shane took a moment to snap his phone into the tripod he'd had the foresight to set up next to his bed. He'd known his little stunt on the ice would make Ilya horny as hell. He'd been counting on it.

When he was settled on the bed, shirtless as instructed, Shane said, in Russian, "Do you have plans for me?"

Ilya's mouth hung open for a moment, and Shane could practically see the bolts of arousal rocketing through him. "Fuck," Ilya said.

Shane bit his lip, pleased with himself. Pleased that he could still make Ilya react like this, could still surprise him, after all these years.

"I think I should get a reward," Shane said, in English. "For perfecting that move."

"Perfecting," Ilya scoffed. "Was just okay."

"The puck went in the net."

"Whatever. Hold on. One minute."

Shane waited while Ilya set his phone up on his own tripod. When he was finished, Shane had a good view of Ilya reclining on his bed, wearing only boxer briefs.

"I hope that's not what you wore to my parents' house."

"I dressed up for your parents. Nice shirt, very respectable boyfriend."

"You don't have to dress up for them. They love you."

Ilya's smile looked soft, and helpless. "I know. They made me chicken parmesan. And there was ice cream."

"Sounds healthy and well-balanced."

Ilya shook his head. "What is the point of life if you are not eating chicken parmesan and ice cream?"

"I can think of some good things," Shane said as he gently caressed himself through his underwear. "Besides food."

"High interval training?" Ilya asked dryly.

"Shut up. I'm trying to be sexy."

"Oh. Okay. I was not sure." He stretched one arm over his head and let his hand drape casually against the pillow. "So what is the plan?"

"Plan?"

"You are in charge, yes? You want a reward? What do you want me to do?"

"Um." Shane wished he could respond to that sort of question without blushing. Ilya always managed to be perfectly filthy without embarrassment. "Touch yourself."

Ilya poked his own nose. "Like this?"

Shane looked skyward in frustration. "Why are you like this?"

"Because it is fun."

"You know what? Fuck this. Take your dick out and get yourself hard while I watch."

Ilya was silent for a moment, blinking at the screen. Then, quietly, he said, "Yes. Okay."

In seconds, Ilya was naked, and Shane could see him from his thighs to the top of his head. Shane was pleased to see his cock was half hard already, the head beginning to peek out of the foreskin. Shane licked his lips.

"I wish you were here right now," Shane said.

"Be weird. With your teammates around."

"Then I wish I was at your house right now. Stop being difficult."

Ilya smiled lazily as he stroked himself. "I want to touch you. I miss you."

"I always miss you." Shane's throat felt tight, which was a ridiculous sensation to experience when watching your boyfriend jerk off. He swallowed hard and said, "You look hot."

"Probably."

Shane's lips curved up and he added, "For a guy who just had his move stolen."

That made Ilya laugh and smile so wide his eyes crinkled. Shane laughed too, and tried not to be terrified by how much he felt for this man.

Ilya's laughter morphed into a sigh of pleasure as he kept stroking his cock. "Is this all you want?"

"Yeah," Shane said, barely above a whisper. "Just want to watch you."

It was true, and it wasn't true. Shane wanted to climb through the phone and sit on Ilya's lap. Watching Ilya stroke himself was a decent consolation prize, though.

"I want you to be here," Ilya said.

"Me too. Wanna touch you. Wanna . . . fuck, I want to see you come."

Ilya spread his legs wider and leaned back more on the pillows behind him. "Put your glasses on, then."

"So I can see better, or because you're hot for my glasses?"

"Both."

Shane reached for his glasses case on the nightstand. He made a show of opening the case, pulling the glasses out, unfolding them, and putting them on. Like a nerdy reverse striptease.

Ilya grinned as his big hand moved in an easy, sure rhythm over his thick cock. Shane took advantage of his own improved vision and let his gaze dart all over the place, from Ilya's broad shoulders, to his twitching pecs, to his swollen balls, to the way his muscular forearms worked as he stroked himself.

"You are so fucking beautiful," Shane said.

Ilya smiled at him in that crooked way that had been making Shane feel crazy for over ten years. "Tell me."

"As if you don't know how hot you are."

"Tell me anyway."

Shane smiled and shook his head, but said, "You're so fucking *big*. Like, everywhere. Your arms, your chest, your fucking thighs. I love how tall you are. I don't even care that you make fun of my height because I fucking love being swallowed up by you when we're together."

Ilya groaned and moved his hand faster.

Shane laughed. "Figures that would do it for you."

"Touch yourself." Ilya's voice was strained, making it sound less like an order and more like a plea.

Shane obeyed, humming happily as he finally gave his rigid cock some attention.

"Were you waiting for me to tell you to do that?" Ilya asked with amusement.

"No," Shane said quickly. "I just wanted to see how long I could wait."

Ilya huffed. "Playing your own game over there, yes?"

Shane shrugged one shoulder. "Needed to do something to keep myself awake. It's not like you're doing anything interesting over there."

"Brat." Ilya let his dick snap backward, slapping hard against his firm stomach.

"Wow," Shane said sarcastically. "You've got tricks now."

They both cracked up. Ilya flipped him off with his left hand while he went back to stroking himself with his right.

"How is this for interesting?" Ilya said when he'd stopped laughing. "I have not come for three days."

Shane's eyebrows shot up. "Jesus. Are you okay?" Shane regularly went at least as long between orgasms without feeling deprived, but he knew Ilya usually needed at least one a day.

Ilya chuckled softly. "Fine. Busy, I guess. Or maybe waiting for this. For you."

"I'll admit," Shane said. "You have my full attention now."

"Good. Please jerk off so we can come together."

"I *am*. For fuck's sake, give me a chance to catch up."

"Like you need it."

*"Like you need it,"* Shane mimicked with his best attempt at a Russian accent.

"That is what I sound like? No wonder you are so hot for me. Sexy."

Shane laughed. "Shut up. Let me focus."

For the next couple of minutes, both men were silent besides their quiet moans and heavy breathing. Jerking off together like this always felt like a competition, even when it wasn't. This time, Ilya had explicitly stated that he wanted them to come together, but even that sounded like a challenge to Shane. Fortunately, challenges were a huge turn-on for him.

"You close?" Shane asked shakily.

Ilya smiled. "That was fast, Hollander."

"I didn't say *I* was close."

"But you are."

"You don't—*ah, fuck*—know anything."

"How long has it been since you came?"

Shane shuddered. "I don't remember."

Ilya's head rolled against the pillow. "I am going to come so fucking hard."

Shane exhaled, relieved that they were done pretending. "Fuck, me too."

"I can't wait to fuck you again."

"Me too. Shit, me too. Ilya, are you—"

"Yes. Come on."

Shane's orgasm hit him so hard that he let out a weird whimpering noise as the first burst of come landed on his stomach. It was a struggle to keep his eyes open through the intense jolts of pleasure, but it was worth the effort to watch Ilya coming spectacularly all over himself.

"Holy shit," Shane said, when he was able to talk again.

Ilya had his eyes closed and was breathing hard through his nose. He was still holding his dick.

"You okay?" Shane asked.

"I think there is more." Ilya started stroking himself again, hard and fast. Shane watched in amazement when, a few seconds later, Ilya's whole body tensed and arched as a small spurt of come joined the mess on his belly.

"That's new," Shane said.

Ilya's chest was still heaving. "Like you said. I have tricks."

They both laughed.

"That was hot," Shane said.

"Yes. Very."

"I really need to take a shower. Again."

"Mm."

"I love you."

Ilya's expression turned serious, and for a moment Shane's stomach clenched as if he expected Ilya to tell him something awful.

But all Ilya said was, "I love you so much, Shane."

Shane knew it, but hearing Ilya say it in such a raw, unguarded way cut through him like a blade. The pain of not being in the same room as Ilya felt physical.

"Ten days," he said. God, *ten*. How was he supposed to endure ten more days without Ilya? And then only have him for one, maybe one and a half, before they'd be apart again.

"Ten days." The number sounded just as enormous when Ilya said it.

They said goodbye, ended the call, and then Shane was alone again, and wishing like hell that there could be a solution to their problem.

# CHAPTER NINE

Ilya woke from another dream about his mother. The same dream. Always the same dream.

He reached a hand out toward Shane's side of the bed, but of course it was empty. He hadn't shared a bed with Shane for two weeks.

He brought his hand to his chest and traced the crucifix around his neck with one fingertip, soothing himself with the familiar bumps and edges of the gold cross.

He had to go to practice. He still felt tired. He always felt tired these days. It could be because he was twenty-nine, which was hockey middle-aged. Or because his terrible team had lost five to one last night. It could be because of the frequent unsettling dreams he'd been having about his mother. It could be because he missed his boyfriend.

*It could be because I'm depressed.*

No. He was fine. Normal. It's not like he ever stayed in bed all day crying.

*Neither did Mom.*

He hauled himself out of bed despite everything in his body

and brain protesting. He'd gotten rocked into the boards last night by a New Jersey defenseman, and he was paying for it this morning. One more thing to deal with.

He missed waking up with Shane. He missed breakfast together, even though Shane only ate extremely healthy food now. He missed making Shane coffee and serving it to him in an Ottawa Centaurs mug. He missed showering together, and tumbling back into bed together after, warm and damp and unable to stop touching each other.

He sent Shane a text. How is St. Louis?

Shane began typing his reply right away. Raining. How's Ottawa?

Ilya gazed out his kitchen window to the river behind his house. The trees were bright with autumn leaves, and the sun was shining.

**ILYA:**
Fine.

**SHANE:**
Did you eat breakfast?

Ilya huffed. Shane worried about the weirdest things.

**ILYA:**
Might go to McDonald's for a McGriddle.

He'd mostly written it to annoy Shane, but now he really did want a McGriddle.

**SHANE:**
You shouldn't be eating that shit.

**ILYA:**
Should I be eating hay for breakfast like you?

**SHANE:**
It's not hay. And yes, probably.

**ILYA:**
I would rather have the sandwich that is made with pancakes as bread.

**SHANE:**
Gross.

Ilya smiled as he imagined Shane's nose wrinkling, bunching up his freckles.

**ILYA:**
Send me a pic.

He had time to pour himself a coffee, fix it with cream and sugar, and take a couple of sips before Shane finally sent a selfie. Ilya wondered how many he'd taken before deciding this one was good enough to send.

It wasn't intentionally sexy. It was just Shane, standing near a window, probably in his hotel room, wearing a light blue Montreal Voyageurs T-shirt, and smiling. His hair was tucked adorably behind his ear on one side.

**ILYA:**
I miss you. It was the only thought in his head, at that moment.

**SHANE:**
I miss you too.

**SHANE:**
Stop stalling. Where's my pic?

Ilya was still shirtless, which was a good start for a selfie. He stretched the arm holding his phone out and raised it a bit, angling down. Then he shimmied the waistband of his sweatpants down until he was nearly exiting the safe-for-work zone. He tucked a thumb into the waistband, tugging down a bit, and snapped the pic.

Wow, Shane wrote back. That was mean.

Ilya wished he could watch the shift in Shane's face now. The way his cheeks flushed and his eyes grew brighter when he was aroused. He was probably biting his bottom lip.

**ILYA:**
If you are alone we could . . .

**SHANE:**
Team meeting in ten minutes.

**ILYA:**
Is that a challenge?

It took Shane forever to reply, and Ilya imagined he'd deleted several responses before finally landing on: I can't. Sorry.

**ILYA:**
ok

**SHANE:**
It's going to be hard to delete that photo.

**ILYA:**
I can take more.

He knew Shane *would* delete the photo. They always deleted anything in their message history that could give away their secret.

**SHANE:**
You gonna watch tonight?

**ILYA:**
Maybe. If I am very bored.

**SHANE:**
I'll try to win for you.

Ilya huffed and wrote, Try to lose. We are in the same division, idiot.

**SHANE:**
Nah.

And *then*, with no warning, Shane sent a pic of his crotch, his semi-hard dick visible under the gray fabric of his boxer briefs.

**SHANE:**
Talk to you later.

Ilya exhaled shakily and wrote, Fucker.

* * *

Shane hated West Coast road trips because they messed up his sleep schedule. They had flown directly from St. Louis to L.A. earlier that day, and had a game at eight tomorrow night, which would feel like eleven at night. Yuck.

Now it was nine thirty Pacific Time and Shane was in bed in his hotel room, trying to ignore the fact that it was only nine thirty. If he were home, it would be past his bedtime, especially before a game day.

But he couldn't sleep.

He could hear Hayden moving around in the room next door. Earlier it had sounded like he'd been watching a movie. Now Shane could only hear footsteps.

He closed his eyes. *Sleep*, he told himself.

He was in the middle of some slow breathing exercises when there was a knock at his door.

"Just a sec," he called out as he hauled himself out of bed and began rummaging through his suitcase for some sweatpants and a T-shirt. Once he was decent, he opened the door.

"Hey," said Hayden. He was pawing the back of his own neck, and his blond hair was thoroughly rumpled. "Can I hang out for a bit?"

"Did you watch a scary movie again?" Shane asked, already stepping back to let him in.

Hayden smiled sheepishly. "It was fucking terrifying."

Shane closed the door behind him. "You need to stop watching those."

"I know." He threw himself onto Shane's bed, making himself at home. "What were you up to?"

"Trying to sleep."

"Oh. Sorry."

"It's cool," Shane said, sitting on the bed beside him. "I wasn't too successful."

"Fucking time zones."

"Yep."

"Wanna watch something?" Hayden asked.

"What? Like, one of the *Saw* movies?"

"No! The opposite of that." Hayden grabbed the remote off the nightstand. "I'll find something."

He landed on a competition reality show about strangers hooking up in some tropical location, which basically *was* a horror movie as far as Shane was concerned. He kept his thoughts to himself, though, and let his friend be comforted by toned young women in bikinis.

"It would be weird to go on one of these shows," Hayden said.

"Mm," Shane agreed.

"I'd probably be good at it, though. I've got a good body, I'm a nice guy. I know I'm not, like, smart, but compared to these dudes I'm a road scholar."

"Rhodes," Shane said.

"Yeah. And I'm rich, so. That would be an edge."

Shane sat up from where he'd been lying back against the pillows. "Sorry. In this scenario, you would be a contestant on this trashy reality show, but also you would still be an NHL player?"

Hayden shrugged. "I guess."

"You would spend a month of your life, or however long it takes to film this show, living in this gross beach house and trying to win ten thousand dollars when you have an NHL salary and, like, barely any vacation time?"

Hayden frowned at him. "You're overthinking this, buddy. Obviously I'm not going on a show like this because I'm married to the best woman in the world and we have . . . four beautiful children."

Shane grinned. "Did you hesitate before you said four?"

"No!"

"Did you actually lose track of how many kids you have?"

Hayden lightly punched Shane's thigh. "Just wait until you're a dad. You'll see."

They watched in silence until the next commercial break, then Shane said, "You think I'll be a dad someday?"

Hayden's eyebrows pinched together. "Sure. You want to be, right?"

"I think so, yeah."

"Well, then."

"It won't be easy. And probably won't be for a long time."

"Parenting is never easy."

"Yeah but, like, obtaining a baby sometimes is. For some people."

Hayden laughed. "It's never been an issue for Jackie and me, that's for sure. Although, she's fixed now, so."

Shane wrinkled his nose. "Fixed?"

"Like, had her tubes tied or whatever they call it. When we had Amber she had it done when she had the C-section. Two-in-one surgeries."

"Efficient." Shane realized it was maybe weird that he hadn't known any of this. He often teased Hayden about his brood of children, but he never really talked to him about his and Jackie's experience with having babies and raising kids. "Was that a mutual decision? Not having any more kids?"

"Definitely. I mean, even if only Jackie had wanted to stop, that would have been the decision made. I would never have pushed for more if she wasn't into it. That would be fucked. But four kids is plenty for both of us." He sighed. "The kids want a dog now."

Shane smiled. "So does Ilya."

"Does he want kids?"

"I think so." Shane's cheeks heated. "We haven't talked about it too seriously. There's not much point right now."

On the television, a very drunk young man started making out with a very drunk young woman. Shane let his eyes unfocus even more than they already were without his glasses, and quietly began to stress out about the logistics of adopting children with Ilya. There were so many things that had to happen first, and they were all terrifying.

"He'd be a good dad, I guess," Hayden said, breaking through Shane's anxiety spiral.

"Who?" Shane asked, in case Hayden meant the drunk gentleman on the TV.

"Rozanov. He's good with kids. Ruby and Jade love him."

"He basically *is* a kid, that's why," Shane said, though inside his heart was glowing. "Do you think I'd be a good dad?"

"Sure. You'd be the responsible one who makes sure they, like, eat vegetables and brush their teeth and stuff. Ilya would be the fun one who buys them Jet Skis for their tenth birthdays."

"Oh god. He *would* do that."

"And you'd return them and buy the kids sensible shoes or something instead," Hayden teased.

"Eat shit. I'd be a cool dad."

Hayden wrapped a hand around Shane's forearm. "Shane. Buddy. You've never been cool about anything ever. And parenting is the most high-stress thing you can do. You'll be an absolute mess."

"Thanks."

"You should still do it, though. Kids are the best."

"Okay."

"Hey, maybe Ruby and Jade will be old enough to babysit *your* kids! Man, that's wild to think about."

It *was* wild to think about. Every aspect of it was wild. "Yeah."

"You got plans for tomorrow?" Hayden asked.

"I'm hanging out with Rose."

"Oh, sweet! Can I come?"

"No. Last time you babbled the entire time like a drooling fanboy."

"Yeah, because she's a giant movie star!"

"She's also one of my best friends. And a totally normal, real person."

"I'll be cool, I promise!"

Shane shook his head. "She's taking me shopping. I don't need a witness to that. I'm weird enough about clothes without you being there."

"Fine." Hayden turned his attention back to the TV. After a minute of watching, he chuckled. "That guy's back tattoo. Sheesh."

Shane squinted at the shirtless white guy who was being yelled at by another shirtless white guy. "What's it say?"

"'No Worries.'"

Shane huffed. "Must be nice."

There were two kids—Willa and Andrew—who lived in the house down the street from Ilya. Almost every home game day, the kids would stand in their driveway and wave at Ilya as he drove by on his way to the arena. Sometimes they wore the jerseys he'd given them. Sometimes they held homemade signs.

Ilya slowed down as he approached their house and rolled down his window. Willa was wearing her jersey, and Andrew had an Ottawa Centaurs foam finger.

"How many goals should I score tonight?" Ilya asked.

"Three!" said Willa.

"Eight!" said Andrew.

Ilya chuckled. "No problem. Will you be there?"

Andrew—the younger one—started jumping up and down. "Yeah! And I'm going to get popcorn!"

"Aw. Lucky," Ilya said. "I never get popcorn at the games."

"Because if you ate popcorn while playing hockey, you would get a cramp," Willa said wisely.

"This is true," Ilya agreed. He noticed the kids' mother sitting on the front steps. "Hello, Kate."

Kate waved. "Good luck tonight, Ilya."

Ilya nodded and gave a final wave, then drove away smiling. There were a lot of things that he found difficult about living and playing in Ottawa, but he absolutely loved this pregame ritual with his neighbors. He loved having neighbors. His penthouse in Boston had been sexy and private, but being on the ground in a house surrounded by other houses was nice.

To be fair, it was a *big* house. With a gate and trees and an enormous semicircular driveway. He still needed *some* privacy.

The drive from Ilya's house to the arena was only about fifteen minutes, and he passed a Starbucks drive-thru on the way, so it was basically a perfect commute. It was a sunny day, so Ilya had decided to take his orange Porsche 718 Cayman, which was the coolest of the cars he had left. These days he mostly drove his Mercedes SUV with all-wheel drive. Sometimes on nice days he rode his Ducati, but both Shane and Yuna strongly disapproved of his decision to buy a motorcycle, so Ilya didn't take it out often.

Shane was so sure Ilya was going to die in a crash. It was annoying.

Ilya drummed his fingers on the steering wheel to the rhythm of the Bad Bunny song that he'd recently added to his pregame playlist. He needed to get his fill of good music now because it was Evan Dykstra's turn to be in charge of the locker room music, and that meant country. Ilya tried to be open-minded about music, and maybe not all country was bad, but the particular songs Dykstra was into were definitely bad.

He pulled into the Starbucks drive-thru, ordered a coffee with cream and sugar for himself and a black coffee for Luca Haas because he'd found that he liked the way Luca got flustered when Ilya gave him any attention at all. Ilya had always been against hazing or making rookies feel uncomfortable or bullied, but he got a kick out of being nice to the starstruck ones.

The first person Ilya spotted in the parking garage at the arena was Wyatt Hayes, who was just getting out of his army-green Jeep Wrangler. It had a Green Lantern logo on the tire cover on the back because Hazy was a fucking nerd.

"Hey, Roz," Wyatt said with a small wave.

Ilya nodded back because he was carrying two coffee cups. "Hazy."

Wyatt fell into stride with Ilya as they walked through the garage. He was about Ilya's height—maybe an inch shorter—with curly blond hair and a wide mouth that almost never frowned. "What kind of crowd do you think we'll get tonight?"

"Is a beautiful evening, so basically no one."

Wyatt laughed. "Yeah. Our numbers will go up when it gets cold."

"A little."

"Maybe they should offer fans a free hot chocolate or something. That would be an enticement."

"Sure," Ilya said dryly. "Or a month's rent."

Wyatt laughed again. "That might get a few people in the seats. Maybe."

As much as the lousy attendance was a running joke amongst his teammates, Ilya honestly fucking hated it. In Boston the arena had been full every game, cheering for their team. In Montreal the arena was sold out well in advance for basically the entire season. Shane didn't know what it felt like to play for a half-empty arena because even when he played in Ottawa the arena was reliably full. Of Montreal fans. With Shane Hollander jerseys.

But tonight they were playing Columbus, so no one was going to be there.

"Maybe we should play shirtless," Wyatt joked. "That could bring in a new audience."

"Would be cold," Ilya said.

"Yeah. And also I would probably die."

"Shirtless goaltending. Bad idea," Ilya agreed.

"I guess we could start winning," Wyatt mused. "That might work."

"I will suggest it at the next meeting."

"Who's the extra coffee for?"

"Haas."

Wyatt snorted. "He's gonna frame it."

"Fuckin' A!" Bood yelled as he slammed into Ilya in the corner, wrapping him in a hug. Ilya had scored early in the first period, making it 1–0 for Ottawa. The goal siren blared, the fans who'd bothered to show up cheered, and the team's goal song started playing (DJ Khaled's "All I Do Is Win," which seemed like an ironic choice to Ilya).

"Your turn next, baby," Ilya said, trying to match Bood's energy. He bumped gloves with their other winger, Tanner Dillon, who frankly wasn't good enough to be on a line with either of them. Ilya dreamed of a day where his right wing linemate was as strong as his left. Maybe it would be Haas someday. He had potential.

But Ilya was tired of waiting. Tired of losing. He wanted a star right wing player on his line *now*.

He wanted a lot of things *now*.

"Great start, fellas," Coach Wiebe said cheerfully when they reached the bench. "Keep it up."

They didn't keep it up. By the end of the second period it was 3–1 Columbus.

"We played against Boston last week," said Jake Pierce, Columbus's star center, as he and Ilya waited for a face-off. "They were really good."

"Cool."

Pierce huffed and shook his head. "I have no fucking idea why you signed with this team."

"Maybe I like the quiet."

"You know we've got rookies who had posters of you on their bedroom walls?"

"Nice. Good taste."

"You shouldn't be here, is all I'm saying."

Ilya's lips curved up. "Next time I sign with a shit team in a boring city, I will choose Columbus."

He could tell Pierce was trying not to smile. "You're a fucking weirdo, Rozanov."

The game ended 4–2 for Columbus. Most of the crowd had left by the middle of the third period.

"Rough one tonight," Harris said to Ilya in the locker room after the press had finally left.

"Rough one every night," Ilya sighed. He remembered when hockey had been *fun*.

"If it makes you feel better, I regrammed this photo of a pumpkin a fan carved your portrait into. It's pretty impressive." He held out his phone so Ilya could see.

"Wow." As far as pumpkin portraits went, it *was* impressive. Ilya loved how weird North American Halloween was.

Then he got an idea. He took a few seconds to weigh the pros and cons, then stood up and announced, "Halloween party this year is at my house, okay?"

Everyone cheered and clapped, which made Ilya smile. He

never hosted parties, and rarely went to them. Because he was a terrible captain and teammate.

He would host this party, and it would be talked about for years. The best party ever. Epic. In Boston he'd been the one who organized impromptu outings. He'd been the guy his teammates called when they wanted to go out and get drunk and dance and get laid. He could be that guy again. He could try.

# CHAPTER TEN

"Holy! What's up, sexy?"

Shane ducked his head so Rose wouldn't see how embarrassed he was. "As if."

"I'm serious! Look in the mirror." Rose grabbed his arm and hauled him in front of a full-length mirror. "Look!"

Shane looked. Rose had convinced him to come shopping with her during his day off in L.A., and shopping with one of the biggest movie stars in the world did not mean, as Shane had expected, going to a mall. It meant private shopping sessions at tiny designer-owned boutiques. He'd also quickly realized that Rose wasn't even looking for clothes for herself, and was mostly interested in dressing Shane up like a doll.

So now he was wearing an ivory-colored silk T-shirt that was basically transparent and cost more than most people earned in a month. It looked more like something Ilya would wear.

"Your body is ridiculous," Rose said. "Look at that ass!"

The dark brown slacks had some stretch in them, and were hugging his thighs and ass in a way that, Shane could admit, looked pretty nice. "The pants are good," he allowed.

"It's *all* good. Trust me. And here. Try this with it." She held out a reddish-brown leather bomber jacket. "It's short so you won't be hiding that juicy butt."

"Stop it," Shane said as he slipped the jacket on. He'd never really been a leather jacket guy, but maybe . . .

"I love this look with your longer hair," Rose said. "You look like trouble."

Shane turned from side to side in front of the mirror, examining himself. He *did* look different, but still himself. Just . . . cooler.

"I like it," he admitted. "Do these pants come in other colors?"

An hour later, he and Rose left the boutique with several bags, all containing clothes for Shane. Rose had insisted on paying for everything, which was completely unnecessary, but Shane allowed it because it seemed to make her very happy.

Shane was vaguely aware that there were people—paparazzi, most likely—taking photos of them as they walked the short distance from the store to Rose's chauffeured car, but Rose didn't mention them so he didn't either. Shane didn't know how she dealt with that level of public scrutiny. It made his own life as a superstar hockey player in Canada seem downright private.

"I'm starving," Rose announced when they got into the car. "You wanna get tacos?"

Shane *did* want to get tacos, but . . . "I'm on a pretty strict diet," he said. "For, like, performance."

Rose laughed. "Aw geez. I thought I finally had a lunch date I could eat real food with. Okay, what can you eat, then?"

After Shane rattled off an embarrassingly long list of forbidden foods, Rose asked her driver—who she seemed to have a very friendly relationship with—to take them to a place that had, according to her, the best poke in town.

"So how are things?" Rose asked once they were at a patio table with their bowls. "With . . . y'know?"

"Great," Shane said quickly. "Really great."

"Yeah? No plans to go public?"

"Not really, no."

"You okay with that?"

Shane took advantage of the fact that he'd just popped a chunk of tuna in his mouth and took his time answering. Most days, he thought he was fine with hiding. They had a long-range plan, and Shane wanted to stick to it. That was easy, and organized. And safe. But some days . . .

"It would be nice to be open about our relationship. Most of the time the hiding doesn't bother me, but sometimes the unfairness of it all makes me furious. The other guys on the team get to talk about their wives and girlfriends, and have them come to team events and stuff. They have kids and, I don't know, *lives* beyond hockey that they can be proud of. I want that."

"And what does *he* want?"

"I don't know. The same, I think." Shane nudged some fish around with his chopsticks. The restaurant had allowed him to substitute the rice for extra kale, which was nice, but also sucked. "He said he wants to wait, but he's also said he'd come out anytime, if I wanted it."

Rose reached across the table and poked him in the arm. "He loves you so much!"

Shane turned the color of his raw tuna. "I know. I'm lucky."

"Do you want my advice? As a person whose entire life is under a microscope?"

"Sure."

"Do what makes you happy. Live how you want, love who you want. People will judge you, hate you, criticize you, but plenty more will support you and love you. And, in the end, no one matters except the people you care about. Your parents support you, your best friends support you. Who are you really worried about?"

"I don't know. The league? The fans? My teammates?"

"Your teammates know you're gay, though, right?"

Shane nodded.

"Anyone being an asshole about it?"

"No. I mean, I can tell some of them don't love it, but they keep quiet about it. I don't know if even the openly supportive guys would be okay with me and, um . . . y'know."

"What about your agent? Does your agent know?"

"We told her in the summer."

"Good. You want your agent on your side if things go sideways. Trust me."

Shane picked up a chunk of fish, then put it down. "Do you think things will go sideways? Are people going to figure us out?"

She smiled sadly at him. "I'm not saying it's impossible for you guys to keep this secret for as long as you want to, but . . ."

"Not likely?"

She wrinkled her nose and shook her head. "Sorry, buddy."

Shane sighed. "Then we should make a plan B, I guess."

"I'd recommend it. Always plan for the worst and hope for the best."

Damn. Shane really didn't want to have to think about the possibility of their relationship being outed. Not more than he already thought about it, anyway.

"What about you?" he asked, hoping to change the subject. "You seeing anyone?"

"Nah. I sort of had a thing going with a pro surfer, but he was a *lot*. Always wanted to talk about deep shit for hours. It was intense. And boring."

"Sorry."

"I think I want to find a nice, normal guy, y'know? No celebrities. I want to meet, like, a bookstore owner."

"Isn't that the exact plot of a movie? I swear I watched a movie like that with my parents."

Rose laughed. "You're right! That's *Notting Hill.* Okay, not a bookstore. Maybe a . . . flower shop. There. Totally different."

"I wish I knew a nice flower shop owner. I'd introduce you."

"Keep your eyes open. I'd also accept a baker. I love bread."

"I miss bread," Shane said wistfully.

"God, I'll bet. Is it worth it, though? Does the clean eating make you feel better?"

Shane frowned at his bowl of kale. "I keep saying it does, but it might be the discipline that makes me feel better, not the food."

Rose's mouth dropped open in exaggerated shock. "Wow. This just turned into therapy."

"Sorry. Ignore me."

"No way. Tell me all about how much you like *discipline*."

"Shut up. It's not a sex thing."

"Hm."

"It's not! I like to practice discipline and self-control, and be rewarded for it. That's all."

"That still sounds like it could be a sex thing."

Shane rolled his eyes. "Eat your poke."

"Is that an order, *sir*?" she asked in a husky voice.

"Holy fuck! That doesn't even make sense. Wouldn't *I* be the submissive one in this fantasy you're making up?"

Rose cackled while Shane wished he could disappear. The truth was, he *did* like it when he and Ilya played a bit with discipline in the bedroom. Shane wasn't into punishment, or shame, but he loved it when Ilya made things . . . challenging. And then rewarded Shane for it.

"I'm sorry," Rose said gleefully. "You're just so fun to tease."

"I've been told."

Late in the afternoon, Rose dropped Shane off at his hotel. She hugged him as they stood next to her car and told him she'd be at his game the next night.

"Oh yeah?" Shane said.

"I'll be in a box, wearing a Montreal jersey."

"That'll cause a scene."

"Maybe the paps will think we're back together."

Well, that wouldn't hurt. Except Ilya would never let him hear the end of it. "I'll see you . . . someday," Shane said. His heart felt heavy. He really wished she lived closer to him.

"Soon," she promised. "I fly to Romania on Monday to start shooting a movie that I already know will be terrible, but maybe we can meet up somewhere after that."

"Definitely."

She hugged him again and said, quietly against his ear, "Say hi to Ilya for me."

"Okay."

"And come up with a backup plan."

"I will."

As he watched her drive away, a ball of tension formed inside his stomach, expanding into his chest. There was no backup plan. If he and Ilya were found out, they were fucked.

"Guess what," Ilya said as soon as Shane accepted his FaceTime request. It was the next morning—early in L.A., almost lunchtime in Ottawa—and Shane was still in bed.

"What?"

"We are getting a team puppy! Harris told us today at practice."

"Oh. Cute."

Ilya looked perfect, sitting on his deck in the early-autumn sunshine. He was wearing a black sweater that looked soft and cozy, and his jaw was covered in thick stubble. The sunlight made his golden-brown hair gleam. "He is too small right now, but when he is old enough he will come to the arena to visit!"

"You gonna let anyone else play with him, or . . ."

"Maybe. Good game last night." He lifted a McDonald's cup and took a long sip of something that was, at best, Coke, but could possibly be a chocolate shake. Shane decided to ignore it.

"You stayed up that late?"

Ilya grinned. "Yes, but, you know. Mostly partying."

Shane smiled back, knowing damn well Ilya had only stayed up late to watch his boyfriend play hockey. "Sure. I saw Rose yesterday."

"Yes, I saw the photos."

"Aw man, did those hit the internet?"

"They say you are back together. Congratulations. Very happy for you."

"*Anyway*, I want to tell you what she said."

"She wants you back?"

"No. Shut up. She said we should maybe make, like, a backup plan. In case our secret gets out."

"Backup plan," Ilya repeated. "What would that be?"

"No idea. I figure we either stick to the plan we have, or our secret gets blown and we're fucked, right?"

Ilya frowned. "Maybe. Yes."

"I know we're careful, but . . ."

"Someone might notice my heart eyes."

"Your *what*?"

"Heart eyes. Hayden said I look at you with heart eyes."

Shane squirmed against his bedsheets. "When did he say that?"

"At camp. I was staring at you and he said—"

"Oh god." Shane palmed his face. "He did not say that."

"Yes. Was probably true. I look at you and I am just . . ." Ilya opened and closed his fist several times in front of his chest. "My heart goes crazy, you know?"

Shane's own heart started going a little crazy. "You should see a doctor about that."

Ilya grinned and shook his head. "Is just being in love, I think."

Shane covered his face with a pillow. He couldn't look at Ilya in that moment. Couldn't let Ilya see him either.

"Come back," Ilya said, laughing.

Shane tossed the pillow aside. "I fucking miss you so much. I wake up alone every day and it *sucks*."

"I know. Four more days."

Shane groaned. "We're not even going to have time to see each other before our game, are we?"

"Probably not."

"God, that's going to be brutal."

"Maybe I will kiss you during a face-off."

"Pretty sure that would be a face-off violation."

"You are a nerd."

"I'm also naked right now."

"Oh yes?"

"Mm. Except my glasses."

Ilya grinned and stood up. "Let's go to my bedroom, then."

# CHAPTER ELEVEN

Ilya bent over the face-off circle in Montreal and smiled at the man across from him. "Hi."

Shane's lips quirked up. "Hi."

They'd done this dance so many times, but this time felt the hardest. Ilya hadn't seen his boyfriend in three weeks, and now he was inches away from him, heart-stoppingly beautiful and completely forbidden.

"Do you have plans after the game?" Ilya asked casually.

Shane's smile grew. "I'm wide open."

Ilya hoped his own eyes showed the promise he was trying to silently transmit: *you will be.* The way Shane licked his bottom lip suggested the message had been received.

The puck dropped, Ilya won the face-off, and the game was on.

During their fourth shift together, Ilya was battling Shane for the puck against the boards. Shane struggled against Ilya's weight as they clashed their stick blades together. "You got any more tricks to show me?" Shane said.

If he was trying to distract Ilya, it worked. Shane wasn't usually the one to try to fluster Ilya with secret sexy messages on the ice. The surprise caused Ilya's body to slacken long enough for Shane to skate away with the puck. Ilya smiled to himself as he chased after him.

The next time Ilya was pressed against him, later in the first period, Ilya answered Shane. "I don't think I need tricks."

For a split second, their eyes met. Shane's were dark and full of promise, but then he said, "We'll see," and shoved Ilya off of him.

Honestly, Ilya wasn't expecting anything too complicated to happen tonight. After three weeks of not touching each other, Ilya would be surprised if they even made it past the living room, or bothered to take their clothes off, before they were both spent and sleepy.

But they did have tomorrow. And the next night.

They hadn't been able to see each other, before the game. The Centaurs had flown into Montreal in the afternoon, after practicing in Ottawa, and he and Shane had both been busy getting ready for the game. Ilya's team was flying back to Ottawa directly after this game, but he wouldn't be flying with them. He'd been nervous when he'd told Coach Wiebe his fabricated story about needing to meet with Shane about their charity tomorrow. He'd never skipped a team flight before, in all of their years of sneaking around, and he was worried it would seem strange now. And obvious.

But Wiebe hadn't even blinked at it. "It's a day off tomorrow anyway," he'd said easily. "Enjoy Montreal."

Ilya loved his new coach.

"Hollander giving you trouble?" Evan Dykstra, Ottawa's best defenseman, asked when Ilya returned to the bench.

Ilya's lips curved up. "Always."

By the second period, the score was two to one for Montreal, which wasn't bad, considering. Wyatt had been making incredible saves to keep Ottawa in the game.

After another highlight reel–worthy glove save, Ilya skated over to Wyatt to tap him on the pads.

"Is it supposed to rain tomorrow?" Wyatt asked, as if he wasn't in the middle of a hockey game and hadn't just done something amazing. "I was thinking about taking my bike out, hitting a trail."

Ilya could only smile and shake his head. "I don't know."

"I'll check later. Hey, score a goal, would ya?"

"No problem."

Three minutes later, Ilya scored a goal, tying the game. He waved to the Montreal crowd as they booed him.

"Stop being an asshole," Shane grumbled as he skated by him.

Ilya blew him a kiss.

"Knock that shit off," said a gruff voice beside Ilya. He turned to find one of the refs frowning at him. "I'll give you an unsportsmanlike conduct penalty if you keep that up."

Ilya rolled his eyes as he skated to his bench. If the ref only knew how much Ilya *actually* wanted to kiss Shane.

He enjoyed a brief fantasy as he sat on the bench of pressing Shane against the glass after scoring a goal and kissing him breathless. That would shut this fucking crowd up.

"Man," Bood said as they skated to the bench, "this town hates you."

"Nah. They wish I played for them."

Bood laughed. "Hollander would hate that."

"My good friend Shane Hollander, you mean?"

"There's no way he likes you that much."

"He loves me," Ilya said plainly. Honestly.

Bood, of course, thought he was kidding. "Now you're really dreaming."

Ilya chomped on his mouth guard to avoid smiling.

A few seconds later, Luca Haas took a long pass and was on a breakaway. Most of the Ottawa bench stood up, Ilya included.

"Get it, Haasy!" Bood yelled.

They all watched as the puck sailed past the Montreal goalie's arm and into the net. His second NHL goal. He jumped up after scoring, arms raised and an enormous grin stretching his boyish face. Then he was engulfed by his linemates.

"The damn kid's got skills," Bood said.

"Good. We need them." Ilya held his hand out for a high five as Haas reached the bench. Haas slapped Ilya's glove, then was pulled into an awkward embrace by Bood that nearly hauled him over the boards and onto the bench.

"Fucking beauty, kid!" Bood yelled in his ear. "Legendary."

Less than two minutes later, Shane scored, making the Ottawa celebrations short-lived.

"That was rude," Ilya said when they bent for the face-off after.

"What? Trying to win?"

"Couldn't even let poor Haas enjoy that for a couple of minutes?"

"Maybe I'll explain to you how hockey works later," Shane said dryly.

"If that's what you want to do," Ilya said, *"later."*

Ilya won the face-off.

Twenty seconds later, Shane had the puck because Ilya's linemate, Tanner Dillon, had fucked up a pass. Ilya really needed a better right wing player on his line.

Shane charged into the Ottawa zone but couldn't get a clean shot, so he went behind the net with the puck. Ilya chased after him, but couldn't catch him before Shane passed the puck to J.J. at the blue line. Ilya moved to the front of the net, and found himself directly in the line of fire when J.J. unleashed his rocket of a slap shot at the net. The puck caught Ilya on the side of the knee, and he went down, swearing loudly.

Wyatt must have covered the puck because play stopped a second later. The same ref who'd gotten in Ilya's face earlier skated over to check on him.

"You need the doctor?" he asked gruffly.

Ilya glared up at him. "No. Give me a second."

He slowly pulled himself up until he was on one knee, the good one planted on the ice. The other one was bent in front of him and felt like a fiery ball of pain.

"That's *my* job, y'know," Wyatt said. "I've got these big pads on my legs." He tapped one with his stick. "So the puck doesn't directly hit my fucking kneecap."

"Was not my kneecap," Ilya said through gritted teeth. "Just the side. Is fine."

"Ah. Like, where you have no padding at all?"

Ilya stood up with some effort. The crowd clapped for him, but he knew it was half-hearted. The Montreal fans would probably prefer to see a puck go clean through his torso.

Shane approached him as Ilya made his way to the bench. "You okay?"

"Great." He flexed his knee a few times, testing it, and winced.

"Wyatt probably woulda stopped that without your help."

"Yes. Thank you."

Shane frowned at him with obvious concern in his eyes. "You sure you're okay?"

Ilya gave him a quick smile that probably looked more like a grimace. "Maybe no kneeling for a few days."

Shane bumped right up against him. "I'll have to make new plans, then."

He skated away quickly, leaving Ilya grinning and shaking his head as he finished his slow journey to the bench.

**SHANE:**

Where the fuck are you?

Ilya huffed at his phone in the back seat of a taxi that was taking him—slowly—to Shane's house.

**ILYA:**
In traffic.

**SHANE:**
Fuck. Where?

**ILYA:**
Montreal? I don't fucking know.

**SHANE:**
Hurry up.

**ILYA:**
Ok. I will ask the driver to make the car fly.

For a full minute, Shane didn't reply. Then he wrote, Are you over the bridge yet at least?

Ilya chuckled and wrote, You seem a bit horny.

**SHANE:**
I'm fucking dying.

The blunt admission made Ilya's cock twitch. He wrote, Get yourself ready for me then.

**SHANE:**
What do you think I've been doing for the past twenty minutes?

Oh. Fuck.

**ILYA:**
You better not come without me.

**SHANE:**
Then you'd better hurry up.

Ilya was getting way too aroused in this unmoving taxi. He should put his phone in his pocket, take some cooling breaths, and think about something else. But instead he asked, Where are you?

**SHANE:**
Bed.

**ILYA:**
Fingering yourself?

**SHANE:**
Yes.

**ILYA:**
How many?

**SHANE:**
3

Ilya sucked in a breath, then wrote, You need something bigger.

**SHANE:**
I know! That's why you need turmeric.

**SHANE:**
Need to hurry, I mean. Fucking voice-to-text.

**ILYA:**

Get yourself close. Right to the edge. But don't come.

**SHANE:**

I already got to the edge once by accident.

Jesus fuck. Ilya could see it so vividly: Shane trying so hard to be good and productive, getting himself ready so Ilya could slide right into him when they were finally together. Working himself open, trying not to touch his cock. Probably giving it a few strokes anyway, until suddenly he'd found himself on the brink of orgasm. Ilya could imagine his panicked expression, the desperate way he'd squeeze the base of his cock, teeth clenched, breathing hard through his nose.

**ILYA:**

But you didn't come?

**SHANE:**

No.

**ILYA:**

Good boy.

Shane didn't always like that kind of praise, and, admittedly, Ilya was usually teasing him when he used it. But not tonight. Tonight, Ilya was proud of him.

**ILYA:**

Can you do it again? For me?

Nothing for a few seconds, and then, Yeah.

Ilya palmed his right knee, pressing his fingertips into the fresh bruise there, trying to calm his dick down. He wasn't even sure how this weird thing he'd asked for was supposed to work.

Ilya poked his bruise, and waited.

He loved playing these games with Shane. Even though they'd been an exclusive couple for over three years, and secret lovers for years before that, their sex life was far from stale. Every kind of sex they had was exciting: the frantic, heated, almost aggressive sex they sometimes had after a game, or after an argument; the unhurried, exploratory sex they indulged in when they had plenty of time and privacy; the playful, competitive sex they enjoyed when one of them challenged the other.

And this. The times when Shane wanted to prove something to Ilya—wanted to be *good* for him. And rewarded for it after. Ilya fucking loved *this* sex.

He wondered what Shane was doing at that moment, as the taxi finally crawled past the accident near the entrance to the bridge. Was he still fingering himself, or was he jerking himself off while he played with his balls? Was he reaching for a toy from the drawer that had gone from housing a solitary dildo to an impressive array of sex toys over the past couple of years? Ilya was fond of buying Shane presents.

Three minutes passed between Shane's last text and the next one.

**SHANE:**

Fuck.

**ILYA:**

Did you do it?

**SHANE:**

Yes. Fuck you. That was torture.

Ilya glanced out the window, then wrote, I will be there in five minutes. One more before I get there, ok?

Obviously, Shane could refuse. Tell Ilya to get fucked. Or lie about it. Ilya knew he wouldn't do any of those things.

**SHANE:**

Ok. You have your key, right?

**ILYA:**

Yes.

He smiled at the thought of making Shane answer the door like this.

Five and a half minutes later, Ilya was thrusting a wad of cash at the driver, thanking him quickly, and exiting the car. He slung his backpack over his shoulder and jogged up to Shane's front door, past the hedges that secluded the house from the street. He'd given up trying to chill his dick out after the last near-orgasm confirmation text from Shane. Now he was rock hard, and desperate to get his hands on his boyfriend.

"Ilya?" Shane called out from upstairs as soon as Ilya opened the door.

"Yes."

"Fucking hell. Get up here."

Ilya practically flew up the stairs, and found Shane sprawled on the bed, naked and flushed and beautiful.

"Chert voz'mi," Ilya muttered. He dropped his backpack on the floor and immediately began tearing off his clothes.

"The last one was a close call," Shane said. "I haven't touched myself since."

He was on his back, legs akimbo, one hand resting on the pillow above his head, the other gently stroking his stomach. There was a bottle of lube on the bed beside him, and Ilya grabbed it once he was fully undressed.

"Is your knee okay?"

"Good enough," Ilya said impatiently as he slicked himself up. "How do you want it?"

"Now," Shane said.

Ilya grunted. "Condom?" They rarely used them anymore, but sometimes Shane preferred them for easy cleanup.

"Fuck no. Come on."

Ilya kneeled on the bed between Shane's thighs, wincing at the pain that shot through him as his bruised knee pressed into the mattress. He forced himself to ignore it, and leaned down to kiss Shane roughly. Fuck, he'd been wanting to do this for so long. He missed kissing Shane possibly more than anything else.

Shane chased his mouth when Ilya pulled away, but Ilya only smiled. Then he gripped Shane's thighs and hauled his hips up off the bed. Shane rested his ankles on Ilya's shoulders as Ilya lined up and drove into him in one smooth thrust.

They both swore loudly, then Ilya made eye contact with Shane, checking to make sure he was good. Shane nodded, and Ilya nodded back. Then, Ilya started pounding into him in a steady, powerful rhythm that had Shane panting and clawing at the bed sheets in seconds.

"My impatient slut," Ilya growled as he fucked him. "Could not even wait for me."

"Just," Shane gasped, "being efficient."

"So good," Ilya said, punctuating his words with thrusts. "At time. Management."

"Wanted your dick."

"You have it. Is it good?"

"Fuck yes. Love it. Harder."

There was a padded leather bench at the end of Shane's bed that Ilya was ninety percent sure could hold his weight. He shuffled toward it, dragging Shane with him, then planted one foot on the bench.

"You want it harder?" Ilya asked.

Shane nodded, his eyes glazed and blissed out. Ilya hauled Shane up until only his upper back, shoulders, and head were on the mattress, then started a steady, ruthless rhythm, driving into Shane hard enough to make them both lose their minds.

"How many days?" Ilya gritted out. "How long has it been?"

"Three, I think? Four? When was the last time we had phone sex?"

"Four days ago," Ilya answered quickly. He didn't need to do the math. He *knew*. The difference was he'd jerked off at least once a day since. Twice most days.

"Can you come like this?" Ilya asked, because *he* sure as fuck was going to.

"Fuck, maybe. You're so deep. Jesus."

Ilya wrapped his hand behind Shane's left knee and bent his leg forward, adjusting the angle of his dick inside him. He gave a few quick thrusts and Shane let out a noise that was almost a sob.

"Right there. Like that. Holy fuck. Let me just . . ." He wrapped a hand around his own dick and started stroking. "Keep going. Don't stop. Don't—"

Ilya never wanted to stop. He jackhammered into Shane, while Shane stared up at him, eyes wide and lips parted as his hand flew over his cock.

"Saved it all for me?" Ilya asked, his voice shaky and strained.

Shane nodded and bit his bottom lip.

"Let me see it," Ilya commanded.

Shane's gaze went to the head of his cock. "Fuck. *Fuck!* I'm going to—oh *shit*."

Shane probably realized the same moment that Ilya did that his face was directly in the line of fire. It was a moment too late, if he wanted to do anything about it. His cock spurted ribbon after ribbon of come over his cheeks, chin, and lips. One stripe landed across his eyebrow.

It was all too much for Ilya. He made a last-second decision, pulled out, and gently lowered Shane to the mattress just in time for Ilya to shoot his load all over Shane's chest.

For a long moment, neither man said anything. They panted together, Ilya looming over Shane on his knees. Shane was absolutely covered in come, which Ilya was sure he'd be grossed out by in about half a second.

"Ugh," Shane said, half a second later. "I'm a mess."

"Sorry."

"Are you kidding? That was hot as fuck. Holy shit."

Ilya watched Shane's glistening chest heave as he waited for his own breathing to steady. "You are okay?"

Shane stretched his arms out in a T shape on the mattress. "I'm fucking great."

Ilya brushed his fingers over Shane's hole, and Shane jerked his hip off the bed. "Not hurt?" Ilya asked.

Shane exhaled slowly. "Not hurt. Feels nice, actually. You touching me there after."

"Yes?"

"Mm. But I need a shower. Or at least a cloth."

After a few more lazy minutes, Ilya went to the bathroom and returned with several warm, damp facecloths. He carefully wiped Shane's face first, then kissed his nose, each eyebrow, and then his mouth. Shane tangled his fingers in Ilya's hair as they kissed, and Ilya sighed into his mouth. It was so fucking unfair that they had to endure so many days without this.

They kissed for a while, then Ilya continued cleaning his boyfriend. He used a new cloth for his chest and throat, then another for his dick, thighs, and ass. He took his time with Shane's ass, since Shane seemed to find the attention to his sensitive flesh soothing. Ilya gently swiped the warm cloth over his slightly swollen entrance more times than was necessary, watching his boyfriend smile and shiver happily.

"You are so beautiful," Ilya said.

"Not bad yourself."

"We can shower in the morning, yes?"

"Yeah. Come here."

Ilya stretched out beside Shane, then rolled him so he could spoon him from behind. Shane curled against him easily—automatically—holding Ilya's hand where it lay in front of Shane's belly.

"Hi," Shane said sleepily.

"Hi."

# CHAPTER TWELVE

Shane was shocked to find it was morning when he opened his eyes. He didn't remember falling asleep, but he must have been wiped out after the game and the mind-blowing sex.

God, and the edging. That had been hot as hell.

He could hear Ilya snoring softly behind him, one strong arm draped loosely over Shane's waist. Shane smiled and snuggled back against him, sighing happily. He was hard, and he could feel that Ilya was too, but he could ignore that for now. Sex was great, but moments like this one, where they could cuddle and caress and just exist alone together in a quiet room, were Shane's favorite thing.

Shane was normally an early riser, and followed a strict routine every morning. But instead of jumping out of bed and into some running clothes, this morning he succumbed to the comfort of being held by the man he loved, and dozed off.

He was awoken sometime later by Ilya trailing kisses along his shoulder.

"Good morning," Shane mumbled.

"It is," Ilya agreed.

Shane rolled to his back and gazed up at Ilya, rumpled and

sleepy and gorgeous in the morning light. "We have the whole day together."

Ilya smiled. "And night."

"What do you want to do?"

"I want you to brush your teeth, because you won't let me kiss you until you do."

"You have to brush yours too," Shane was quick to add.

"Yes, yes." Ilya lifted Shane's hand to his mouth and kissed his knuckles.

"And we have to shower."

"I *know*. But then I want to make you a gross, healthy breakfast." He kissed Shane's palm. "And I want to spend the whole day touching you."

"Okay."

They brushed their teeth, then made out in the shower together. They were both in good moods, smiling and laughing easily. Ilya made poached eggs with sliced up fruit while Shane made protein smoothies and coffee.

"That ESPN doc about us airs next week," Shane said.

"Yes."

"You think it'll be weird watching that?"

Ilya shrugged. "Maybe."

"I think my interviews were terrible. I was so awkward."

"Of course you were."

"Answering so many questions about you, and our, y'know, professional relationship. While hiding our actual relationship. It was tough."

"Mm."

Shane held out a mug of coffee, which Ilya took. Then, as casually as possible, Shane asked, "What did you say about me?"

Ilya chuckled and went to the fridge to get some of the coffee cream that Shane had bought specifically for him. "Watch the documentary and find out."

Shane let out a long, exasperated breath. "Just tell me one thing."

"No."

Shane glared at him, then stomped angrily over to the kitchen table. "Fine."

Ilya put the cream away and headed for the sugar bowl. "I said you come really fast when I suck your balls."

Shane threw a strawberry at him. "You're an idiot. And it's not even that fast."

"Okay."

They sat at the table together, and Ilya sniffed his smoothie with open disgust on his face.

"It's packed with protein and nutrients," Shane promised him. Ilya didn't seem to think that was a good enough reason to drink it. He set it aside and went for the eggs instead.

"I said nice things about you," Shane said as he watched Ilya devour his eggs.

"Did you?" He sounded disinterested, but Shane knew it was a front.

"Yup." Shane sipped his smoothie, and waited.

"What did you say?" Ilya said.

Shane smiled. "You'll have to watch and see."

Ilya huffed. "Fine."

The triumph of victory didn't last long. Shane poked at his eggs and said, somewhat pathetically, "I wish you'd tell me one thing you said."

"Why?" Ilya snapped, his voice loud and sharp enough to startle Shane. "Was boring. I could not say any of the things I wanted to say. I said you were a great hockey player. A nice guy. Very competitive. All of the shit that any of your teammates could have said." Ilya sighed loudly, then continued in a quieter tone. "When you watch it, this is what you will see. Me saying nothing. I wanted to say you are fucking *everything* to me. Everything. Okay?"

Shane swallowed hard. "Oh."

He wasn't sure, after years of being together, how he could still be surprised by the depths of what Ilya felt for him. By the plain, unguarded way Ilya would occasionally reveal what he held in his heart. Maybe English being Ilya's second language made it harder to dress up his feelings with fancy words, but the raw honesty left Shane thunderstruck every time.

Ilya let out a shaky breath. "But I am still not drinking that smoothie."

Shane laughed, glad to be rid of some of the tension that had built inside him. Then, quietly, he said, "You're everything to me too."

Ilya held his gaze for a long moment, and Shane thought his eyes looked a bit sad. Then Ilya said, "Of course."

An hour later, they were tangled up together on Shane's couch. Shane couldn't even remember the planned activity that had brought them here—watching a movie? video games?—because it had been instantly shoved aside in favor of kissing. Shane was straddling Ilya's lap, facing him, and kissing him while he held his face in both hands.

"I missed you so fucking much," Shane murmured against Ilya's lips.

Ilya squeezed his ass, and kissed him hungrily. They were both fully clothed and hard as hell, but neither was in a hurry to escalate things. Maybe they'd keep kissing and caressing each other until neither of them could stand it anymore, then Ilya would bend him over the sofa and rim him and finger him until Shane was begging for it.

Shane groaned thinking about it, which made Ilya laugh.

"What?" Ilya asked.

"Nothing." Then, he gathered up some courage and said, "Thinking about you fucking me."

Ilya licked Shane's Adam's apple. "I am thinking about it too."

Shane's phone rang on the coffee table behind them.

"Don't answer it," Ilya said.

Shane turned and grabbed the phone. "It's Hayden."

"Then definitely don't answer it."

Shane noticed that he also had a bunch of missed texts from Hayden. He answered the phone while Ilya thunked his forehead against Shane's chest.

"What's up, Hayden?"

"Thank Christ," Hayden said. "Listen, Jackie broke her ankle."

"No, I didn't!" Shane heard Jackie yell in the background.

"Well, it's sprained or something. She tripped on a toy and I have to take her to the hospital."

"Shit," Shane said. "Sorry to hear that. I hope she's okay."

"Me too. But, like, can you babysit the kids until we're back?"

Shane's gaze met Ilya's. He could tell immediately that Ilya had heard the entire conversation. Normally Shane loved hanging out with Hayden's four kids, but today was supposed to be just for him and Ilya.

But Ilya smiled excitedly and nodded.

"Sure, no problem. But, um . . . Ilya is here."

"Oh," Hayden said. "Sorry. You're probably, like, making up for lost time, right?"

Gross. "No, it's fine. We can do it. I'm just saying, Ilya is coming too."

Hayden exhaled loudly into the phone. "How soon can you get here?"

* * *

Ilya had been to the Pikes' house only once before, for an olive branch in the form of a barbecue. He'd suspected at the time that it had been Jackie's idea more than Hayden's.

Jackie, who at the moment was lying on the Pikes' large sectional sofa with her right foot resting on a stack of pillows. An ice pack was draped over her ankle. "Hi, Ilya," she said.

"Tripped over a toy?"

She rolled her eyes. "I tripped over Hayden's stupid remote control car."

Ilya laughed, delighted by this new and important information. "It was Hayden's toy?"

"One of the kids left it out," Hayden insisted from the other side of the room. "It wasn't me!"

Ilya shared a *look* with Jackie.

"Come on." Ilya offered her his hand. "I will help you to the car."

She tried to move her swollen ankle, then winced.

"Are you sure it is not broken?" Ilya asked.

"It's not broken. It just hurts."

She reached for his shoulder, and Ilya decided to make this easier for her. He bent and hovered one hand near her bent knees. "May I?"

"Go for it."

Ilya lifted her into his arms. She wasn't a tall woman, but she was fit and strong. He was still able to lift her easily.

"Hey, I can do that!" Hayden insisted as he strode across the room.

"Good grief, Hayden," Jackie said. "Just get the door."

Ilya carried Jackie to the Pikes' SUV and helped her get comfortable in the back with her leg elevated across the seat. Shane exited the house with all four kids trailing behind him.

"You good?" Hayden asked her as he got into the driver's seat.

"Do you have her health card?" Ilya asked.

"Shit."

"It's in my purse," Jackie said. "On the kitchen counter."

"Got it," Shane said, jogging back to the house.

The kids swarmed the car, asking a million questions at once.

"I'm fine," Jackie assured them. "Mommy just needs a doctor to look at her ankle. He'll patch me up and I'll be good as new!"

"But you were going to paint our nails," one of the twin girls—Ruby, Ilya was pretty sure—said with a pout.

"I can do that later," Jackie promised her.

"I can do it," Ilya said. He looked at Ruby and tapped a finger against his lips. "Wait. What color?"

"Purple. With sparkles. And pink. And blue."

He smiled. "No problem."

Shane returned with the purse, and handed it to Jackie.

"Thank you for doing this," Jackie said. "I know we ruined your day."

"Not ruined," Ilya said honestly. "Just more interesting."

Amber, the youngest Pike child, started crying when Ilya tried to close the car door.

"Oh, sweetie," Jackie said. "It's okay. Mommy will be home soon and you'll have so much fun with Uncle Ilya."

"Uncle Ilya?" Hayden grumbled.

Ilya picked Amber up and smiled at her. "Shane told me that you are a great chef."

The three-year-old stared at him with wide, wet eyes, then nodded.

"If you like plastic food," Hayden said, "you're in luck."

"Better than what Shane eats," Ilya said, winking at Shane.

Hayden actually laughed at that.

★ ★ ★

"Sparkles on all of them?" Ilya asked.

Ruby nodded without hesitation and Ilya got to work. He'd already painted her nails a bold combination of dark purple, neon pink, and light blue, but obviously the sparkles were necessary.

"How's it going?" Shane asked as he entered the kitchen.

"Amazing. Look at this great job I am doing."

Shane bent over the table and inspected Ruby's manicure. "Wow. I'm jealous."

"I'm next," said Ruby's twin sister, Jade, claiming her spot before Shane tried to butt in line.

"Is Amber asleep?" Ilya asked.

"Yeah. Conked right out after a solid hour of preparing food for us."

Ilya smiled, remembering how seriously Amber had presented each of their plastic meals. "Was surprised you ate the hamburger. Red meat, you know."

Shane lightly punched his shoulder. "Idiot."

"That's not nice," Jade said.

"You are right," Ilya agreed. "That is not nice, Shane."

"Sorry." He sat at the table between Jade and the middle child, Arthur. The Pikes' only son was a remarkably quiet kid, seemingly content to watch whatever was happening around him. He seemed to be fascinated by his sister's nails.

"Do you want nail polish, Arthur?" Ilya asked.

The five-year-old blinked at him, then nodded.

"He can't!" Ruby insisted. "He's a *boy*."

"Boys can wear nail polish," Ilya said. "Watch." He carefully brushed a coat of the pale blue color on his thumbnail. "See?"

"Dad said it's just for girls," Jade said.

"Well, *Dad* is a—"

"Your dad doesn't know a lot of boys who wear nail polish," Shane cut in just in time. "But plenty do."

Ilya painted the rest of the nails on his left hand and admired his work. "This is nice. I should have sparkles too maybe."

"Here," Shane said. He took Ilya's hand in his, then grabbed the bottle of glitter polish. "It's easier if someone else does it. Probably."

Everyone watched as Shane bent over Ilya's hand, concentrating intensely as he brushed polish on each nail. Ilya's heart fluttered at the sweetness of it.

"Is he your husband?" Ruby asked.

Ilya flinched, nearly making Shane's brush slip. "No."

"Are you *his* husband?"

"That's not how—" Shane said, then stopped himself. "We're not married."

"Are you going to get married?"

Shane locked eyes with Ilya, and Ilya saw the silent plea for help in them.

"Do you think we should?" Ilya asked.

"Do you love each other?"

"We're friends," Shane said stiffly at the same time Ilya said, "Yes."

Jade grabbed her sister's arm. "We could have a wedding today!"

Ruby jumped and clapped, probably making a mess of her nails. "Yeah! Can we?"

Ilya grinned at Shane. "What do you say, sweetheart?"

Twenty minutes later, Shane was standing in the Pikes' living room wearing a magician's cape, a top hat, and holding a pink plastic heart-shaped ring. Ilya was standing next to him wearing a red sequined bow tie and a headband covered in flowers. He was holding an identical purple ring.

Across from them stood two seven-year-old girls wearing princess dresses, and behind them was a large assembled audience of stuffed toys and Arthur (wearing a firefighter costume and a freshly painted blue manicure).

Arthur pressed a button on a toy that played fifteen seconds of a song from *Moana*, and they were ready to begin.

"This is the wedding of Shane Hollander and Ilya . . ." Jade narrowed her eyes at Ilya.

"Rozanov," he supplied.

She nodded. "Rose-noff."

Shane snickered, and Ilya nudged him. "Shane. Keep it together. Is our wedding day."

"Shane, do you promise to love Ilya and be his husband forever?" Ruby asked.

Shane gazed at his ridiculous-looking boyfriend, who smiled back at him. One of the flowers on his headband was holding on by a thread, dangling in front of Ilya's raised left eyebrow. Suddenly—absurdly—Shane's throat felt tight.

"I do," he said quietly, and with an embarrassing amount of feeling.

"Ilya," said Jade, "do you promise to love Shane and be his husband forever?"

"I do," Ilya said. "Forever."

There was a slight tremor in Ilya's voice, which surprised and relieved Shane. At least Shane wasn't the only one getting inappropriately emotional.

"Okay," Jade said. "Do the rings now."

Ilya took Shane's hand, and slipped the child-size purple heart ring onto his pinkie, down to his second knuckle. Shane huffed out a shaky laugh.

He took Ilya's hand and smiled at his painted nails. He wiggled the ring onto the end of Ilya's pinkie, barely able to get it past the tip. He glanced up, and caught Ilya blinking rapidly.

"I now pronounce you husband and husband," Ruby said.

Jade elbowed her. "*I* was supposed to say that!"

"No you weren't! You say the kissing thing."

"Oh yeah. You may now kiss."

Shane raised his eyebrows at Ilya, silently asking *You wanna?*

Ilya leaned in and kissed him quickly on the mouth while the kids whooped and threw handfuls of paper they'd ripped up into the air. Arthur hit play on the *Moana* song again.

After the kiss, Ilya pressed his forehead against Shane's, and they just stood there like that, frozen in the moment.

"Does this mean tonight is our honeymoon?" Shane asked quietly.

"Let's pretend it is."

Shane was having a difficult time getting his key to work because Ilya wouldn't stop kissing his neck.

"Quit it for a sec, would you?" Shane said, tipping his head to the side to try to block Ilya's attacks.

Ilya wasn't deterred. He switched to the other side and nibbled under Shane's ear. Shane let out a childish-sounding giggle and pretended to try to get away when Ilya wrapped an arm across his chest from behind.

"Give it to me," Ilya said, snatching the key from Shane's hand. He deftly inserted the key in the lock and turned it while continuing to make a meal of Shane's neck.

"Show-off," Shane complained.

"Always." Then Ilya scooped Shane into his arms, bridal style. The same way he'd carried Jackie to the car earlier that day.

"What the hell?" Shane said, though he knew he sounded more delighted than outraged. "Put me down!"

Ilya grinned at him, and nudged the door open with his foot. "Is our wedding night."

"This can't be good for your knee."

"My knee is fine," Ilya scoffed. "And you are very light."

"I'm two hundred pounds!"

"Sure you are."

"I am!"

"Like you are five-ten."

"I *am* five-ten!"

Ilya shook his head and stepped over the threshold.

The Pikes had been at the hospital for hours, but thankfully Jackie's ankle was, as she'd repeatedly told her husband, only sprained. She'd hobbled through the door on crutches around dinnertime, Hayden hovering close behind looking exhausted and concerned. Ilya, Shane, and the kids had been gathered on the sofa, watching *Frozen 2*. Ilya's arm had been wrapped snugly around Shane, which had been nice, in the presence of others. Hayden hadn't even seemed bothered by it, but that may have been because he'd been distracted by the floral headband Ilya had still been wearing.

It had been a thoroughly enjoyable day.

Ilya carried Shane to the living room, then stopped and glanced around. "Now what?"

"Now you put me down!"

"This is how it works? I thought maybe I put you on our bed? With rose petals?"

"God, fuck off." Shane squirmed until Ilya had no choice but to release him. Shane landed on his feet, but stumbled forward and almost collided with the coffee table. When he turned around to glare at Ilya, he found him smiling at him with the same soft expression Shane had seen on his face during their make-believe wedding vows.

"What?" Shane asked.

"Nothing." Ilya scratched the back of his own neck. Looked away. Looked back at Shane. "Today was nice."

"It was." Shane took his hand and tugged him closer. "I mean, not the part where Jackie sprained her ankle, but the rest of it."

"She is lucky it was not broken."

"*Hayden* is lucky," Shane said. Hayden was his best friend and a wonderful father, but Jackie took care of about ninety-nine percent of everything that went on in that family.

"I like those kids," Ilya said. "I can't believe Hayden made them."

"You're great with kids." Shane brushed their noses together, then kissed Ilya's mouth. He tasted like the lemonade Shane had declined at the Pikes' house but that Ilya had happily drank two glasses of. Shane guiltily enjoyed the taste now, sweet and tangy.

When they broke the kiss, Ilya said, "You will be a good dad."

Shane rested his forehead on Ilya's shoulder and smiled. "Not as good as you."

Ilya huffed. "Not everything is a competition with us."

"We'd find a way to make parenting a competition."

Strong arms tightened around Shane. "No. It will be together. Peaceful."

Shane, feeling brave, admitted, "There were moments today where I felt like I was looking into our future."

Ilya pulled back to meet Shane's gaze. "And it was okay?"

"It was amazing."

Shane saw joy flash in Ilya's eyes, and then he didn't see anything because Ilya was kissing him thoroughly. Shane lost himself in it, enjoying the familiar but still exhilarating heat of Ilya's mouth. Shane touched him everywhere: the rough scratch of Ilya's ever-present stubble, the soft curls of his shaggy hair, the long line of his neck and the mounds of his muscular shoulders. He slid a hand up under Ilya's T-shirt and glided his palm over Ilya's abs, his perfect bellybutton, and the neat trail of hair beneath it. Then up to his broad chest, over his chest hair and stiff nipples, finally resting over his heart and his stupid bear tattoo.

"I love you," Ilya murmured against Shane's lips.

"I love you too."

"But we are not having four children."

Shane laughed. "God no. Of course not."

"It would be too much. With the dogs."

"Um. I think you mean cat."

"I did not mean cat. Definitely not."

"How many dogs exactly?"

"Some. Maybe one, to start. And then he needs a friend, so two. Maybe they don't like each other so we get number three to be, um . . ."

"A mediator?"

"Okay. Maybe, yes."

"And if they don't like that one?"

"The fourth dog will—"

Shane stepped out of Ilya's arms. "No."

Ilya laughed. "One dog."

"One dog," Shane agreed.

"You will want more. Just wait."

*Just wait.* The words rang in Shane's ears as he made his way to the kitchen. He believed in their relationship, and was confident that they would have everything they wanted when the time was right. But sometimes he wished the right time was now.

"Are you hungry?" Shane asked.

"Yes."

"I have a premade lasagna. I just have to bake it."

Ilya's face lit up with interest. Then, just as quickly, his face fell. "What are the noodles?"

"Zucchini."

"No!"

"It's good, I swear. You won't even notice the difference," Shane lied. He turned on the oven, and decided not to tell Ilya what the stand-in for the cheese was.

Ilya grunted as he sat on Shane's sofa, and Shane glanced over with concern. "How's your knee?"

"It fell off," Ilya said dryly, clearly done with Shane asking the same question over and over.

"Let me look at it."

"You saw it this morning." Ilya had his sore leg stretched out on the sofa. "Is still just bruised."

Shane was already at his side. He tried to slide Ilya's pants leg up, but the tapered cut of the fancy jogging pants made it impossible. "Pull your pants down."

"You are terrible at foreplay," Ilya said, but he lifted his hips and slid his waistband down to his shins. The outer part of Ilya's left knee was entirely dark purple and swollen.

"Jesus," Shane said. He brushed his fingers over the bruise. "Maybe *you* should have seen a doctor today."

"I saw the team doctor last night. Is bruised. Have you not ever had a bruise?"

"I'm getting you some ice."

Ilya made a vague grunting noise that Shane translated as *Ice would feel amazing but I am absolutely not going to admit that.*

Shane left and returned with an ice pack, some ibuprofen, and a glass of water. He carefully placed the ice on Ilya's knee while Ilya took the pills.

"Thank you, moya gazonokosilka."

This was a game Ilya liked to play where he used random Russian words as pet names, to test Shane. Shane thought hard for a moment, trying to guess the word's meaning, but ultimately surrendered. "No idea what that one means."

"Is, um . . . for cutting the grass."

"Lawnmower?"

"Yes."

"Weird."

Shane felt something digging into his hip when he bent to kiss Ilya quickly, then remembered the plastic heart rings that the kids had insisted he and Ilya keep. He took them out of his pocket and placed them on the coffee table, and was about to return to the kitchen when Ilya said, quietly, "The kids didn't care."

"About what?"

"About us. They knew, and they did not care."

"Yeah. That was a surprise." Shane had no idea how Ruby and Jade had been so certain that Ilya and Shane were a couple—he was sure their parents hadn't told them, it would be risky giving young children that information—but they'd known and accepted it and had insisted on making honest men of them both.

"Maybe more people would not care," Ilya said. "If they knew."

"I think most people would care way too fucking much," Shane said dismissively.

Ilya's expression shuttered, then he began to aggressively adjust his ice pack. Shane felt like he'd said something wrong, but what else could he have said? He didn't honestly believe that many people would accept them as a couple. They could only stick to the plan, which was continuing on in secret until they were both retired. Or at least until one of them was, but Shane hoped they would retire together. The idea of playing in a league without Ilya seemed strange and hollow.

Shane put a tentative hand on Ilya's shoulder. "What's wrong?"

Ilya crossed his arms over his chest and mumbled something in Russian.

"Huh?"

"I think *you* care too fucking much."

"About what? Us?"

"No. About everyone else. Opinions."

"Aren't we both concerned about that?"

Ilya didn't answer, and Shane felt like he was missing something important. "We can talk about it if you—"

"No," Ilya grumbled. "Is nothing."

"Okay." It wasn't the first time Ilya had seemed randomly upset about something he refused to talk about. Shane worried, sometimes, that there were a lot of things Ilya wasn't telling him.

Ilya sighed. "Sorry. I am tired. Forget what I am saying."

Shane brushed a thumb across Ilya's cheek. "I love you."

Ilya's lips quirked up. "Good. Because we are married now."

Still not sure what any of this was about, Shane picked up the remote from the coffee table and handed it to Ilya. "We can eat on the sofa. Find a movie or something."

He got to work making a salad to a soundtrack of heroic music and loud explosions coming from the living room. Ilya loved action movies. The lasagna still needed to bake for a while after Shane finished the salad, so he joined his boyfriend on the couch, letting Ilya rest his feet in his lap.

"What movie is it?"

"I don't know. But Rose is in it."

Shane squinted at the TV and wished he had his glasses. "Oh yeah. I've seen this one. It's kind of bad."

"Rose looks beautiful, though."

"She always does." They watched in silence while Shane absently rubbed Ilya's feet.

"You could have had it all," Ilya teased when Rose was on the screen in a particularly sexy evening gown.

Shane snuggled closer against him. He'd had a question on his mind for weeks. He didn't want to ruin this cozy moment, but he couldn't hold it in anymore.

"Ilya?"

Ilya must have heard the caution in Shane's voice, because his body tensed. "Yes?"

"Are you . . . okay?"

"Fine. Is just a bruise."

"No, I mean . . ." Shane gnawed on his bottom lip, unsure of how to proceed.

"Shane?"

He decided to just go for it. "I feel like, maybe, you're not okay. Sometimes."

Ilya removed his arm and turned toward him. "Not okay how?"

Shane sat up and faced him. "You've been through a lot, and I know our . . . thing . . . isn't easy. And I'm just wondering if you maybe need to deal with some of that." He steeled himself. "Professionally, I mean."

Ilya narrowed his eyes. "Why are you saying this?"

Shane put a hand on his arm, and Ilya flinched under his touch. Shit, Shane was fucking this up. He tried again. "I'd never thought much about, y'know, mental health stuff, before we started the charity. But sometimes you seem . . . sad. Or, I dunno, withdrawn."

"Withwhat?"

"Withdrawn, like, um, quiet."

"Everyone is quiet sometimes." Ilya turned back to the TV. "You should try it."

Shane huffed out an exasperated sigh. "Fine. We don't have to talk about it. Just know that if you want to talk, or want to maybe see someone about it, I'll support you. And if you don't want to, I'll support that too. But I'm worried sometimes."

For a long time, Ilya didn't say anything. Shane watched the hinge of his jaw twitch. His lips were a hard line.

"You should not worry," Ilya finally said, his gaze staying on the television. "I am okay."

Shane took his hand and squeezed. "You don't have to deal with anything alone, all right?"

Ilya swallowed hard. "Yes. Fine." His hand was trembling.

"I'm serious," Shane said.

Ilya stood, pulling his hand away. "If there is something, I will tell you. But there is nothing. So let's eat bad lasagna and shut up about it, okay?"

That really didn't sound like nothing was bothering Ilya, but Shane had promised to support him if he didn't want to talk. He stood too. "It's not bad lasagna."

Ilya managed to smile a bit at that. "We will see."

# CHAPTER THIRTEEN

"What are you doing tonight?" J.J. asked.

"Nothing," Shane said, then immediately regretted it. Ilya had left yesterday and Shane was feeling the loss. He didn't want to do anything social tonight.

J.J. placed one hand on the wall of Shane's locker room stall, above where Shane was sitting, boxing him in. "Sweet. You should come out with me. I'm meeting some friends at this amazing cocktail bar that my buddy Benoit opened."

"I don't drink," Shane reminded him.

"Still?"

"Yes. Still." Shane resumed untying his skates, hopefully indicating that the conversation was over.

"Okay, well, they have other stuff to drink. I'll bet they make, like, bomb mocktails."

Shane almost reminded him that he didn't consume most of the probable ingredients in a mocktail either, but decided to just shut the whole thing down instead. "I'm gonna stay in. But thanks."

J.J. sighed and sat in the stall next to Shane. Hayden's stall, but Hayden was in the shower. "It's not healthy," he said, in French.

When J.J. switched to French with Shane, it usually meant he was about to get real. Or that he was drunk. "What do you do besides come to practice—" he waved a hand around the locker room, indicating the activity they'd just finished "—play games, work out, and sleep?"

"Lots of stuff," Shane argued, hoping he wouldn't be asked for specific examples.

"Like what?"

"I . . . see friends."

"Friends," J.J. said flatly. And skeptically. "Like who? Your parents?"

"No," Shane said quickly, then scrambled for examples. "Hayden?"

J.J. frowned at him, then said, "Come out tonight."

"Why?"

"Because . . ."

Oh god. "Because why?"

"There's someone I want you to meet."

Shane bent and yanked his skate off. "Nope. No way."

"He's super nice, and, y'know, handsome. He's a personal trainer, and I figured you'd probably be into that."

"And let me guess: he's gay and single."

"Well, yeah."

Shane wanted to snap at him that just because a man was gay and single and handsome and a personal trainer didn't mean that Shane would—okay, well, under different circumstances Shane probably *would* be into all of that, but that wasn't the point. The *point* was that Shane had a perfectly good secret boyfriend, so obviously it was rude of J.J. to try to set Shane up with other men. Even if J.J. didn't know Shane was with anyone, and probably assumed Shane hadn't had sex in years. Or ever.

The truth was, it was kind of sweet that Shane's NHL teammate was trying to find him a man to date.

After a slow exhale, Shane said, "I appreciate it, and I'm sure he's very nice."

"And handsome," J.J. reminded him. "Even *I* can see that."

"Sure. But I'm really not looking for a date right now." There. That was straightforward. And honest.

J.J.'s eyes were full of concern, which made Shane doubt that he was going to let this go. "Why don't you want to date anyone? It doesn't have to be serious. You could just get laid, y'know?"

Shane glanced around the room nervously, but no one seemed to be paying attention. "I'm fine," he said tersely.

J.J. laughed. "If being wound so tight you seem like you are going to fly apart at any second is fine, then sure."

"I'm not!" Shane said in the tone of someone who was about to fly apart. "Do the other guys think so? Do I seem distracted or something? Is it affecting my game? Is that what this is about?"

J.J. switched to English. "No! Buddy, no. This is me, as a friend. You're a great guy and I want you to be happy. That's all. I promise."

Shane leaned back in his stall until his head bumped against the wall. "Okay."

"Okay, you'll meet David, or . . ."

"David?" Shane decided to play this up as an end to the conversation. "My dad's name is David. I can't date a David!"

J.J. took Shane's objection seriously. "Shit. Sorry. I didn't even think of that. You're right." He stood, looking dejected.

"Hey," Shane said, "I do appreciate it. Really."

J.J. brightened at that. "So if I meet any nice single gay guys who aren't named David . . ."

"Introduce them to David," Shane said. "Really. I'll let you know if I'm ever looking, okay?" Which would hopefully be never.

J.J. nodded. "I'll mind my own business. Got it."

He left just as Hayden returned from the shower, wearing only a towel wrapped snugly around his waist. Hayden watched J.J. leave, then turned to Shane. "Did he try to set you up with that guy?"

"He *told* you?" Shane did not like the idea of his love life being a team concern.

"Yeah, he told me."

"Why didn't you, like, discourage him?"

"Because the dude sounded perfect for you." Hayden held his arms out when Shane's mouth dropped open. "What? I think you can do better!"

"For fuck's sake. Thanks, Hayden."

Hayden sat next to him, and nudged his arm with his elbow. "I'm kidding. Mostly. Besides." He leaned in. "I know you and Ilya are married now, so . . ."

Shane closed his eyes. "Oh my god."

"Jade told me it was a beautiful ceremony. I'm a little hurt that I wasn't invited but, y'know. I'm happy for you kids."

"Shut up."

Hayden laughed, and eventually Shane joined him.

"You know," Hayden said seriously, "even though I give you shit about him, I do hope that I'd be invited. If you ever did get married for real."

Shane stared at him, simultaneously touched by Hayden's support and baffled that he thought Shane wouldn't invite him to this hypothetical wedding. "Of course you would be. Don't be fucking stupid."

Hayden grinned. "Good. Just making sure."

"I kind of doubt we'd ever have, like, a traditional wedding with all the stuff, but if we have anything at all, you're on the list, all right?"

"Cool. Is Rozanov on the list, or . . ."

"Fuck off," Shane laughed. "You're off the list now."

"No way."

"Yup. All the way off."

"Nuh-uh. I'm your best man. And the MC."

"Absolutely not."

"Shit, I'll get, like, annulled, or whatever. Marry you guys myself."

"Do you mean *ordained*?"

"Sure. Okay."

"Annulled means ending a marriage, dumbass. Do you want to end your marriage and marry both of us? Because that's how that sounded."

"Fuck no! First of all, Jackie rules, and second of all, I would never marry Rozanov."

"So you'd marry me?"

Hayden turned a little pink. "No! I'm not—no!"

Shane decided to go easy on him, because this was getting weird. "You're my best man, Hayden. One hundred percent."

"Fucking right." Hayden held out his fist, and Shane bumped it. "I've gotta go film a FanMail."

"What the hell are you talking about?"

"FanMail! It's a website where fans pay money to have their favorite celebrities send them little video greetings. Or to send videos to other people, like their dads or whatever."

"Seriously? You do this?"

"Uh . . . yeah. I get a hundred dollars a pop for wishing randos a happy birthday. Of course I do it."

"Does it cost extra if you're only wearing a towel?"

Hayden grinned. "I was gonna get dressed first! Jesus, dude."

"Maybe you should be on that other site? The porn one."

"*The* porn site? Like, the one and only porn site? Is that the one I should be on?"

"Shut up. You know the one I mean."

"Sure. Is it porno site dot com?"

"OnlyFans! That's the one I mean! Isn't that where people, like, do sex stuff for money?"

Hayden laughed so hard Shane worried he would lose his towel. "You are so innocent. I love it."

"I am not." Why did everyone act like he was a total prude? Even Ilya—the man he had actual sex with on the regular—teased him about it.

"Sorry," Hayden said, still laughing. "I'm sure you're wild in bed."

"You think I'm not?"

Hayden held up his hands. "Please don't tell me."

Fuck Hayden. Shane could be wild in bed. He wasn't always uptight. "You sure? Because the other night—"

"Nope!" Hayden backed away. "Hard no. Super no."

Shane shook his head. "Get dressed, dickhead."

Hayden began rooting through his bag for clean clothes. "It's okay if the magic is gone. That happens after you get married. Sometimes. Not to me, obviously."

"You're such an idiot," Shane said, but he was fighting a smile. And he was already brainstorming ways to show a bit of his wild side to Ilya next time he had a chance.

Ilya was surrounded by beautiful women. They were all married to his teammates, but still. Beautiful.

His teammates were beautiful too. Everyone and everything was beautiful. He caught a glimpse of himself in the giant mirror that hung on one wall of his spacious living room. Swirling colorful disco lights glinted off his breastplate and wrist cuffs as he danced. Stunning.

He was maybe a little bit drunk. And a little bit high. A distant, annoying voice in the back of his brain—a voice that sounded a lot like Shane Hollander's—suggested that he might not be setting the best example for the younger players at the moment, as team captain.

But a louder voice said this was a party, in Ilya's own home, and he was having fun and so was everyone else. Because Ilya knew how to throw a party.

The song that was pulsing on the sound system was good. Ilya didn't know what it was, or who had taken over the music.

Evan Dykstra was dancing next to him, dressed like a bee. He did not look stunning. His wife, Caitlin, was dancing with him, wearing a butterfly costume. She had her arm around Evan's neck, and they were smiling at each other like they were the only ones in the room. This was a rare night out for the two of them, now that they had a baby at home.

Ilya decided to take a break from dancing. His costume was heavy and much too warm for a crowded house party, and his cape was all twisted.

"Going to get some air," he said in the general direction of Evan and Caitlin. They didn't even look at him. He noticed, as he walked away, that the makeshift dance floor was full of couples. He must have been the only one dancing alone.

He had to swat plastic skeletons and bats out of the way as he headed for the back of the house. He'd gone big with the Halloween decorations. He'd gone big with every element of the party because Ilya didn't socialize with his teammates nearly enough.

Despite the brisk chill in the air, Ilya's back deck was full of guests, talking and laughing. He found an empty seat in the corner of his outdoor sectional sofa, between Zane Boodram and Wyatt Hayes, and plunked himself down. Wyatt was dressed as a superhero that Ilya didn't recognize. Zane was dressed like a pirate, maybe? A sleeveless one so he could show off his tattoos. He had a scarf that probably belonged to his wife tied around his head.

“Good party, Maximus,” Bood said, grinning lazily. “You should throw them more often.”

Ilya stretched his arms across the back of the sofa. “I won’t.”

“You’ve got this giant fucking house and never invite anyone over,” complained Tanner Dillon, Ilya and Bood’s linemate, from an armchair across from the sofa.

“Why would I?” Ilya asked flatly.

Wyatt laughed and handed him the joint they’d been passing around. “Have you seen the kids? They can’t believe they’re in *Ilya Rozanov’s house*.”

“You are making me feel old,” Ilya complained, though, if he was being honest, the youngest players on the team did seem like kids to him. There was less than a decade between himself and Luca Haas, but the gap felt far wider.

Ilya shifted and brought his legs up to rest on Wyatt’s lap. The knee-high sandals he was wearing looked fantastic, but were very uncomfortable. Wyatt didn’t even protest, just kept smiling at him as Ilya took a pull off the joint. Ilya tilted his head back so he could gaze up at the stars for a moment as he savored the sharp sensation of smoke filling his lungs.

“Where’s your shield?” Wyatt asked.

“I don’t know. Somewhere,” Ilya said, exhaling as he tilted his head back down. “What are you supposed to be?”

“I’m Adam Strange,” Wyatt said excitedly. “He was an archaeologist who got teleported by a Zeta-Beam to the planet Rann and then—”

“No,” Ilya said, holding up a hand. “Is fine. Enough.” He took another long drag off the joint, then passed it to Tanner, who’d already had his arm outstretched, waiting for it.

“Oh, this pass you can take?” Ilya quipped as he handed the joint over. Wyatt and Bood cracked up.

“Dick,” Tanner said.

Wyatt’s wife, Lisa, walked over to the couch, and tapped Ilya’s shins where they were resting on her husband's lap. "You're in my spot," she said.

Ilya moved his legs, and Lisa perched herself on Wyatt's knee. She was dressed like Wonder Woman, a superhero Ilya actually recognized. She frowned at the joint Wyatt had just been handed by Tanner.

"You don't approve, Doctor?" Ilya guessed.

Lisa, a doctor at the local children's hospital, said, "It's the sharing germs that bothers me, not the weed. But you guys are full-time disgusting, so I guess it doesn't really matter."

"We're not disgusting," Bood argued.

"Dude," said Lisa, "I watched you pick up your mouth guard with your gross hockey glove, carry it around for a minute, and then put it back in your mouth. Last night."

Bood shrugged. "It was on the ice. The ice is clean. My gloves just have my own sweat on them. It's all part of this beautiful body."

Everyone laughed. Zane Boodram did have a beautiful body, with light brown skin, a six-pack that he was very proud of, and muscular arms that were sleeved in tattoos celebrating his Trini heritage.

"I can't believe you're going to be a father," Lisa teased.

"Look, I still can't believe I'm *married*," Bood said with a grin. He glanced across the patio to where his visibly pregnant wife, Cassie, was talking to Nick Chouinard's wife, Selena. "But everyone else was doing it, so I figured what the hell." He nudged Ilya. "Except this guy."

"Roz is never settling down," Tanner said cheerfully. "He's a fucking legend."

"Nah. He'll meet the right one someday," Bood said. "Boom! Head over heels. Won't even know what hit him."

There was more laughter, then the conversation shifted to something else. Ilya found, after several minutes, that he was no longer paying attention, and was suddenly overwhelmed with the need to be alone. He stood and said, "I am going to . . ." as he waved a hand in the general direction of the house. He left without waiting for their reaction.

He walked straight through the party and upstairs to his bedroom, closing the door behind him. Again he caught a glimpse of his reflection in the large mirror that stood in the corner, but he didn't still think he looked stunning. He thought he looked ridiculous. And sad.

He removed the cape and tossed it on his bed before picking up his phone from where it was charging on his nightstand. There was a message from Shane from over an hour ago. **Don't take that costume off.**

Okay. Whatever that meant.

**ILYA:**
How is your night?

He waited several minutes for a reply, then gave up. Sighing, he fell backward onto his bed, wincing as he landed weird on his fake sword. He removed it and tossed it across the room as if it were the source of all his problems. He just needed a few minutes alone, then he could return to the party.

He'd already met the love of his life, and he *was* head over heels, and he couldn't tell anyone and it fucking sucked.

He let himself sulk for twenty minutes, then forced himself to stand up, adjusted his expression so he looked less miserable, and headed back downstairs. He left the cape and sword behind. The costume looked sexier this way anyway, with only the straps from the breastplate crisscrossing across his bare back.

By midnight, most of the guests had left. Babysitters needed to be relieved, and morning fitness schedules needed to be kept to. The stragglers—mostly kids—made after-party plans and called cabs when they noticed Ilya glaring at them. He may have tarnished his reputation as a fun party guy, but he didn't care.

At twelve thirty, Ilya received a text from Shane. Party still going?

**ILYA:**

No. Everyone is gone.

Ten minutes later, his doorbell rang.

Shane was standing on the doorstep in a puffy jacket, looking a little embarrassed.

"I didn't want to use my key and scare the shit out of you," he said. "Oh wow. That costume is even better in person."

Ilya blinked, unable to find words.

Shane let out a shaky breath. "This is probably so stupid. I have to be back in Montreal for a practice tomorrow morning and—"

He didn't get to finish that sentence, because Ilya was hauling him into the house and kissing him at the same time. He pressed Shane against a wall inside the door and devoured him while Shane ran his hands over Ilya's mostly bare back. He couldn't believe he was here. All night he'd been dying inside, wishing he could have the man he loved at his side. Wishing Shane was in his arms, in his lap, in a ridiculous costume, in front of everyone.

"You smell like weed," Shane said when Ilya finally let him breathe.

"You'd know."

"I know what *weed* smells like," Shane said testily.

Ilya grinned at him. "You're here."

"Yeah." Shane smiled shyly. "Is that okay? You sent that photo and I've just been—fuck, I missed you so much."

Ilya kissed him again, then said, "You want to get fucked by a gladiator, Hollander?"

Shane gazed up at him through his dark lashes. "I put a plug in before I left."

Holy shit.

With a growl, Ilya began stripping Shane of his puffy jacket, and then all of the rest of his clothes. "Fucking help me," Ilya snarled as he tugged at Shane's track pants.

Shane laughed and pressed his smile into Ilya's neck as he toed off his sneakers, then stepped out of his pants and underwear. Once Shane was naked, Ilya grabbed his thighs and hitched him up until Shane's strong legs wrapped around Ilya's waist. Ilya carried him to the living room like that, kissing him the entire way. He slid a hand down to Shane's ass, found the base of the plug, and pressed on it.

"Oh fuck," Shane gasped.

"You drove the whole way here with this in?"

"Uh-huh."

"That," Ilya said as he carefully tugged at the toy, "is very slutty."

"Not as slutty as that costume." Shane relaxed his legs from around Ilya's body and stood back. He ran his gaze appreciatively over Ilya. "Jesus."

Ilya smiled. Maybe the costume wasn't so ridiculous after all. "Worth the drive?"

"Fuck yeah." Then Shane was back in Ilya's arms, kissing him with a hand gripping the back of Ilya's neck.

Ilya played with the toy some more, tapping the base, then pulling it nearly out before slowly pushing it back in. Shane shuddered, then whimpered, then bit Ilya's shoulder.

"Is it safe even," Ilya asked, "to wear a plug for so long?"

"Yeah," Shane said breathlessly. "I Googled it."

Ilya grinned, imagining it. He was going to tease him some more about it, but Shane cut him off by dropping to his knees.

"Been thinking about this all night," Shane said, gazing up at him with dark, lust-drunk eyes. Then he flipped the front of Ilya's skirt up and hauled Ilya's underwear down. Ilya hadn't even finished stepping out of them before Shane wrapped his lips around his hard cock.

"Shane," Ilya breathed. Shane didn't need any costume pieces to look like a fantasy. He was absolutely beautiful, on his knees for Ilya. He was always so beautiful.

Ilya's eyes prickled with tears as he watched him, which was weird and alarming. He closed his eyes, hoping Shane hadn't noticed. Ilya had felt oddly fragile all night, and the wonderful surprise of having Shane here combined with the fervent way his dick was being worshipped was too much.

Enough. Time to take control of himself and this situation. He took a step back, enjoying the way Shane fell forward a bit, chasing his dick, and said, "Did you come here for this, or did you come here to get fucked?"

Shane blinked up at him. "Shit," he said quietly.

Ilya smiled. "Stand up. Turn around."

Shane obediently got himself in position, gripping the arm of the sofa, and Ilya grabbed a packet of lube from a discreet little box on the mantel behind him. He'd learned to keep lube in most rooms of the house.

He slicked himself up, then played with the toy in Shane's ass a bit more, pressing on it, and turning it slowly. Shane moaned and wriggled his hips, then gasped when the toy bumped up against his prostate.

"How did you drive all this way," Ilya asked, "without coming?"

"It was close," Shane gritted out. "I had to pull over once and—*fuck*—readjust."

Ilya chuckled, and twisted the toy again. "So dangerous. Driving in that condition. Irresponsible."

"Fucking hurry up," Shane complained.

Ilya complied by sliding the toy out of him in one steady pull while Shane gasped and arched his back. Ilya tossed the toy on the floor and lined himself up. "Is this what you came here for?"

"*Yes.* Come *on.*"

Ilya pushed into him, gripping Shane's hips tightly to hold him steady. Shane's body welcomed him, already loose and open. It felt like heaven.

Shane cried out, and Ilya started a steady rhythm, thrusting into Shane so hard the couch slid a few inches across the floor. The room that had so recently been full of people and music and drunken laughter was now filled only with the slap of Ilya pounding into Shane, his own rough breathing, and Shane's moans of pleasure.

"Fucking love you so much," Shane panted. "Needed this."

Ilya grunted, and planted a hand between Shane's shoulder blades, pushing him down until his arms buckled and his chest rested on the arm of the couch.

"Holy—" Shane gasped. "That's perfect. Oh my god. Don't stop."

Ilya didn't want to stop, but he could feel his orgasm building already. He reached for Shane's cock, wrapping his hand around it, and started stroking.

"Wait," Shane gritted out. "Wanna see you."

Ilya didn't argue. He pulled out and flipped Shane over, then tilted him back until he fell onto the couch cushions with his ass resting on the arm. Ilya grabbed his thighs, pulled him up and toward him, and sank back into him.

"Harder," Shane demanded. "Want to feel this for days."

Ilya grunted, and began snapping his hips so vigorously that he was almost worried he was hurting Shane. Except Shane was smiling like he'd never felt anything so wonderful.

"Ilya," he panted. "So perfect. Love this."

"Make yourself come," Ilya ordered, somewhat frantically. *"Now."*

Shane stroked himself furiously, his gaze fixed on Ilya's face. His eyes were huge and shiny and Ilya wanted to dive into them. He wanted to stay buried in Shane forever, making him come again and again and again.

"I'm coming. Holy fuck. Ilya, I'm—" Shane's words dissolved into a groan as he spurted all over his own stomach.

"Yes," Ilya said quietly. "So beautiful."

It only took a few more thrusts before he was emptying himself into Shane, bracing himself with one hand on the back corner of the couch.

"Wow," Shane rasped.

A weird giggle erupted out of Ilya. He covered his mouth quickly.

Shane grinned. "Oh my god. What was that?"

"Nothing. I don't know." Ilya distracted himself by carefully pulling out of Shane.

Shane slowly got to his feet, placing a hand on Ilya's shoulder for balance. "Gotta say, that was totally worth the drive."

"With a plug in your butt," Ilya reminded him. His insides felt like they were vibrating, and he realized his hand was shaking.

"I just really needed to see you," Shane said seriously.

Ilya nodded, then wrapped him in a tight hug. His eyes were burning with tears again, which was embarrassing and inappropriate after amazing sex.

"Thank you," he said into Shane's hair. It was so unlike Shane to be impulsive like this. To drive to Ottawa in the middle of the night for some quick sex.

But it was also unlike Ilya to cry after sex, so everyone was experiencing new things tonight.

"I like the decorations," Shane said after a minute of Ilya breathing in the scent of him.

"Yes. They are good."

"Very spooky."

"Mm."

"We should probably get cleaned up. There was come on my belly. Now it's on your costume."

Ilya sniffled, and hoped Shane didn't notice. "We will take a shower. Then bed. Then morning sex."

"I have to leave before seven."

Ilya squeezed him tighter. "No. Skip practice."

"I can't."

"I know." Ilya sighed, and let Shane go. "Very early morning sex, then."

Shane grinned. "'What we do in life echoes in eternity.'"

"What?"

"It's a quote from *Gladiator*!" Shane gestured at what was left of Ilya's costume. "Come on!"

"Okay, nerd."

"I only know it because Comeau has it tattooed on his arm."

"Of course he does."

Shane flicked Ilya's left pec, over the breastplate. "You're in no position to be making fun of other people's tattoos." He smiled up at Ilya, and Ilya smiled back, overwhelmed by how much he loved this man.

"Go," Ilya said gently. "Upstairs."

Shane kissed him quickly, then turned and headed for the stairs. Ilya watched him go, giving himself a moment to take some deep breaths and try to settle whatever was happening inside him.

* * *

The next morning, when the sun had just begun to rise, Ilya watched Shane drive away. He stood on his front step for several minutes after, staring in the direction the car had gone, and shivering in his gym shorts and T-shirt. Then, he went inside, closed the door, and burst into tears.

When he'd finished crying, some uncertain amount of time later, he felt more exhausted than he had after any hockey game. He was crumpled on the floor, slumped against his front door, and standing up seemed like an insurmountable feat.

He decided that, yes. He should probably get some professional help.

# CHAPTER FOURTEEN

*November*

Ilya paced the waiting room outside Dr. Galina Molchalina's office. He was alone, but he still had his plain black ball cap pulled low over his eyes, and kept his head down. He'd tried sitting, tried reading one of the magazines on the squat coffee table in front of the cheerful blue sofa with the yellow and white throw pillows. He'd examined the abstract art on the walls. He'd done whatever he could to distract himself from how badly he wanted to leave.

He wasn't sure if Dr. Molchalina was even a *good* therapist. She just happened to be the only one in Ottawa who spoke Russian. And, during their brief phone conversation, she'd acknowledged that she knew who Ilya was without making a big deal about it. That had been a plus.

Finally, the door opened and Ilya stood with his back to whoever was exiting the room, wanting to avoid being recognized and to offer the other person the same privacy. He pretended to be fascinated by a tall plant in the corner.

He heard the outer door open and close, and then his new therapist said, in Russian, "The plant is fake, I'm afraid."

Ilya turned to face her. "That makes sense, I guess," he said, also in Russian. He gestured to the walls. "No windows."

"Sometimes it's better to not have the distraction of the outside world," she said with a small smile. "And it's better for privacy."

"Oh."

She held out her hand to him. "I'm Galina. It's nice to meet you, Ilya."

Ilya shook her hand. She was a small woman, probably in her forties, with dark blond hair that she wore in a neat ponytail. Ilya wondered when she'd left Russia, and why. "It's nice to talk to someone in Russian."

"Has it been a while?"

Ilya considered it. He couldn't remember the last time he'd had a full conversation in his native tongue. He hadn't been in Russia since his father died years ago, and he never talked to his brother anymore. Ottawa didn't have any other Russian players, and he didn't have any Russian friends. The only person he ever spoke Russian to was his friend with former benefits, Svetlana, but she lived in Boston and they hadn't spoken much since Ilya had moved to Ottawa. He felt bad about that almost every day. He missed her.

"It's been a long time." He smiled wryly. "I may not be able to shut up."

"That's what I'm here for. Would you like to come in?" She took a step toward the open door of her office.

"Of course, yes."

He walked past her into the small, cozy room. As described, it had no windows, but did have very nice lighting, a comfy-looking light gray couch and matching armchair, and more fake greenery. It was about what he'd imagined a psychologist's office to look like.

"I sit here, right?" Ilya asked, gesturing to the couch.

"Most people do. Are you nervous?"

Ilya figured lying wouldn't be the best way to start his therapy journey. "I'm very nervous. Is that weird?"

"Not at all. Though I hope you'll find there's no reason to be. Please make yourself comfortable."

Ilya sat in the middle of the sofa, hands folded in his lap, knees spread apart. Every muscle in his body felt tense, and he tried to take a steadying deep breath.

"Are many of your clients Russian?" Ilya asked.

"A few. I'm the only Russian-speaking psychologist in town, I believe. As you probably know, mental health isn't a popular concept among our people."

Ilya was very aware of that. "No. It isn't. Not for hockey players either."

"That's true. But you're a Russian hockey player, and you've been outspoken about mental health issues. The charity you started is doing good work," she said. "I've been following your progress with it. I'm very impressed."

Ilya twisted his fingers together. "Oh. Thank you."

"You told me you haven't tried therapy before, even though you seem to be quite knowledgeable about mental health. What made you decide to book this appointment?"

Okay, so they were just going to . . . start. Ilya tried not to overthink his reply, and said the first thing that popped into his head. "I think I might be depressed. Sometimes."

She waited for him to say more, but he didn't. He'd never said those words out loud, in any language, so he just let them sit there like an anvil.

"Your mother suffered from depression," she said.

Ilya nodded. It wasn't a secret anymore. Not since Ilya had

spoken about her illness during the press conference where he and Shane had launched the charity they'd started in her name.

"Would you like to talk about her?" Galina asked gently. "That might be a good place to start."

Ilya had been expecting this, but he still wasn't sure if he was ready. He stared at his folded hands, and noticed his knuckles were white from how hard he was gripping his fingers together.

"I'll try," he said.

He started talking, and he didn't stop for almost forty minutes. By that point his cheeks were wet with tears that he hadn't even noticed were falling until Galina had silently handed him a box of tissues. There was now a small pile of used, crumpled tissues beside Ilya on the couch. His ball cap was next to the pile, because he'd started raking his fingers through his own hair as he'd been rambling. He'd never talked so much about his mother. He'd shared his fondest memories of her, and the way she'd tried to hide how bad her depression had gotten, always ready with a reassuring smile for Ilya. He'd noticed, even as a child, that her smile was often sad.

He told Galina about finding his mother's lifeless body when he'd been twelve years old. How he'd thought she was resting, as she often was, until he'd gotten closer. It was her hand that he'd noticed first. The way it was flopped over the side of the bed, fingers dangling.

He talked about his father sternly telling Ilya that his mother's death had been an accident. She had taken too many pills for her headache, that was all.

"Did you believe him?" Galina asked.

"No. Not at all. But I didn't say anything." He took a slow, shaky breath. "He moved on so quickly. He wanted to forget about her. Wanted me and Andrei to forget her too. It was like . . . he was disgusted by her." Ilya's throat tightened again.

"I missed her so much. I still . . ." He covered his mouth with his hand as the room turned blurry.

"I'm sorry," Galina said. "That's a horrific thing for anyone to go through. Especially a child."

Ilya could only nod miserably. He knew it was. He tried not to think about it too often, because what good would it do, but he knew.

She gave him time to collect himself a bit. Finally, when his eyes were dry and his throat had relaxed, he said, "I might be done for today. That was a lot."

"It was. How do you feel now?"

Ilya assessed himself before he answered. "Tired. But better, maybe. I would like to do this again."

They figured out a date and time for Ilya's next appointment, then Ilya gathered his tissue pile up and found a waste bin in the corner. He paused at the door before leaving and blurted out, "Do you think there is something wrong with me?"

"Wrong?"

"Am I depressed? Mentally ill? Am I . . . going to get worse?" He closed his eyes, embarrassed that he'd said all of that, but needing to know.

"You're here," she said kindly. "I'm afraid I can't give you any answers this early on, but being here is an important step in the right direction."

"Slow and steady, right?" Ilya said, in English, with an attempt at a smile.

"Exactly."

He sighed. "I hate slow things."

That made her laugh. "I've heard you like fast cars. Maybe you can think of this as building a Ferrari, instead of driving one."

Ilya was hoping he was more like a Ferrari that needed a bit of a tune-up, rather than one that needed to be built from the ground up, but he understood what she was saying. The important thing was to avoid the scrap yard.

Ilya walked around Ottawa for a long time after his appointment. He'd hoped that speaking to a professional would give him some clarity, but instead his brain was a jumbled mess, and his chest felt hollow. He pulled the hood of his sweatshirt up over his head to block out the cold autumn wind, and to hide his ragged expression.

Was he supposed to feel this way? Was therapy useful at all? He didn't think he could keep it up if he was going to be this badly shaken after each appointment.

As he walked, he cautiously examined his feelings, searching for any improvement. It had been good, perhaps, to talk about his mother, as much as it had wrung him out. Maybe therapy, like so many things worth doing, hurts when you first start. Ilya knew about pushing through pain.

He'd see Shane tomorrow afternoon. They would have a night together. Ilya was excited about it, but now he felt weird about it too. He didn't think he could tell Shane about therapy. Not yet. But he was worried Shane would notice how raw Ilya was. He didn't want to tell Shane the truth: that he'd felt off for a while now, and that it was getting worse. That the things that used to help weren't helping anymore. That he was worried this was how it had started for his mother.

That some days he missed Shane so much it felt like claws were digging into his heart.

He ended up walking along the canal, his back to the wind. Ottawa was cold in November, but he'd never lived anywhere warm, so it didn't bother him.

He kept his head down as he walked, but was still recognized by some fans who, fortunately, only wanted to shout out his name and wave and didn't ask for selfies. Ilya did not have a selfie face at the moment.

There was a bench facing the water with no one around, so Ilya sat. He pulled out his phone and opened his saved photos. He didn't keep his photos very organized, but he had one album he'd named "Boring." He opened it now, and scrolled through the six photos it contained. They were all more or less the same, taken years ago during the NHL Awards. Ilya and Shane had been presenting an award together, and the scripted banter had involved Ilya asking Shane for a selfie. Ilya had used his real phone, and he'd taken real photos. Six of them.

Back then, Ilya's hair had been longer, and that night he'd had it tied back. Shane's hair had been short and tidy. He looked annoyed in the photo, lips almost pursed, dark eyes full of impatience. Ilya had his arm around his shoulders and was grinning broadly, hamming it up for the audience.

Ilya couldn't possibly guess how many times he'd looked at these photos in the years since he'd taken them. He had other photos of Shane. Newer ones. Ones that had been taken since he'd finally gathered the courage to tell Shane he loved him, and Shane had said it back. He didn't need to cling to these old ones, as he once had, as the closest thing he'd thought he'd ever have to being Shane's boyfriend.

But these photos reminded Ilya of that night. It reminded Ilya of the way Shane had put on a show, later in the privacy of Ilya's hotel room. He'd stroked himself, fingered himself, writhed on the bed, while Ilya had watched from a chair at the end of the bed. Shane had clearly been nervous, but he'd done it. Because Ilya had asked him to. It remained one of the hottest things Ilya had ever experienced.

He also loved the photos because they reminded him of how

he'd felt back then. The overwhelming, inconvenient longing he'd secretly carried for Shane. The way he'd tried so hard to convince himself he didn't feel anything extraordinary for Shane. That he'd only wanted to fool around with him because it was forbidden and sexy.

Ilya looked in the eyes of his younger self in the photos and laughed. "Who were you kidding?" he said quietly, in Russian.

He'd been an idiot then. He still was, really, when it came to Shane Hollander.

Impulsively, Ilya sent Shane one of the photos. He'd never shown them to him before; embarrassed, maybe, that he still had them.

Less than a minute later, Shane replied: Wow. I forgot about those pics. You still have them?

**ILYA:**
Obviously.

**SHANE:**
Should I cut my hair? Did I look better like that?

Ilya huffed. Of course that would be Shane's reaction to Ilya revealing how fucking soft he was for him. How soft he'd always been. Ilya had been carrying these photos around like precious treasure for years, transferring them to each new phone. And Shane was concerned about his hair.

**ILYA:**
No. I like your hair now.

**SHANE:**
Ok.

**SHANE:**

I just remembered what night that was!

**ILYA:**

It was a good night.

**SHANE:**

I'm glad you don't have any photos of THAT.

God, Ilya wished.

**SHANE:**

Are we watching the doc tomorrow?

**ILYA:**

If you want.

**SHANE:**

Yeah. Let's do it.

**SHANE:**

I have to get ready for the game. I'll see you tomorrow!!!!!!!!!!!!!!!!!!!

Ilya sent back a heart emoji, followed by several eggplant and peach emojis. He ended it with a kissy face. Then he stood and began walking back to his parked car, feeling lighter. He decided to stop at the weird healthy grocery store on the way home.

# CHAPTER FIFTEEN

As usual, Shane found himself pinned against a wall as soon as he entered Ilya's house. Ilya was kissing him hungrily, one hand under Shane's thigh, Shane's leg wrapped around Ilya's ass. Shane still had his jacket and shoes on.

"Miss me?" Shane said with a laugh against Ilya's lips.

"No," Ilya said, then went back to kissing him.

They kept it up for a while—kissing, touching, rubbing, getting hard against each other—while Shane grew uncomfortably warm in his outdoor clothes.

"Wait," he panted. "Let me . . ." He fumbled for the zipper on his jacket, not wanting to interrupt things but needing to remove some layers.

Ilya released Shane's thigh and stepped back. His eyes were shining and his lips were swollen, and Shane regretted trying to take the jacket off.

"We should stop," Ilya said.

"What? Why?"

"Because." He smiled. "We need to make dinner."

When Shane had his jacket and shoes off, Ilya took his hand

and led him to the kitchen. The counter was full of fresh vegetables, a box of organic farro, and a bowl of cooked salmon.

"What's all this?" Shane asked.

"We are cooking together. Like we used to. I found a recipe that is okay for you."

He picked up his iPad off the counter and showed Shane the recipe. Shane read it carefully, touched that Ilya had gone to this much trouble. "Looks good," Shane said.

Ilya beamed.

Shane went to the sink to wash his hands, suddenly realizing how hungry he was. "This is very romantic, Ilya."

"Is just food."

"How long did it take you to find that recipe?"

Ilya didn't answer him.

They worked together, and it was nice. Shane missed cooking with Ilya, and regretted that his nutrition plan made it more difficult. They cooked the farro, and chopped, seasoned, and roasted the vegetables, then assembled it all into bowls, topping the grains and vegetables with chunks of salmon and fresh herbs.

"This is not bad," Ilya conceded when they were eating at the kitchen table later. Ilya had lit a candle in the middle of the table, which Shane found adorable.

"Clean eating doesn't have to suck," Shane said. "I eat lots of delicious stuff."

Ilya shot him a skeptical look, then took another bite of salmon and spiced cauliflower. "Not as good as chicken parmesan," he said, after he swallowed.

Shane couldn't argue that. Secretly, he'd fucking kill for some crispy chicken, smothered in cheese. Maybe with some pasta and alfredo sauce on the side. Maybe a beer to wash it down with. Some garlic bread . . .

But garlic bread wasn't important. Winning was important. Playing in the NHL for as long as possible was important.

"For dessert," Ilya said with a slight quirk of his lips, "we can look at a picture of cake."

Shane rolled his eyes.

"Or . . ." Ilya leaned in suggestively. "Maybe there is something else you are craving?"

"Like your dick, you mean?" Shane asked dryly.

Ilya grinned. "Is that part of your diet?"

"Gross."

They both laughed, and Shane's heart flipped happily in his chest. He loved quiet, domestic moments like this with Ilya. He loved joking about sex and laughing together. He loved that Ilya had looked up a recipe and bought fussy ingredients for it. That he'd given them this moment.

"I love you," Shane said, the words out before he'd known he was going to say them.

Ilya's smile turned bashful and sweet. "I still like to hear that."

"I still like saying it." They smiled at each other for a long moment, sappy as shit, then Shane said, "So. Are we watching the documentary tonight?"

"If you want."

"You didn't watch it already, did you?"

Ilya glared at him. "No."

"But you remembered to record it?"

"Fuck, Shane. Yes."

"Okay. Sorry."

Ilya took a sip of water, then said, "We don't have to watch it."

"I want to." Shane's lips twitched. "I want to see what you said about me."

"You mean the thing about how much you like having your balls sucked?"

Shane heaved an enormous sigh, then stood up to bring his empty plate to the sink.

"Because I definitely told them about that," Ilya said.

"Okay."

"And that you squeak when you are trying not to come."

"I don't *squeak*."

Ilya shrugged. "This is why we need a sex tape. So you can see."

"No way. You would leak it immediately."

Ilya grinned. "Can you blame me?"

"Have you heard of this FanMail website?" Shane asked as they were getting settled on the couch later.

"Yes. Is like, people pay to have famous people pretend to care about them."

"That's a bleak way of putting it, but sort of. I'd never heard of it until Hayden told me he'd been doing them and—"

Ilya slammed the remote onto the sofa cushion beside him. "Hayden is on FanMail?"

"Yeah."

Ilya launched off the sofa and darted away.

"What the hell are you doing?" Shane asked.

"Getting my phone." He returned a moment later with his phone in his hand, grinning at the screen. "A hundred dollars!" Ilya said. "Who would pay this for a video from Hayden?"

"Lots of people," Shane said defensively. "He films them all the time."

"I am going to buy one."

"Ilya, no. Don't be a dick."

"Dear Hayden," Ilya said aloud as he typed. "My boyfriend is sad because he has a very annoying coworker and needs to be cheered up. Could you send him a video and sing him his favorite song, 'O Canada'?"

"That is *not* my favorite song."

"What is?"

Shane didn't have an answer ready for that, so he crossed his arms instead. "Please don't send that."

"Too late."

"He's going to know it's you. What email address did you use?"

"Don't worry about it." Ilya sat beside Shane and picked up the remote again. "Let's watch this stupid thing."

There was nothing particularly surprising or even interesting about the documentary. It was mostly a collection of their career highlights, with a few talking head interviews mixed in to create a bit of a story.

Ilya had been right: it wasn't really about *them*.

But it was nice, having all these clips and interviews put together in a one-hour package. It was even nicer to be able to watch it curled up together on Ilya's couch.

Suddenly a clip appeared that Shane had never seen before.

"Don't watch this," Ilya said. His tone was dead serious.

"Is this—oh." On the screen, Shane had just been laid out by Cliff Marlow during a game against Boston. He winced. He'd never been able to remember that hit, but he sure remembered the injuries it caused.

Ilya's body tensed against him as they both stared at Shane's unconscious body on the ice.

"Spoiler," Shane said with a shaky laugh. "I wake up."

"I know," Ilya said quietly.

In the video, Ilya was crouching over Shane's body. The camera caught a close-up of Ilya's face as he glanced over his shoulder and began to frantically wave medical staff over. His skin was ashen and his eyes were wide and terrified.

A crowd formed around Shane's body seconds later, but Ilya didn't leave. He stood, just outside the scrum, like a guardian. He was talking, but no one seemed to be listening to him.

A spinal board and a stretcher were brought onto the ice.

Ilya had to be shoved out of the way by one of the medics, but that didn't keep Ilya from staying as close as he was allowed, his eyes never leaving Shane's body.

"Was I awake then?" Shane asked quietly. "I don't remember."

"Yes. Barely." Ilya's voice sounded small and unsteady. "You were trying to talk to me."

Ilya never fucking left. Even though Shane's teammates were all, sensibly, huddled near the Montreal bench, out of the way of the medics, Ilya stayed. He'd stood there in his Boston uniform, making sure Shane knew he wasn't alone.

Shane squeezed his hand, now. Because Shane wasn't the one reliving a traumatic moment by watching this.

"How could they not know?" Shane said. "How could anyone have seen this—seen *you*—and not known about us?" Ilya had displayed his heart so openly, smashed against the ice as unmistakably as Shane's broken body.

"I don't know," Ilya said.

Ilya needed to stop watching this, so Shane climbed into his lap and kissed him. He'd never thought much about how scared Ilya had been. He'd been relieved that his injuries weren't career-ending, and hadn't thought much about the incident beyond that. But he knew if their situation had been reversed, Shane would have been a wreck. Injuries were part of the game, but getting knocked out cold was scary. He hoped Ilya never scared him like that.

"I'm sorry you went through that," Shane said. "And I'm sorry I never knew about it."

"Is fine," Ilya said, even though his eyes were glistening with tears. "Was scary, but you are okay."

"I'm okay," Shane agreed.

Beside them, Ilya's phone lit up. He picked it up, probably welcoming the distraction, and laughed.

"What?" Shane asked.

"Hayden texted me a picture of his middle finger."

Shane woke up from a dream where he and Ilya were fucking at center ice. It had been ridiculous, and obviously fucking on ice would be difficult and uncomfortable, but it had also been hot as hell and now Shane was rock hard and felt about three strokes away from orgasm.

Jesus. What if he'd actually shot his load in his sleep? Ilya would never let him live it down.

He turned his head to find Ilya sprawled out on his stomach beside him, deep asleep with his mouth hanging open and hair covering most of his face.

Shane's heart swelled. This beautiful man was all his.

He closed his eyes and reached down to ruthlessly squeeze the base of his own cock, then did some deep breathing. No point in being this fired up if Ilya was dead to the world.

When he finally got himself under control, he opened his eyes and found Ilya grinning at him.

"Trying not to come?" Ilya asked.

Shane palmed Ilya's face, pushing his stupid grin away. "You were asleep! What the fuck?"

"I woke up," Ilya said simply. "And you were meditating with your dick in your hand."

Shane shoved him onto his back and climbed on top of him, straddling him so he could look down at his smirking boyfriend and try to gain some dignity back. "I was not *meditating*."

"Okay."

"I had a sexy dream, that's all. And I woke up all . . . aroused, or whatever."

Ilya folded his arms behind his head. "Tell me about this dream."

"No way."

Ilya's mouth fell open in mock offense. "You will not share?"

"Nope."

"It was about another man, then. Was it Hayden?"

Shane threw his head back and groaned. "For the last time, I'm not attracted to Hayden."

"Too bad for Hayden."

"Hayden is *straight* and not attracted to me!"

"If you say so."

Shane rolled his head in a dramatic fashion until he was glaring down at Ilya again. "I guess all I had to do to get rid of this hard-on was wake you up. Now I'm too annoyed to be turned on."

"I don't think that is true."

And, no. It wasn't true. Not now that Shane was finally cluing into the fact that he was straddling his very handsome boyfriend's naked body. He couldn't resist being aroused by Ilya's crooked smile and sleepy, half-lidded eyes.

"You're so fucking hot," Shane said helplessly, sliding his palms up to Ilya's chest.

Ilya's smile grew. "Tell me about the dream."

"It's embarrassing."

Ilya pulled one hand from behind his head and cupped Shane's mostly soft dick. "Tell me one thing."

Shane's breath hitched as Ilya began to slowly massage his cock. "I—we were . . . fucking."

"Wow," Ilya said dryly.

Shane wasn't going to sit here and be accused of having unimaginative sex dreams. He swallowed his shame and added, "At center ice."

Ilya's eyebrows shot up.

"I know that logistically," Shane continued quickly, "it would be, y'know, basically impossible, but dreams are weird. So, yeah. Center ice."

"Were there people there? A crowd?"

Shane's cheeks heated. "I don't think so. Maybe it started as a game, but then we were naked and alone, I think."

"Interesting." Ilya moved his hand down to caress Shane's balls. "I have had dreams where we are fucking in front of people. Like we are showing off."

Shane gasped as Ilya gently tugged at his sac. "You'd love that, wouldn't you?"

Ilya chuckled. "Do you think so?"

"Sure. You've probably gone to sex parties and fucked in front of a captive audience before, right?"

A second later, Shane found himself on his back, with Ilya looming over him. Ilya bent low and kissed Shane's throat.

"No," Ilya said. "No sex parties." He kissed a trail down Shane's chest and stomach, then lifted his head. "Wait. How many people is a party?"

Shane narrowed his eyes at him, and Ilya grinned broadly. Shane never knew when Ilya was being serious about his sexual past, or when he was just talking shit to get Shane riled up. He knew that, ultimately, it didn't really matter how many people Ilya had slept with, but it did fascinate Shane that the number could really be anywhere between two and a million.

It was definitely more than two.

Probably less than a million.

"Tell me what you think a sex party is," Ilya teased. His eyes danced with glee.

"No."

"Please. I have to know."

"Weren't you about to—"

"Yes. In a minute. Is there, like, balloons?"

Shane rolled his eyes, then moved like he was going to leave the bed. Ilya laughed and pinned him down, hands wrapped around Shane's wrists. As he gazed down at Shane, his expression shifted from teasing to something softer.

"I am so glad I met you," Ilya said quietly.

Shane's heart clenched. It was such a simple statement, but it was so open and honest, and it instantly made Shane think of the flip side of those words.

What if they'd never met?

But they had, and they were perfect for each other in a way that probably only they would ever understand. Their relationship wasn't easy, but it *existed*. They'd made it happen, against all odds, and they'd protected it.

Shane couldn't find words, so he tried to lift his arms and Ilya let him, releasing his wrists immediately. Shane wrapped his arms around him, pulling him down, and held him. They stayed like that for several minutes, breathing against each other and saying nothing.

"Now, then," Ilya said, then kissed Shane's throat. "I want to blow you while you think about getting fucked at center ice."

Shane let out a shaky laugh. "I don't actually want to be fucked at—*ah*." His back arched when Ilya wrapped his plush lips around the head of Shane's cock.

Shane didn't think about being fucked at center ice or anywhere else while Ilya took him apart with his mouth. He reached for Ilya's hand and held it tight, fingers woven together. There was absolutely nowhere else Shane wanted to be.

Shane was determined not to say anything as he watched Ilya slather about a pound of cream cheese on a sesame seed bagel. If Ilya wanted to eat nothing but empty carbs and saturated fats, that wasn't any of Shane's business. Instead, Shane bit the inside of his cheek, and continued to measure out protein powder for his breakfast smoothie.

"Oh come *on*," he cried, about thirty seconds later when Ilya started adding a layer of Nutella to the mountain of cream cheese.

"What?" Ilya asked.

Shane waved a hand at Ilya's breakfast. "That's how you're going to start your day?"

"No," Ilya said, dipping his knife back into the Nutella jar. "I started my day by blowing you. Remember?"

Yes, Shane remembered. But he wasn't going to let that stop his outrage. "Are you seriously going to eat that?"

"Are you seriously going to drink *that*?" Ilya said, pointing his knife with its glob of Nutella at Shane's blender.

"This is balanced and contains a ton of nutrients and protein. *That* contains nothing but sugar and fuck knows what else."

"Chocolate," Ilya said helpfully. He finished smearing the Nutella on, then grabbed a banana and waved it in Shane's face. "Look. Healthy."

Shane watched as Ilya peeled the banana and began slicing it over the bagel. "Whatever," Shane sighed, and went back to making his smoothie. He didn't want to see what Ilya added next. Probably sprinkles. Or onion rings.

While they were eating at Ilya's breakfast bar, Shane checked his email and was shocked to find one from the NHL's league commissioner, Roger Crowell. He was even more surprised when he read that Crowell wanted to meet with him when Shane traveled to New York later that week.

"Holy shit," he said aloud.

"What?" Ilya asked through a mouthful of bagel and chocolate.

"Crowell wants to meet with me."

"Why?"

"I have no idea." Shane wrote back right away, confirming that of course he would. Then he immediately spiraled into a panic about what the meeting could possibly be about.

"He doesn't say why?" Ilya asked.

"No."

"That is weird."

"I *know* it's fucking weird! Why me?"

"Is it just you?"

"I—" Okay, Shane didn't actually know. "Maybe? It sounded like it. He didn't mention anyone else."

The commissioner was the single most powerful person in the NHL, overseeing basically everything. He wasn't a particularly popular man among players. Shane had always regarded him with an appropriate amount of respect, mixed with a bit of wariness.

"What if he knows about us?" Shane asked, jumping to the worst-case scenario.

"Why would he?"

Shane chewed his lip. It was true that there was no way Crowell would know about his relationship with Ilya. It probably wasn't that.

"Maybe he wants to give you a special award," Ilya said. "Second-best hockey player."

Shane ignored him. "I've met him, but never actually, y'know, *met* him. Like, I've never had a real conversation with him. Is this something he does?"

Ilya shrugged.

"Is it about the documentary, do you think?"

"Possible."

Shane exhaled. "It's probably nothing to worry about, right?"

"Probably not. But I like how worried you get." Ilya bumped his shoulder against him affectionately.

"Whatever."

Ilya leaned in for a kiss, and Shane dodged him. "No way. Not after you ate *that*."

"Come on," Ilya said, grinning as he leaned in again. "You can taste chocolate again."

"No."

In the end, Shane couldn't resist kissing him. It was better than chocolate.

# CHAPTER SIXTEEN

A few days later, Shane was sitting in a waiting area outside Crowell's office. He had never been to the NHL's headquarters in Manhattan before, and the sleek lobby that had greeted him when he'd stepped off the elevators, with its fortieth-floor view of the Hudson River, was impressive. And intimidating.

"Commissioner Crowell can see you now, Mr. Hollander," said the receptionist.

Shane nodded at her without quite making eye contact. He found her intimidating too.

When Shane walked in, he was greeted warmly by Crowell. "Shane! Come in. Thank you for meeting with me. Short notice, I know."

Roger Crowell was a tall man, solidly built, with thick silver hair and heavy eyebrows over calculating, pale blue eyes. He'd never been a hockey player, but he'd played football in college, back in the seventies, and he clearly still kept in shape. If he weren't so fucking scary, Shane would say he was handsome.

"No problem," Shane said as he shook Crowell's offered hand. "The offices are nice."

"You've never been here before?"

"No."

Crowell's face shifted into a confused expression that seemed a bit theatrical to Shane. "Is that so? I'm surprised to hear it. Well, welcome."

"Thank you."

Crowell gestured to one of the leather chairs facing his desk, and Shane perched on the edge of the seat. Crowell sat in his own high-backed executive desk chair, leaning back in it comfortably. "Montreal's had a great start to the season."

"Yes. Not bad."

"Always tough, defending a title," Crowell said. As if he knew.

"It can be, yeah."

"And how's that charity doing? The one you started with Rozanov?"

"Good. We've been able to fund some very worthwhile organizations and initiatives." Shane knew he sounded like he was reading directly from the Irina Foundation's website, but he was too nervous to care. Where the hell was this conversation going?

"Glad to hear it. Your camps are doing good work too. Very . . . inclusive."

"Yes. We try to make sure of that. It's important to both of us."

"That's good. That's good. We like to see that. Diversity is important."

"It is," Shane said cautiously.

"It can be hard sometimes to find a balance," Crowell continued. "If you know what I mean."

Shane definitely didn't. "Balance?"

"Of course we, as a league and as a sport, want to talk about inclusion and diversity in hockey. We want to see things move in the right direction. But too much talk about that stuff can be . . . distracting."

"Um."

Crowell held out one hand. "Now I've heard, and you don't have to confirm this, but I've *heard* that you are . . . homosexual."

"I, uh—" Shane's stomach clenched. He *was* a homosexual, but the way Crowell said it made it sound icky.

"Like I said, you don't have to tell me. But let's say the rumor is true."

It wasn't so much a rumor as something that Shane had told his teammates, and had willingly admitted to anyone who asked. He kept his mouth shut now.

"So maybe you've told your teammates, your friends, your family. Maybe you have a partner, I don't know. The point is, I don't *need* to know, and neither does anyone else."

"Okay."

"Nothing against Scott Hunter, of course. He's a great player and a great ambassador for the game, but that approach can be a lot, y'know?"

"Approach? You mean his activism?"

"Activism, sure. Or just being loud about your personal business. What I'm saying is I appreciate the way you handle yourself, Shane. I know you put hockey first, and keep your private life private. That keeps everyone comfortable, and keeps the focus on hockey."

Shane had no idea what the fuck they were talking about. Was Crowell telling him not to come out publicly? Was that what this meeting was truly about? "I admire Scott Hunter," Shane said. "What he's done over the past few years has been important to LGBTQ hockey players and fans, especially young players."

"Of course. Like I said, the NHL absolutely supports Scott Hunter and the LGBTQ community one hundred percent." Crowell said "LGBTQ" slowly and carefully, as if he were repeating a phone number he needed to memorize. "Did you know we sell Pride merchandise year-round on our website now?"

"Does the money go to LGBTQ charities?"

"And we're expanding our Pride Nights," Crowell said, ignoring Shane's question. "Every team has them now, and we're planning the first joint Pride Night game."

"That's a good first step, but—"

"I know that, historically, hockey hasn't been the most inclusive sport, but obviously *anyone* can make it to the very top if they work hard enough. I mean, you're proof of that."

Shane wasn't sure if Crowell was referring to his rumored homosexuality, his Japanese heritage, or both. He really wanted to get the fuck out of this office.

"What I wanted to say, Shane, in person, is that the league is proud of what you're doing with your charity. Mental health is so important. And you can tell Rozanov that too. Just great work, both of you."

"Okay. Thank you."

"And, if you want to be more vocal about your . . . personal life, maybe the NHL can help you with that. We can plan something together. We'd be happy to do that with you. For you."

"I'll . . . think about it."

Crowell smiled like a panther. "Fantastic." He stood, so Shane stood as well. "Always a pleasure sitting down with one of the league's best players, Shane. You know, you're my nephew's favorite."

"Oh. That's cool."

"Good luck this season. Lydia can show you out."

"Okay. Thank you. Um . . . thanks. Bye."

Shane followed Lydia—the receptionist—to the elevators in a daze, his stomach clenching and his skin crawling with disgust. He wanted a shower, or a treadmill, or soundproof room he could scream into.

He stood in the elevator and miserably watched the doors close, blocking out the large glass NHL logo on the other side.

Ilya woke up from his pregame nap to find about a hundred texts from Shane on his phone. Most of them asking him to call as soon as possible. But also assuring him he was fine. But to call him. Soon. Now, if possible.

Ilya called him.

"Jesus. Finally," Shane said.

"I was asleep. What is it?"

"I met with Crowell."

Ilya propped himself up on an elbow. "Oh yes?"

"It was weird."

"Weird how?"

"He basically said—I don't even know what he said. He's really intimidating."

"Tell me one thing he said."

Shane exhaled loudly. "First of all, he told me we were doing good work with the Irina Foundation. He asked me to tell you that."

"Okay."

"But he also, like, told me not to come out, maybe?"

Ilya sat all the way up. "I don't understand."

"He said he's heard *rumors* about me being gay and basically that he'd like them to stay rumors."

"He said this?"

"Not exactly. Like I said, it was weird. The way he talks, it's friendly and scary at the same time. I hated it."

Ilya was starting to get angry. Mostly at Crowell. A little bit at Shane. "What did he say?"

"I think he doesn't want another Scott Hunter. He doesn't seem to be a fan of activism in hockey. Or anything that isn't hockey in hockey, really."

"He is a fan of money in hockey," Ilya said.

"He was talking about how great diversity is, and about the league's LGBTQ initiatives, but also that he hates distractions from the game. The whole meeting felt like an indirect threat. Like, he wanted to make sure I wasn't going to surprise anyone by coming out on social media or something."

"Or kissing your boyfriend on TV."

"Right. I mean, obviously I'm not going to do either of those things."

"Obviously." Ilya said it bitterly, but Shane didn't seem to notice.

"But also it was like he was daring me to accuse the league of not being, like, queer-friendly or something. By listing all the stuff they do."

"Gross."

"It was, a bit. Yeah."

"So what are you going to do?"

"Nothing. I wasn't going to do anything anyway, but I still feel slimy after that meeting."

Ilya's jaw clenched. He knew all too well Shane had no intention of going public about their relationship, but if there had even been a chance and Crowell had crushed it . . .

"Anyway," Shane said, "I just needed to tell someone about it. So thanks."

"No problem."

"Good luck tonight, okay?"

"Sure. You too."

"I love you."

Ilya's heart felt like lead. "I love you too."

"Last time we met," Dr. Galina Molchalina said, in Russian, "you told me quite a bit about your mother. Would you like to talk about your father today?"

"No," Ilya said, without hesitation. Then, "I'm glad he's dead."

If Galina was shocked by this statement, her face didn't show it. "He died a few years ago, right?"

"Yes. I'd been expecting it. He had Alzheimer's, and had been deteriorating quickly. My brother pretended it wasn't happening."

"Are you and your brother close?"

Ilya barked out a surprised laugh at that. "Andrei? No. Not at all. I haven't talked to him since I went home for the funeral. He's a clone of Dad."

Galina leaned back in her chair and crossed her legs, waiting. Ilya sighed. He supposed he *did* need to talk about his goddamned father.

"Dad was a cop. Very highly decorated, very proud. He climbed the ranks all the way to an important job at the Ministry. He was about fifty when I was born. Andrei is four years older than me. And my mother was still only in her twenties when I was born, so."

"Quite an age gap between your parents."

"Yes." Ilya hated to imagine what circumstances made his young, beautiful mother have to marry a joyless old man and bear his children. "My father hated her, I think. He always thought she was cheating on him, or planning to leave him. I wish she could have left."

He didn't want to get into some of his darker memories of his father terrorizing his mom, and Galina must have sensed it. She asked, "Was your father proud of your hockey career?"

"Not really. He was a big KHL fan. He thought the Russian league was superior to the NHL, and did not want me going to America. He never followed my NHL career too closely, but he was always interested when I played for Team Russia in any tournament. If Russia won gold, he was proud of me. Anything less was an embarrassment."

"That must have been very hard," she said, and Ilya wondered if she was thinking of the disastrous Sochi Olympics.

"My mother loved watching me play, when I was little. I liked playing for her. After she died, hockey became an escape for me. It got me away from home, and it was a way to get out some of my anger, I guess." He smiled. "And I was very good at it."

Galina smiled back. "It's good that you had that. Were there other things you did to escape at that time?"

Well. Yes. And Ilya supposed there was no reason to be shy about it. Not here.

"Sex," he said bluntly. "When I was old enough, sex was the other thing I did to keep my mind and body busy. *Sex and Hockey* could be the title of my autobiography. I'm not complicated." He stretched his arm along the back of the couch, trying to show how relaxed and uncomplicated he was. It probably wasn't convincing.

"May I ask when 'old enough' was?" she said.

"Fourteen, I think. Something like that." He hesitated a moment, wondering if he was ready to reveal this, then decided to just go for it. "It was girls only, at first. Then boys too. Not as many, but some."

Again, her face didn't show any surprise. She jotted something on the notepad she balanced on her lap, then glanced back up. "That would have been risky, especially in Russia," she said.

"I think that was part of what I liked about it."

"Those desires didn't scare you?"

Ilya considered the question before answering. "No. They never did. It just seemed like an opportunity for more sex." It was the truth; maybe if he hadn't been attracted to girls first, he would have been scared, but being attracted to men as well had always made him feel . . . evolved.

She scribbled more notes while Ilya watched.

"I'm bisexual. Just to be clear." He said it casually, as if he said those words all the time. He'd barely said them ever.

She nodded. "What has it been like, being a bisexual NHL player?"

Ilya shrugged. "Normal. I don't advertise it."

"It's never been an issue?"

"No." Ilya frowned. He was lying, which was pointless here. "Well, yes. It's made it hard to be . . ." He wasn't sure how much he should reveal here. His therapist was sworn to secrecy. This was a safe space. But he still felt like he should have Shane's permission to talk about their relationship to someone else. So, he said, "I'm . . . seeing someone. In secret."

"A man," she guessed.

"Yes."

"For how long?"

Ilya almost laughed. "Ten years, give or take."

For the first time during their session, Galina looked surprised.

"Off and on," Ilya explained. "It was casual for years. Secret hookups, that sort of thing. But then I fell in love with the guy."

"And . . . did he feel the same?"

Ilya couldn't stop the giddy smile that spread across his face. "He did. He does."

She acknowledged his smile with one of her own. "How does your relationship work now?"

"We see each other when we can. He lives in . . . a place not too far away from here. We're both busy, but we spend as much time together as we can. Especially in the—" Ilya cut himself off. He was revealing too much.

"In the summers?" Galina guessed. "When you aren't playing hockey."

"Right. Yes."

A silence hung in the room, heavy and full of mutual understanding. She knew who his boyfriend was, and she knew *he* knew. And no one had to ever say his name aloud.

"So," Ilya said. "That's another thing. In my life."

"Does anyone know?"

"A few people. His parents know. Maybe five other people besides. Mostly Sh—" He pressed his lips together just in time. "Mostly his friends."

"None of *your* friends?"

"Not yet. No."

"That doesn't sound even. He has more support than you do in this."

Ilya knew that. Of course it had occurred to him. Sometimes he was even angry about it. "I know."

"Who would you tell, if you could?"

Everyone. Ilya would tell the whole world if he could. "I don't know. My teammates might not understand. I don't have many friends who aren't teammates."

"There are other queer NHL players," she said. "And ex-NHL players. Are you friends with any of them?"

"Some. Sort of. I think even they would be bothered by—" He caught himself. After a moment's hesitation, though, he decided there was no point in pretending she didn't already know the next part. "By rival players secretly dating. A gay hockey player is still a hockey player, and there are unofficial rules. A code."

"Are there *official* rules?"

"I don't think so. I don't know. I'm sure the league will make some up in a hurry if they find out about us. Either way, things would get very difficult for us."

"What do you think the worst-case scenario is?"

Ilya took a moment to think before answering. "My worst fear is having to go back to Russia. Especially since, in that scenario, I would have been outed as bisexual."

"Do you think that's likely?"

Ilya sighed. "I don't know."

"What would need to happen, for you to have to leave Canada?"

"I guess I think . . . if I wasn't allowed to play hockey, I would be unemployed. And I haven't lived here long enough to apply for citizenship."

"But there are other ways," she said reasonably. "And it's unlikely you'd be banned from the NHL, especially given who you are."

She was right. Ilya had considered the fact that, even if the worst happened and he and Shane were kicked out of the league—or shunned by every team, if not officially kicked out—then he could seek out other ways to stay in Canada. He could find other work. He could . . . get married.

"Worst-case scenario," he said slowly. "Actual, realistic worst-case scenario: our NHL careers are over, but we can get married, and live a quiet life together in Canada."

"How does that make you feel?"

"Angry that we would have our careers cut short like that. But also . . . I don't know. Relief, maybe. Sometimes I feel like I might scream, it's so hard keeping this secret. I love hockey, and I deserve to have the career I want for as long as I want it. I've earned that. But if I had to choose . . . I'd choose him."

Galina made another quick note.

"But," Ilya said quietly, "I shouldn't have to choose."

"What's the best-case scenario?" she asked.

Ilya blew out a breath. "No idea. We announce we're together and everyone cheers? I win three more Stanley Cups and celebrate each one with my husband watching? I don't know."

"What's a realistic best-case scenario?"

Ilya considered it, and smiled. "We keep going, same as we are now, except everyone knows we're together and it's fine. No big deal."

"Is that what you both want?"

Well, that was the big question. Ilya thought that was what Shane wanted, but he was also pretty sure Shane was happy to hide until they were both retired. "I hope so."

# CHAPTER SEVENTEEN

In the middle of November, without warning, Ilya got a new, unwanted teammate. Troy Barrett was definitely a talented forward, and a potential upgrade to Ilya's current linemate, Tanner Dillon, but he'd also always seemed like a total prick to Ilya.

"I hate this," Ilya complained on the phone to Shane. "My team was perfect. Now we have this asshole."

"Your team is terrible," Shane reminded him.

"Yes, but, you know. The *vibes* are good. Barrett has bad vibes."

"I know. Sorry."

"Harris was bringing the new team puppy to practice today! Now Barrett is there too. Ruins everything."

"I still can't believe he called Kent out," Shane said. "Maybe he isn't so bad?"

The reason Toronto had quickly traded Barrett to Ottawa for a few draft picks—far less than the all-star player was worth—was because Troy had gotten in a fight with his even shittier teammate, Dallas Kent. Kent, a homophobic bully and one of the most repulsive people Ilya had ever met, had recently been accused of rape and assault by numerous anonymous women online. Apparently that had been a bridge too far for his former best friend, Troy Barrett.

"Yes, well. What is the saying about a broken clock? Wyatt says it."

"It's right twice a day."

"Yes. He is right about one thing. Probably still mostly bad."

"Maybe he'll be a good linemate. I've been listening to you complain about Tanner Dillon for as long as you've played for Ottawa."

"I still don't want him."

"I know. I'm just trying to cheer you up." Shane sighed heavily. "I have to go. Team meeting."

"Okay. How is Buffalo?"

"Amazing," Shane said flatly.

Ilya laughed. "Good luck tonight."

"Good luck with Troy Barrett. I can't wait to hear all about him."

"So nosy."

"I love you. I'll call you after the game tonight."

"I will be waiting. I love you too."

They ended the call, and Ilya immediately texted Harris.

**ILYA:**
You are bringing the puppy today yes?

**HARRIS:**
Yup!

Ilya exhaled slowly. At least this day wouldn't be total garbage.

"So how was he?" Shane asked. He was sprawled out on his hotel bed, completely exhausted after the game.

"So cute, Shane. You should see him!"

"What?" Troy Barrett was an attractive man, sure, but that was an unexpected reaction from Ilya.

"He licked my face with his little tongue!"

"Uh."

"His ears are so floppy, and he is so soft. I wanted to carry him around all practice."

Oh. "I meant *Troy*, idiot. Not the puppy."

Ilya huffed. "Who cares? Puppy was great. His name is Chiron. He is black and small and—"

"Okay. Puppies are cute. Agreed. But what was Troy like?"

"Was fine. Quiet. Whatever."

Shane grinned at the ceiling. "Do you have a photo of the dog?"

"Of course. Did you not see my Instagram?"

"No." Shane was not particularly invested in social media, though he knew that Ilya was posting random things all the time. Shane mostly reposted official team posts, and info about the Irina Foundation.

"There are photos, videos. So many things. Chiron is great."

"I'm glad you made a new friend."

Ilya sighed. "I wish I could get a dog."

Yeah, Shane wasn't sure how that would work. "Someday," he offered.

"Everything is someday. I am tired of waiting for someday."

"I know. But we're still young. We've got lots of time."

"Are we? I feel a thousand years old sometimes."

"I imagine Luca Haas isn't helping. What's he like?"

"Nice kid," Ilya said. "Possibly has a crush on me. I will let you know."

Shane refused to acknowledge his own jealousy. "He's a good player. Smart, y'know?"

"Very smart. But so young. Too young."

"We were younger than him when we started," Shane pointed out. They'd both been nineteen during their rookie seasons.

"I was never as young as Haas. He is, like, seven."

Shane chuckled, and it turned into a yawn.

"You are tired," Ilya said. "That game looked tough."

"Oh, you watched, did you?"

"Of course not."

Shane smiled. "Talk to me in Russian," he said. "Just wanna listen to you for a bit."

"You are going to fall asleep."

"Probably." Shane rested the phone on his pillow, and rolled onto his side to face it. It wasn't a video call, so he closed his eyes and let his boyfriend lull him to sleep with words that Shane mostly didn't understand, but made his heart flutter all the same.

# CHAPTER EIGHTEEN

Ilya was absolutely not going to buy cigarettes.

He was just going for a walk. After dark. In Vancouver. Alone. With no particular destination in mind. Enjoying the crisp night air—warmer than the nights were now in Ottawa—and letting clean, mountain oxygen fill his lungs.

He stopped into the first convenience store he came across, paid for a pack of cigarettes and a lighter with cash, and slunk back into the night.

Using the lights of the cranes at the shipping docks as his guide, Ilya walked toward the harbor. He loved the way city lights reflected off black water at night. It reminded him of the view from his old apartment in Boston.

He found a small park with long wooden docks that stretched out into the harbor, complete with benches. He walked out to the end of one, then pulled the cigarettes and lighter from his pocket.

Shane's voice nagged him in his head as he took his first drag. He smiled as he exhaled, welcoming the company. Maybe he only ever smoked so he could hear that voice in his head.

Ilya almost never smoked these days, and he felt like a failure whenever he gave into the urge. But for the few minutes between lighting the cigarette and stamping the smoldering butt out, he was incandescently happy.

*I will never fucking forgive you if you get lung cancer and die.*

Ilya watched another cloud of smoke disappear into the night sky. *I know, sweetheart,* he replied silently. *I know.*

He imagined Shane would be similarly unforgiving if Ilya took his own life. Not that Ilya ever would. Unless he couldn't help it.

*I'm trying to get better.*

He finished the cigarette, stamped out the butt, then picked it up and put it in his coat pocket. Smoking was one thing, but littering was one bad habit too far.

When he got back to the hotel, he felt somewhat better. Alone in his room earlier, his mind had been reeling and he'd felt claustrophobic after the long plane ride. It was late now, though, especially when translated to Ottawa time, and he needed to get as much sleep as possible before their game tomorrow.

Troy Barrett was standing by the elevators, holding a paper bag that couldn't more obviously be concealing a liquor bottle. Ilya hadn't spoken much to Barrett since he'd joined the team earlier that week. He should probably talk to him now, as team captain.

The elevator doors opened and Barrett stepped on. Ilya didn't move. He knew he was being irresponsible, but he was too exhausted to care. And it seemed hypocritical of him to be lecturing anyone about vices right now.

Truthfully, he wanted to ask Barrett to share whatever was in the bottle.

Deciding he needed to focus on himself tonight, Ilya waited for the next elevator.

Ilya woke later than he should have the next morning, but not late enough to miss breakfast. He filled his plate with scrambled eggs and various breakfast meats from the buffet line and joined Wyatt and Bood at a table.

"You find some trouble last night or what?" Bood asked.

Ilya smiled mysteriously. He'd learned that the best way to hide his secrets was to pretend he was hiding entirely different ones. "Did you see your sister?" he asked Wyatt. "And your nephew?"

"Yep! Saw the whole gang. They'll be at the game tonight, so I've gotta put on a show."

Ilya glanced around the banquet hall the hotel had provided for their private team breakfast. "Have you guys seen Barrett?"

"This morning?" Bood asked. "No."

Wyatt shook his head. "Haven't seen him since yesterday when we arrived. Why?"

"No reason." Ilya hadn't been a good captain last night when he hadn't stopped Barrett from taking a bottle of alcohol back to his hotel room, but maybe he could be a good captain today by respecting his privacy until Ilya had a good reason not to.

When he'd finished eating, he headed to the hotel lobby to see what kinds of chocolate bars they were selling in the little shop there. As he was crossing the middle of the room, where all the couches and chairs were for guests to lounge on, someone called his name.

"Ilya Rozanov."

Ilya stopped walking, and turned in the direction of one of the couches. He couldn't think of anyone he wanted to talk to who would call out his full name in a busy public place.

He found three men he didn't recognize—two sitting, and one standing—grinning at him. "Yes?"

The standing man strode over to him like they were friends. He was older than Ilya, probably in his fifties, with piercing blue eyes, gray-flecked dark hair, and a reasonably fit physique for a man his age, though he was several inches shorter than Ilya. He extended his hand when he reached Ilya.

"Curtis Barrett," he said in a loud, confident voice. "Troy's father."

"Oh. Okay," Ilya said, and shook his hand. "I have not seen your son yet today."

"Knowing him, he's probably trying to kick some girls out of his hotel room." He laughed, and it was horrible. "Fun's over, ladies, right?"

Ilya wasn't sure if he liked Troy, but he *definitely* didn't like his father. "I can tell him you are here," Ilya offered, mostly to get away from him.

"Sure, if you see him. I've been calling and texting all morning, but he forgot how a phone works, I guess."

Ilya smiled tightly. "I will let him know. If I see him."

He left quickly, continuing his journey to the store at the other side of the lobby. He bought himself a Caramilk bar and, after a moment's consideration, added a bottle of Gatorade.

He checked the room assignments on his phone while he rode the elevator back up to the team's floor, then walked directly to Troy's room and banged on the door. "Barrett. Wake up."

"What is it?" called the tattered remains of Troy's voice. "What?"

"Open the door."

Ilya heard moaning, and creaking, and shuffling, and then a bleary-eyed, and mostly naked, Troy Barrett opened the door. He reeked of alcohol and sweat, and his room was a mess. But he was, as Ilya had suspected, alone.

Ilya didn't wait for an invitation. He pushed past Barrett, wrinkling his nose as he took everything in. "Smells terrible. You got drunk last night."

"A little," Troy mumbled.

"Not good, Barrett." Ilya was legitimately annoyed. Troy had joined the team less than a week ago and already he was letting them down. Ilya held out the Gatorade. "Drink this." Then, because Troy looked like he was about to topple over, Ilya added, "Sit down."

Troy sat down heavily on the bed with a sigh and opened the Gatorade.

"I saw you in the lobby with the liquor store bag. Heading for the elevators," Ilya explained before Troy could wonder how he knew what he'd been up to last night. "You were in a hurry, it looked like."

Ilya spotted the cause of Troy's condition—a bottle of horrible, cheap vodka on the nightstand, nearly empty. "This is something you do a lot?" he asked as he inspected the bottle's label. He sniffed at the liquid inside. Disgusting.

"No," Troy said miserably.

"We play tonight."

"I know. It was stupid."

"Yes." Ilya wanted to be angry with him, but he found it difficult when Troy looked so pathetic, sitting on his bed in his underwear, curled over a bottle of Gatorade that he was clutching like it was precious.

"It won't happen again," Troy said in a small, tired voice. Ilya noticed the shimmer of tears in his eyes before Troy looked away. "I'm sorry. It was—"

His voice broke, and he pressed his lips together. The last of Ilya's annoyance with him evaporated. "This is your town, yes? Where you are from?"

"Yes," Troy said, barely more than a whisper.

"Your personal life is personal. If it does not affect your game, it does not matter to me. Coach will say the same thing." About that, Ilya was confident. Coach Wiebe was kind and fair.

Troy didn't really know Coach Wiebe yet, though. "Are you going to tell him?"

"Not this time." It sounded a bit threatening, but Ilya couldn't help that. He needed Troy to understand that this couldn't be a habit.

Troy didn't say anything. He just stared into the Gatorade bottle, probably hoping Ilya would leave.

"You look like shit," Ilya said. "Practice is optional this morning. You are opting out."

Troy didn't protest. "Okay."

Now Ilya had to give him the news he suspected Troy did not want to hear. "Also your dad is in the lobby."

Troy's face went even paler than it had been before. *"What?"*

"Yes. He introduced himself to me." Ilya probably wasn't able to hide how he'd felt about *that* interaction. Nevertheless, if Troy needed someone to get rid of his father, Ilya could stomach talking to the man again. "He is still there, but I can tell him you are . . ."

Thankfully, Troy refused his offer, insisting that he deal with his father himself. Ilya wasn't sure it was the best idea, given Troy's condition, but he didn't argue. Troy thanked him for the Gatorade, and Ilya suggested he spend the day resting before the game.

Before he left the room, Ilya paused and said, somewhat awkwardly, "Family can be hard. Fathers."

Troy seemed to understand. "Yeah. Sometimes."

Ilya nodded and left. It was possible he had more in common with Troy Barrett than he would have guessed.

# CHAPTER NINETEEN

Shane wondered, as he traveled the dark highway between Montreal and Ottawa, how many times he'd done this drive in his life. He could almost do it with his eyes closed, and was in fact in danger of doing that now. It was after midnight, and he was exhausted.

He could have waited until tomorrow morning to make the drive. He'd just finished a game in Montreal, and Ilya had played in Winnipeg tonight. His plane back to Ottawa was still in the air, meaning it would be another couple of hours at least before Shane would see him. Waiting until morning would have made sense.

But Shane couldn't wait until morning. Not when he hadn't seen Ilya for two weeks. Even if all they did was fall asleep on each other tonight, it would be worth the drive.

He listened to a Russian language lesson podcast as he drove, which kept his mind alert as he concentrated on translating as much as he could. The podcast wasn't quite as effective at keeping him awake as the butt plug had been. Shane smiled to himself, still surprised he'd actually done that. Seeing Ilya in that ridiculous gladiator costume had fried his capacity for rational thought. One moment he'd been telling himself it would be absurd to drive all the way to Ottawa for a quick fuck, and the next he'd been exiting Montreal city limits with a plug in his ass.

Ilya was a bad influence. But maybe Shane had needed that in his life. Needed it as much as he'd needed someone to stroke his hair, to make him laugh, to show him how good sex could be.

As much as he'd needed the warmth that filled his heart whenever he watched Ilya work on jigsaw puzzles with Dad.

Ilya texted as Shane was pulling into his driveway. Just landed.

**SHANE:**
I'm here.

Ilya sent back a heart emoji.

Shane let himself into the house and hung his coat up in the closet. He tucked his shoes away underneath. He'd gone home to change out of the suit he'd left the arena in before driving here, and was now wearing the fancy silk T-shirt Rose had bought him and a pair of dark jeans. He checked himself out in the full-length mirror in Ilya's living room and fixed his hair a bit.

It would be another hour at least before Ilya walked through the door. Shane decided to make himself comfortable on the couch and turned on the TV, flipping around until he settled on an Australian rugby game that may or may not be live. He barely understood rugby, but the men were certainly hot enough to keep him awake until Ilya got home.

"Shane."

He heard the name but couldn't place where it was coming from.

"Hollander." Something pushed on Shane's shoulder.

Shane opened his eyes, which was his first clue that he'd

fallen asleep on Ilya's couch. Ilya was standing over him, smiling softly, still wearing his suit.

"Shit," Shane said groggily as he sat up. "Sorry."

"Is okay." Ilya sat beside him. His hair was a mess of curls, likely because he'd shoved his shower-damp hair under a toque in Winnipeg before getting on the plane. In the low lamplight of the living room, his hazel eyes looked almost golden.

"Hi," Shane said.

"Hi."

Shane fell into his arms. The usual rush of relief flooded through him as they kissed for the first time in two weeks.

"I missed you," Ilya said unnecessarily.

"Yeah." For several long moments they just held each other. Shane buried his nose in the crook of Ilya neck and inhaled deeply, enjoying his familiar scent, and the solid weight of him in his arms.

"This shirt feels nice," Ilya said.

"It's silk."

"Fancy."

Shane pulled back and examined Ilya's face. "You look tired."

"Well. I was not the one asleep on the couch."

Shane frowned at him the way he always did when Ilya was being snarky when Shane needed him to be serious. "Rough trip?"

Ilya glanced down at the sofa cushions. "You know it wasn't good."

Yes, Shane knew that Ottawa had lost all four games on the trip, but that wasn't what he meant. "You okay?"

"I have not been sleeping well," Ilya admitted.

"Then let's go to bed." Shane stood and extended his hand. Ilya took it, and they walked upstairs together.

In the bedroom, Shane turned on one of the bedside lamps,

keeping the lighting low. Ilya stood at the end of the bed and watched him, then continued to watch as Shane began to undress him. Ilya's eyes were hooded, but more with exhaustion than lust, Shane suspected.

"You won tonight," Ilya said as Shane slid his dark gray suit jacket off of him.

"It was Buffalo," Shane said, almost apologetically. "Nothing to brag about."

"Buffalo beat us last time we played them," Ilya pointed out.

Shane didn't know what to say to that, so he silently loosened Ilya's tie and removed it, laying it on the bench at the end of the bed, on top of the jacket.

When he was halfway through unbuttoning Ilya's shirt, Ilya stopped him by capturing Shane's hand in his own. Shane glanced up and found Ilya staring at him like he had something important to say.

"What?" Shane asked, when Ilya didn't say anything.

"How long can you stay?"

"Until Friday morning. We've got a practice, then we're flying to Dallas."

Ilya's fingers clenched around Shane's hand. "And when is the next time?"

"I'm home for almost two weeks after this road trip. You?"

"Away when you get back."

"Oh." Shane forced himself to sound cheerful. "We'll have Christmas together, though." All NHL players had a few days off at Christmas, and he and Ilya had spent it in Ottawa the past few years, sharing the holiday with Shane's parents. Christmas didn't mean much to Ilya, but he generally loved food and presents, so he always seemed to enjoy it.

Ilya smiled, but it looked forced. "Yes. Will be nice."

Shane understood how he felt. Their scattered days and

nights together during the hockey season were never enough. He placed the hand that wasn't being held in a death grip on Ilya's cheek. "Hey," he said softly. "I'm here now."

Ilya's tight smile relaxed into something more genuine. "Yes," he agreed, and leaned in to kiss him.

Shane couldn't imagine anyone in the world being a better kisser than Ilya. Commanding and tender at the same time, just on the edge of filthy, but still managing to make Shane feel adored and precious. Shane was always just trying to keep up.

Ilya released Shane's hand and moved his own to the back of Shane's head, fingers tangling in his hair and pulling gently. "Love this long hair," he said in a low rumble that made Shane's toes curl.

Shane hummed happily in response, then slid his newly freed hand up Ilya's spine, over the slick material of his dress shirt, then curved his palm around the back of Ilya's neck. Shane's dick, which had been surprisingly chill so far, thickened hopefully against Ilya's thigh. Shane tried to angle his hips back so it wouldn't be obvious—Ilya needed sleep more than sex—but Ilya chuckled into his mouth and moved his thigh forward to bump against his erection.

"Happy to see me," Ilya murmured against Shane's lips.

"Always. But you can ignore . . . that."

"This?" Ilya asked, and dropped a hand to squeeze Shane's dick through his jeans.

Shane closed his eyes and grunted softly. "Yeah. You need sleep. We both do."

"Sex helps me sleep," Ilya argued.

Shane laughed and batted his hand away, then resumed unbuttoning Ilya's shirt. He continued removing clothing until Ilya was down to his boxer briefs and socks.

"I'll let you take the socks off," Shane said.

"And you will help with the underwear?" Ilya asked with a crooked, sexy smile.

"Maybe."

Shane got himself undressed, and Ilya crawled into bed. Shane went to the bathroom to brush his teeth, and when he came back, Ilya was already asleep.

Shane smiled and got into bed beside him, stretching an arm across Ilya's chest and snuggling close. "Good night, sex machine," Shane said quietly.

Ilya didn't reply. He just turned his head so his nose was buried in Shane's hair, and breathed.

# CHAPTER TWENTY

"Found you."

Shane nearly toppled off the stability ball he was balancing on at the sound of Ilya's voice. "Jesus."

He steadied himself and managed to hold his position, standing with his knees slightly bent on top of the large blue ball. It would have been easier—and would have made more sense—to simply hop off the ball, but he felt like showing off a bit.

"Impressive," Ilya drawled. In the mirrors that lined one wall, Shane watched him saunter across the floor of the spacious home gym that took up most of Ilya's basement. "How long have you been on there? Two hours?"

He leaned against the weight rack next to Shane, and their eyes met in the mirror. Like Shane, Ilya was wearing only workout shorts, his feet bare.

"I don't know," Shane said tersely. "You made me lose count."

"Aw."

"Good morning, by the way."

"Yes."

"Seems like you slept well." Shane had been awake for over an hour, but had left Ilya to sleep.

"Very well. Full of energy now." Ilya's gaze raked over Shane as he said it, and Shane wobbled on the ball.

"Are you hungry?" Shane asked.

"Always." Ilya pushed off the weight rack and parked himself in front of Shane. His lips were twisted into that damn half smile that always meant trouble.

"Go away."

"You are the perfect height for kissing now. Taller than me, even."

"Don't."

Ilya leaned in. "Can you do it? Kiss me without falling?"

Probably not, but that didn't mean Shane wouldn't try. "Bring it."

Ilya tilted his head and brought his lips close. When it became apparent that he was going to make Shane come to him, Shane huffed and closed the distance. For one magical second, they were kissing. Then Shane fell forward, and Ilya, the asshole, stepped backward.

"Thanks, shithead," Shane grumbled as he pulled himself off the floor.

Ilya was laughing, one hand planted on the mirror.

"That's going to leave a handprint," Shane said, which, yes. Even *he* could hear how insufferable he sounded.

"Oh no," Ilya teased, but he removed his hand.

"Did you come down here to work out?"

Ilya walked over to the weight rack and sat on the bench tucked inside. He spread his legs wide, showing off his muscular thighs and the bulge that pressed against the front of his shorts. He stretched his arms over his head, grinning lazily at Shane. "No."

Shane's gaze embarked on a journey, starting with the long fingers brushing the barbell that rested near the top of the rack, then down Ilya's sculpted biceps and forearms. Then it traveled to his broad, lightly furred chest and the chain that glinted next to his bear tattoo, and finally down to his impressive abs and the trail of hair that disappeared into the waistband of his shorts.

Jesus. His boyfriend was fucking stunning.

Shane stepped into the wide V of Ilya's legs. Their thighs brushed together, and Ilya placed firm hands on Shane's waist, guiding him closer.

"I don't understand your fitness regimen," Shane said as he combed his fingers through Ilya's rumpled curls.

"Why?" Ilya leaned forward and kissed Shane's stomach. Then did it again, and again. Gentle caresses of his lips against Shane's bare skin that sent sparks shooting down to Shane's toes.

"Because you don't have one," Shane said, though his voice sounded less admonishing than he wanted and a whole lot more trembly.

"I have one. Is just normal, not like yours." He kissed the jut of Shane's pelvic bone, where it stuck out above his shorts. "More running and weights. Not . . ." He waved a hand in the direction the ball had rolled off to. "Standing on balls."

"Stability and balance," Shane argued through quickening breaths, "are just as important as mass and endurance."

"Mm." Ilya slid his hands around to Shane's inner thighs, then pushed up under his shorts. His thumbs glided over the length of Shane's new and unsurprising erection, and Shane let out an equally unsurprising gasp.

"I like mass," Ilya purred. "And endurance."

"Ugh," Shane said, but it was followed by a sharp inhale when Ilya curled his fingers to cup Shane's balls.

"Maybe I *should* have more balls in my workout," Ilya mused.

"You are the absolute worst."

Ilya only replied with a wicked grin, then he tugged Shane's shorts and underwear down until they pooled around his ankles.

"Fuck," Shane said.

"Yes." He took Shane's cock in his hand and stroked him with loose, gentle fingers. It made Shane feel like his bones were melting.

Ilya kept his gaze turned up, locked on Shane's. His eyes were dancing with amusement and possibly simple, unchecked joy, which made Shane realize it had been a long time since he'd seen Ilya looking so happy. Shane smiled back at him, heart fluttering, as he allowed himself to let go of everything that wasn't *this*. Wasn't *him*.

"I love you so fucking much," Shane said. He smoothed a thumb over one of Ilya's thick eyebrows. "I was counting the minutes all week. Couldn't wait to see you again."

"I could tell. By how you drove here in the middle of the night."

"Don't try to make me feel weird about that. You love it when I'm eager."

Ilya rubbed his thumb lightly over the head of Shane's cock. "I sleep better with you," he admitted.

Shane was struggling to focus on the conversation, but he forced himself to. It was important. "I wish we could sleep together every night."

"I know. Now turn around."

"Turn around? Why?"

Ilya grinned and rotated one finger in the air. Shane still didn't understand, but he turned his back to Ilya as instructed and . . . then he understood.

"Oh god," he whispered, staring at himself in the wall of mirrors, naked except for the shorts pooled at his feet. His rock-hard cock was pointing directly at its own reflection.

Ilya stood behind him and kissed the side of his neck. Then he wrapped an arm around Shane's waist and took his erection in hand.

Shane closed his eyes. He couldn't—

"No," Ilya said in a low voice. "Watch. See how beautiful you are like this."

"I don't think I can. It's too much."

Another soft kiss to his neck, and then to his temple. "Stay there. One second."

Ilya left, and Shane cracked one eye open. He turned to watch Ilya, and to avoid looking at his own reflection. Ilya was standing near the stairs, and a second later, the overhead lights dimmed by half.

"Better?" Ilya asked.

Shane glanced back at the mirror. It was less intense, with the lights dimmed. "Why do you have sexy mood lighting in your gym?"

"You have it in yours."

"Yeah. For yoga and meditation. Two things you don't do."

"But you do them. So I have lights that dim. For you."

Shane's heart wobbled. "Oh."

"And—" Ilya returned to his position behind Shane, wrapping an arm across Shane's chest and pulling him back to rest against Ilya's bare torso "—is good for this."

It was still too much for Shane. He relaxed his eyes so he couldn't see himself too clearly, and focused on Ilya's hand on his cock, and his solid body behind him.

Ilya released him, then pulled something from his own shorts pocket. Shane turned his head to see.

"Do you always bring lube packets to workouts?" he asked dryly.

Ilya only smiled and opened the packet. He squeezed the lube into his palm, then returned his hand to Shane's dick. "Is a shame you don't have foreskin," he said.

"Why? Because if I had some you wouldn't have to walk around with pockets full of lube?"

"Why did your parents cut it off?"

"I don't know! It's not like we talk about it."

"Maybe I will ask them."

"You'd better not!"

Ilya laughed, and kissed behind Shane's ear. "We do not talk about these freckles on the back of your neck enough."

"I'm not—" Shane's breath hitched as Ilya increased the speed of his strokes. "I'm not too familiar with them."

"They are just here. A little group of them." Ilya's lips brushed the base of Shane's neck, making Shane shiver. "Adorable."

"Oh." Shane closed his eyes and rocked slightly into Ilya's hand. His ass bumped against Ilya's erection, which he was keen to do something about, but for now he was happy to let Ilya do whatever this was.

Ilya kept murmuring things in his ear as he stroked him, telling him how beautiful he was, how sexy. Some of his praise was in Russian, and Shane felt himself sink into a place where he didn't feel quite so ridiculous being on display like this.

"Do you see," Ilya asked, "how you look when you are gone like this? Stunning, Hollander."

Shane opened his eyes and gasped at what he saw. He'd never seen himself like this. He'd seen *Ilya* like this—eyes hazy with lust, mouth slack, cheeks flushed—but never his own face. Even when they jerked off together over FaceTime Shane always closed the window that showed himself. He wondered if Ilya left his own open.

It was weird, watching himself being pleasured, but it was also hot as hell. Ilya was watching too, gaze fixed on the mirror, eyes blazing intensely.

"Ilya," Shane said breathlessly.

"You see," Ilya said. He gently tugged the elastic at the back of Shane's head, and the hasty ponytail Shane had pulled his hair into for his workout fell apart. Ilya nuzzled into the long strands that now brushed the tops of Shane's shoulders.

Shane reached one arm back, looping it around the back of Ilya's neck. He twisted his head and caught Ilya's mouth in a messy, urgent kiss. Ilya allowed it for a moment or two, then guided Shane's face back to the mirror.

"You are going to watch yourself come," Ilya said.

"Fuck," Shane said, but nodded. He was way too far gone to do anything but watch and feel his orgasm build, hot and pulsing in his stomach, in his spine, in his balls.

Ilya pinched one of Shane's nipples, and Shane hissed and writhed against him. "Want," he moaned, not sure at all what he was asking for.

Ilya chuckled softly against his neck. "I know. Almost there, yes?"

"Yes. So fucking good." Shane tilted his head back slightly, still watching himself in the mirror. "Want to make you feel good too."

"You are. I love this." Ilya brought his lips to Shane's ear. "I love when you let go like this."

Shane loved it too. Loved that Ilya could do this to him. It was terrifying and wonderful to feel so free in this man's arms.

"Ilya," Shane panted. "Ilya. I'm going to come." He squeezed his eyes shut as the dam began to break inside him.

"Open your eyes," Ilya commanded softly. "Watch."

Shane's eyes flew open at the same moment his cock began to spurt over Ilya's fist and onto the floor. He could see how tight the muscles in his chest were, the way his abs and thighs trembled as his whole body rocked with pleasure.

When it was over, he slumped back against Ilya and huffed out a slightly hysterical laugh. "Fucking hell."

"Good?"

"Yeah," Shane sighed. "Yeah. That was just a *lot* before breakfast, y'know?"

Ilya nipped his earlobe. "It was very hot." He wiped his hand on Shane's stomach.

"Ugh. Gross," Shane said, and squirmed out of his arms. He stepped out of his shorts and then used them to wipe the floor. He knew Ilya was probably rolling his eyes behind him about how fussy Shane was about mess, but he didn't care.

"Take a shower, Hollander. I will make breakfast."

"What about . . ." Shane stood and gestured to the very obvious tent in Ilya's shorts.

"Later." Ilya smiled. "We have all day."

Shane kissed him. "Okay."

"Is chocolate pancakes good for breakfast?" Ilya asked.

"Uh—"

"I am kidding. I will make your gross protein shake."

"It's not gross," Shane lied.

"Go. Shower."

# CHAPTER TWENTY-ONE

*December*

“Do you have many friends?” Galina asked.

“Tons,” Ilya replied quickly, slightly offended. It was his third appointment with his therapist, and he wasn’t sure he was making much progress.

“I mean, do you have many people you can confide in? That you trust?”

This time Ilya didn’t answer so quickly. “I love my teammates. We have fun together, and support each other, but, no, I don’t talk to them about . . . myself.”

“What do you do, when you aren’t playing hockey, and when your boyfriend isn’t around?”

Ilya shrugged. “Not much. Stay home. Watch TV. Play video games.”

“Is that how you’ve always spent your free time?”

He shook his head slowly. “No.”

“What did you used to do, when you played in Boston?”

Ilya huffed out a laugh. “I had sex. Like, all the time. I went out, picked up. I went to clubs and parties and had a great time.”

"But now you're in a monogamous relationship?"

"Yes. And I'm glad. I love being with . . . him, and I don't miss . . ." He rotated one hand in the air. "Sleeping around. It was fun at the time, but I only want . . . him."

Ilya and Shane had talked about *other people*. A couple of years ago he'd told Shane, as casually as possible, that if he wanted to have sex with other men when they were apart—which was most of the time—he could. Since Shane had figured out he was gay around the same time he'd realized he had fallen in love with Ilya, it wouldn't be unreasonable for him to want to explore sex beyond what Ilya could give him. What did it matter as long as his heart belonged to Ilya? That's what Ilya had told himself.

Shane hadn't taken Ilya's offer well. He'd thought it had been Ilya's backhanded way of letting Shane know that he'd cheated on him, or that he wanted to. Ilya had told him that he didn't believe in cheating because he didn't *own* Shane. It had ended with Shane storming out of Ilya's house in Ottawa and driving back to Montreal, which had been a horrible waste of a rare night they could have had together. He'd ignored Ilya's texts for three days after.

Then, on the fourth day, he'd called Ilya from his hotel room in Philadelphia and said, "You really wouldn't mind if I had sex with someone else?"

And that was when Ilya had realized how much he *would* mind it. He'd felt sick at the idea of someone else touching Shane, and he hadn't been sure if Shane was asking because he'd already done it, or if he was about to or what. Maybe someone had been heading to his Philadelphia hotel room at that very moment.

But all Ilya had said was, "Of course not. If that is what you want."

"I *don't* want, you fucking moron," Shane had spat. The relief had been so intense that Ilya had nearly sunk to his knees in his living room.

"We're happy together," Ilya said now, to his therapist.

"But when you're apart?"

"I'm miserable," Ilya admitted. "More than he is, I think."

"Why do you think that is?"

"He has friends, family. He lives near where he grew up, his best friend knows about us. He has another close friend who knows about us. He's not alone."

She nodded and made some notes. "Is there someone on your team, or maybe another person, who you feel like you could open up to? Maybe not the whole truth, but someone you could share part of yourself with?"

Ilya wasn't sure. Harris was certainly a possibility. He was openly gay, super nice, and easy to talk to. But he also worked for the team and was, honestly, a bit of a gossip.

For some reason Troy Barrett came to mind. Ilya had noticed, over the past few weeks, that Troy might not be entirely straight. For one thing, his gaze had lingered on Ilya's bare chest more than once (not that Ilya could blame him), and for another, he kind of obviously had a crush on Harris.

It was possible that Troy needed someone to talk to too.

"Maybe," Ilya said finally. "It would be good, I think. To try."

He was sure none of his teammates would be bothered if they knew Ilya was bisexual, but he was also sure that revealing that part of himself would make it too easy for people to guess the rest of it. If they knew he was bisexual, and that Shane was gay—because most of the league had at least heard that rumor by now—and knew that he and Shane worked together in the summers . . .

Well. It didn't take a genius.

Better to let the hockey world think that Ilya was all about the ladies, and that he and Shane had a tenuous friendship based mostly on running a charity together. It had been working so far.

"It seems somewhat imbalanced," Galina said. "Your boyfriend—"

"Shane," Ilya said, suddenly finding the way they were both dancing around the obvious annoying. "You know who it is. His name is Shane."

As usual, no surprise showed on her face. "Shane," she repeated, "seems very comfortable in his life. Whereas you have made a lot of changes for him."

"For both of us," Ilya corrected her.

"Of course. But maybe you need more things in your life that are specifically for you."

Ilya considered this, then huffed. "I almost bought a car yesterday. A Lotus Evora. Cyan blue. It is an absolutely ridiculous car for driving around Ottawa, and I sold most of my car collection when I moved here. But I just wanted . . . I don't even know. To feel like my old self, maybe."

"What made you decide not to?"

"I knew it wouldn't make me happy, I guess. I had it all picked out and was about to call my dealer when I decided I was being stupid. I still would have been sad, but with a blue car in my garage."

"A lot of people find shopping to be therapeutic. Buying things we don't need." She smiled. "For me, it's usually new bedsheets, but we might be in different income brackets."

Ilya smiled back and said, in English, "Money doesn't buy happiness, yes?"

She laughed, then continued, in Russian, "Why did you sell your car collection when you moved to Ottawa?"

"The cars didn't make me happy anymore. When I thought about my collection, it seemed gross. So much money spent on cars I barely had a chance to drive. I put all of the money I made from selling them into the Irina Foundation."

"It had nothing to do with how Shane felt about your cars?"

Ilya couldn't honestly say it hadn't. Shane had thought the collection was ridiculous, certainly. He didn't understand the obsession, and he was terrified that Ilya was going to die in a high-speed crash. Maybe Ilya had sold them because he'd wanted to be a better person. The kind who owned a sensible SUV with all-wheel drive for winter conditions.

"Maybe a little."

"Have you made many changes based on how Shane felt about things?"

Ilya didn't like where this was going. "He isn't demanding. He didn't ask me to sell the cars, or to stop going out. He wants me to be happy."

"Does he know you're not?"

Ilya thought back to the one time Shane had expressed concern for Ilya's mental health, and how quickly Ilya had shot him down. "I don't know."

"Is it something you could talk to him about?"

"Isn't that why I'm here?" Ilya asked with a hint of irritation. "So I don't have to burden him with this? I thought I could talk to you and fix myself so I can be good enough for him."

A heavy silence hung in the room for a moment. Then, Galina said, very gently, "What do you think Shane would say, if he heard those words? If he knew you didn't want to burden him, or didn't think you were good enough for him?"

God, Ilya could imagine Shane's face so clearly, all twisted into his scrunched confusion expression. "He would say, 'What the hell are you talking about? You're already good enough for me.'" Ilya smiled. "He would say, 'You're perfect for me.'" His smile fell. "He doesn't understand, though. There are some things I can't talk to him about."

"It is completely fine and understandable to not share everything that we talk about here with him, but hiding your feelings from Shane—letting him believe you're happy when you're not—that will only build a wall between you. He's on one side with his friends and family, while you're on the other side, alone."

Ilya swallowed thickly. "It wouldn't be like that." Though now that she'd said it, he could see it was already starting to happen.

"I think you should talk to him. Does he know you've been seeing me?"

"No."

"That might be a good place to start."

Of course Ilya knew he should tell Shane that he was seeing a therapist. Shane would probably be relieved—he'd suggested it, after all. But would Shane ask questions? Would he want to know what they talked about? Ilya couldn't drag all this stuff to the surface again. Once was excruciating enough.

"I'll try," Ilya said. It was all he could promise.

It was too cold to walk around Ottawa after his appointment, so instead Ilya went to the arena to work out. He thought it might be good to see some other people.

As it turned out, the only other member of the team there was Luca Haas, doing kettle bell swings in one corner. Haas's eyes went wide when he spotted Ilya, and he nearly dropped the kettle bell.

Ilya nodded at him, then hopped onto an exercise bike to warm up. He stared hard at himself in the mirror in front of him, trying to get what Galina had said about Shane out of his head.

*He's on one side with his friends and family, while you're on the other side, alone.*

It wasn't true. Shane's parents were right there with Ilya. He probably saw them more than Shane did. Ilya was a part of their family now, he knew that, and he loved them.

And he had friends. He had . . .

. . . a Swiss weirdo staring at him. Ilya could see him in the mirror.

Ilya stopped peddling and dismounted. He turned toward Luca, who looked terrified.

"Hello?" Ilya said.

"Sorry," Luca said in his crisp Swiss-German accent. Unlike when Ilya had been a rookie, Luca's English was nearly perfect. "Was I staring?"

Ilya smiled. "I look good on a bike. I understand."

Luca's pale, baby-smooth face turned pink. "No! I wasn't—"

"Was a joke." Ilya walked toward him. "You are here alone?"

"Yes. I like the quiet, sometimes."

Ilya sat on the weight bench beside him. "I understand that."

"If you want to be alone I can—"

"No, no. Is not what I meant." Ilya smiled at him. "You seem a bit scared of me."

"I still can't believe we are on the same team."

Ilya chuckled. "How long until you believe it?"

"Years, maybe?"

Ilya held out his hand. "Ilya Rozanov. Normal guy. Nice to meet you."

After a moment's hesitation, Luca shook his hand. "Luca Haas. Embarrassing fanboy."

Ilya gestured to the weight bench a few feet away, and Luca sat facing him.

"How do you like Ottawa?" Ilya asked.

"In some ways it reminds me of Zurich, but in others it is very different."

Ilya nodded. He'd been to Zurich once and remembered the river that wound through the city, the low buildings, and the museums. He could see the similarities.

"Was it hard for you?" Luca asked. "When you left home?"

Ilya answered honestly. "No. I couldn't wait."

"Oh." Luca frowned at his folded hands.

"But," Ilya amended, "there was . . . adjustments. It was not so easy, with the language and the culture. I had no Russian teammates, and, like you, there was many expectations for me to be great right away."

Luca nodded. "Yes. It's a lot of pressure."

"I *was* great right away. Made it easier," Ilya joked.

Luca laughed. "That would help."

Ilya stretched out a foot and nudged Luca's sneaker. "You are also doing great. The fans love you. You see how much Harris posts about you. Can't get enough. I see Haas jerseys all over town." That was a bit of an exaggeration. He'd seen two.

"Thank you."

A silence fell between them that was interrupted by Ilya's favorite sound: a dog barking.

He stood and looked toward the door of the gym. "Is that Chiron?" he called out.

A second later, the team puppy came charging into the room, followed by Harris. "It sure is," Harris said, smiling as usual. "I heard you were in here and I thought—"

"Yes!" Ilya exclaimed, crouching to greet Chiron. He'd never needed a puppy in his arms so badly. He let Chiron sniff and lick his fingers, then scooped him up and cuddled him against his chest. "He is already so big!"

"Yup," Harris agreed. "He's a beast."

Luca approached cautiously. "Can I pet him?"

"Yeah, man," Harris said. "Get in there."

Luca scratched the top of Chiron's head with one finger.

"Okay. Hold on," Harris said. He pulled his phone out of his pocket. "This is way too cute." He snapped some photos that Ilya knew would kill later on Instagram.

"Hey, guys," called out a cheerful voice from the doorway. Coach Wiebe sauntered in wearing workout clothes. Ilya couldn't help but notice that he looked good in them.

"Coach," Ilya and Luca said at the same time.

"I am ninety percent sure dogs aren't allowed in here," Wiebe said. "But ninety isn't a hundred, right?" He took over head-scritching from Luca, except he used his whole hand.

"You like dogs?" Ilya asked.

"Love them. We've got a big ol' golden retriever at home. Lollipop. The kids named her, so don't look at me. We call her Lolly, mostly."

"I need to meet Lolly," Ilya said seriously. "Bring her to work someday."

"She's anxious around new people," Coach said. "She was a rescue from a bad situation, so she mostly sticks to home and her regular walk route. Sweetest thing, though."

Ilya almost laughed. His coach was seriously the nicest guy on earth.

"Are you boys going to the hospital visit this week?" Coach asked. The team visited the local children's hospital every December. Ilya wouldn't miss it for the world.

"Of course," Ilya said. "I have been training for my Mario Kart rematch."

Coach laughed. "And how about our star rookie?"

"Yes," Luca said. "I will be there."

"I hope Barrett's going," Coach said. "I know it'll be a rough week for him, with the game in Toronto after, but I think it would be good for him."

Ilya agreed, and he'd make sure Troy would be there.

They all played around with Chiron for about twenty minutes, then Harris announced that Chiron's trainer was there to pick him up. Ilya watched miserably as Harris left with the puppy.

"Do you think the other dogs are nice to him at his school?" Ilya asked no one in particular.

"Only the best of the best get to be in that place," Coach assured him. "It's like the NHL of dogs."

"Yes, but there are huge assholes in the NHL."

Coach laughed and clapped him on the shoulder. "Yeah, but not in Ottawa."

"I came out to Troy Barrett," Ilya said, a week later.

Shane nearly choked on the sip he'd just taken of his smoothie. *"What?"* he asked after a fit of coughing. He was glad this wasn't a video call.

"I told him I am bisexual," Ilya said calmly, as if he'd told Troy that he liked pizza or something. As if he revealed his sexuality to people all the time when Shane knew he'd barely told anyone. Ilya had told Shane that Troy wasn't such a bad guy, now that he was getting to know him, but it still seemed fucking nuts that Ilya would choose him of all people to share this closely guarded secret with.

"When? Why?"

"Last night. I wanted to tell someone."

All right. Shane didn't know that this had been weighing on Ilya, and that made him feel like a shitty boyfriend. But he could worry about that later. "Why him?"

For a moment, there was silence. Then Ilya said, "You can't tell anyone this."

"Tell anyone what?"

"Promise me."

"Fine. I promise. What?"

"He came out to me first," Ilya said.

Shane blinked. "I'm sorry. *What?*"

"He told me he is gay. I don't think he has told many people. Maybe no one. So it felt like I should, you know. Share back."

"Troy Barrett is *gay*?" Given the fact that Troy had always seemed like a homophobic douchebag to Shane, this was a lot to process.

"Yes. But that is a secret."

Shane closed his eyes. Okay. Troy Barrett was gay, and also he was friends with Ilya now. Weird. "Of course I won't tell anyone."

"I know."

"Why did he tell you?" It suddenly occurred to Shane that the reason Troy had come out to Ilya was because he was *interested* in Ilya.

"I took him out last night. To the Kingfisher. Was his first gay bar, he said." Then Ilya laughed. "You'd like him. You are both very bad at being gay."

"Hilarious," Shane said flatly. "So what happened at the bar?"

"We had a nice talk with the queer New York hockey players."

"Scott and Eric were there?"

"Yes. They own the bar."

"I know, but—" Shane sighed. "Okay. So you had a queer NHL player meeting."

"You feel left out?"

"I mean, yeah. Kind of. What were you guys doing there?"

"Just talking. Drinking beer. Having a fun time. You would have hated it."

"Did Troy come out to everyone there?"

"No. Just me. Was after. We were walking to the hotel."

"Sounds romantic," Shane grumbled.

"Shane. He is in love with Harris. Not me." There was a beat of silence, then Ilya added, "That is also a secret. Though not a good one because Troy is very obvious about this crush."

"Just to recap," Shane said. "Your new friend Troy Barrett is gay and in love with your team's social media manager?"

"Yes."

"Were you surprised when he told you? Because I'm pretty fucking surprised."

"No. Because of the crush on Harris thing. And also he was checking me out a few times."

Shane exhaled slowly. "I don't think I like Troy."

"Why? You have a lot in common. You both are short, gay, and both think I am hot."

"Your favorite qualities in a man."

"You are both very pretty. Nice dark hair. Troy also does not have chest hair."

"Let's stop talking about Troy Barrett."

Ilya laughed. "It is cute how you are jealous."

"I am absolutely not jealous of Troy fucking Barrett." Except for how Troy got to spend so much time with Ilya, play hockey on the same line as him, and, apparently, check him out in the locker room and go to gay bars with him.

"I only am telling you," Ilya said in a more serious tone, "because it was nice. To talk about this with someone."

Wait. "You didn't tell him about *us*, did you?"

"Of course I didn't fucking tell him about us!" Then Ilya mumbled something in angry Russian. Shane only caught about half of the words.

"What was that?"

"Only you can tell your friends about us, right? This is how it works?"

"What the hell are you talking about? And since when is Troy your closest friend?"

Ilya exhaled loudly into the phone. "I have to go. Practice soon."

Shane didn't understand why they were both so angry, but ending the call before one of them said something they couldn't take back was probably a good idea. "Fine." He winced at the bitchiness of his tone, then said, more gently, "Call me after practice?"

"I might be busy having sex with Troy," Ilya said tightly.

"Ilya . . ."

"I have to go."

The call went dead.

Shane slumped against his kitchen counter and started thinking about all the ways that conversation could have gone better.

Ilya didn't call Shane after practice. Instead he took a nap, ate dinner, and got ready for his game that night against the New York Admirals. The Admirals were the best team in the league, so Shane would understand why Ilya would need to focus.

Not that he cared if Shane understood. Shane certainly hadn't understood why it had been important for Ilya to tell someone—anyone—that he was bisexual. And why it had felt so good to have his teammate come out to him. How good it felt to be making a new friend, and to have earned that friend's trust so quickly.

Maybe Ilya shouldn't have told Shane. Maybe he should have saved all this for his next session with Galina. Not that he would out Troy to his therapist, but he would find a way to talk about it. Galina would understand why this was important to Ilya. She knew how lonely he was.

Jesus. Ilya hadn't even told Shane that Troy had almost guessed that he and Shane were a couple. It was alarming how quickly Troy had started to put the pieces together in his head once Ilya had told him he was bisexual. If Shane knew about *that* he'd probably lose his shit completely.

Ilya carried his bad mood onto the ice that night for the match against the Admirals. At first, his anger seemed useful, pushing him to battle hard and even open the scoring early in the first period. But as the game went on, and as New York kept scoring, Ilya's anger caused him to take stupid penalties and make costly mistakes.

After the game he'd been quiet and sulky. He hadn't talked to anyone in the dressing room, and no one had talked to him. Probably because they didn't want to get snarled at.

That night, there was an unexpected knock on his hotel room door.

"Hey," Troy said when Ilya opened it. "Thought you might wanna watch a movie or something."

Ilya took in Troy's uncertain expression, aware that gestures of friendship were probably outside Troy's usual comfort zone. Ilya nodded, and stepped back to let him in.

Twenty minutes into the climate disaster action movie Ilya had found on television, Troy said, "Even when I played for Toronto, we hardly ever beat the Admirals."

Ilya just grunted.

"I wish Scott Hunter wasn't such a decent guy," Troy continued. "I'd love to just hate him, y'know?"

"You wish he wasn't hot," Ilya said.

Troy's eyes widened in surprise, as if he'd forgotten that he'd come out to Ilya already. Then he huffed out a laugh and said, "Yeah. That too."

Ilya smiled for the first time in hours.

They watched the movie in silence for a while, then Ilya blurted out, "I am a shitty captain."

"What? No you're not."

"Anyone on the team would be a better captain than me."

"As if," Troy scoffed. "I'll bet you've been captain of every team you've ever played for."

Well. Yes. "Does not matter. I am a bad captain for this team. Now."

"No way. You're a fucking legend. All the young guys idolized you growing up, and they still do. *I* fucking idolized you, man."

This time Ilya scoffed. "I am not so much older than you, Barrett."

"I just mean, when I played junior, everyone wanted to be like you. Guys like Hunter and Hollander, they're amazing, but you look like you're having fun out there, y'know? You're a leader, but you're also, like, cool."

Ilya's eyebrows shot up. "Cool?"

Troy's lips curled into something that was almost a smile. "Compared to Hunter and Hollander."

Ilya laughed out loud, which made Troy laugh. "Wow," Ilya said. "Is that a compliment?"

"Totally."

"I am hotter than them too."

Troy raked his gaze over Ilya appraisingly, and for an uncomfortable moment, Ilya thought he may have come here to seduce him. Then Troy wrinkled his nose and said, "Meh. I wouldn't say that."

They both laughed again, and Ilya hit him with a pillow.

"I am no Harris," Ilya teased.

Troy's cheeks darkened. "Shut up."

"Why? Is cute."

"It's embarrassing. I can't believe you know about that." Troy buried his face in the pillow Ilya had hit him with.

"Harris should know about it," Ilya said.

"No way. Never."

"That is dumb. He is nuts about you."

"Well, then *he's* dumb." Troy settled the pillow in his lap, then started nervously kneading it with one hand. "You think he likes me, though?"

"I am never wrong about these things." He wasn't lying. Ilya had always been an expert at detecting when someone was attracted to him, or to anyone else. Harris was definitely crushing on Troy.

Attraction, sex. Those things were easy. Relationships, feelings, *love*. Ilya was still working on how to navigate that stuff.

Troy left when the movie ended, which was far later than either of them should have been awake with a game to play in New Jersey tomorrow, but again, Ilya was a bad captain.

A tiny voice in his head, that maybe sounded a bit like Shane, told him that bad captains don't make new teammates feel comfortable coming out to them. Or feel comfortable knocking on their captain's hotel room door in the middle of the night just to hang out.

When Ilya was in bed, but before he went to sleep, he typed out a text to Shane: I'm sorry.

He deleted it. He wasn't really sorry for anything. Instead he wrote, I miss you, then deleted that too.

After staring at his phone for several minutes, he typed a red heart emoji, and sent it.

He was surprised when Shane replied almost right away. He'd expected Shane to be asleep.

**SHANE:**

I've been working on an apology text for over an hour.

Ilya smiled and wrote, How many words do you have?

**SHANE:**

Too many. I'm really sorry about what I said. I'm glad you told Troy. I'm glad you have a friend you trust.

Ilya felt immediately lighter. He wrote, Thank you. It feels good, to have someone know.

**SHANE:**

I was being a jealous prick.

**ILYA:**

I know.

Then, because he couldn't help himself, Ilya added, He is very hot. I understand.

**SHANE:**

You're the worst.

**ILYA:**

Maybe he is up for that threesome you pretend you don't want.

**SHANE:**

Good night, Ilya.

**ILYA:**

Would be a nice Christmas present . . .

He watched the three dots for what seemed like forever as Shane typed. Finally, Shane's reply appeared: For Troy, maybe.

# CHAPTER TWENTY-TWO

"It's fucking Christmas, Hollander," Ilya groaned. "Eat a cookie."

Shane bit back a whole speech about how even one cookie would fuck up all his hard work. He wasn't on a *weight loss* diet, he was following a complicated nutritional regimen designed to enhance physical performance.

But Shane didn't want to explain all of that *again*, so instead he rolled his eyes as hard as he could.

"I don't *want* a cookie." It was a lie. It was a fucking lie. He wanted a cookie so bad.

"Yuna," Ilya called out. "Tell your son to eat a cookie."

"Leave him alone," Yuna called from . . . whatever room she was in at the moment. She moved around so much it was hard to keep track. "We love Shane even without carbs."

Shane would really like it if everyone stopped talking about his diet. It shouldn't be a big deal. He was a professional athlete who was treating his body as if he were a professional athlete. His nutritionist had worked with some of the top athletes in the world, and they all swore by him. Maybe Ilya was getting away with eating like a stoner teenage goat for now, but he'd be thirty soon, and that would change. Shane preferred to stop any physical deterioration before it started.

"You don't even celebrate Christmas," Shane said grumpily.

"I celebrate cookies," Ilya said, then crammed an entire thumbprint cookie in his mouth.

"Gross."

"It has jam!" Ilya said through a mouthful of cookie.

Ilya did love jam. Especially raspberry. He had a spot of it on his cheek that Shane decided not to tell him about.

"Here," Yuna said as she emerged from the garage. She tossed something that Shane barely managed to catch. "I got you a treat."

Shane frowned at the pomegranate in his hands. "Thanks."

Ilya laughed. "Take a bite!"

"You don't bite into a pomegranate, dumbass."

"No? There isn't important fiber and nutrients in the, um, shell?"

Shane huffed and took his pomegranate to the kitchen. The whole Christmas day so far had been weird, and sort of tense. They'd been sniping at each other since Shane had arrived at Ilya's yesterday morning.

They'd woken up together after a somewhat competitive evening playing foosball on the new table Shane had bought as a Christmas gift for Ilya. It had been delivered earlier that day, and Ilya had been thrilled with it. So that had been okay.

Their heated foosball battle had turned into heated making out, and then sex, which had also been okay. Normal. Overall a decent Christmas Eve.

In the morning, Ilya had grouched about Shane not being fun to make breakfast for, and Shane had told him he didn't *ask* Ilya to make breakfast for him. They'd argued back and forth while Shane made a smoothie and Ilya made himself scrambled eggs with toast and sausages. Then they'd glared at each other across the kitchen table while they ate.

Before they'd left for Shane's parents', Ilya had grumbled something about giving Shane his present later, and Shane didn't know what that meant. Ilya hadn't seemed excited about it, that was for sure.

There were things, Shane suspected, that Ilya wasn't telling him, which made Shane anxious and a bit angry. Why would Ilya keep anything from Shane? He'd thought they were beyond that. If Shane didn't know better, he'd think Ilya was cheating on him or something. Or that he wanted to break up.

But, Shane kept assuring himself, he *did* know better. Maybe Ilya's mood was purely hockey-related. Shane would certainly be in a pissy mood if his team sucked as much as the Ottawa Centaurs.

Whatever it was, Shane was getting tired of it. If Ilya had a problem with Shane, or with anything, he should talk to Shane about it. Not dig into him about his diet or his friends or whatever else Ilya decided to make fun of him about.

Ilya entered the kitchen as Shane was irritably extracting seeds from the pomegranate. "Need help?" he asked.

Shane sighed, releasing some of the tension in his shoulders. Maybe he was being annoyed with Ilya for no reason. "I'm good." He pinched a seed between his finger and thumb and held it out. "Want one?"

Ilya opened his mouth, and Shane slipped the seed inside. Ilya closed his lips around Shane's fingers for a second, which made Shane smile. He really did love Ilya so much.

"Good," Ilya said when he'd swallowed the seed. "Not as good as the cookies, but good."

"Yeah, yeah."

Ilya opened the fridge and pulled out a carton of eggnog.

He glanced at Shane as he made his way to the cupboard where the glasses were, as if waiting for him to say something about the nutritional horrors of eggnog.

*"What?"* Shane asked testily.

"No lecture?"

Shane slammed the pomegranate half he was working with down on the cutting board. Juice flew everywhere. "Would you please fuck off? I don't give a shit what you or anyone else eats, Ilya."

Ilya snorted. "This is not true. You bitch at me all the time."

"Because you always start it!"

Ilya didn't reply. Instead, he pulled a large glass from the cupboard and poured himself about a gallon of eggnog.

Shane's pomegranate-stained fingers curled into fists. He was *not* going to say anything.

Ilya raised the glass in a toast, and took a long haul of eggnog, which was disgusting to watch. Shane stared him down anyway.

Ilya finished with a loud, obnoxious "Ahh," then wiped his mouth with the back of his hand. Shane turned his back to him, grabbed a dishcloth, and began cleaning the spattered pomegranate juice from the counter.

"Your parents want to exchange presents now," Ilya said.

"Okay."

"Come to the living room when you are done, yes?"

"I *know* where we exchange presents on Christmas." God, Shane knew he sounded like an absolute bitch, but he couldn't help it.

He could hear Ilya leave the kitchen as Shane continued to aggressively wipe the counter.

The tension followed them home, neither man saying much to the other. Shortly after they got back, Ilya thrust a neatly wrapped present at Shane, then plopped himself grumpily on one end of the couch.

Shane sat on the opposite end, glanced at Ilya with a mixture of apprehension and apology, and carefully unwrapped the gift.

It was a framed photograph that he'd never seen before. He knew immediately when it was from, though. It was an outtake from their first ad campaign together, the one they'd shot in the dingy rink in Toronto the summer before their rookie seasons. The day when they would eventually hook up for the first time. Kiss for the first time.

In the photo they were nose-to-nose in full hockey gear, cropped close from the shoulders up, simulating a face-off. Unlike the intense, serious photo that ran in the campaign, however, in this one they were both laughing. Shane's nose was scrunched up, and Ilya's eyes were crinkled, but they still held each other's gaze.

"How'd you get this?" Shane asked quietly.

"I found out the photographer's name and his email. I asked if he still had those. He sent me some and that one was my favorite."

Shane traced a finger over his own giddy face in the photo. At the time he'd felt embarrassed and unprofessional about not being able to keep a straight face. But now he felt a thrill shoot through him as he remembered all of the details of that day: the heat between them, the civil war that had raged inside Shane as he'd fought to ignore his attraction to Ilya. The cliff they'd been just about to jump off together.

"It never occurred to me that these existed," Shane said now.

"I have always wondered."

Shane pulled his gaze away from the photograph to look at the present-day version of Ilya. He looked effortlessly beautiful, as always, but also anxious, and a bit sad.

"Ilya," Shane said. He set the photo carefully on the coffee table, then held his arms open for his boyfriend. Ilya came to him immediately.

"Thank you," Shane said into Ilya's hair.

"You are hard to buy for."

"I know. I love this, though. I'll bring it to the cottage."

Ilya stiffened slightly in his arms. "The cottage. Yes," he said quietly.

Shane felt like he needed to explain why it might be risky to display photos like this one in his Montreal home, which was ridiculous. Of course Ilya knew the reasons. So instead, he kissed him, and it escalated as it usually did. They went up to the bedroom and had sex, but Shane still felt like they'd become dry kindling, waiting for the spark that would destroy them. Like there was something important that wasn't being said, and they were both waiting for the other person to say it, but neither of them knew what it was.

Ilya spent most of Boxing Day working up the nerve to ask Shane a single question. Finally, early in the afternoon, he broached the subject.

"Bood is having a party tonight."

Ilya said it casually, as if there were no particular reason he was letting Shane know. As if his stomach wasn't a mess as he anticipated Shane's reaction.

"Zane Boodram? He's having a party on Boxing Day?"

"Yes. Not a big party. It will be chill. Mostly just the team and partners. Bood has fun parties."

"Oh."

Ilya held his breath.

"Did you want to go or something?" Shane asked, clearly confused. "I could stay here, I guess. Or head back to—"

"I want you to go too," Ilya said. "I want you to come with me to the party."

Shane twisted around so they were facing each other on

Ilya's couch. "You want me to go to a party with your teammates? Why?"

*So they can fucking meet my boyfriend*, Ilya wanted to scream. But instead, he kept his tone light and said, "They are cool people. You might have fun."

"But . . . wouldn't it be weird, if we showed up together?"

Ilya shrugged easily, as if this was a normal thing for him to suggest. "They know you would be in Ottawa for Christmas. We are friends, so I invite you to a party. No big deal."

Shane's face scrunched up in confusion, then he shook his head. "Too weird. I don't think so."

The dismissal, though expected, irritated Ilya. No, irritated was too small a word—it *infuriated* him. For a moment, Ilya didn't react. He stared at Shane, stony-faced, while anger scorched through him like lava. Then, before he said anything he may regret, he stood up and walked out of the living room.

Shane caught up with him in the kitchen. "You can go," he said. "It's fine."

"Great," Ilya snapped.

"What's wrong?" Shane sounded so genuinely clueless about why Ilya might want him to meet his friends that it only angered Ilya further.

"What isn't wrong?"

"What does *that* mean?"

Ilya spun around to face him. "It means I have a boyfriend who doesn't want anyone to know I am his boyfriend."

Shane's eyes widened in surprise. "Uh, sorry. Did I miss something? I thought we were on the same page about this."

"We are not on the same anything."

"I don't fucking understand you."

"Sorry," Ilya said sardonically. "My English, you know."

"That's not what I—" Shane threw his hands up. "Could

you please explain what the fuck is happening? Because last I checked we didn't go to each other's team parties. Or tell anyone about our relationship."

"No. *I* don't tell anyone about our relationship. You tell Hayden, and Jackie, and Rose, and your parents, and who the fuck knows who else."

"That's literally everyone! You know that."

"It is five more people than I have told," Ilya said, omitting his therapist, because that was a whole other conversation.

"What about . . ." Shane waved a hand around as he searched for a name. "Ryan Price?"

"Oh yes. My best friend Ryan Price. I have not talked to him since the last camp."

"Well—" Shane didn't seem to have anything to add to that.

"I have *no one*," Ilya said. "No one I can talk to about us."

"That's not true. My parents love you."

Ilya threw his head back and walked to the living room. Shane followed immediately.

"It's not easy for me either, you know," Shane said, clearly angry now. "We're both hiding, and we've both made sacrifices that—"

Ilya spun around. "What sacrifices, Shane? What have *you* given up?"

"Seriously? If we get outed, our fucking careers might be over! Everything I care about—" Shane snapped his fingers "—gone."

"Everything," Ilya said flatly.

Shane rolled his eyes. "Not *everything*. But hockey is pretty fucking important to me."

"No shit."

"Oh, fuck you. Sorry I still want to win cups instead of smoking weed with my teammates between losses."

The words hit Ilya like a crosscheck to the teeth. Shane truly didn't understand anything. Not what Ilya had given up for him, certainly. Ilya could be in Boston right now, leading one of the top teams in the league to more Stanley Cups. He could be breaking more records, and winning more awards. Instead he'd *chosen* to come to Ottawa, when he could have gone to almost any team in the league. He'd chosen a team that hadn't made the playoffs in over a decade. He'd chosen it because it was Shane's hometown, and close to where Shane lived. He'd chosen it so he could build a life in Canada with the man he loved.

And Shane thought he had, what? Come to Ottawa so he wouldn't have to work so hard? Ilya wanted to punch a wall.

"You wouldn't even choose me, would you?" Ilya said. "If it is between me and hockey."

"Of course I would," Shane said, though not as confidently as Ilya would have liked.

Ilya studied his face, and saw Shane flinch. "*Would* you?"

Shane tilted his chin up defiantly. "Would *you* choose *me*?"

Ilya let the question hang in the air, his whole body trembling with rage. He couldn't believe Shane would even ask that, after everything.

Finally, quietly, Ilya said, "You should go."

"What? No way. Fuck that. Answer the question."

"No," Ilya said firmly. "Go home, Shane. We can talk . . . later."

Shane's brow furrowed, and he seemed unsure about whether Ilya was serious, so Ilya made it clearer. "I don't want to look at you right now. I don't want to talk to you. Go home."

Because Shane couldn't leave anything alone, he asked again, "Would you choose me?"

Suddenly, Ilya had Shane backed against a wall. Ilya hadn't realized he'd moved until he was looming over Shane, one hand planted firmly on his chest. Ilya pulled his hand away quickly and moved it to the wall. He would never hurt Shane, he was sure of that, but his own fury was scaring him at the moment. He'd never been this close to flying apart.

If Shane was scared at all, his face didn't show it. He kept his sharp black eyes fixed on Ilya's, refusing to back down from this fight.

Ilya didn't want to fight. He was exhausted, and miserable, and his boyfriend was breaking his fucking heart.

Quietly, in a voice that couldn't disguise his pain, he said, "I already chose you, Hollander."

He stepped back, and watched Shane's eyes widen. After a moment, Shane's lips parted as if he had something to say, but Ilya didn't want to hear it.

"Go home," Ilya said. "Please." Then he turned and walked quickly upstairs.

# CHAPTER TWENTY-THREE

Shane had no idea how he got back to Montreal. He couldn't remember a minute of the drive, he'd been so consumed by a whirling storm of anger, shock, fear, and shame.

*I already chose you, Hollander.*

The words kept repeating in his head, continuing even as he made his way into his house, up the stairs, and finally collapsing on his bed.

He should have stayed. He should have stayed and fought for himself, or . . .

Fuck.

It would be ridiculous to say this was their first fight—their entire relationship seemed like one unending fight sometimes—but this was the first one that had left Shane feeling terrified. Obviously he had fucked something up. He hadn't been paying attention to Ilya, or to what Ilya had given up for him, and he now realized that Ilya had given up a whole fucking lot for Shane. For *them*.

Of course he resented Shane. Ilya had left his home country, his family—even if only a brother he hated remained—his team, his friends in Boston, his entire fucking life, really. He'd changed everything.

Meanwhile Shane was comfortable in Montreal, playing with the same team he'd started with. Winning Stanley Cups. He had friends he could talk to about Ilya—a teammate even—and his parents lived nearby. He'd set his boyfriend up in his hometown, not far from Montreal, because that was convenient for him. Everyone he loved all in one tidy circle.

And in the summers they went to Shane's cottage. God, their entire relationship was about Ilya fitting into Shane's life as easily as possible.

But Shane really hadn't had any reason to believe Ilya resented it. Ilya loved the cottage, loved Shane's parents, loved *Shane*. He liked his teammates in Ottawa, and told Shane all the time that it was a great organization, better than Boston had been. He'd been the one to tell Shane, way before they'd talked about making any big life changes, that he wanted to become a Canadian citizen. Ottawa made sense.

But even knowing all of this, Shane had clearly missed something important.

He didn't know what to do. He wanted to drive right back to Ottawa and apologize, but Ilya had made it clear that he wanted space, and Shane should respect that. Maybe they could talk tomorrow. Or tonight. Or . . .

Shit. Shane really wanted to call him right now. Or at least text him. The season resumed tomorrow and they wouldn't be able to see each other for who knew how long. At least a week or two.

He typed out a message to Ilya. I'm sorry. Call me when you want to talk. Please.

God, was that pushy? Should Shane just leave him alone?

Fuck it. Shane hit send. Ilya could ignore it if he wanted, but Shane really hoped he wouldn't.

He waited a few minutes, just in case Ilya decided to call him right away. But Ilya didn't even text, and Shane's heart sank.

Needing to talk to *someone*, he called his mom.

"I messed up," Shane said as soon as her face filled his phone screen.

"What? With your coach? It's a day off. How could you—"

"No. With Ilya."

The concern left her face immediately. She even smiled. "There's nothing you could do to ruin things with him. What happened?"

Shane sat up and swung his legs over the side of the bed. "I take him for granted. Everything he's given up, and everything he's changed." He rubbed at his forehead in frustration. "He's lonely, y'know? And I'm living my life, happy as can be, assuming that our rare times together are enough for him."

"He told you this?"

"More or less. I mean, no. But he said enough to help me figure out the rest." He exhaled. "I'm the worst boyfriend."

"That's not true. And Ilya would agree with me, so don't start."

Shane pressed his lips together, trying to fight the lump that had formed in his throat. "I don't deserve him."

Mom fixed him with an exasperated glare. "Shane."

"He's going to break up with me," Shane said miserably. "This was never going to work. It's too hard. I'm asking too much of him."

"He's an adult," Mom said. "And he loves you. Against all odds, you boys *are* making this work. I know it's not ideal, but I'm proud of how hard you've both worked to be together. It's powerful." She laughed softly. "I wish I could brag about it to everyone I meet."

Shane shook his head. "Nothing to brag about now. I've been a complete asshole. Shit, I'm so selfish. I thought being closer together would make things better for both of us, but he was happier before."

"This is a conversation you need to have with him. For what it's worth, he likes being in Ottawa. He told us that he likes this team better than his old one. He loves his teammates, and his new coach."

Shane's heart lifted a bit. "He said he likes Ottawa?"

"More than once. And honestly I think he'd live in the city dump if it meant being closer to you. He's head over heels."

"But that's the problem! If he's making all of his decisions based on me, he's going to resent me. He already does."

"Talk to him," Mom said patiently.

"He doesn't want to talk."

"You've tried? He said that?"

"He ignored my text."

"Uh-huh," Mom said flatly, clearly not convinced. "When did you send it?"

Shane's cheeks heated. "Like, twenty minutes ago."

"Good grief, Shane. He could be in the shower. Or on a treadmill. Or asleep. Or charging his phone. Relax!"

Shane huffed a laugh. "You sound like Ilya."

"Because we're very much aligned in our views when it comes to you."

"You both think I'm an uptight wet blanket."

"We both love you to death, and want you to be happy. And we both know you can be your own worst enemy."

"Well. I had another enemy, but then I fell in love with him."

Mom laughed. "Talk to him. Give him time to respond, and if he doesn't, then try again. And for god's sake *listen* to him."

"I will. And if he won't talk to me, I'll . . . drive to Ottawa and stand outside his door until—"

"Or you could just be cool for once in your life."

Shane's mouth dropped open. "Oh my god. Ilya is such a bad influence on you!"

"He'll call. I promise. Be patient."

"Okay."

"I love you."

"I love you too."

"And Ilya loves you."

Shane nodded, hoping those words were still true. "Thanks. Bye."

He stared at his phone for several minutes after the call ended, trying to will Ilya to text him back. When no messages came, Shane opened Instagram and scrolled through Ilya's posts. He never paid much attention to them, especially since Ilya mostly posted photos of random things he saw, and rarely posted selfies.

The most recent post was from yesterday—Christmas—and it was of the foosball table Shane had given him. No caption. He scrolled and found a photo of the exercise ball Shane had been balancing on in Ilya's gym. One of the latest puzzle Ilya had completed with Shane's dad. One of Ilya's loon tattoo.

One of the two plastic heart rings, together on Shane's dresser.

Shane realized that most of Ilya's posts were, in weird cryptic ways, about Shane. His entire account was like a secret diary of their relationship, full of inside jokes and little references that only Shane would understand.

And Shane hadn't even bothered to look at it before. Not really.

He looked now. He scrolled until his eyes were so blurry he had to give up and sob into his hands instead. How could Shane have doubted for a second how fiercely Ilya loved him?

"This isn't working," Ilya said as soon as Galina closed her office door behind him.

"Our sessions, you mean?"

"Yes. I feel worse than ever. Everything is fucked." He knew he wasn't being cool, but it had been a rough twenty-four hours and he was barely holding himself together. He'd turned his phone off yesterday as soon as Shane had left his house. He'd spent a couple of hours lying on his bed, staring at the ceiling and trying to nap. Then he'd gone to the gym in his basement and rode his exercise bike hard. After that he'd punished his heavy bag for a while.

He hadn't seen Shane's text until this morning, and he hadn't replied yet. He didn't know what to say. He'd already had his appointment with Galina booked for today, so he'd decided to talk to her before reaching out to Shane. He wasn't above wanting someone to tell him what to do because he was fucking lost.

"Why don't you sit down?" Galina said calmly.

"No," Ilya snapped. He pointed an accusing finger at her. "You said I would feel better. You're supposed to fix me."

Galina didn't react to the anger in his voice, or the absurd finger-pointing. She only looked at him with quiet interest, and maybe a hint of amusement. "You've been coming to see me for less than two months. I'm good, but I'm not that good."

Ilya put his finger away, but despite feeling foolish, he needed her to understand how urgent the situation was. "I can't do this if I am going to feel worse. I have to focus on hockey, and I have to be a good boyfriend, and I can't do either of those things if I'm this fucking sad."

"Ilya," she said firmly. "Sit."

Ilya sat, sighing heavily as he did so. "What's wrong with me?"

Galina sat in her own chair and crossed her legs. "You are a human being with a lot of responsibilities and pressure. You play a physically taxing, dangerous sport for a living. You are hiding a very big secret while also living your life in a spotlight. You are in love with a man you aren't allowed to be in love with. You are carrying trauma from your childhood that you've never allowed yourself to process properly. And also you feel things very deeply. Deeper than maybe anyone realizes."

Ilya blinked. He hadn't actually been expecting an answer. Especially not one that was so . . . thorough.

"Is that all?" he said dryly.

"I think you are depressed."

Ilya hugged his own chest protectively. "Like my mother."

"Not necessarily. Depression is complicated and manifests in many different ways. And there are many ways to treat it."

"Drugs." Ilya didn't want drugs. Other than painkillers that were absolutely necessary, he avoided pills. Pills could be a weapon.

"Again, not necessarily. Antidepressants can be very helpful for some people, but they aren't the only thing that helps." She waved a hand in the air, indicating her office. "This helps. Being here. Talking. Some people respond well to things like exercise."

Ilya snorted. "I can't exercise more than I already do."

"No," she agreed, "but you can do physical activity that is purely for you. Not for hockey. A hike, or a long bike ride. Tennis with a friend. That sort of thing."

"In Ottawa? In the winter?"

She smiled. "It doesn't have to be exercise. We haven't known each other for very long, but I think you need to do more things that are just for you in general. Your priorities seem to be divided between hockey and your boyfriend."

"I like those things," Ilya argued.

"Last time we met I suggested you talk to Shane about the things you've given up for him. Did you do that?"

"Yes!" Ilya practically shouted. "That's why everything is fucked!"

"He didn't take it well?"

"We had a fight. Yesterday. I haven't spoken to him since because he doesn't understand anything. He asked if I'd choose him over hockey and I couldn't believe he even asked, you know?"

"What made him ask that?"

Ilya chewed the inside of his cheek for a moment, wishing he didn't have to say the next thing. "I asked him first," he mumbled.

Galina's eyebrows rose slightly. "And why did you ask him?"

"Because . . ." Ugh. This was embarrassing. "He hurt my feelings. I asked him if he wanted to go to a party at my teammate's house." He sighed. "It was stupid. Of course he was right to say no. We have never done anything like that before, and it would have been ridiculous to bring him but . . . I wanted to. I want to introduce him as my boyfriend to my friends."

"That would be an enormous step," Galina said. "One that would require some serious discussion beforehand, I would imagine."

"Yes, well. We didn't discuss. I asked him, he said no, and I got angry."

Galina made some notes while Ilya stewed in his own humiliation for a moment. "I take it," she finally said, "that Shane is not ready to go public."

"No. I don't even know if *I'm* ready. But some days I think I'll scream or die if I have to keep this secret any longer."

"Does he know that?"

"No. I . . . haven't talked to him much about my feelings still. I still have not told him that I'm seeing you." Ilya's eyes began to burn with tears. "I don't know when I'll see him again. Not for a week at least. We both have busy schedules, and road trips." He swallowed. "I'm scared. I think I've ruined everything. I shouldn't have mentioned that party."

"I think you need to talk to him. Really talk. I'll bet you've been keeping important things from each other because you don't want to ruin the precious time you have alone together."

Ilya nodded. "Yes. Exactly."

She smiled. "You might have to suffer through a tough conversation. I suspect you'll both feel better on the other side of it."

Ilya knew she was right, but he couldn't imagine how to start the conversation with Shane. At the same time he felt a strong urge to leave the appointment and call him right away.

"What do you want to say to him?" Galina asked. "If you could say anything."

Ilya considered her question for a long time, scrolling through the long list in his head of things he should probably discuss with Shane.

His lips curved up on one side. "Are you going to pretend to be Shane?"

She smiled back. "Not exactly."

"Good. You'd have to be much more annoying."

"I doubt that's what you want to tell him."

"No. I tell him that he's annoying all the time."

Galina waited patiently for Ilya to get serious. Finally, Ilya took a slow breath, in and out, closed his eyes, and started talking.

Shane was about to head to the arena for his game against Toronto when Ilya finally called him.

"Oh my god. Hi." Shane didn't even pretend to be chill. "Ilya, listen, I—"

"Is okay," Ilya said. "I should have let you stay. We need to talk, I think."

Shane sighed with relief. "Definitely. Can we FaceTime? I want to see you."

"Yes."

A FaceTime request popped up and Shane clicked on it, realizing only after the video feed opened that he probably looked like shit. He'd barely slept, he was wearing his glasses, and his hair was in a very hastily made bun.

But he stopped caring about any of that once Ilya's face filled his screen. He looked so tired but so soft at the same time, his lips curved just slightly upwards on one side. His cheeks and the tip of his nose were pink, like he'd just come in from the cold.

"Ilya," Shane said, because he couldn't think of any other words.

"I'm sorry I asked you to go to the party," Ilya said. "And that I was mad that you said no. It was . . . not reasonable."

"No. It's fine. I mean, yes, I was surprised and confused, but I was such an asshole to you. You've given up so much and I don't appreciate it enough. I get that."

"I would give up more," Ilya said simply. "Anything for you."

"I don't want you to. God, are you okay? I know you hate talking about your feelings, but I'm worried."

Ilya's jaw worked for a moment, as if he was trying to decide what to say. Then he said, "I have been seeing a therapist."

"Oh," Shane said, unsure if that was good news or bad. "Like, a psychologist, you mean?"

"Yes. Not the team one. One who speaks Russian. Is good. She has been helpful, I think."

"She speaks Russian? That's great."

"Yes. Much easier to talk that way."

Not for the first time, Shane felt terrible about not learning Russian fast enough. "So, it's been . . . good?"

"I think so. Slow, but good."

"How long have you been going?"

"A couple of months."

Jesus. Why hadn't Ilya told him? Shane wanted to ask, but it would probably sound like an accusation. "I'm glad you're getting help. If you need it. And that you found someone you can talk to." He couldn't disguise the hurt in his voice, even though he had no reason to feel hurt.

"Shane," Ilya said gently, "I have told you things I have not told anyone. You *know* me. Therapy is . . . different."

"I know," Shane said. He did know. He was just mad at himself for not being a better listener.

"There is one thing I should tell you." Ilya sounded nervous, suddenly. "She knows. About us. I told her."

Shane couldn't help the shock that he was sure showed plainly on his face. "You did? Like, you used my name?"

"Yes. I am sorry, but . . . I did not want to lie in that room the same as everywhere else."

Shane supposed he could understand that. What good was seeing a therapist if you needed to lie to them? "Okay. I mean, she's, like, sworn to secrecy or whatever. So that should be fine."

"Yes."

Shane sat on his bed. "You don't have to tell me, if you don't want, but what made you decide to see a therapist?"

Ilya's lips pulled into a tight smile. "Big question."

"I know. Sorry. Forget I asked."

"No. I want to tell you everything, but . . . not now, maybe."

Shane nodded. "I get that."

"It's a lot, you know?"

Shane didn't know, but he said, "Yeah. For sure."

"But I am sorry I made you leave. I had a very nice Christmas with your family, as always. And I wasted a day and a night we could have been together."

"I'm sorry for basically everything I said. Like, so fucking sorry. I love you."

"I know, moya lyubov."

Shane grinned. "I know that one."

"Ah," Ilya said in mock despair, "then you know my secret."

"That you love me?"

"That I am very mushy inside."

Shane laughed. "I knew that too." He glanced at the clock beside his bed. "Shit. I have to go."

"Okay."

"I wish our schedules weren't fucked. But maybe a bit of distance is good right now?"

"I think so. Yes. We will talk when we are in the same room again."

They smiled sadly at each other for a few seconds. Shane's heart felt heavy, and he was anxious thinking about their impending conversation, but he was more confident that things were still good between them.

"Try not to win too many games," Ilya joked.

"You too."

Ilya winked. "We never do."

# CHAPTER TWENTY-FOUR

*January*

Ilya wasn't able to keep his promise to Shane for very long. After losing a road game in Buffalo, and then two home games, the Centaurs won the first game of their southern road trip, an afternoon match against the much higher-ranked Carolina team.

"Fucking right!" Bood yelled as the team returned to the dressing room at the end of the game. "New year, new energy. We're gonna be unstoppable, baby!"

Ilya hoped so. He *really* hoped so. He believed in this team, despite their long history of losing. He had great teammates and a great coach. He was playing on a line with Bood and Troy now, and they were really starting to click. It felt great to have a player on his right who could keep up with him. The team just needed a few wins to gain confidence. Maybe this would be the road trip that changed everything.

Troy seemed happy about it too. Or maybe he was mostly happy that Harris had traveled with the team for this southern road trip. It wasn't something Harris did often, but Ilya was glad he was getting a working vacation to some warmer climates.

The team was heading directly from the arena to the plane that would take them to Tampa Bay. They'd have the rest of the night and all of tomorrow off to enjoy the warm Florida weather.

Harris was shooting video of the celebration in the room while Troy grinned at him from his stall, completely moony-eyed. Ilya sat next to Troy. "Still haven't told him?"

"Not going to either."

Ilya scoffed. "This would be a good chance. Romantic day together in Tampa tomorrow, maybe?"

Troy's cheeks darkened slightly. "As if."

"Think about it."

"No."

Coach Wiebe entered the room, and everyone cheered.

"Huge win tonight, guys," Wiebe said with a huge smile. "I'm proud of you. Barrett with two beautiful goals? Are you kidding me? Amazing stuff, Troy. And where are our all-stars? Wyatt, Roz? Massive saves tonight, Wyatt. Absolutely incredible. And a goal and two assists from our captain? Can't ask for more than that. Love it."

Ilya stood and waved, which made everyone laugh. He realized he was actually in a great mood for the first time in a long time.

"All right," Coach said, and clapped his hands together once, "let's go to Florida, folks!"

The room erupted in cheers.

The party continued all the way to the plane. Everyone was rowdy and laughing, and Ilya soaked it in like a sponge. He'd missed this feeling.

Ilya was sitting alone, across the aisle from Harris, who seemed to be hard at work on his laptop. Near the end of the flight, Troy moved to sit in the empty seat beside Harris. Ilya smiled to himself, and looked out the window to hide the wistfulness that had probably crept into his expression. If things worked out with Harris and Troy, Ilya couldn't promise he wouldn't be a little bit jealous. It would be amazing to have your boyfriend so close.

The plane dipped suddenly—some unexpected turbulence. Everyone laughed at Bood, who had been standing in the aisle and was now on the floor. Ilya hastily wiped at his shirt, where Coke had splashed from the can he was holding. Ugh. He shouldn't have worn a white shirt.

He pulled out his phone and checked to see if there was any score yet in the game Shane was playing tonight. It had just started, so no. Nothing yet.

They hadn't spoken much since their phone call over a week ago. Ilya missed him, but he also thought the space from each other was good. They would talk—really talk—when they saw each other again, but for now Ilya needed time to think about what actually needed to be said.

He loved him, he knew that. He wanted to make sure Shane never doubted it. He didn't expect their impending conversation to be easy, but whatever was said, he needed Shane to know he loved him. That he was still willing to do whatever it took to be together. But he also needed Shane to know all of the reasons why Ilya had decided to see a psychologist. He needed the man he loved to know the worst about himself.

A bang louder than any noise Ilya had heard during a flight rocked the plane. Everything shook violently for a moment, and Ilya's can of Coke fell to the floor. He didn't have time to worry about it before the plane fucking *dropped.*

Ilya was screaming. He knew he was screaming and that he should probably stop, but everyone around him was screaming too. He gripped the arms of his seat and closed his eyes, as if either of those things would help.

*We're going to crash.*

*I'm going to die.*

*I'll never see Shane again.*

*We were going to have dogs and kids.*

The plane leveled out with another horrible shudder. Suddenly, the screaming stopped, and the cabin of the plane was eerily silent, as if everyone was holding their breath at once.

The pilot made an announcement. Ilya's brain was too panicked to translate all the words, but he heard "engine" and "emergency landing." He focused on the word *landing*. Pilots were trained to deal with this, right? He'd *know* if Shane hadn't been such a pill about Ilya wanting to get his pilot's license.

Shane.

What if Ilya died? What would Shane do? How would he mourn?

Several rows behind him, Ilya heard Nick Chouinard yelling about a fire. He didn't want to look.

Fuck. This was really happening. They were going to die, and Ilya would never get to have the big conversation with Shane. Would never get to tell him everything that Ilya had been hiding in his heart.

If only Shane wasn't playing a game right now. Ilya could—well, not call him, but talk to him somehow. He wished he could text, but all he had access to was Wi-Fi.

Fuck it. Ilya opened Instagram and started typing a new private message to ShaneHollanderHockeyPlayer.

Shane, he wrote, then stopped. He had no idea what to say. There was no possible way to put everything he needed to tell Shane into words.

But the plane was on fire, and Ilya didn't have time to think. He wrote what was in his terrified heart: You are the best thing in my life.

His eyes were blurry, making it hard to type. He quickly swiped at his eyes and kept writing.

I love you. Always. Maybe from the first time I saw you.

He let his mind take him away from the nightmare happening around him and back to a rink parking lot in Saskatchewan. Ilya couldn't remember what Shane had said, exactly, that first time they'd met. He only remembered freckles splashed over rosy red cheeks. He remembered Shane's hand being unfairly warm when he shook it. He remembered being studied by dark, earnest eyes.

It was entirely possible that Ilya *had* lost his heart in that moment. It took his brain a long time to catch up, but his heart had known right away.

He wished Shane could respond. He hated thinking about Shane seeing these messages . . . after.

He'd keep them forever. Ilya knew he would. Fuck. He had to say something really good.

I am thinking only about you right now. A million memories. Thank you for those.

Whatever happens, I am with you. Safe in your heart. I believe it.

He did. Ilya only had vague ideas of the afterlife and any gods who may be waiting there, but he believed his soul would stay with Shane, however it could. He believed the people you loved stayed with you until it was your time to go. He often felt his mother with him, and he knew he'd do the same for Shane.

And maybe he'd see his mother again soon. That was a nice thought. Ilya pressed his palm to his chest, feeling the crucifix pendant through the fabric of his shirt. He prayed, quietly and with no real structure. He murmured requests for whoever was listening to keep Shane safe, to let him live a long, happy life.

To please not let this plane crash, because Ilya had wasted so much fucking time hiding how much he loved Shane—from the world, from Shane, from himself. He needed more time. He needed to love Shane properly.

The plane tilted to one side, then the other, and a moment later came the glorious thud of wheels touching down on solid ground.

The jubilant roar from his teammates was earsplitting. Probably because Ilya was cheering louder than anyone. He looked out the window and saw flashing lights from various emergency vehicles but holy shit, the pilots had managed to land on the actual runway, safe and sound.

"Thank you," Ilya said, gazing at the ceiling of the plane. "I won't waste it."

Montreal lost their game in Washington, which was annoying. Shane saw that Ilya's team had won big against Carolina that afternoon, and he fully expected Ilya to give him shit about it.

He didn't check his phone until he was on the bus, heading back to the team's hotel. He had one text and one missed call from Ilya. The text said: Sorry about the Instagram messages. Call me.

Shane hardly ever checked his Instagram messages, but sometimes Ilya used that when he was on a plane and couldn't text.

Shane checked them now.

The messages were . . . intense. Romantic, certainly, but weird.

"Whoa," J.J. said. "The Centaurs' plane had to make an emergency landing."

Shane turned to where J.J. was sitting across the aisle. "What? Is everyone okay?"

J.J. thumbed at his phone screen. "Sounds like it. Must have been scary, though."

Shane read the messages from Ilya again. Holy shit. Those were meant as, like, his *last words*.

"But they're okay?" Shane asked again, panic rising even though he knew Ilya was okay. He had the evidence right there in his hand.

J.J. looked at him with amusement in his eyes. "Yeah. I said they're fine. Landed safely."

But dread had already clawed its way into Shane's heart, filling his head with horrific alternate outcomes. What if those messages had been Ilya's last words? What if they'd been all Shane had left?

He texted Ilya. **I heard about the plane. Are you ok?**

Ilya replied right away. **Yes. Can I call you?**

Shane glanced around the bus at his teammates. A lot of them were wearing headphones, but there was no way Shane was going to be able to sound calm about this.

**SHANE:**

I'm almost at the hotel. I'll call when I'm there. Sorry. I can't do this with my teammates around.

Ilya texted back a heart emoji.

Shane read his Instagram messages a third time.

Whatever happens, I am with you. Safe in your heart. I believe it.

But he wouldn't have been. He would have been fucking *gone*. Who was Ilya's next of kin, even? The brother he never spoke to? Would Shane have been allowed to spread his ashes somewhere that Ilya would have liked? Maybe at the cottage, or maybe he'd prefer to be buried in Moscow with his parents. God, they'd never talked about this sort of thing.

Anger flared through Shane's body, hot and sudden. They had lots of reasons to keep their relationship a secret, but those reasons seemed extremely unimportant now. What if Ilya had *died*? What if he had fucking *died*?

Shane would have died too. Alone, and secretly, and for the rest of his life.

He clutched his phone to his chest, and turned his head to face the window so his teammates didn't see the way his lip was trembling.

Ilya knew, as team captain, that he should be at one of the tables in the hotel bar with his teammates. He should be making the rounds, checking in with everyone. Especially the rookies.

But he just . . . couldn't.

The adrenaline had worn off quickly, and now he was standing alone in the parking lot outside the lobby, smoking a cigarette. Sure, his New Year's resolution had been to quit smoking for real, but he'd *earned* this cigarette.

His phone rang when his lungs were full of smoke. He exhaled too quickly, which made him start coughing.

"Hi," he said, and then coughed again.

"Ilya. Jesus. Are you okay?"

"Yes. Fine." He coughed again, and thumped his chest with his fist.

"Where are you? What's going on?" A pause. "Are you smoking?"

"No," Ilya said, and stamped out what was left of his cigarette on the ground. "I am in Tampa. At the hotel. The team is all together in the bar."

"It must have been terrifying."

"Yes. It was scary, but we are okay now. Everyone is okay. Maybe a little . . ." He waved his hand around in the air. "Shaken."

"You can tell me if you're not okay," Shane said gently.

Ilya smiled tightly. "I think I am . . . crashing maybe. A bit."

"Adrenaline is wearing off. Yeah, that makes sense."

"Yes."

"Are you . . . in the bar now?"

"I wanted some air, so I am outside now."

"You *are* smoking!"

"I am enjoying the warm Florida night!" He sighed. "And also smoking a little."

"Well," Shane said, "I'll allow it."

"Great," Ilya said flatly.

Shane laughed, which made Ilya's heart race. What if he'd never heard Shane's laugh again?

"Can I see you?" Shane asked. "Can we FaceTime?"

"Yes. Of course. One second." Ilya bent to retrieve his cigarette butt, pocketed it, and started walking to the other side of the parking lot. On the way, he sent Shane a FaceTime request.

He could tell right away that Shane had been crying.

"Oh," Ilya said softly. "Sweetheart. I am so sorry." They didn't use pet names very often, beyond the nonsensical Russian nouns Ilya liked to throw at Shane, but Ilya said this one with his whole heart.

Shane gave a fragile, trembling smile. "You should be." Then he covered his mouth with his hand as his eyes filled with tears.

"I am okay," Ilya assured him. "Still here. I should not have scared you with those texts."

Shane only shook his head in response, mouth still hidden by his hand. Ilya hated seeing him so upset, but he loved seeing him. Loved his freckles and his little nose.

"I did mean what I wrote," Ilya said. "All of it."

Shane lowered his hand, cleared his throat, and said, "So a little brush with death and you turn into Mr. Poetry?"

Ilya laughed softly. "Was it too much?"

"No. Fuck you, it was beautiful. And I'm glad it wasn't . . ." Shane stopped talking. Then he took a steadying breath and said, "I'm glad it wasn't . . . necessary."

Ilya's eyes started to burn. "Yes. Me too."

"You're not allowed to die, Ilya. Not before I do."

"Do you have to win *everything*?"

"I have to not lose you." His voice cracked on the last word.

"Shane," Ilya said soothingly, "it is okay. I am okay. Is over."

"You're so far away," Shane said, sniffing hard. "I want to rent a car and drive there."

"Would be a long drive," Ilya said with amusement, "from Washington."

"Thirteen hours." Shane smiled sheepishly. "I looked it up. Right after I looked up available rental cars in Washington."

Ilya chuckled fondly, which made Shane laugh too.

"Maybe you could play for us against Tampa," Ilya joked. "Give us a chance of winning."

"I doubt I'd play very well, to be honest." He exhaled. "God. I just keep thinking—"

"I know," Ilya cut him off before he could say it. "But I didn't. I'm here. I'm fine."

Shane nodded. "I wish you were here with me right now. I want to hold you. I want to, fuck, feel your heart beating."

"Now who is the poet?"

"Shut up."

They both laughed again, then smiled at each other for a few silent moments.

"You look way too good," Shane said, "for someone who just went through a harrowing ordeal."

Ilya was too tired to translate those last two words, so he replied with, "I love you." In Russian.

Shane repeated it back. Then said, in English, "You should go be with your team."

Ilya sighed. "Probably. Yes."

"Call me tomorrow. Or later tonight if you want. I'll just be, y'know, freaking out in my hotel room."

"Don't. Jerk off or something instead. Send me pictures."

"While you're hanging out with your teammates? Absolutely not."

"I won't *show* them."

"Good night, Ilya."

"I almost died!"

"I'm really not ready to joke about that yet."

"Sorry. Good night, moy pomidor."

"Tomato, right?"

"Yes."

"Weird. I love you."

"I love you. Send pictures."

They ended the call, and Ilya went back inside the hotel. He considered joining a table, and he considered going up to his room, then he spotted Troy sitting alone at the bar. Why Troy was sitting there and not upstairs making out with Harris was beyond Ilya.

He left Troy alone, and joined one of the tables. He picked the one that had the most pitchers of beer on it, and immediately poured himself a glass. Time to get fucking drunk.

# CHAPTER TWENTY-FIVE

The next morning, as Shane was putting the few things he'd unpacked back into his suitcase, there was a firm knock on his hotel room door. When he opened the door, he found J.J. there, holding two coffees.

"That for me?" Shane asked, stepping backward to let him in.

"If you don't want it I can drink two."

Shane took the coffee, and set it on the dresser. "Thanks."

He wasn't sure why J.J. was here, or why he'd brought him coffee. He was one of Shane's closest friends, but this specific situation was unusual.

"So." J.J. leaned against a wall with his own coffee. "You seemed kind of fucked up last night. About the Ottawa plane thing."

Shane pulled an imperfectly folded T-shirt out of his suitcase and began refolding it. "No, I wasn't. It was just, y'know, surprising."

He realized his shoulders were hunched, so he made an effort to relax them.

"Uh-huh," J.J. said. "You want to tell me the truth now?"

Shane frowned at the shirt he'd just folded, then shook it

out and began folding it again. Part of him wanted to tell J.J. everything. Part of him *needed* to tell him. Needed to tell the whole world because having to hide suddenly felt so fucking unfair. Shane wasn't sure he *could* tell him, but he could tell him *something*. "It's nothing. I got some texts from . . . from Ilya. Rozanov."

"I know which Ilya," J.J. said with amusement.

"He sent them when the plane was . . . when he thought they were going to crash."

A heavy silence filled the room, giving Shane a moment to realize how weird that must have sounded to J.J. Ilya thought he was about to die, so he'd texted *Shane*.

"He, um—" Shane started, but how on earth could he explain without admitting everything? "He's—"

Shane squeezed his eyes shut. He was so fucking tired of lying. He could be *grieving* right now. If that plane had crashed, J.J. would be sitting in Shane's hotel room right now watching him fall apart completely. There would have been no way Shane could have hidden his agony.

"He's okay," J.J. reminded him.

"I know."

J.J. took the shirt from him before Shane could start folding it again. "Look, I know you've got this . . . thing . . . for Rozanov."

Shane's stomach dropped. "What do you mean?"

J.J. smiled sadly at him. "Why do you think I keep trying to set you up? Having a crush on a straight man is no good, buddy."

Wait. What?

Shane was completely stunned, and needed to think fast. This was a lie he hadn't considered hiding behind before: an unrequited crush. It made *sense*.

It fucking hurt, but it made sense.

"Is it obvious?" Shane sat on the bed. The misery in his voice was real, but not for the reason J.J. thought.

J.J. set his coffee on the dresser and sat on the bed next to Shane. "Sorry, buddy. I'm not saying everyone sees it, but not much gets past me, y'know?"

"Right," Shane said, nodding fervently.

J.J. clapped a giant hand on Shane's shoulder. "The good news is, you can do *way* better than Rozanov."

Shane pressed his lips together to keep from laughing.

"I get that he's attractive, but come on. That guy is annoying as fuck."

Shane couldn't hold back the laughter anymore. "You're right. I should aim higher."

"And it's not like you guys could date or whatever anyway. Like, it would be impossible."

Shane stopped laughing. "I know."

"Can you imagine? Dating your rival? What a fucking scandal."

Shane turned his gaze to the floor and said nothing.

"Hey," J.J. said gently. He ducked his head so their eyes met. In French, he said, "I'm not making fun of you. It hurts to love someone who can't love you back, and I'm sorry you've been dealing with that. You can always talk to me about it."

He was being so earnest and sympathetic that it made Shane feel like a scumbag for lying. "Thanks."

"And if you need someone to take you out, be your wingman or whatever . . ."

Shane's smile returned. "I'll consider it."

J.J. stood and stretched his arms wide for a hug. Shane stood and was quickly engulfed by his friend.

"I'm glad Rozanov is all right," J.J. said when they separated. "Seriously. He's not entirely terrible."

"Not always, no."

"And Wyatt, geez. He woulda been on that plane too. I love that guy." J.J. frowned. "I'm going to go call him."

J.J. had never been a big fan of texting. He loved talking too much. "I'm sure he's been waiting for your call," Shane said dryly.

"Stay strong, friend," J.J. said as he opened the door to leave. "We'll get you through this and out the other side, okay?"

"I mean, you don't really have to—"

But J.J. was gone.

Fucking hell. *The other side.* Shane wanted to haul the door back open and tell J.J. that the other side was a life together with Ilya. That there was no unrequited crush. That he was so fucking in love with Ilya it felt like his heart would burst sometimes, and that Ilya felt the same about Shane.

That when Shane finally saw Ilya again—in two days, hopefully—he was going to . . . god, he didn't even know what he wanted to do.

Except he did know. He knew exactly what he wanted. He wanted to reach the other side. He wanted that life together. Not in ten years, but now. Because ten years suddenly seemed like an impossible wait.

Ilya pulled into his driveway just after two in the afternoon the day his team flew home from Florida. It felt like two in the morning, he was so drained.

But Shane's Jeep Cherokee was there, at least an hour before Ilya had been expecting it to be, which gave him a sudden burst of energy. He parked his own SUV next to Shane's, not bothering with the garage, and jogged to the front door. It opened as soon as he reached it, and there was Shane, looking perfect in nice pants and a soft, dark blue sweater.

"Our plane got in earl—" But that was all Shane managed to say before Ilya grabbed his face with both hands and kissed the hell out of him.

And Shane let him. Right there on Ilya's front step, mostly secluded but still partially visible from the street. Shane kissed him back with equal urgency and, if he felt the same as Ilya, relief.

Ilya wanted to tell him so many things, but he couldn't seem to stop kissing him. It was bitter cold all around them, but Shane's mouth was warm and nothing about this place felt like Florida, so Ilya would happily stay here forever, kissing Shane in the snow.

Eventually they broke apart, and Shane managed only to say, "Come inside," before they were kissing again.

Finally, finally, Shane took Ilya's hand and led him inside. It was only then that Ilya realized Shane hadn't been wearing a coat.

"I'm sorry," Ilya said. "You must be freezing."

"I'm fine." Shane watched him remove his outerwear, chewing his lip and sliding his hands in and out of the pockets of his dress pants. He seemed uneasy.

Ilya tried to kiss him again, but Shane took a step back and said, "Follow me?"

Ilya smiled. "Anywhere."

Shane let out an oddly nervous laugh, which made Ilya laugh. Then Shane took his hand again, and they walked together to Ilya's living room, where—

"What is this?" Ilya asked. The drapes were drawn across the large windows that normally looked out to the river, and the room was dark. Except for the glow of about a million candles.

They were everywhere: on the tables, on the floor, on the mantel, even on the arms of the furniture. It was beautiful and . . . weird.

"Are you trying to burn my house down?" was what Ilya finally said.

Shane's lips curved up. "They're electric. Fucking relax, Rozanov."

Ilya's heart started to race, but not because he was concerned about fire safety. He'd once told Shane, years ago, that one day he would cover the dock at his cottage in candles. That he'd bring Shane down there, then ask him to marry him. It had been a joke, sort of. But now he was really standing in a room full of candles and—

Shane sank to one knee in front of him.

Ilya had enjoyed watching Shane go to his knees in front of him many times over the years, but he knew immediately that this was different. He suddenly felt winded. And dizzy. And maybe a little queasy.

"What is this?" he whispered.

Shane gazed up at him, his expression steady and determined, and said, "I've been doing a lot of thinking."

Ilya swallowed. Why was it so hard to swallow? It was like he had no saliva at all.

"We've wasted so much time," Shane continued. "Years of denial, then years of hiding what we are to each other."

"Shane—"

"Could you not interrupt?" Shane said with a teasing smile. "For once in your life?"

Ilya pressed his lips together.

"I don't have a plan for anything beyond this," Shane confessed, "but I know what I want. There's nothing in my life that matters to me more than you, Ilya." He slid his hand into his pants pocket again. He had to lean awkwardly to one side to fit his fingers inside.

Then, Shane was holding a ring, pinched between two fingers, in the space between himself and Ilya.

"Shane," Ilya said again, unable to stop himself.

"I choose you, Ilya. I promise I will always, always choose you." Shane's eyes began to shimmer. He took a deep breath and said, "Ilya Grigoryevich Rozanov, will you marry me?"

Ilya wasn't sure how much time had passed before he realized he hadn't said anything. He hoped it had only been a second or two, but judging from the fear in Shane's eyes, it must have been longer. Finally, in a tight, trembling voice, he said, "You know my middle name."

"It's on Wikipedia. I kind of fell down a rabbit hole learning about the Russian tradition of using the father's name to—"

"Yes," Ilya interrupted.

"Sorry. I'm babbling. You know how Russian names work."

"No," Ilya clarified. "Yes."

Shane stared at him with obvious confusion. Ilya nodded to the ring.

"Yes," Ilya said again. "I am saying yes, Hollander."

"Oh." Then Shane's lips spread into a wide grin. "Yeah?" He scrambled to his feet and into Ilya's arms.

They kissed, and Ilya said, "Yes." They kissed again, and Ilya said, "Of course."

They kissed some more, and Shane said, "I love you."

By the time they finished kissing they both had tears streaming down their cheeks. "Is this because I almost died?" Ilya teased.

"No. It's because *I* almost died."

Ilya brushed the tears on Shane's face with his thumb. What could he even say to that?

"So, um," Shane said, after a long, fragile moment, "the ring."

"Yes, right." Ilya took the ring from Shane and inspected it for a moment. A simple black band with a gold interior. Very classy. He smiled at Shane, and attempted to slip it onto his own finger. It didn't quite fit.

"Nuts," Shane said, looking disappointed. "I didn't know your ring size."

"Is okay." Ilya removed the ring with some effort. "Am I supposed to wear it now? Or is it for after we are married?"

"You know," Shane said, "I have no idea. I just thought I should have a ring for this."

Ilya handed the ring back to Shane, then loosened and removed his necktie. He opened the top buttons of his shirt, then reached back and unclasped the gold chain around his neck. He removed it, then held out his palm for the ring.

"Oh," Shane said, then handed him the ring. Ilya slipped it onto the chain until it nudged up against the crucifix pendant that had been his mother's.

"Here," Shane said, and reached for the chain. Ilya turned his back to him, and Shane fastened the necklace back in place.

"Did you buy one for yourself?" Ilya asked. "Or is that my job?"

"I was going to buy the matching one. I just . . . wanted to make sure I needed it first."

Ilya raised his eyebrows as he turned back to face Shane. "You thought I would say no?"

Shane at least had the decency to look embarrassed about it. "I don't know. I just didn't want to be cocky about it."

Ilya laughed, a little wetly because he was still a mess, then cradled Shane's face with both hands. "Buy the ring."

They were both half crying as they kissed, their breath stuttering and their lips stretched into wide smiles. A terrible kiss in theory, but Ilya had never experienced one better. Shane Hollander was going to be his *husband*.

Shane untucked Ilya's dress shirt from his suit pants and slid his hand underneath. He pressed his palm to Ilya's chest, over his heart.

"God," Shane whispered.

Ilya covered Shane's hand with his own. "Still alive. I told you."

Shane kissed him again, but this time there was an edge of desperation to it, a ferocity that Ilya easily returned, clutching at Shane's sweater, at his skin, at his hair.

Their breathing changed from hitched and snuffly to heavy and panting. Ilya helped Shane out of his sweater and the shirt underneath, then they worked together on removing Ilya's shirt.

"Ilya," Shane said reverently. His eyes were dark and anguished. Ilya couldn't have that, so he kissed him again. He pulled their bodies tight together, letting every sense fill with Shane. Letting Shane know he was solid and real and alive and extremely interested in fucking him.

They fumbled with each other's belts, got their pants and underwear and, with a bit of unavoidable awkwardness, their socks off. Shane smiled at him when they were both naked, wide and bright and beautiful. He was staring at Ilya's chest, and Ilya glanced down to see the ring there, glinting in the light of a million candles.

"Yours," Ilya said.

"Mine." Shane crashed into him again, kissing him hungrily.

There was a coffee table covering most of the plush rug in the middle of Ilya's living room. Without breaking the kiss, Ilya used one foot to push it aside. He heard the soft thump of several candles hitting the carpet, and was thankful Shane had chosen to go electric.

"What—" Shane asked. Then, "Oh," as Ilya scooped him up and laid him on the rug.

Ilya took a moment to just look at Shane, laid out like that in the magical lighting he'd worked so hard to create. His long hair fanned out under his head, and his dark eyes danced with joy and desire. His freckles were all bunched up because he was smiling so widely his nose was wrinkled.

Ilya took one of his hands, tangled their fingers together, and pinned it on the rug over Shane's head. The ring dangled in the air between them.

"I love you so much," Shane said softly.

Ilya swallowed. "I will be very proud to be your husband."

He leaned down and captured Shane's mouth in another slow, luxurious kiss. Shane gripped his fingers tighter and rolled his hips under him, sliding their erections together. It felt fucking incredible, simple and explosive at the same time. Ilya'd had every intention of fucking Shane right here on the rug, but he didn't want to stop what they were doing. He wanted to be pressed this close to Shane, touching everywhere. He wanted Shane to rock against him just like this, chasing his pleasure while getting Ilya closer to his own release with each slow, controlled grind of his pelvis.

It was the control that was unraveling Ilya more than anything. This wasn't frantic rutting—this was Shane loving Ilya with his body. Careful, steady thrusts that matched the rhythm of their pounding hearts.

Ilya realized they weren't even kissing anymore. Their gazes were locked, lips parted as they both huffed and shuddered into the inches between them.

"Is this okay?" Shane whispered.

"Yes. Perfect," Ilya assured him.

Shane's eyes fluttered closed for a moment, his head tipping back on a gasp. He opened them again and smiled shyly. "Feels so good."

"I know."

Ilya kissed his throat, his jaw, and then his mouth again. His own orgasm was building, and he was torn between urging it on and wanting to pull back. He didn't want this moment to end.

Except there would be more moments like this. A whole lifetime of them.

"Shane," he breathed.

"Yeah," Shane said shakily. "Me too."

The steady movement of their hips began to lose its rhythm as they both teetered on the brink of climax. They breathed into each other's mouths, foreheads pressed together, until Shane whimpered and Ilya felt the first hot splash of his release on his skin. It was enough to break the dam inside him, and his own release surged and erupted.

Shane wrapped his arms and legs around Ilya's trembling body, pulling him even closer. They kissed sloppily, and laughed about it. Finally Ilya rolled onto his back, and Shane immediately rested his head on his chest. He traced a fingertip around the ring that was now resting up near Ilya's throat.

"I was thinking summer," Shane said.

"Summer for what?"

Shane lifted his head and met Ilya's gaze. "For everything. Coming out. Going public. Getting married."

Ilya's heart flipped. "Yes?"

"Yeah. I know it's going to be a shitshow, but I'm tired of being scared of being found out. I want to tell people, on our own terms. I think I can handle anything that happens, as long as going public is a choice we made ourselves. Together."

"That is what I want," Ilya agreed. "We tell people ourselves. Together."

Shane smiled. "I might have already told my parents that I was going to propose to you."

"Did they approve?"

"Of course. I think we already are married, as far as they're concerned. But they're also a little unclear about our plan. So am I, but we'll figure it out."

"We will," Ilya agreed. "And until summer?"

"I guess more of the same? Except maybe we could . . . be less careful?"

Ilya's eyebrows went sky high.

"I mean," Shane said quickly, "we could hide in plain sight a bit? I think it would work. I just learned that J.J. thinks I have an unrequited crush on you."

"Un-what?"

"Like, he thinks I'm in love with my straight friend."

Ilya laughed. "That must be very hard for you."

"I'm just saying, people *really* think you're straight."

"And if I told people I am bisexual? Would that ruin everything?"

Shane frowned as he seemed to consider it. Then he said, "If you want to come out, you should."

"I can wait. Until summer. Is not long."

"No," Shane agreed.

They kissed, then Shane went back to resting against Ilya's chest. Ilya stroked Shane's hair, enjoying the quiet and the excitement that was crackling through him. Summer! Not ten years from now, but *this summer.*

After several quiet minutes, Ilya said, "You have tomorrow off, yes?"

"Mm."

"I am skipping practice."

"Is it optional?" Shane murmured sleepily.

"I don't care."

# CHAPTER TWENTY-SIX

Ilya felt like a fucking superhero as he got dressed for his next game.

The press of the ring that hung around his neck against his chest, under the layers of jersey, pads, and athletic shirt, was still foreign, but it sent a thrill through him every time he felt it. No one had asked about the ring. Probably no one had noticed it. Ilya wouldn't give a straight answer if anyone did ask. He had a reputation for being mysterious anyway.

He'd met with Galina that afternoon after Shane had left, and they'd mostly talked about his near-death experience. He hadn't told her that he'd gotten engaged. It still felt too new, too precious, to share with anyone.

Galina had probably noticed the change in him, though. He knew an engagement ring wasn't a cure for depression, but he was happy to ride this high for as long as he could.

Which was why he hadn't exactly gotten into his mental health concerns with Shane, like he'd planned. He was still optimistic that he could fix himself without troubling his future husband. It was probably stupid, but, well, Ilya had been feeling a bit stupid these past few days.

Tonight's game was at home, and they were facing the number one ranked New York Admirals. Ilya wasn't intimidated. He was Ilya fucking Rozanov, and it was time for his team to start winning.

He walked to the middle of the locker room. "Everyone listen."

The room immediately fell silent. Ilya wasn't surprised. He rarely gave speeches, preferring to lead with action more than words. Admittedly, he had no idea what he was going to say now, but he needed to say *something*.

He decided to start with something attention-grabbing. "The New York Admirals are not a better team than us."

As he expected, his teammates began to scoff and laugh at that. Ilya talked right over it. "They are *not*. They have Scott Hunter, we have *me*."

Across the room, Ilya could see Troy's lips curve up. He kept going. "They have Tommy Andersson—a good goalie. Young, talented, yes. We have Wyatt Hayes—a *great* goalie." He found Wyatt and grinned at him. "Old, talented."

That caused the room to erupt into laughter and applause. Wyatt smiled back at him and said, *"Experienced."*

Ilya continued until he'd named every player in the room, pointing out what made them great. What made this *team* great.

"I am fucking tired of losing. Enough. We are going to win this game tonight, and we are going to keep winning." Since he was already making lofty promises, he decided to aim even higher. "We are going to fill every seat in this fucking arena. We are going to surprise *everyone* and we are going to the playoffs this year. Not next year. Not in the future. *This fucking year.*"

Not one person in the room rolled their eyes or waved his bold predictions away. They all cheered, and it made Ilya's heart soar. He loved this fucking team.

"We went through something together. It was fucking scary. But we are alive. We are all alive and I don't plan on wasting another second of it." No more losing, no more hiding his feelings, no more hiding his boyfriend. No more being afraid of his dark thoughts. No more being afraid of flying.

He finished the speech with, "Let's fucking go."

The roar of his teammates was deafening.

They won the fucking game.

Ilya scored, Troy scored, Luca scored. Even fucking Tanner Dillon had scored. Wyatt made great saves all night. And every minute had been *fun*.

They partied in the locker room after, then moved the party to Monk's. This time, Ilya had gone too. He wouldn't have missed it.

"You are so bad at pool," he chirped at Bood while bending to take a shot. "How am I supposed to do this when there are so many of your balls in my way?"

"That's my strategy," Bood said with a grin.

Ilya huffed, took his shot, then watched in dismay as one of Bood's balls went into a side pocket. Bood cracked up. "See? You do my work for me."

"Like on the ice, you mean?"

Bood pointed his cue at him menacingly. "Okay. You can fuck off now."

They both laughed. Ilya was in a great mood. Not only had the game been a blast, and he was having a great time drinking with his teammates, but he'd seen Troy leave the bar with Harris a few minutes ago. Plenty to celebrate.

Ilya went to pour himself another beer and found the pitcher empty. "Another?" he asked Bood.

"Nah. I have to get home. Cassie is about to have a baby any second."

"Yes. Of course. Tell Cassie I say hello."

Bood hugged him, then thumped him hard on the back. "Good game tonight."

"You mean the hockey game, yes? Not the pool."

"Not the pool," Bood agreed. "Have a good night, Roz."

Ilya wasn't quite ready to go home yet. He was worried the good vibes would end as soon as he was alone. He went to the bar, ordered another beer, then carried it to a table where a bunch of guys were watching Luca Haas do . . . something.

"Did you know that Luca could draw like this?" Evan Dykstra asked when he saw Ilya. "This is amazing."

"Let me see," Ilya said, and leaned over the table. Luca was working on a pencil drawing of Spider-Man. It looked professional.

"Holy shit," Ilya said. "Incredible. I cannot draw at all."

"And he's, like, half drunk," Dykstra said proudly.

"It's not that good," mumbled Luca. "I messed the webs up on his shoulders." He sighed and grabbed the eraser that was sitting on the table next to him.

"No!" Ilya protested. "Don't erase it."

"I'm just going to fix it," Luca said with a little smile. "This is for Nick's son. Do you want me to draw you a Spider-Man next, Ilya?"

Ilya kind of wanted to say yes. He sat in the only empty chair and watched with fascination as Luca fixed whatever had been bothering him about the drawing.

"Is this what you have in that backpack you always carry?" Ilya asked. "Drawing stuff?"

Luca pushed his glasses back up his nose with the end of his pencil. "Mostly, yes." He finished the drawing, signed it, then shook his hand out. "I'm taking a break. My fingers are cramped."

"Why are you not an artist for a job, Haas?" Ilya said.

Luca laughed. "I think hockey pays better."

"You should design my next tattoo," Ilya said. "Like, a cool animal."

Luca stared at him. "Are you serious?"

Ilya shrugged. He hadn't thought much about his next possible tattoo, but it would be nice to have one designed by a teammate. "Sure."

"That is a lot of pressure," Luca said.

"If it is too much I will get someone else to do it," Ilya teased. "D, do you want to design my tattoo?"

Dykstra grinned. "You want a stickman or a heart?"

Luca stood and stretched his back, twisting from side to side. "I am getting another beer."

"Get a pitcher," Ilya said. "We can share."

"Oh," Luca said, then he smiled. "Yes, okay."

Now that the art show was over the other guys started to leave the table to mingle. By the time Luca returned with the pitcher and a stack of glasses, Ilya was the only one left.

"So," Ilya said after Luca had sat down, "how are you enjoying being the fan favorite?"

Luca poured himself a beer. "I am *not* the favorite. You are, of course."

"I am old news. You are new and exciting."

"I am new and nervous. And probably disappointing."

"Disappointing? How? You have been playing less than four months."

Luca's eyebrows rose above his glasses. "How many goals did you score in your first four months in the NHL?"

Ilya smiled and took a sip of beer. He didn't need to answer. He was sure Luca knew.

Luca sighed. "I should not compare myself to . . ." He waved a hand at Ilya. "Of course you are the best."

"Of course," Ilya agreed playfully.

Luca leaned forward, and for the first time Ilya noticed that he did seem a bit drunk. "I had your poster on my wall. When I was a kid."

"When you were a kid," Ilya teased. "Like when? Last year? Four months ago?"

Luca huffed and took a sip of beer.

"Which poster was it? Did I look handsome?"

"You always look—" Luca's cheeks flushed bright red. "It was just a hockey picture. With all your gear."

Ilya mentally filed that slip-up under *Interesting*. "Is the poster still on your wall?" he asked. "Be honest."

*"No."*

"Did you bring it with you? I can sign it if you like."

Luca laughed and shook his head. "Yes. I have it over my bed," he said sarcastically.

"This will be distracting for people you are trying to have sex with."

Luca laughed again, this time more of a shocked sputter. "Maybe that is the problem."

Ilya leaned in. "Problem?"

"Nothing. I was joking." Luca pressed his lips together and looked away, as if deciding whether or not to admit something. Then he said, to his beer, "It is hard to meet people to, um, do that with. Lately."

Ilya had not expected to be pulled into a conversation about sex with his rookie, but he supposed he was an expert. "Is it? Do you go out? Or use apps? I am sure most of Ottawa wants to fuck you."

Luca coughed. "That is, um—I have tried apps a bit, yes."

"No luck?"

"Not really. I am a bit nervous about meeting people."

Ilya smiled. "No shit."

"You never had this problem, I am guessing."

"No," Ilya said honestly. "But it can be . . . complicated. Being very young and famous and wanting sex but wanting to be, um . . ." He searched for the right word. "Careful?"

Luca nodded. "Yes. Careful."

"I was maybe not so concerned with careful," Ilya said. "I had a lot of sex with many people."

Luca's cheeks pinked. "Yes. I have heard."

"Was fine. No problems. Most people want to hook up and move on with no drama. Even when you are famous."

Luca fiddled with a coaster. "I am not so much looking for hookups."

"Oh. You don't like sex?"

Luca turned redder. "I like it, yes. I am, um, particular. Maybe. Or shy. I don't know." He let out a nervous giggle. "This is not a conversation I thought I would have with you."

Ilya grinned. "But I am right beside your bed, watching you have sex!"

"Dude! I did *not* just hear that!"

Ilya turned to see Dykstra standing behind him, laughing. "Stop spying."

"Stop watching the rookies have sex, then?"

Ilya glared at him. "He has a poster of me. Is a joke."

Dykstra's brow furrowed, and he looked at Luca. "You have a poster of Roz beside your bed?"

"No! When I was a kid I did."

Dykstra laughed. "Dude, you *are* a kid."

"I am older than I look," Luca explained with the earnestness of a drunk twenty-year-old.

"Yeah," said Dykstra. "My one-year-old daughter is older than *you* look." He laughed at his own joke. "Speaking of which,

I'm out." He fist-bumped both of them, then headed toward the exit.

"You look older than one," Ilya assured Luca.

Luca snorted and shook his head. "They say never meet your heroes."

Ilya grinned and decided he liked this kid a lot.

# CHAPTER TWENTY-SEVEN

"I don't know what you are trying to prove," Ilya said.

"That I'm the fastest skater in the league. Obviously."

Ilya huffed. There was no way Shane was the fastest skater in the league. Even if it were a competition between only the two of them, Ilya had always been considered the faster skater. He could admit that Shane was a better stick handler, but Ilya was faster. No question.

"We will see," Ilya said.

They were sitting together on the Eastern Conference team bench at the NHL All-Star Skills Competition, which was mostly a fun night that no one took too seriously. No one except Shane Hollander.

Shane and Ilya liked to enter the same event each year, so they could compete directly. The league liked that too, as did the fans. For whatever reason, Shane had wanted to enter the fastest skater competition this year. Ilya suspected it had a lot to do with Shane's impending thirtieth birthday.

Ilya wasn't nervous—he *was* a fast skater. He'd done this event once before, years ago, and he'd won. Shane had been injured that year and hadn't been at the All-Star Weekend. Ilya's victory had probably been bothering Shane ever since.

"Ready?" Ilya asked as they watched the ice crew set up the last of the pylons for the event.

"Absolutely."

"It can be dangerous," Ilya warned. "Watch those corners."

"I know how to skate."

"Are your blades sharp? Good edges?"

Shane gave him a withering look. "Worry about your own skates, Rozanov."

Ilya smiled. Game fucking on.

They watched as a rookie for Vancouver broke the previous leader's time by four tenths of a second. The other players tapped their sticks against the boards to congratulate him. The Western Conference bench engulfed the kid in hugs and back slaps and noogies.

"Are you going to break that poor kid's heart?" Ilya asked.

"Yep," Shane said, and leaped over the boards onto the ice.

The crowd went nuts as Shane took his place at the starting line. The event was very simple: one lap around the perimeter of the ice surface, and the fastest time won. Ilya always thought the fastest skater competition was a little ridiculous because there was usually less than a second dividing first and last place, so essentially it was a tie.

He still wanted to win, though.

But mostly he didn't want Shane to break his ankle trying to shave a fraction of a second off his time by going too hard in the corners.

The start signal sounded, and Shane was off. He whipped through the first two corners like he was being slingshotted, then pumped his legs hard down the straight length of the ice. No one wore helmets for the skills competition, so Shane's long hair flew behind him as he charged toward the final two corners. Ilya's heart was in his throat as he watched, terrified and dazzled at the same time.

Seconds later, Shane cleared the finish line, unharmed, and with the new lead time.

Well.

When Shane returned to the bench, he was met with more teasing and chirping than hugs.

"Wow, Hollander," laughed a defenseman for Pittsburgh. "Couldn't even let the kid finish celebrating before you destroyed him, huh?"

"Jesus Christ," grumbled Wyatt, "you can't just be the best player in the league, you've gotta be the *fastest* one too?"

"Hey!" Ilya protested. "He is not the best player in the league. Or the fastest."

"Prove it," Shane said with a sexy grin. Ilya wanted to devour him.

"When it is my turn, I will."

The next three skaters failed to beat Shane's time. Finally it was Ilya's turn, as the last competitor in the event.

"Good luck," Shane sing-songed as Ilya swung his legs over the boards.

"Maybe I will do it backwards," Ilya said. "So it will be a challenge."

Shane scowled at him, and Ilya laughed. Shane would never speak to him again if Ilya didn't give this everything he had.

He skated slowly to the start line, waving at the crowd as he went. He'd do his best.

His best, as it turned out, was a fraction of a second too slow. Shane was declared the winner.

But, for real, it was basically a tie. So whatever.

Shane didn't act like it was a tie. He flashed Ilya a smug little smile, as if Ilya even gave a shit about this thing.

"Congratulations," Ilya said when Shane had stopped celebrating. "You are like one thousandth of a second faster than me. In this one race."

"I won. That's all that matters."

Ilya wanted to say something obnoxious about how all of Shane's food restrictions and self-sacrifice translated to exactly point one three seconds' worth of athletic supremacy, but he decided to let Shane enjoy his victory instead.

Besides, winning stuff always made Shane horny, so Ilya considered himself the real winner.

Unfortunately, they had to watch Dallas Kent win the shot accuracy competition next, which was a real boner killer. Except the way Shane was huffing angrily beside Ilya was kind of hot.

"I fucking hate him," Shane said.

"Yes."

"I want to . . . I don't know. I want him to be punished."

"That would be nice," Ilya agreed.

Shane glanced up to the box where Commissioner Crowell was sitting. "I wish *he'd* do something."

Ilya snorted, then realized he hadn't told Shane the latest thing he'd heard about Crowell. "He will not help. He called Troy, a few days ago, and told him to stop posting about sexual assault on his Instagram."

Shane's head whipped around to face Ilya. "What? Wasn't Troy just posting about, like, where victims could seek help? And about charities people could donate to?"

Ilya nodded. "Only helpful things, yes."

"Why the fuck would Crowell want him to stop?"

Ilya nodded in the direction of Dallas Kent. "I think because it hurts Kent's feelings."

Shane's mouth dropped open. "Seriously? Jesus fucking Christ."

"Or because it makes the league look bad."

Shane scoffed. "Probably."

At that moment, Kent skated by them. Ilya glared at him, and he was sure Shane was doing the same.

"I meant to tell you," Shane said, once Kent was out of earshot, "I was impressed with what Troy was doing."

"Did you forget to tell me, or did you not tell me because you still hate him?"

"I don't hate him."

"Hm."

"I'm glad you're friends, or whatever," Shane grumbled.

"I will tell him you said that," Ilya said, "next time we are showering together."

Shane elbowed him in the arm. "Shut up. I'm trying to watch this."

"They are setting up pylons. Is that what you want to watch?"

Shane ducked his head, which meant his cheeks were turning pink.

Wyatt suddenly appeared in front of them and leaned one elbow on the boards. "How's it going, fellas?"

"Shhh. Shane is watching the men set up pylons."

"Would you fuck off?" Shane snarled.

Wyatt glanced at the ice. "That's cool. The ice crew's hard work isn't appreciated enough. Except the Zamboni drivers. Talk about all-stars." He slapped the boards. "There should be a Zamboni competition. With obstacles and stuff."

Ilya blinked at his goalie. "Yes. Great idea, Hazy."

"Congrats on winning the skating thing, Shane."

"Thanks."

"It was a tie, basically," Ilya said.

"That's not what the clock said," Shane argued.

"If we did it again right now, I would probably win."

"Well, you should have won the first time, dickhead."

Wyatt furrowed his brow at them. "You know, you two don't have to sit together."

"Hello, Hunter," Ilya said cheerfully as he sat in the chair next to Scott Hunter. A bunch of the players were gathered in the hotel bar, most of them sitting at large tables.

"Rozanov," Scott said with a wary nod.

Ilya plunked his pint of beer on the table and leaned back in his chair. "Too bad about the thing you lost."

Scott huffed. "The stickhandling event is stupid anyway. It's designed to make us look bad."

"Mm. Someone still won, though."

Scott narrowed his eyes. "You didn't win your event either. Hollander smoked you."

"Was basically a tie."

Scott took a sip of his own beer and seemed to glance around for someone else to talk to. Finally he sighed and said, "Your team's been playing well lately."

It was an understatement. Ottawa had been on fire since returning from their nearly ill-fated trip to Florida, and was enjoying a franchise-record winning streak. "We're making the playoffs this year," Ilya said.

"Might be a bit early to be stating that as fact."

"I don't think so. We are very good. Remember when we beat you? We haven't lost since then. Since that time we beat you."

Scott snorted. "Man, you're annoying."

Ilya grinned. "Hollander told me you want to coach our camps."

"One of them, maybe. Yeah."

"What are your qualifications? We have a boring guy already: Hollander."

"You know what? I might be busy this summer after all."

Ilya nudged him. "We are happy to have you. Really. The kids will be very excited."

Scott eyed him suspiciously. "Okay?"

"Yes. And bring Kip. We go out at night sometimes and have fun. Ryan Price brings his boyfriend."

Scott's face relaxed a bit. "Kip said he'd like to see Montreal."

Ilya gasped. "Ottawa is also good!"

"Yeah, but Montreal is Montreal."

Ilya couldn't argue that. He glanced across the room and spotted Shane, talking to Colorado's team captain, Matheson. Shane was wearing that sexy silk T-shirt that Rose bought him—the one that was practically transparent—and Ilya had been stealing glances at him all night.

Ilya briefly rubbed his own chest, searching for and finding the round outline of the ring hidden under his shirt.

"How is married life?" he asked.

Scott's expression shifted back to suspicious. "Good . . ."

"You are happy? Kip is happy?"

"Last I heard."

Ilya raised his eyebrows.

"This morning!" Scott clarified. "I was talking to him this morning! He was going to come with me, actually, but he's doing some volunteer work in Brooklyn this weekend instead."

"Nice of him."

"Yeah," Scott said defensively. "He's *nice*."

"Good." Ilya took a drink of beer. Shane was laughing at something Matheson said. His eyes were all crinkled. "Is Kip happy you are retiring this year?"

"Fuck off. I'm *not* retiring this year."

Ilya widened his eyes in mock surprise. "No? But your body is so old!"

"Okay," Scott said, and began to stand. "Good night, Rozanov."

"Do you remember where your room is?"

"Shut up."

"Do you need help?"

Scott kept walking and didn't reply. Ilya couldn't help but admire his hulking body as Scott walked away. In all honesty, he looked like he could play hockey for many years to come.

Ilya finished his beer, then stood. He caught Shane's eye right away, and nodded in the direction of the elevators. Shane gave the barest suggestion of a nod in reply, which was enough.

Shane rode the elevator with a Finnish rookie from Vancouver—the same one who'd been in the fastest skater competition—who Shane didn't know at all. He seemed to be more interested in his phone than in Shane, though. Shane gave him a brief, friendly smile, then stared straight ahead at the elevator doors.

The All-Star Weekend was always fun, but also a little exhausting between the interviews and the events and the socializing with other players. The weekends also involved a lot of high-risk sneaking around, which was stressful. Well, stressful and a bit sexually thrilling, if Shane was being honest. It had been hard to focus on anything Matheson had been saying to him because Ilya had been sitting across the room, drinking a beer and looking so fucking hot that Shane had been internally struggling to tamp down an erection for the past half hour.

Shane went to his own room first. Partially because the rookie was still walking behind him, and partially because he wanted to freshen up a bit.

When he pulled his phone out of his pocket he saw a text from Ilya: Where are you?

Shane smiled to himself and decided not to reply. He liked an impatient Ilya.

Once Shane had changed, brushed his teeth, fixed his hair, and had gotten himself clean everywhere he wanted to be clean, he made his way to Ilya's room down the hall.

He knocked as gently as possible on the door, and Ilya opened it immediately.

"Finally," Ilya said. He stepped back so Shane could enter and quickly shut the door behind them.

"Did I keep you?"

Ilya stepped into his space. "You are too slow."

"Not according to the skills competition."

Ilya exhaled hard through his nose, then kissed Shane furiously.

It always felt like *before* whenever they met in a hotel room. Hotels had been their go-to meeting place for years, grabbing a precious hour or two together when they were in the same city. Now their cities were so close that their teams rarely stayed in town after the games. Sneaking into Ilya's hotel room like this set Shane on fire like nothing else.

He hooked his leg around Ilya's ass and gripped his shoulders, practically trying to climb him. Ilya huffed out a laugh into his mouth and slid a hand under Shane's ass to help support him. "Talking to Matheson made you horny," Ilya said.

"Looking at *you* made me horny," Shane corrected him. "Not being able to touch you. Just—*fuck*—just shut up, okay?"

Ilya, thankfully, went back to kissing him, and Shane sank back into the wonderful, rare sensation of not giving a fuck about anything except Ilya's hands on his body and Ilya's tongue in his mouth.

Shane was, of course, as hard as granite already and knew, distantly, that he was thrusting a bit against Ilya's thigh, and that he should probably stop because it would be embarrassing if he shot his load already. But he also kind of didn't care.

Fortunately, Ilya cared. He broke their kiss and extracted himself from the embrace of Shane's leg wrapped around him. "Sometimes faster is not better," Ilya said with a crooked smile. He took Shane's hand, then lifted it to his lips and gently kissed his knuckles.

"Yeah, but—oh." Shane's argument was cut short when Ilya flicked his tongue between two knuckles. For some reason the sensation sent ripples of pleasure throughout Shane's body. How did Ilya know? What made someone even decide to do that?

"We are going slow tonight," Ilya informed him. Shane could only nod, his head as wobbly as the rest of him.

Ilya tugged on his hand and led him to end of the bed. He paused there, and began lightly playing with the ends of Shane's hair with one hand, while the other rested on Shane's hip.

"I want to look at you," Ilya said. "Everywhere. And touch you. And kiss you. I want to take my time until you are dying for it."

Shane's tongue felt heavy. "You'd better make it worth the wait."

"I will." Ilya trailed a fingertip delicately along the line of Shane's jaw. "Because I will be dying for it too."

Shane hadn't touched alcohol for a year, almost, but he felt a bit drunk in that moment. Ilya's hand on his hip was possibly the only thing that was preventing him from toppling forward onto the floor. "Sounds like hard work for you."

Ilya's lips curved up. "It is your reward. For winning today."

"Oh," Shane said thickly. "Fuck."

Then they were kissing again, Ilya's big hand gripping Shane's face, his thumb pressing into the hinge of his jaw. Shane pressed his own hands to Ilya's chest and found the ring there.

He wanted to see it. He wanted Ilya's shirt off. He wanted all of their clothes off. He wanted Ilya inside him and—

"Relax," Ilya chuckled. Shane realized he'd been grabbing at Ilya's shirt, possibly trying to tear it off.

"I fucking want you," Shane said. It sounded whiny.

"I know." But instead of doing anything to speed things along, Ilya lightly kissed his forehead, then his right eyebrow, then his cheek.

Shane let out a long, slow breath and closed his eyes. He needed to accept that Ilya was in charge here. He stood very still and let Ilya kiss his jaw, his chin, his throat. He focused on Ilya's breath against his skin, the fingers in his hair, and the steady beating of his own heart.

Ilya only wanted to pamper him. The least Shane could do was let him.

A sudden burst of yelling and laughter came from the hallway, outside the door. Loud male voices of their peers—Shane was pretty sure one of them was Dallas Kent. He flinched at the reminder that they were dangerously close to the rest of the hockey world here.

"Ignore them," Ilya whispered.

"I'm trying."

Ilya licked at the hollow of Shane's throat, then kissed down until he reached the low collar of Shane's shirt. "I like this shirt," Ilya said.

"That's why I wore it."

Ilya peeled it away and kissed the newly exposed skin of Shane's collarbone and chest. He kissed his shoulders as he gently pushed Shane backward onto the bed.

Shane shuffled on his back until his head reached the pillows. Ilya followed, hovering over him and continuing to drop soft kisses wherever he liked. It was luxurious and indulgent for Shane to just lie there while Ilya made him feel wonderful. It did feel like a prize he'd earned, and that fucking *did it* for Shane. He loved being rewarded like this.

Ilya kissed his chest as he undid Shane's belt, and then the button on his shorts. He caught Shane's right nipple in his teeth as he pulled his zipper down.

"Ah," Shane gasped. He lifted his hips so Ilya could slide his shorts and underwear off and to the floor. Shane's cock was hard and lay flat against his stomach, hoping for attention.

Ilya, of course, ignored it.

He continued to sweetly torture Shane with light kisses and caresses that made Shane's toes curl and his blood thrum. He felt like he was sinking into the mattress, or floating to the ceiling. His head was cloudy with lust and happiness. He could still hear people—fellow NHL stars—talking loudly in the hall, but it seemed distant and unimportant. Nothing mattered but Ilya. The man he loved. His future husband.

"You *are* going to fuck me," Shane murmured, "right?"

Ilya kissed Shane's hipbone. "Maybe."

Shane shivered. *"God."*

Ilya laughed against his skin. "You work so hard on this body. You should like this attention."

Shane *did* like it, dammit. "Take your shirt off?" He sounded pathetic.

Ilya sat up and pulled his T-shirt off over his head, then tossed it behind him. The ring glinted on its chain against his dark chest hair, and god, sometimes Shane *forgot*. It seemed impossible to be able to claim this man *forever*.

Shane reached out with one hand. "Come here. Kiss me."

Ilya lowered himself and nipped Shane's bottom lip, then pecked one corner of his mouth, then the other. When he finally took Shane's mouth, he kissed him with maddening patience and control. Shane tried to take charge, desperate to move things along, but Ilya wouldn't let him.

*Be good*, Shane instructed himself. *Let him do this for you.*

He wished Ilya would touch his cock. It was *right there*, but Ilya had positioned himself so he was mostly beside Shane, leaving Shane's erection alone and miserable.

Shane tried to sneak a hand down to give himself a little relief, but Ilya grabbed his wrist and pinned Shane's hand firmly on the pillow, above his head, then did the same with the other one.

"Stay," Ilya said, his voice a low, delicious rumble.

Shane nodded, then said, to his embarrassment, "Please."

Ilya's lips curved up. "Please what?"

Shane didn't even know. "Touch me. Whatever you want. Just . . . need you."

"You have me, sweetheart."

The first time Ilya had used that particular pet name, Shane had felt like he'd been struck by lightning. It had been so unexpected and earthshaking and *hot*. Shane could never get away with calling anyone sweetheart, but the word rolled effortlessly off Ilya's tongue, in his sexy fucking accent. Despite that, Ilya rarely said it, so every time he did, it knocked Shane on his ass.

Ilya slid down the bed and began kissing Shane's thighs, and up the crease along his groin. Shane shivered and gasped, but he kept his hands on the pillow and didn't ask for more. After several minutes, he was rewarded for his good behavior when Ilya, without any real warning, sucked one of Shane's balls into his mouth.

"Oh fuck," Shane whimpered. Ilya was an expert when it came to Shane's balls. He knew exactly how to roll them in his mouth, how to press his tongue along the seam of Shane's sac, and how to use his fingers on the sensitive area just below. He'd made Shane come just from this, many times, but Shane didn't think that was the plan tonight. He hoped not. "Fuck, Ilya. So good."

Ilya hummed, which sent sparks shooting up to the tip of

Shane's dick. He released Shane slowly, letting the delicate orb slip out between his glistening lips. He stood and went to his suitcase in the corner of the room. A moment later he returned with a bottle of lube.

"Thank fuck," Shane sighed.

Ilya smiled. "Turn over."

Shane didn't hesitate for a second. He went up on his knees and forearms and waited. He was expecting the welcome pressure of a slick finger, so he nearly yelped when he felt the warm, wet brush of Ilya's tongue.

"Holy—yes. Fuck yes," Shane panted.

Ilya was so fucking good with his tongue. He switched between long, confident strokes and soft flutters against Shane's hole while he gripped Shane's ass cheeks in his strong hands, pulling them apart to get deeper. Shane dropped his head to the pillow, mouth slack. He couldn't focus his eyes on anything.

"You were so fucking beautiful today," Ilya said, then kissed Shane's right ass cheek. "When you were skating, with your hair."

"You too," Shane slurred. "Love watching you skate."

He heard the click of the lube bottle, then felt the gentle press of Ilya's finger against his entrance. "Can I tell you a secret?" Ilya asked.

Shane tensed, his stomach flipping in anticipation. "Yes."

Ilya slid his finger inside. "You are a better hockey player than me."

Shane gasped, both from the intrusion and the admission. "I'm just—just on a better team."

"No," Ilya said calmly. "You have always been better. Always."

God, why was Ilya saying this? Did he really think so? Did it matter?

"It's," Shane gritted out as Ilya stroked his prostate, "a tie."

Ilya chuckled. "Yes. Okay."

Shane relaxed into the pillow and against Ilya's fingers. He felt absolutely perfect, loose and happy and safe, not focused on anything except opening for Ilya. And even that wasn't a chore because Ilya knew exactly how to get him there. His strong fingers sank inside him, twisted, curled, gently stretched apart while Shane breathed and sighed and sank deeper into the sensations.

Loud knocking jolted Shane out of the moment. The knocking was followed by the voice of Cliff Marlow. "Rozanov! You in there?"

All good feelings left, abruptly replaced by pure panic. Shane craned his neck to peer at Ilya over his shoulder. Ilya winked at him, gave Shane's prostate another stroke, and called out, "Yes."

Shane mouthed *what the fuck?* at him, but Ilya only grinned and continued to finger fuck him.

"We're going out," Cliff said. "I need my wingman, let's go." He sounded more than a little drunk.

"Where?" Ilya asked, and added a second finger.

"I don't know. Some club. Can you open the fucking door?"

Shane wanted to die. But he also was oddly turned on by this weird situation. Which also made him want to die.

Of course Ilya decided this was the perfect time to finally touch Shane's dick. He wrapped his hand around the shaft and Shane's whole body jerked. Unfortunately, Shane also let out a loud moan.

"Shh," Ilya scolded, as if any of this were Shane's fault. Then, to Cliff he said, "I can't right now. Sorry."

There was silence, and then Cliff jumped to a slightly wrong conclusion. "Shit. You've got a girl in there with you, right? Sorry, man."

"Maybe," Ilya said.

Shane rolled his eyes.

Cliff laughed. "Probably two or three. Have a good night, you fucking legend."

Shane bit his own forearm to keep himself from saying anything.

When Cliff was finally gone, Shane said, "Two or three, huh?"

Ilya huffed. "Cliff cannot even count to two or three."

"I can't believe you fucking *chatted* with him while you were *fingering me*," Shane hissed. "What the fuck is wrong with you?"

"Wrong with *me*? I am not the one who fucking loved it."

"I did not."

Ilya rubbed his thumb over the head of Shane's leaking cock, making Shane suck in a breath. "Your cock loved it."

"My cock loves being touched, not whatever weird shit you're into. Could you please fuck me now?"

Ilya released him and slid his fingers out of Shane's ass. Shane flipped onto his back so he could watch him finish undressing. In less than a minute, Ilya was naked and slicking his own cock with lube, so maybe he was in more of a hurry than he'd been letting on.

Shane thought Ilya would haul him to the end of the bed so he could stand while fucking him. Shane loved it that way, with Ilya able to use all of his power and strength and Shane able to watch him and touch him and stroke himself for him.

But instead, Ilya left Shane where he was—relaxed against the pillows—and lowered himself carefully over his body. He kissed him in a slow, adoring way that absolutely annihilated Shane's brain every time. Then, when Shane was fully reduced to a quivering mass of pure need, Ilya finally entered him.

Shane watched Ilya's face as he pushed inside. His eyes were wide like the sensation still surprised him, after all these years. Like he hadn't been expecting Shane to welcome him inside so easily. Like he somehow didn't know he belonged there.

"I love you so much," Shane whispered.

Ilya could only nod, his teeth biting hard into his bottom lip to keep himself quiet.

When he started moving, he used slow, deliberate strokes that weren't enough, but were also too much. Every nerve in Shane's body was buzzing. Ilya peppered Shane's face with gentle kisses, his breath dancing across Shane's skin in ragged puffs. Shane wrapped his legs around Ilya's back, urging him to go deeper, and faster.

There was more noise from the hallway—more NHL players being drunk and rowdy—and Shane tried to ignore them. Or at least tried not to let their proximity turn him on even more. Because Ilya hadn't been wrong; there was something hot about doing this surrounded by their peers.

Ilya finally sped up. He grinned at Shane, as if he knew what he'd been thinking about. "What if they could see?" Ilya's voice was low and quiet and his words made Shane's cock twitch. "If that wall was a window."

Shane squeezed his eyes shut, which only helped him to imagine it. "Fuck," he said.

"They could see how well you take it. How much you love it."

"Stop," Shane said weakly, not meaning it at all.

"They would be so jealous of me. Getting to have you like this."

Shane opened his eyes. "They'd be jealous of *me*. You're so fucking beautiful."

"Stroke yourself," Ilya commanded, then began thrusting harder, snapping his hips and tipping his head back.

Shane loved this moment, when Ilya began to lose control and started to desperately chase his own release. Shane obediently stroked himself, biting his own lip to keep from crying out.

He came first, his release splashing onto his stomach at the exact moment someone in the hallway let out a loud whoop, which was a weird coincidence that Shane, unfortunately, found very hot.

Ilya was laughing, almost hysterically, but he was still thrusting and interrupting his own laughter with frantic grunts until finally, "I'm going to come, Hollander. Fuck."

Shane wished he hadn't said his name, but he stopped caring about it immediately because watching Ilya Rozanov's face when he climaxed was Shane's favorite thing in the world.

Ilya managed to stop himself from crashing down on top of Shane, and instead carefully pulled out and rolled to his side, breathing heavily.

"That was," Shane said, "fucking hot."

Ilya wrinkled his nose. "Ehn. Was okay."

Shane let out a shaky laugh and lightly punched Ilya's chest. "Fuck you."

They took turns getting cleaned up in the bathroom. Shane got back into bed, still naked, as he waited for Ilya. He was thankful they'd managed to keep the sheets relatively clean.

"You are staying," Ilya said.

Shane opened his eyes and found him standing outside the bathroom, also still naked.

"Well," Shane said, gesturing to the hallway where they could still hear loud male voices. "I'm not going out *there*."

"They will not assume we were having sex," Ilya said reasonably.

"I *know*."

"Maybe we watched a movie," Ilya said as he sauntered toward the bed. No one should look that elegant naked.

"Who?" Shane asked dryly. "Me and the two or three women you were having an orgy with?"

Ilya gave him a crooked smile and slid under the covers beside him. "Two or three people is not an orgy, Shane." He tilted Shane's chin up with a finger and held him there while he kissed his lips. "I am glad you are staying."

"I'm not saying I'm not nervous about it."

"I know. But I hate when you are so close but not in my arms."

Shane's heart wobbled. "I suppose we're almost married. So."

"Yes," Ilya agreed. "Next year we will be the first married NHL All-Stars."

Shane's whole body tensed. "Oh my god."

"What?"

"I hadn't even thought of that."

Ilya kissed him again, but it didn't stop Shane's brain from spinning out of control.

"Oh my *god*," Shane said again when Ilya finished kissing him. "I'm so focused on marrying you and being a couple and stuff and dealing with the blowback from the hockey world that I never even thought about, like, being married *and* playing hockey."

"Scary?"

It was fucking terrifying, but Shane didn't want to say that. "We'll deal with it," he said with not nearly enough confidence.

"Deal with it?" Ilya said with a smile. "I can't fucking wait."

# CHAPTER TWENTY-EIGHT

Ilya and Shane had just finished a boring press conference together the morning of the All-Star game. When they were finally able to exit the room, Ilya was surprised to see Commissioner Crowell in the hallway. He was alone and looking at his phone, and Ilya, without even thinking, took a purposeful stride toward him.

Shane stopped him with a hand on his arm. "What are you doing?"

"I am going to talk to Crowell."

"The hell you are! Don't be stupid."

Ilya grunted, shook Shane's hand away, and continued walking toward Crowell.

"Commissioner," Ilya said when he was a few feet away.

Crowell glanced at him, and furrowed his brow. "Mr. Rozanov. How are you enjoying the weekend?"

"Fine. But I was talking to my friend Troy Barrett, and he said you called him."

"I did."

"As his captain," Ilya said, trying to force some importance into his title, "I am . . . concerned."

Crowell's lips formed something close to a sneer. "Are you?"

Now that Ilya was standing in front of Crowell, he wasn't entirely sure what he wanted to say. And he had a feeling he may stumble through his English sentences more than usual. Crowell was intimidating.

"Barrett has been doing good work. Trying to help," Ilya said.

"I assume you're talking about his recent social media activity," Crowell said. His tone was almost bored, but with a dangerous edge to it. "He's become quite the activist *all of a sudden*."

"Yes. This is what I mean. He is trying. After what Dallas Kent did—"

Crowell held up a hand. "After what Dallas was accused of doing. *Anonymously*."

Ilya narrowed his eyes. "Barrett was his friend. He knows him."

"Does he? Because when I spoke to him he told me he didn't, in fact, know anything about the accusations. He didn't witness anything. It had never even *occurred* to him that his best friend was capable of such things. Seems strange, doesn't it? I would say it's more likely that people on the internet make stuff up than it is for someone to not know their best friend at all."

Ilya felt like the ground was crumbling beneath his feet.

"Commissioner Crowell," came a voice from behind Ilya. Shane had approached. Fuck. He didn't need to get dragged into this terrible decision.

"Shane," Crowell said in a way that was warm and cold at the same time. "Are you also here to defend Troy Barrett's personal vendetta against Dallas Kent?"

Ilya could see the anxiety all over Shane's face, but Shane straightened his shoulders and said, "I think he was doing good work. Using his voice to help people."

"Barrett should be using his *hockey skills* to win *hockey games*," Crowell said. "That's what he gets paid millions of dollars to do.

I have no patience for unnecessary drama. You two have always kept your rivalry on the ice. None of this petty social media bullshit."

"I don't think it's petty," Shane argued. "I think Barrett legitimately cares about the issues he's bringing attention to. He's doing what the *league* should be doing."

Oh shit. Ilya could not believe Shane just said that. He took a step closer to him, as if to protect Shane from whatever the response from Crowell would be.

Crowell stared at Shane balefully. "Is he? Should I be taking time out of my busy schedule of running the entire fucking National Hockey League to make sure we post about every goddamned issue in the world? You know what happens every time a player decides to be an *activist*?" He said the word *activist* like it was the worst insult he could imagine. "Journalists start looking into the league's history with whatever issue they're going on about. Suddenly a team with a hundred-year history isn't so great because they had a coach that said something once that was maybe a bit racist. It's ridiculous and I don't have time for it."

"Like when Scott Hunter came out?" Ilya asked, his voice surprisingly steady. "This was annoying for you?"

Crowell looked slightly thrown by this. "Of course we support Hunter. We support his entire community. Hockey is for everyone."

Ilya managed to keep himself from rolling his eyes. "But you would like Hunter to shut up now, yes?"

"I never said that. I only think there's a time and place where advocating for personal things is appropriate. Hunter often crosses the line."

"And you do not want others to cross the line," Ilya said. "One gay player is enough?"

Crowell's glanced at Shane, and then back to Ilya. "We've had other players come out."

"You mean Baldwin and Lundin," Shane said, naming the Vancouver and Los Angeles players who had come out shortly after Scott Hunter had. "Baldwin was never offered another contract, and Lundin ended up moving back to Sweden."

Crowell scoffed. "Baldwin was at the end of his career anyway, and as for Lundin, lots of Europeans choose to cut their careers short to return to their home countries."

Ilya didn't personally know either of the players in question, but he'd certainly suspected that their decisions to leave the NHL had more to do with the way they'd been treated by their teams than their ability or desire to play hockey. The only other queer players he knew of—Ryan Price and Eric Bennett—were both retired and hadn't advertised their sexuality when they'd played. Troy Barrett was the only other active queer NHL player that Ilya knew besides Hunter. And Shane.

It was a pretty small group.

"Anyone who feels the need to come out is welcome to do so," Crowell said. "But I don't see why it has to be such a big deal." He laughed without humor. "It hardly matters these days, does it?" His gaze landed on Shane again.

"It matters," Shane said firmly. His jaw was clenched. Ilya wanted to hold his hand.

Crowell looked between them for a silent moment and said, "Well. I have a very full schedule today, so I'm afraid I have to end this *unexpected* conversation now." He straightened his suit jacket, and gave them both one last cold glare before turning and walking away.

"That was probably a terrible idea," Shane said, once Crowell was out of earshot.

"Probably," Ilya agreed. "But I would do it again."

"Me too."

# CHAPTER TWENTY-NINE

*February*

"Where have I seen you before?" Ilya asked.

The Detroit defenseman, Kerr, looked confused. "The fuck are you talking about, Rozanov?"

Ilya pointed a gloved finger at him. "Oh! I know. From that gif. I see it all the time. From last season when I deked around you like you were a fucking statue and scored."

Kerr shoved him. They were behind the Detroit net, after a stoppage in play. "I wouldn't be fucking bragging if I played for Ottawa."

Ilya leaned back against the glass, still smiling. "Weird because it's like 3–1 for us right now."

"Whatever." Kerr skated away.

"Rozanov," an exhausted-sounding ref said, "could you give it a rest for once?"

"Anything for you."

Bood joined Ilya as he skated toward the bench. "Are we sure we're in the right building?" he said over the roar of the crowd. "This can't be Ottawa."

It was midway through the second period of the first home game since the All-Star break and the arena was packed. And *loud.* Even now, when nothing was happening on the ice, the crowd was fired up.

"I guess we just had to start winning," Ilya said.

"Damn, we should have tried that sooner," Bood joked.

Ilya laughed, because he was in a great fucking mood. Hockey was fun again, and he was happy for Bood, who had been with Ottawa for his entire career and had never known how it felt to be on a good NHL team. He was happy for Wyatt, who was way too good to be the goalie for a losing team. He was happy for the rookies, and Coach Wiebe, and for Troy, who had been smiling a lot lately, though that probably had more to do with Harris.

Ottawa ended up winning the game 5–2 after Troy scored an empty net goal with less than a minute to go. A great effort all around. And definitely worthy of a team outing to Monk's to celebrate.

Ilya was sitting at a table with Troy Barrett, Evan Dykstra, and three pitchers of beer. He was already most of the way through one of the pitchers. "Do you know why I think we are winning so much?" he said, his words a bit sluggish as he drunkenly stumbled through the English language. "Because Dykstra has not been the DJ. In the locker room."

"Hey!" Evan said. "My music is totally fucking good."

"No," Ilya groaned. "Is terrible."

"Where's Hazy?" Evan said, looking around. "He'll back me up."

"Does not count. Hazy likes everything."

Bood approached the table, holding a beer in one hand and a pool cue in the other. "Who wants to get destroyed at pool?"

"Sure," Evan said. "Ilya's being a dick."

"No!" Bood said, feigning shock. "Ilya *Rozanov*?"

"Isn't your wife having a baby right now?" Ilya asked.

"Not yet, but I'm leaving after I kick Dykstra's ass. Y'know. Just in case."

Evan left with Bood, and Troy, who'd been quiet all evening, said, "Dykstra's music really is awful."

"Right?" Ilya took a long sip of beer. "Are you okay?"

Troy frowned at the table. "Yeah. I'm just . . . thinking about something."

"Harris?" Ilya guessed.

Troy's lips curved up a bit. "No. I mean, yeah. Kind of." He glanced up at Ilya. "We're together now, by the way."

Ilya beamed and put a hand on Troy's shoulder. "This is great! Where is he now?"

"Still working. But he'll be here soon he said." He fiddled with a paper coaster on the table. "So, I'm thinking about coming out. Like, all the way out. Publicly. Maybe the day of the Pride Night game."

Holy shit. For a moment Ilya was speechless as a confusing swirl of excitement, shock, and jealousy rose inside him. The Pride Night game was at the end of February, only a couple of weeks away. "Oh yes?" was what he finally managed to say.

"Yeah. I'm tired of hiding. And now that I'm with Harris, I don't think I *can* hide, y'know?"

It was true. Ilya was sure the whole team would notice how Harris and Troy looked at each other soon, if they hadn't noticed already. "I am very happy for you. And for Harris. And of course I will support you. The whole team will."

"You think so?"

"Troy! Yes. Of course. This team is the best."

A silent question hung in the air: Then why wasn't Ilya out? Ilya let it hang.

"The Pride Night game," Troy said. "It's against Toronto. So. That sucks."

Ugh. That *did* suck. It was hard enough for Troy to face his former team without anything else added to it.

"The Pride Night game is just a league thing, you know? Is not, like . . . it does not have to be when you come out." Ilya was doing a terrible job of explaining what he meant. "Like, is for show, kind of. Do not feel pressure to have to come out."

"I know. I just think it would be nice, maybe?"

Ilya could see that. Pride Night games had always felt weird to him. Performative, mostly, but also uncomfortable because he felt guilty for not being out.

"Then you should do it," Ilya said. "And we will make sure to embarrass your old team that night."

"You are such a big boy now," Ilya said as he scratched Chiron's ears. "You are like two Chirons."

Harris had brought Chiron into the locker room at the end of practice to visit the team, but Ilya suspected he had an ulterior motive. His suspicions were confirmed a moment later when Harris asked, "Was Troy not here today?"

Ilya smiled at the dog. "He is here somewhere. Showers, probably."

Harris glanced toward the showers, but managed to keep himself from running in there to get an eyeful of wet, naked Troy. "Chiron got some bad news last week," he said. "I mean, maybe he's not too sad about it."

A million horrible possibilities flashed through Ilya's brain. "What news? What is wrong?"

"Turns out he's not therapy dog material. At least according to the trainers."

"Impossible," Ilya said, because clearly Chiron was the best dog in the world and the trainers were fucking idiots if they couldn't see that. "What will happen to him?"

"Nothing bad," Harris assured him. "He's still going to be

the official team dog, but he'll need a home away from the arena."

Ilya almost offered to take him. He wanted to so badly. But there was another option that made way more sense. "You will adopt him," he told Harris.

Harris, as it turned out, had already been thinking the same thing. So Ilya was doubly glad he hadn't tried to steal Harris's dog.

Ilya smiled at Chiron. "You are going to be the happiest dog ever." He meant it. Harris loved dogs, and his family had a big farm that Chiron could visit and run around at.

Troy emerged from a back room—not the showers—looking sweaty and, yes, sexy, so Harris's attention left Ilya immediately. Ilya sat on the floor and played with Chiron, still wearing most of his gear. He removed one of his elbow pads and waved it around, letting Chiron chase it and chomp on it when he caught it.

He definitely needed a dog.

A few minutes later, Troy stood on the bench in his stall and tried to get the room's attention. It didn't quite work, so Ilya decided to help. "Everyone shut up and listen to Barrett."

The room got very quiet as everyone turned their attention to Troy. Ilya could only think of one thing that Troy could be announcing, with Harris at his side, so he held his breath and waited.

"Just one thing," Troy said. "I'm dating Harris. We're together. I'm gay."

Ilya had to respect how efficient the speech was. He began to clap loudly, and everyone else joined in, cheering and whooping. Ilya loved this team. He watched Troy step down off the bench and into Harris's arms. Then he bent Harris backward and kissed the hell out of him, in front of everyone.

Ilya's heart twisted, partly with happiness, partly with jealousy.

He was thrilled for Harris and Troy, but at the same time he knew he'd never get a locker room full of hockey players cheering for his and Shane's relationship. And of course he shouldn't resent Troy for being able to come out, announce his relationship with Harris, and basically adopt a wonderful dog all on the same day.

"It's okay," he said to Chiron in Russian. "My day is coming."

But he wondered sometimes, even with Shane's ring hanging around his neck, whether he was fooling himself.

"I thought you'd given up on me," Galina said, in Russian, as she waved Ilya into her office.

"Sorry," Ilya said. He'd let five weeks go by without an appointment because he'd been feeling more like his old self. He'd been hoping, absurdly, he knew, that he was fixed. But seeing Troy and Harris kissing in the team locker room had sent him spiraling back to a dark place, so he'd made an appointment.

"Busy?" she asked as she sat in her chair opposite the couch.

"Yes," Ilya said, taking his usual place on the center cushion. "We might be heading to the playoffs, if you can believe it."

"I know, I've been following. It's very exciting, as a fan."

Ilya smiled. "And as a player."

"So hockey is good," she prompted.

"Hockey is great. I'm having fun again." He looked away from her. "I thought, maybe, that would be enough."

"You thought you didn't have to see me anymore because you felt happier."

"Yes." He forced himself to look at her. "Stupid. I know."

Her lips curved up. "I wish it were that easy."

"Me too."

"I take it your good mood didn't last?"

"Not exactly, no. I'm still having fun playing hockey, and I love the time Shane and I have together. And I'm . . ." He paused, but decided he should probably tell her this. "I'm engaged. He asked me to marry him, and I said yes."

"Congratulations."

Ilya nodded. "It's everything I want, and we are planning to come out this summer and maybe get married then too. No more waiting until we are both retired."

Galina made notes and said, "This is a big change for you guys."

"Huge," Ilya agreed. "I'm excited and happy, but I'm also scared."

"Of how people will react?"

Ilya pressed his fingers to the ring that lay hidden under his T-shirt. "I'm scared Shane will change his mind. Or that he won't, and it will affect his career, and he will hate me for it. Maybe not for a while, but eventually."

"Does it seem likely that he'll change his mind?"

"I don't know," Ilya said honestly. "He spooks easily, sometimes. Panics."

"But he proposed to you. That probably wasn't a decision he made lightly."

Ilya happily remembered Shane going to one knee, surrounded by the candles that he'd bought and carefully decorated the living room with. "No. I think he was very serious about it."

"Does the second scenario seem more likely? Where he resents you?"

Ilya grabbed one of the throw pillows next to him and hugged it against his stomach. "I don't know. My brain tells me it's likely, but my brain has lied to me before."

"Brains can be jerks that way."

Ilya gave a small smile. "Yes." He curled his fingers into the pillow. "There's another thing. One of my teammates just came out as gay. To the team, I mean. But he's planning on coming out publicly on the day of our Pride Night game next week."

"Wow. That's exciting. How does that make you feel?"

"I'm very happy for him. He's dating the team's social media manager. A great guy. I'm happy for both of them. The team all supports them. It's been nice."

Galina didn't say anything, just waited for Ilya to continue.

"But," Ilya added, "I'm jealous, I guess. It's made me think about how much harder it will be for me and Shane."

"Do you remember," Galina said slowly, "in one of our earlier sessions, I'd asked about your other friends?"

"Yes."

"Have you told anyone yet, about Shane?"

"No," Ilya admitted.

"You seem to be trapped in this cycle of wanting to be openly in a relationship with Shane, but also dreading it. I think it would help if you told a friend—someone you trust. Someone on your side."

"Maybe," Ilya said, though it also sounded like a good way to lose a friend.

"Try it," she urged. "A teammate, or an old friend. Just one person, and see how you feel after."

"Okay," he said. "I'll try."

"Fuck you, Rozanov!"

It was probably the one millionth time Ilya had heard that phrase, or similar, during the afternoon game in Boston. This time it was from a charming middle-aged woman behind the penalty box he was currently serving a two-minute minor in.

Beside him, Dykstra, who was serving his own penalty, said, "You gotta love Boston."

"She probably used to wear my jersey," Ilya said. "Used to love me."

"That was before you turned traitor, though." Dykstra laughed. "Did you see the guy who actually added 'fuck' to the back of his Rozanov jersey? He's sitting near that corner somewhere." He gestured with his stick. "That's a commitment to hate that you have to respect."

Ilya squirted Gatorade in his mouth. If he offered to sign the "Fuck Rozanov" jersey he'd bet the guy wearing it would be thrilled. Deep down, this city probably still loved him.

"We were talking about getting dinner somewhere after the game," Dykstra said. "We figured you'd know all the good Boston joints."

"I can suggest something, but I cannot join you. I am meeting a friend."

"Oh yeah? A friend, or a *friend*."

Ilya only smiled.

"So you're still alive."

Ilya grinned at his old friend and hugged her. "Still alive."

Svetlana swatted his shoulder. "Then why the fuck haven't I seen you in three years?"

"I'm sorry," Ilya said, meaning it. He switched to Russian. "It's a long story, but it's mostly because I'm a terrible friend."

"You were always a terrible friend, but you were a fantastic lay and I miss you."

"I missed you too." Ilya offered her his arm. He'd met her on the sidewalk near the Beacon Hill restaurant they were having dinner at. She'd stepped out of the taxi looking like a movie star in a long black fur-trimmed coat, her white-blond hair swept into an elegant knot at the back of her head. "You look stunning."

"Probably."

"Are those boots practical for Boston winters?" Ilya asked, eying the tall, narrow heels on her knee-high leather boots.

"Of course. They're like ice picks. And don't change the subject. We're still talking about how terrible you are."

"I thought we were talking about how great I am in bed."

"How great you *were*. It's been years, Ilya. *Years.*"

"I know," Ilya said seriously. He opened the door to the restaurant and held it for her. "Let's order drinks. Then I'll explain."

Once they were seated at the most private table in the elegant Italian restaurant, and martinis had been ordered, Svetlana glared at him expectantly.

Ilya sighed. "If it makes you feel better, you're not the only one I lost touch with."

"It does not," she said sharply.

"I've been . . . a bit closed off, since I moved to Ottawa."

"What does that mean? You're not sleeping your way through North America anymore?"

Ilya huffed a laugh. "No. Not anymore."

The server brought their martinis. Ilya had never been so happy to see a cocktail.

"What a loss to women everywhere," Svetlana said dryly.

"Hopefully they can get over it." Ilya sipped his martini, which was perfectly cold and crisp. "How have you been? Where are you working?"

"I finished my MBA." She smiled. "I have been offered a job by the Boston Bears."

"Perfect!" Svetlana knew more about hockey than anyone. More than Shane. Possibly more than Yuna. "You're going to take it?"

"I think so. They're excited to have Sergei Vetrov's daughter working for them." Vetrov had been a superstar for Boston in the '90s.

"And what does Sergei think?"

"That I am a princess who should get whatever I want. We have that in common."

Ilya laughed. "Were you at the game today?"

"Yes. You couldn't hear me booing you?"

"Not over everyone else booing me. Boston hates me now."

"Of course we do. You left."

And that could be a segue into *why* he left, but he was struggling to make himself bring it up. Shane knew about and supported Ilya's decision to tell Svetlana about their relationship, and Ilya knew he could trust her, but finding the words was difficult.

Instead, he picked up the menu beside him. "What's good here?"

Svetlana reached across the table and pushed his menu down with one beautifully manicured finger. "Why did you sign with Ottawa, Ilya?" she asked in her usual blunt way. "I have never understood it. No one does."

Ilya took his time answering. "To be closer to someone." Then, like a coward, he took another sip of his drink.

Svetlana's vivid blue eyes widened. "Someone? Like, someone you are dating? Are you actually with someone? In a real relationship?"

"Yes."

Her face lit up. "My god. She must be spectacular. Who is it? Where did you meet? In Ottawa? Is she Russian?"

The server returned to take their orders. "We need more time," Svetlana said, not unkindly, but a bit impatiently.

The server left with a polite, "Of course."

Svetlana rested one elbow on the table and tapped her red fingernails against her red lips. "Why have I never heard of you dating someone? Is it a secret?"

"You are asking a lot of questions."

"Answer the last one first."

"We should look at the menu—"

"Ilya."

Under the table, Ilya's fingers flexed against his dress pants. "Yes, it's a secret."

"This is intriguing. Are you having an affair? Is it a teammate's wife?"

"No," Ilya said quickly, slightly offended. "Nothing like that. Of course not."

"Didn't you tell me once you'd slept with your teammate's girlfriend? Back in Moscow?"

"Yes, but he was an asshole to her, and also I was seventeen. I would never do that now."

Svetlana hummed thoughtfully. "It's a secret, but it's not an affair. Maybe your coach's daughter?"

"My coach's daughter is eleven."

"The owner's daughter, then. Or *is* it the owner? Isn't one of the owners of the Centaurs a woman?"

"It's not the owner."

She smiled over the rim of her martini glass. "This is a fun game. I like this." Suddenly her eyes went wide. She leaned forward and whispered, "Is it a man?"

Well. That hadn't taken long. Ilya answered with the slightest tip of his head as he brought his glass to his lips.

Svetlana covered her mouth with one hand, eyes still wide. He could tell she was smiling, though.

"Ilya," she finally said. "Holy shit."

"Yes."

She grinned wickedly at him. "Did you fuck every woman in Canada and had to move on to men?"

Ilya rolled his eyes. "That's not how it works."

"So who is he?"

Ilya's cheeks heated, which he hoped wasn't noticeable in the dim lighting of the restaurant.

"You're blushing," Svetlana said, delighted. "Ilya Rozanov, are you in *love*?"

Ilya couldn't stop the smile that crept across his face. "Extremely."

The server came back then, so Ilya and Svetlana both hastily looked at the menu and ordered. Ilya wasn't entirely sure what he'd chosen, but it had scallops, so it couldn't be terrible.

"Anyway," Ilya said casually, after the server had left, "how's your father doing?"

"Fuck you, Rozanov," Svetlana said. "As if we're not still talking about you falling in love with a man."

"Is it that interesting?"

"Who is he?"

Ilya glanced sideways. "You don't know him."

"Of course not. I've never been to Ottawa. What's his name?"

Okay. There was no dodging this question. Not unless Ilya wanted to lie, which he didn't. What was the point, really? They were going to tell everyone soon enough, and Svetlana was a friend. She may be shocked by what he was about to tell her, but Ilya didn't think she'd go to the tabloids or anything.

"His name," Ilya said calmly, "is Shane."

"Not Russian, then. Too bad. What does Shane do?"

Ilya somehow managed to keep himself from laughing. "He's an athlete."

Svetlana narrowed her eyes. "Which sport?"

Ilya rolled the stem of his martini glass between his thumb and forefinger. "Hockey."

Svetlana huffed. "I don't understand. Unless you're in love with Shane Hollander, I can't think of any—" She stopped, and then she lunged forward, practically resting her whole torso on the table. "Is it Shane Hollander?" she hissed.

"I'm afraid so. Yes."

"Can I bring you another drink?" asked the server, who'd suddenly reappeared.

Svetlana seemed to realize she was basically lying on the

table, and slid back into her chair with as much grace as possible. "We'll need several bottles of wine, I think."

Ilya grinned. "Let's start with one."

Three hours later, Ilya and Svetlana were waiting arm in arm outside the restaurant for their separate cabs to arrive.

"I really am disappointed we aren't going to have sex," Svetlana sighed. She was slumped against him, head resting on his shoulder. They'd both had a lot to drink.

Ilya chuckled. "You can't convince me that you're hard up for sex."

"I'm not," she agreed. "But men are so boring. Why are you all so boring?"

"I thought I was exciting."

"You *were*. Now you're going to marry a Canadian. Boring."

"I don't know how many people would describe my secret relationship with my rival boring."

She laughed. "I don't suppose you have a cigarette."

"I quit."

"Of course you did. Boring."

A car pulled up. "This one is yours," Ilya said, and stepped forward to open the door for her.

She placed a hand on his shoulder, and stood face-to-face with him. "I'm glad we got to catch up. I've really missed you, and I want to be friends, even without fucking."

"I would love that. Come to Ottawa sometime. Meet Shane."

She smiled. "I will. Until then, text me. Keep in touch."

"I promise."

She kissed his cheek, and got into the car. Ilya smiled to himself, feeling like he'd gained back a piece of himself, as he waited for his own car.

# CHAPTER THIRTY

Shane hadn't been expecting to see Ilya the night of Ottawa's Pride game, but he wasn't surprised to find him on his doorstep after midnight.

"Come here," Shane said, arms open. Ilya collapsed into them.

Shane pulled him inside and closed the door. For a long while, he just held him in the dark, rubbing his back while Ilya breathed against him.

Shane had watched the game. It had been amazing, seeing the support from the fans for Troy Barrett. All the banners celebrating his decision to come out. Shane had watched the coming out video Troy had posted to his Instagram too. He'd even teared up a bit, watching it.

He knew Ilya was happy for Troy too. He'd seen how emotional Ilya had been during the long standing ovation Troy had gotten before the game had started. It had been a huge day for hockey.

But Shane also understood why Ilya needed to be held right now.

"Are you okay?" Shane asked quietly.

"No," Ilya said, his voice muffled by Shane's shoulder. "I am crashing, I think."

"I get it."

"It was a wonderful night. I should be happy."

"It's okay to feel weird about it. I do."

"Yes?"

"Yeah. Like when Scott Hunter kissed Kip on TV. It was amazing, but also . . . fuck, right?"

Ilya laughed. "Yes. Exactly that."

All Shane wanted to do was take care of Ilya, however he could. Ilya always knew exactly what to do when Shane was a mess. "What do you need?"

"Need you," Ilya said simply. "Just . . . need to stop thinking."

Shane stepped back, but squeezed Ilya's hand. "Come upstairs. I've got some ideas for how to distract you."

Ilya smiled and removed his coat, stuffing his toque into one of the pockets, and hung it up. He was still wearing the suit he'd left the arena in, including the dress shoes he was now sliding his feet out of.

"Did you drive here straight from the arena?" Shane asked as they walked upstairs together.

"Yes."

Shane reached a hand behind him, and Ilya took it.

"You know I showered after the game, yes?" Ilya said with a gentle, teasing smile when Shane led him to the bathroom and its giant rainfall shower.

"This shower will be better."

Shane turned on the water and let the room fill with steam as they both undressed in the bedroom. It took longer than it needed to because they kept pausing to make out a bit.

"Come on," Shane said softly. "Shower."

Ilya always looked spectacular when he was naked and wet. Shane had no idea how his teammates were able to shower with him without losing their shit. Shane certainly hadn't been able to, all those years ago.

"Is this shampoo new?" Ilya asked as Shane washed his hair. Ilya had to bend forward slightly so Shane could reach.

"Yeah. You like it?"

"Smells nice. Like the ocean."

"It has seaweed or something in it."

"Even your hair is healthy."

"Shut up. Rinse."

Ilya obediently tipped his head back and rinsed his hair. The suds trailed down his body, dipping into the curves of his pecs and abs, and over and around his muscular shoulders. His cock was mostly soft, and Shane hoped to seize the opportunity that had been presented to him.

"Can I suck you?" he asked. "Wanna feel you get hard in my mouth."

Ilya's expression melted into pure desire. "You should hurry."

Shane sank to his knees, running his hands over Ilya's solid body. He mouthed gently at Ilya's soft dick before taking it fully in his mouth. Ilya hissed and began to stiffen immediately. Shane kept his mouth loose, his tongue barely touching Ilya's hardening flesh, and just enjoyed the sensation of being filled up.

When Ilya was fully hard, Shane pulled off and worshipped his cock with little kitten licks and kisses, then spent some time sucking gently under the head. Ilya murmured sweet nothings in Russian, his fingers tracing lightly along Shane's cheeks and into his wet hair.

"So sweet for me," Ilya murmured, in English.

Shane responded by locking his gaze on Ilya's and sliding his lips down, taking him deep.

He was pretty excellent at sucking dick these days. Like all things he wanted, he'd worked hard at it. He'd studied, practiced, and visualized being able to do this. Being able to take his boyfriend's cock into his throat and feel it grow even harder, nearly choking him. He loved how it felt, but more than that, he loved what it did to Ilya.

"Yes," Ilya sighed quietly, the word almost lost in the sound of rushing water.

Shane slid his hands around to Ilya's ass, gripping into the firm muscle and pulling him closer. His knees were already starting to hurt, but he could endure it. Maybe he should keep a yoga kneepad in the bathroom . . .

"Fuck, Hollander. That fucking mouth. Made for this," Ilya growled above him, breaking Shane's boring train of thought. Shane hummed around him, because yes. He *was* made for this. For anything Ilya needed from him.

He dipped his fingers into the crease of Ilya's ass and inquisitively brushed against his hole. Ilya wasn't always into this, but sometimes he was *really* into it, and Shane had a feeling . . .

"Yes," Ilya said. "Keep going."

Shane pulled back slightly on Ilya's cock so he could focus on doing two things at once, while also being able to breathe. He sucked the head of Ilya's cock while he traced circles on Ilya's rim with one fingertip. Ilya moaned quietly above him. His eyes were closed and he looked like he might fall over, swaying slightly on his feet.

Shane gave his dick a parting kiss, then stood, keeping his teasing finger on his rim. "Why don't we get you in bed, and I'll give you whatever you need?"

Ilya nodded, and Shane turned off the water.

Shane dried Ilya off with a fluffy gray towel, starting with his hair, then his chest and arms and stomach, then down between his legs until he was once again kneeling at Ilya's feet.

Ilya tangled his fingers in Shane's wet hair and tugged slightly. "I need too much from you tonight."

"You can have it. Anything."

A soft sound escaped Ilya's lips, close to a whimper. "Take me apart, Hollander."

Shane dried himself off at lightning speed and followed Ilya to the bed. Ilya was already sprawled out on his stomach, a pillow under his hips, ass raised, making it clear what he needed. After three years of being an exclusive couple, they knew each other's bodies well, and they knew each other's limits. Ilya wasn't interested in bottoming any more than Shane was interested in topping, but sometimes Ilya liked it when Shane gave his ass some attention. Sometimes Ilya just wanted to be taken as far out of himself as he could go, and this seemed to do it for him.

Shane started with his tongue. He kept it light and soft, fluttering his tongue the way he liked himself. Ilya groaned and seemed to sink deeper into the mattress.

They didn't talk. Shane kept his mouth busy and Ilya, he hoped, was too out of his head to form words. Shane soaked up his moans and gasps and sighs as he increased the pressure of his tongue. Ilya was so tight, but Shane was finally, after several minutes, able to poke the tip of his tongue inside.

"Oh," Ilya gasped.

Shane should offer to do this more often. Ilya rarely asked for it, but maybe Shane had been missing times where Ilya had *wanted* to ask for it.

Shane pulled back and admired his work so far. He suspected Ilya was ready for something deeper. "You want fingers?"

"Mmff."

Shane laughed. "Gonna need an actual word."

"Da. Yes. Fucking come on."

Shane fetched a bottle of lube, then paused as he stared into the nightstand drawer. "You want to try a toy maybe?" Ilya hadn't been a fan of the dildo Shane had tried on him once, two years ago, but they had smaller things now. Little vibrating prostate massagers and plugs.

"No," Ilya said. "Just want you."

Shane dropped a kiss on Ilya's temple. "Okay." He drizzled lube on his fingers. "Um. So, do you want . . ."

"Fingers, Hollander. Put your fingers in me. And fucking relax."

Shane scoffed. "You're the one who needs to relax here."

"You are the one who is taking forever."

"I liked it better when you couldn't talk."

"Then make me forget how to."

Shane playfully bit Ilya's ass cheek, then pressed a slick finger against Ilya's hole. He worked him slowly, carefully, until he could slip inside without much resistance, up to the second knuckle. He searched around until he found the spot that made Ilya's whole body jolt.

"Holy fuck," Ilya panted. "I always forget."

Shane smiled and started a rhythm. After a few minutes, Ilya was a trembling mess.

"Good, right?" Shane said softly. "Like waves. I love riding this feeling."

"It is . . . a lot."

"Yeah. Like you're gonna come but not exactly. It feels so fucking good."

"You come like this, sometimes."

"I do," Shane agreed. "And it's fucking amazing."

Ilya whimpered.

"You wanna try?" Shane asked.

"I . . . Yes. Fuck. Feels like it will kill me. Rip me in half."

"It won't. Let it happen."

Shane knew Ilya was humping the pillow a bit, which was

technically cheating, but it still took a surprisingly short amount of time before Ilya said, "Don't stop. Oh fuck. Shane," then clenched hard around Shane's finger. His body rocked as he moaned and cursed, then finally stilled.

Shane extracted his finger and kissed Ilya's spine while he waited for him to come down. Finally, Ilya said, "I hope you did not like that pillow."

Shane laughed. "That bad, huh?"

"My whole body just shot out of my dick."

"Do we count that as a lower-body injury?"

Ilya rolled to his back and grinned up at Shane. "Come here so I can jerk you off."

Shane knee-walked until he was straddling Ilya's waist. "I can do it. Your limbs are all noodly."

Ilya folded his hands behind his head. "My favorite show."

Shane smiled and poured more lube into his palm, then got to work. Less than a minute later, he was on the brink of orgasm. "Sorry," he gritted out. "I can't—"

"Is okay," Ilya said. "Come on."

Shane stopped trying to fight it, and let his orgasm slam into him, spilling all over Ilya's chest. Then, Shane collapsed forward and kissed him messily. "Love you," he murmured against Ilya's lips. "So much."

Later, after they'd cleaned up and Shane had put the unfortunate pillow in the laundry for tomorrow, they cuddled up together in bed. It was late and they were both struggling to stay awake.

"Did I tell you," Ilya said, "that Bood and Cassie had their baby?"

"No."

"They had a boy," Ilya said. "Milo."

"Nice name."

"Mm. I saw him. Very cute."

Shane fiddled with the ring on Ilya's chain. "What would you name your son?"

"Roger Crowell."

Shane cracked up. "He'd love that."

"Roger Crowell Rozanov."

"Stop."

"Or . . ." Ilya rolled on top of him, grinning. "Roger Crowell Rozanov-Hollander."

"God, that's a mouthful," Shane said as his heart melted into goo. "Hollander-Rozanov is alphabetical, though, so . . ."

"Sounds worse."

"Maybe we could combine our names. Hollanov. Rozander."

"Roger Rozander. Terrible name."

"We're not naming our kid Roger, you sack of shit!"

They both laughed, and then kissed until exhaustion made their mouths sloppy and slow. Ilya fell asleep first, and Shane listened to his steady breathing as his own body fizzed with happiness.

# CHAPTER THIRTY-ONE

*March*

Ilya was, of course, happy to see all the support Troy got during the week following the Pride Night game. He was sure there was plenty of the other side being vocal online, but those people were getting drowned out, and they didn't matter anyway. It made Ilya hopeful that things might be okay when he and Shane announced their relationship.

He was only a little jealous when he saw how much lighter Troy seemed. How easily he smiled now. How openly Troy and Harris were affectionate with each other, knowing they didn't need to hide. Knowing they had the support of the team. Ilya imagined it felt wonderful.

When they were on the ice, waiting for practice to start, Troy approached Ilya. "Hey."

Ilya nodded at him. "Barrett."

Troy snatched a puck that was against the boards and began moving it around with his stick blade. "So, I want to, um, thank you."

"For what?"

"Giving me the push I needed, I guess. Being . . . supportive."

Ilya stole the puck from him. "It is called being a friend."

"Yeah, well. Not in my experience."

Ilya passed the puck back to him. "How has it been? Being out?"

Troy smiled. "Amazing."

There was a twist of jealousy in Ilya's chest, but he ignored it. "Good."

"And also, Harris was wondering if you . . ." His voice dipped to a nearly inaudible mumble.

"What?"

Troy sighed and straightened his shoulders. "Harris wants you to come to dinner at his family's farm this Sunday. As a thank-you."

This was completely unnecessary, and possibly more than Ilya could deal with right now, emotionally. He was ready to politely decline, but something occurred to him. "Will Chiron be there?"

Troy's lips curved up a bit. "Yeah. And a bunch of other dogs."

Well. Ilya could probably make time for a bit of dinner.

"Aah! Harris, who is this good boy? He is even bigger than Chiron!" Ilya was crouching in the driveway in front of the Drover family farmhouse with an enormous brown dog's paws on his shoulders.

"That's Mac," Harris said. "He's trouble."

Ilya rubbed Mac's face with both hands. "He is not trouble. He is very good."

Ilya had been to Harris's family's apple farm once before, but not to the house. He'd gone to the grand opening of Harris's sisters' cidery, which was also on the property. That had been nice, but the farmhouse looked fucking adorable.

And there were *so many dogs*.

"Why do I have a house?" Ilya joked as a second, smaller dog bumped its nose on his thigh, looking for attention. "I could live in a tent here and be so happy."

"You should come inside," Troy called from the front porch. "It's freezing out here."

"I have not met everyone yet," Ilya argued as he twisted around to greet a third dog. "Who is this one?"

"Not sure yet," Harris said. "She just got here."

The unnamed dog was medium-sized with long hair that was a mix of brown and white and gray. She had floppy ears, big brown eyes, and the sweetest face Ilya had ever seen.

"You are new!" Ilya said to her as he scratched her soft ears. "You will love this farm."

"She was found by one of our neighbors," Harris said. "People tend to bring strays here because my parents are good with them. Mom took her down the road to see Linda to get her checked out."

"Linda is a vet," Troy supplied.

The dog licked Ilya's fingers, making him laugh. "Not shy at all, are you?"

"She's in good shape," Harris said, "considering she was alone outside in the cold. Linda thinks she was found pretty quickly, thank god. She's super friendly—the dog, I mean. Shannon's been taking good care of her."

"Shannon's that dog," Troy said, pointing to the smallest dog there.

"No one owns her?" Ilya asked as he stood up. The unnamed dog squeezed between his legs.

"Not that we've been able to find. We know everyone around for miles." Harris's face turned angrier than Ilya had ever seen it. "Sometimes people drive dogs they don't want out to the country, though."

"And *leave* them?" Ilya asked, horrified. He'd grown up in Moscow and had seen plenty of stray dogs, but the idea of someone abandoning a dog that loved them—a part of their family and their home—was monstrous.

Harris nodded. "Yeah. It's gross."

"It's fucking horrible," Troy said.

Ilya headed toward the front door with five dogs all around him. Chiron walked in front, but kept turning to make sure Ilya was following. The new dog stayed close to Ilya's ankles.

The house smelled amazing, and it was just as charming as Ilya had imagined. Packed with family history and people laughing and, yes, dogs.

"I think most people are in the living room," Harris said, leading the way.

"Buckle up," Troy muttered, "it gets loud in here."

There were five people sitting in the living room. Harris went around the room, reintroducing Ilya to his two sisters and their husbands. When he got to his mom, Ilya interrupted him.

"How could I forget?" he asked silkily. "The best dance partner I have ever had."

"Oh, stop it," Mrs. Drover said. She was a short woman with gray hair that was cut into a stylish bob. He'd enjoyed a dance with her at a team charity event last year, which had thrilled Harris. Like her son, she was funny and easy to talk to.

"Is true," Ilya insisted. "No one else has come close. Are you still with your husband?"

"I'm afraid so," said a booming male voice behind Ilya. He turned and saw Harris's dad grinning in the doorway.

Ilya sighed theatrically. "Too bad."

Harris's sister, Margot, stood to offer Ilya her armchair, but Ilya waved her off and sat cross-legged on the floor. "Are you sure?" Margot asked.

Ilya already had three dogs trying to climb into his lap. "Yes," he said. "All of my friends are down here."

Eventually they all moved to the dining room, where they crowded around a table and ate an incredible meal that included baked ham, scalloped potatoes, and, to Ilya's delight, fresh-baked rolls.

"Dad made those," Harris said. "They'll go fast."

For dessert there was chocolate cake. "This is so good," Ilya exclaimed after his first bite. "Who made this cake?"

"Troy did!" Harris said proudly.

"With a *lot* of help," Troy added quickly. "I've never baked a cake before. Or anything, really."

"You bake together!" Ilya said, grinning. "That is very cute."

Troy dipped his head, but Ilya could tell he was blushing.

After dinner, Troy asked Ilya if he wanted to go outside with him. Ilya understood that he was looking for privacy, so he nodded and grabbed his coat and hat.

As soon as they were on the front porch, Troy blew out a breath that floated into the frigid darkness as a white puff. "I love that family, but man."

Ilya laughed. "Is a lot of talking. Like a whole pile of Harrises." He paused. "You would probably like to be in a pile of Harrises."

Troy nudged him with his elbow. "Shut up." He gripped the railing at the front of the porch and gazed up at the night sky. There were already a zillion stars visible. "You know something? This has been the best week of my life."

"Good to hear."

"I never thought—" Troy shook his head. "I just didn't think I could have this, y'know? Have all of it. Being openly gay. Playing hockey. Being with someone as great as Harris. I feel, like, a million pounds lighter."

Ilya suspected he knew why Troy was telling him this. "You think I should do the same."

"I'm not going to tell you what to do, but yeah. I think you should."

Troy didn't know the whole truth, though. He was right, that Ilya coming out as bisexual wouldn't be such a big deal. Not in a bad way, anyway. But that wasn't the biggest secret Ilya was hiding.

"I've gotten so many messages, or whatever," Troy said. "People online replying to my posts. Telling me how much it means to them that I came out. I don't read them, really, but Harris tells me about them. It's nice."

"That part is very good," Ilya agreed.

"I understand hiding, but if I knew how good it felt to be out, I may have done it sooner." He turned to face Ilya. "So that's why I'm telling you. So you know."

Ilya looked at him seriously. "It is not only my secret to tell."

Troy's brow furrowed. Then his eyes widened. "Oh. Oh! You're with someone."

"Yes."

"Who's also closeted?"

"Sort of. Yes."

"Is it . . . is it who we talked about before? In New York?"

Troy had almost guessed that Ilya was dating Shane, back in New York in December when Ilya had come out to him. It had confirmed Ilya's suspicion that anyone who learned Ilya was bisexual would figure out pretty quickly that Shane was his boyfriend.

Ilya didn't say anything now, just like he hadn't said anything in New York. He wanted to tell Troy that Shane would be his husband soon. He could, probably. Maybe. Except Ilya still couldn't quite believe it was actually going to happen.

"It's none of my business," Troy said, breaking the heavy silence. "But, um, if it was someone like that, I can see how that would be . . . complicated. Yeah."

Ilya turned his attention back to the sky, and changed the subject. "Look. The Big Dipper, yes?"

The door opened behind them and Harris stepped out. Chiron, Mac, and the new dog followed him onto the porch. The new dog immediately went to Ilya, sniffing his sneakers.

"She likes you," Harris said.

Ilya bent and gave her some pats. "I am hard to resist." She really was cute. And soft. And she seemed like she'd be a good listener.

"So," Harris said slowly, "we're going to have to find her a new home, probably." He and Troy shared a *look*, and Harris added, "We love dogs here, but we don't have room for one more at the moment."

Ilya narrowed his eyes. "Harris. Are you trying to set me up? Is this a blind date with a dog?"

Harris smiled. "I have no idea what you're talking about, pal. This is just a friendly dinner with a sweet dog who needs someone to love her and give her a big, fancy house to explore."

Ilya glanced down at the sweet dog in question, who was gazing at him with her tongue lolling out of her mouth. Could he? There had to be a way to make this work. There were dog daycares, right? Ilya had no idea if they were any good, but he could look into it.

"How do I do it?" he asked. "I have not ever had a dog."

"Good thing you're friends with me, then," Harris said cheerfully. "I'm an expert. And we can keep her here at the farm for a bit until you're ready to bring her home."

The dog put her front paws on Ilya's shin, her mouth stretched in a smile as if she knew what Ilya was thinking.

"Anya," Ilya said, smiling back at her. "I think her name is Anya."

* * *

Shane had no idea what to expect when he pulled into Ilya's driveway nearly two weeks after he'd last seen him. Ilya had said he had a surprise for him, and the level of excitement in his voice suggested it was a big one. If they weren't already engaged, Shane would have thought he might be about to be proposed to.

Ilya's front door opened as Shane approached. Ilya stood there wearing sweatpants, a loose T-shirt, and an enormous smile.

"What's the big surprise?" Shane asked.

Then he heard a curious bark behind Ilya. A second later, a smallish fluffy dog trotted out between Ilya's legs.

"Who's is this?" Shane asked, eying the dog warily. He wasn't great with animals. "You dog-sitting for someone?"

"No," Ilya said, then bent to scoop the dog up in his arms. He cuddled her close to his chest, and the dog licked his cheek lovingly. "This is Anya. She is my dog."

"You—what? How?"

"Someone abandoned her. In the cold. Monsters," Ilya growled. Then he kissed the top of Anya's head. "She needed a home. I needed a dog."

There was a list of reasons as long as the Rideau Canal why this was not the best time in Ilya's life to become a dog owner. Shane was about to start listing them, but Ilya's mouth was stretched wide in one of his rare unguarded smiles, and it made all the reasons float away.

Shane reached out a tentative hand and stroked one of Anya's ears. "Man. She's so soft."

"She just had a bath," Ilya said. "I took her to the dog spa. Full treatment."

Shane smiled. "She's going to be so spoiled."

"Oh yes. Terrible. Come see all her toys I bought."

It was not a small amount of toys. As soon as Shane reached

Ilya's living room he spotted at least a dozen brightly colored things on the floor, and on the couch, and there was what looked like a chunk of rope on the coffee table. There was also a luxurious dog bed near the fireplace.

"So, um," Shane said. "When did you get Anya?"

"Yesterday."

Shane laughed. "Glad you didn't go overboard shopping for her or anything."

"The dog spa sells toys."

Ilya set Anya on the floor, and she immediately ran over to a stuffed seal and began chomping on it happily. Shane didn't know much about pets, but he would have expected a dog that had been abandoned to be more timid and rough-looking. Shane hugged Ilya from behind. "I love you, but I have to ask this: Are you sure you didn't steal someone else's dog?"

"No! Listen." Ilya told Shane about how Anya had been found out in the country, and how Harris's family had looked after her. They'd continued to look after her after Ilya decided, more or less immediately, to adopt her, until he had enough downtime to properly get her used to his house.

They spent the rest of the morning playing with Anya on the living room floor. She was tireless, joyfully chasing after anything they tossed and proudly returning it to them. When they took breaks, she would wiggle her way into one of their laps for pets, completely shameless and adorable. Shane realized he was more into dogs than he'd thought. They took her for a walk, which meant strolling around Ilya's neighborhood together, but that was okay. Shane smiled at the little red boots Ilya put on Anya's feet.

"Is to protect from the salt," Ilya explained. "And keeps her little paws warm. At the spa they said she does not need a sweater because her hair is long. Too bad because there was a sweater that looked like a strawberry and was so cute."

"They didn't have one in your size?" Shane teased.

They walked beside each other on salt-crusted sidewalks. Shane itched to hold Ilya's hand, so he kept his own hands stuffed firmly in his coat pockets. Soon, he reminded himself. Soon they'd be . . . well, a family, he supposed. Now that Anya was in the picture.

"So," Shane asked carefully, "when you're on the road . . ."

"There is a place that can take her," Ilya said. "Like a hotel for dogs."

"A kennel?"

"A *hotel for dogs*. I have already talked to them, booked time. I went a few days ago to tour it. Very nice. She will be okay there."

That seemed like an easy enough solution. Although Shane suspected Ilya would worry about Anya whenever they were apart. "Does the hotel have a live camera so you can watch her?"

"Of course it does," Ilya said.

"You know you can't use the coaches' iPads to check on her during games, right?"

Ilya was silent a few seconds too long, then said, "I know."

They didn't have sex that night because when Shane had tried to get things started, Anya had started whimpering outside Ilya's bedroom door.

Shane paused in the middle of the trail he was kissing up Ilya's inner thigh. "Go get her," he said, smiling and sighing at the same time.

Ilya bolted out of bed and opened the door. "Anya, sweet girl. What is wrong? Are you lonely?" He picked her up and carried her to the bed.

Shane was sure this was setting a bad precedent, but Ilya was lying on his back with Anya's head resting on his bicep and it was really hard to care about rules.

Shane lay on his side, perpendicular to Ilya, and rested his head on Ilya's stomach. He joined Ilya in petting Anya, enjoying the soothing feel of soft fur and warm dog under his fingers. He put a hand on her back and felt the soft rise and fall of her tiny body as she breathed.

The room was quiet, and so full of love it was almost suffocating. And if someone had told Shane that morning he'd rather pet a dog until she fell asleep than have sex with his boyfriend, he never would have believed them. But life was full of surprises.

"I think she's asleep," Shane whispered.

The only response from Ilya was a sigh that sounded a bit like a snore. Shane raised his head, and smiled at his sleeping boyfriend, who looked happier and more at peace than Shane had seen him in months.

# CHAPTER THIRTY-TWO

Ilya was relieved to learn that Anya enjoyed car rides. He was nervous, when, about a week after adopting her, he drove with her for the first time to Montreal.

"Did the stuff arrive that I ordered?" Ilya asked Shane over the phone as he drove. "The bed, and the—"

"The one million dog toys? Yeah, they arrived."

"Was not one million. Did you set the bed up? Maybe near the fireplace?"

"Yes, it's all set up. Don't worry. And listen, I may have mentioned that you got a dog in front of Jade and Ruby, and now the Pikes want us to visit."

"Today?"

"Yeah. Maybe this afternoon?"

Ilya hadn't seen Hayden's kids since they'd officiated his and Shane's "wedding."

"Yes, okay. But if Anya is freaked out, we will leave."

"If anything freaks Anya out, it's going to be this weird creepy-faced stuffed banana toy you bought her."

Ilya heard the squeak of a toy being squeezed over the phone.

"Do not wear out the toys before Anya gets to play with them, Hollander."

Shane laughed and squeaked the toy twice more. "Better hurry, then."

"Aw, man. Now they're *really* gonna start asking for a dog," Hayden lamented.

Ilya, Shane, and Hayden were standing together in Hayden's living room, watching the four kids and Jackie play with Anya. Ilya had been worried about the number of new people, especially kids, but Anya had made fast friends with everyone.

"Get one," Ilya said. "You would not even notice, with all these kids."

"I'd notice," Hayden sighed. "And Jackie would *definitely* notice having someone else to look after while I'm on the road."

"Anya stays at a hotel for dogs when Ilya's away," Shane said.

"Like a kennel?"

"No," Ilya said irritably. "Is a *hotel*."

"He takes her to a spa," Shane said.

Hayden laughed. "Jesus, I'm jealous of this dog."

Ilya folded his arms. "So is Shane, I think."

Shane bumped lightly against him.

"Oh shit," Hayden said, looking at his phone. "I forgot about a thing I have to—um. Be right back."

"FanMail emergency?" Ilya asked with a teasing smile.

Hayden glared at him. "It's not an *emergency*. I just promised a twenty-four hour turnaround. Twenty-three and a half hours ago."

"Are you going to wear that shirt? There is sauce on it."

Hayden glanced down. "Shit. That's from breakfast. Thanks." He darted away.

"Who needs a message from Hayden in such a hurry?" Ilya wondered aloud.

"You'd be surprised," Jackie said. "He gets so many requests! Between us, though, I think it's because he's the only Montreal Voyageur on FanMail."

Ilya laughed. "You should join, Shane. Give him competition."

"Absolutely not."

"Mom?" asked Arthur in a quiet, trembling voice. "Where's Chompy?"

Jackie's brow furrowed. "Oh no . . . wait! He's in the car, I'll bet. Let me go—"

"No," Ilya said. "I will get him. Where are the keys?"

Jackie gave him a grateful smile. "Hanging by the door in the mudroom, that way. Chompy's in the Mercedes, I think. Back seat."

"Will you come with me?" Ilya asked Shane. "I do not want to hunt an alligator alone."

Shane rolled his eyes. "Sure."

Of course, Ilya was only trying to steal a moment alone with Shane. They stepped outside, through a secluded side door that led to a concrete path that wrapped around to the front of the house. A row of thick trees ran along the edge of the yard, blocking the view from any neighboring houses.

Perfect.

Ilya turned to stand in front of Shane and placed a hand on his waist.

"I assume you have an ulterior motive for inviting me on this adventure," Shane said. He gazed up at Ilya flirtatiously through his lashes, and Ilya made a silent promise to figure out a way to have sex with his boyfriend tonight. Anya was just going to have to deal.

"Maybe," Ilya said.

Shane smiled, then leaned in and kissed him. It was so soft

and sweet and warm despite the air around them being so cold. Ilya sighed happily and deepened the kiss, sinking his fingers into Shane's hair, dipping him back slightly.

"Wow," Shane said breathlessly when they broke apart. "That was a good one."

His cheeks were pink and his eyes were as bright as his smile. Ilya helplessly kissed him again. Shane laughed against his mouth, then stepped back. "Later, okay? Any more of that and I won't be able to go back inside."

"Yes, okay." Ilya's voice was shaky. He took a steadying breath and said, "We have a job to do now."

"Mm. Operation: Chompy."

Ilya gave him a lazy salute and turned toward the driveway.

Shane had a list of ways he wanted to spend the morning before Ilya had to drive back to Ottawa. They could stay in bed for most of it, or maybe take Anya to a park. Maybe work out together. Maybe all of that.

None of his plans involved his doorbell ringing at nine in the morning.

He immediately stopped kissing Ilya and shot him a quizzical look. "Did you order more dog toys?"

"No."

Anya was barking, and then the doorbell rang a second time. Shane sighed and rolled off of Ilya. "I'd better see who it is."

He pulled on some pajama pants and a T-shirt and jogged downstairs, Anya at his heels. He was surprised to find Hayden when he opened to door.

"Hi?" Shane said. Then he noticed how ashen Hayden's face looked. "What happened? Is everyone all right? Come in."

Shane carried Anya into the living room, and Hayden followed close behind. Ilya was standing at the top of the stairs, wearing only sweatpants. "Hayden?" he said.

"Sorry to show up like this, but um . . . can we sit, maybe?"

Shane sat immediately on the couch. "What's going on?"

A moment later, Ilya sat beside him. Hayden sat in an armchair opposite.

"Have you guys been online at all today?" Hayden asked. "I'm guessing not."

"No," Shane said. "Why?"

Hayden blew out a breath and scratched the back of his neck. "Okay. So, um, you know how I did that FanMail video yesterday?"

"Yes," Shane said impatiently. This was sounding less important by the second.

"The thing is. I was in a room that I kind of use as, like, a trophy room. Nice room. Big windows, lots of shelves, mirrors. Really looks good in the videos."

"Very interesting," Ilya said flatly.

"So the windows look out to the side of the house with the trees. And I wasn't standing in front of the windows, because that always looks a little weird to be backlit like that . . ."

"Hayden," Ilya said with a hint of warning. "What happened?"

"I was standing next to the trophy wall with the big mirror and the angle was, like, you could see out the window, in the mirror. I didn't notice when I was filming, or, um, after I sent the video. But in the mirror you can see . . ."

Shane's stomach plummeted. "What can you see?" he asked faintly, already knowing the answer.

Hayden scrubbed his face with one hand. "You guys. Kissing. Like, *really* kissing. A lot."

Shane swallowed with difficulty. "Is it obvious? That it's us?"

Hayden nodded. "Very."

Fuck. *Fuck*. There had to be a way to fix this. "You only sent this video to one person, right?"

"Yep," Hayden said. "And that one person posted it on Twitter."

Shane couldn't breathe. He couldn't swallow. He was going to die from choking on his own saliva.

"I'm so sorry, Shane," Hayden said. "I don't really watch the videos before I send them. I never would have sent it if I saw, but I really fucked up."

Shane couldn't react. He didn't know *how* to react. Eleven years of keeping this a secret and *this* was how they got discovered. A fucking FanMail video.

Jesus, was Ilya going to punch Hayden? Ilya was being oddly silent, but there was no way he wasn't furious. Shane wanted to pre-emptively defend his friend, but he couldn't. He was choking on rage and fear and humiliation, and trying to remember how to swallow.

They'd been so close to telling the world on their own terms. A few months. *Fuck.*

"Please say something," Hayden said miserably. "I know you hate me. Just say it. I deserve it."

Shane opened his mouth, then closed it. He wanted to say something before Ilya said something worse.

"It is okay," Ilya said quietly.

Hayden looked at him with wide, surprised eyes. "What?"

"It is okay," Ilya said again. "You have been a good friend. Kept our secret for years. This was an accident, and it is our fault for not being more careful."

One of the knots inside Shane's chest loosened. He forced himself to nod. "Ilya's right. Of course we don't hate you." He managed to finally swallow and breathe. "So how bad is it?"

"Bad," Hayden said. "The video is fucking everywhere."

"What are people saying?"

"Mostly, like, 'what the fuck?' or 'holy fucking shit' or 'is this a fucking joke?' That kind of thing."

"Oh god," Shane said, and buried his face in his hands.

Ilya placed a hand on his back. "What are your teammates saying?"

"Mostly the same sort of thing," Hayden sighed. "Practice is gonna be weird this afternoon. No question."

"If I'm even allowed at practice," Shane moaned.

"There are definitely people on the internet who think you shouldn't be," Hayden said. "But, y'know. Fuck 'em."

"I don't ever want to look at my phone again," Shane said to his hands. "I'm going to throw it in the river."

"We should call Farah," Ilya said wisely. "She can help."

"Right. Yes. This is definitely a job for our agent." Shane dropped his hands to his lap. "God, this sucks."

"Yes, but it is not so different," Ilya said calmly. "We were going to tell people ourselves, but now we do not have to."

"Because they saw us *kissing on the internet*."

"At least they know we are great at kissing."

"It *was* a pretty top-tier kiss," Hayden agreed.

Shane refused to acknowledge that. "The playoffs start in two weeks. This is such bad timing."

"Especially since it's looking like our teams will meet in the first round," Hayden added. Then he hunched his shoulders and said, "Sorry. Not helping."

Shane stood and started pacing. "Fuuuuuuck," he said, and kicked a dog toy that hit the wall with a squeak. Anya stared at him in what looked like admonishment, like Shane had no right to take out his frustration on innocent dog toys.

"Jesus Christ, what are we going to do? Fuck, what does J.J. think? Oh god."

"Yeah, you're gonna have to talk to him," Hayden said. "He's, um, not into it."

Shane met Ilya's gaze for a moment, and saw concern there.

"He'll come around," Shane said, mostly trying to convince

himself. "It's a shock. I get it. I don't expect everyone to understand, but J.J.'s one of my best friends."

Hayden stood, then bent to scratch Anya's ears. "He's not too happy with me either right now. I think his feelings might be hurt for being left out, y'know?"

Shit. Shane should have told him sooner. "Well. That's on me. I'll talk to him."

Hayden left a few minutes later, but not before Shane gave him a reassuring hug. Hayden *had* done a good job keeping their secret. He didn't deserve to feel shitty about this.

When Shane went back to the living room, he found Ilya staring at his phone with one hand over his mouth.

"Are you watching the video?" Shane asked.

Ilya nodded.

"Is it bad?"

"Terrible. Hayden needs to write down what he is going to say in these videos. He is all over the place."

Shane dropped on the couch beside Ilya. Anya hopped into Shane's lap, and he held her there, stroking her back and trying not to look at the video.

"There we are," Ilya said. He was quiet a moment and then said, "Oh yes. This would be hard to deny." He huffed. "We are really going for it."

"This is a fucking nightmare," Shane said faintly.

The couch began to shake, and Shane realized that Ilya was laughing. "It's *not* funny."

"Is very funny!" Ilya squeaked out. "Hayden's stupid Fan-Mail video. Oh my god. This was somebody's birthday greeting. Someone named Brad."

"Sorry, Brad," Shane mumbled.

That made Ilya absolutely lose it. He fell over on the couch, howling with laughter. Anya whimpered with concern.

"Stop laughing!" Shane said, but now he was laughing too.

Anya leaped to the floor and starting pacing back and forth in front of the coffee table while Shane fell on top of Ilya and laughed until his body ached with it.

"We are so fucked," Shane sighed when he'd finally calmed down. "How many messages are on your phone?"

"A lot. We should call Farah now."

Shane nodded slowly. "Probably. Okay. Yeah. Call her."

Ilya tapped his phone, then set it on the coffee table on speaker mode. Both men crouched forward, waiting for her to answer.

"Ilya. God. How are you holding up?" Farah said as soon as she did.

"Oh. You know."

"Is Shane with you?"

"Yes," Ilya said.

"Hi. Hello," Shane said.

"I'm so sorry this happened. You guys must be devastated."

"I think I'm more . . . dazed?" Shane said. "I don't know. It doesn't feel real."

"I wish it wasn't, but I'm here to help."

"What do you think the league is going to do?" Shane asked.

"Legally, I'm not sure they can do much. But Crowell will try to do something, that's for sure."

Shane's stomach cramped. Ilya huffed angrily beside him.

"If he does, he'll be hearing from me," Farah continued. "If that's what you want."

Shane wasn't sure. The one thing he knew is that he wanted to keep playing in the NHL, and Crowell had the ability to make that difficult, or at least uncomfortable. Shane was pretty sure Crowell couldn't actually kick him or Ilya out, though.

He glanced at Ilya, who only shrugged. "Hopefully it won't come to that," Shane said, though he doubted they'd be so lucky.

"What should we do next?" Ilya asked.

"First," Farah said, "I'm going to write an official statement. Unless you want to write it yourselves."

"Nope," Shane said at the same time Ilya said, "No way."

"I figured. I'll get that written and send it to both of you when I'm done. I think we should post it as soon as possible."

"Okay," Shane said, "but I want to wait until after practice this afternoon at least. I need to talk to my team."

"That's reasonable. But we should release it tomorrow at the latest, probably."

"All right. Yeah."

"What about your team, Ilya?" Farah asked. "Have you spoken to anyone there?"

"Not yet. But I think it will be okay."

"I think so too. But I'm sorry this happened," Farah said. "It's awful. Hayden must feel terrible."

"He does," Shane said, "but we talked to him. It's not his fault."

"Good. Okay, let me get cracking on this statement. I know things are bleak right now, but it will die down. We'll steer things back your way, I promise."

Shane stared at the phone for a while after the call ended, still numb. Ilya rubbed his shoulder.

"Farah will help," Ilya assured him.

"I'm worried she can't."

"I know." Ilya sighed. "I have to go back to Ottawa now. Our plane leaves in a few hours."

"Right. Shit."

"I am sorry to leave you now. Will you be okay?"

"I mean, no. I'll be a fucking mess." He blew out a breath. "I need to try to talk to J.J. before practice."

"Do you think your team will be okay?"

"I have no idea. Probably not at first. I don't think Coach

is going to be okay with it. Or management. Or, like, anyone." Shane sighed. "I'll find out this afternoon, I guess."

Ilya took his hand and brought it to his lips, kissing Shane's knuckles. "One thing at a time."

Shane shifted closer until his face was hovering over Ilya's. "One thing at a time," he agreed. He kissed him, and realized this was it. Ilya was going to leave the safety of Shane's house soon, and walk into chaos. The secret wasn't a secret anymore, and it was time to face whatever was about to happen next. Together.

"Fuck," Ilya said when he spotted the black SUV parked outside the gates at the end of his driveway. He didn't know who owned the vehicle, but he was sure they were here to bother him. Probably an overly ambitious journalist. He didn't need this right now. He needed to pack, get Anya to the dog hotel, and then get to the team plane.

He pressed the remote button that opened his gate and steered into his driveway. When he stepped out of the car, he heard a familiar voice behind him.

"Ilya," Coach Wiebe called out from the end of the driveway. "You got a minute?"

Ilya sighed, nodded, and gestured for his coach to follow him to the house. May as well get this over with.

When they got inside, Anya stood in front of Ilya's legs and barked menacingly at Coach Wiebe. Ilya bent and petted her head. "Is okay, Anya. He is a friend."

Ilya glanced up and locked eyes with his coach, silently asking, *Right?*

Wiebe crouched too and offered Anya his hand to sniff. "Nice to meet you, Anya. I'm just here to talk to your dad." He smiled at Ilya. "She's cute."

"She is the best."

Wiebe stood. "Can we sit, maybe?"

Ilya stood as well. "I can make coffee."

"Now we're talking."

They went to the kitchen, and Ilya used his espresso machine to make them each an Americano. It was faster than brewing a pot. Wiebe waited until they were both sitting at the kitchen table before he got down to business.

"So," he said, with a hint of amusement in his eyes, "I'm guessing your, um, appearance in Pike's video was unintentional."

"Yes."

"Sorry." Wiebe looked genuinely sympathetic. "That's terrible."

Ilya sipped his coffee, not saying anything.

"Is it serious?" Wiebe asked. "You and Hollander?"

"You mean, was it a joke?"

Wiebe shook his head. "No way a kiss like *that* was a joke. No, I mean, are you two an item?"

The ice shelf that Ilya had built up in his chest began to crumble and slide away. "I love him," he said quietly.

There was a long silence. Ilya stared at his coffee and waited.

"And I'd say the feeling is mutual," his coach finally said. "Based on that video, anyway."

Ilya's lips curved up. "It is very much mutual." His tentative smile only lasted a moment. "How bad will this be?"

Wiebe exhaled slowly. "I don't know," he said. "Crowell has ordered that you both be benched for a bit. He wants it *dealt with*, whatever that means."

Jesus. Shane was going to lose his mind.

"I'm sorry," Ilya said, not really meaning it. He wasn't sorry he'd fallen in love with Shane. Wasn't even sorry he'd made the mistake of kissing him when he'd thought no one could see. But he was a bit sorry that Coach Wiebe needed to deal with this. He was a good guy.

"I'm not going to pretend this isn't complicated as hell," Coach said, "but you don't need to apologize to me."

"No?"

"No." Wiebe smiled. His smiles were always warm, with a hint of mischief. "I mean, the timing isn't great. I'm a rookie coach, Roz! Come on!"

"Sorry," Ilya said again.

"The thing is, because I'm a rookie coach—and not particularly popular with Crowell—I don't know how much help I can be. But know that you have my support, whatever happens."

That was . . . more than Ilya had expected from his coach. "Thank you," he said, sincerely.

Wiebe studied him for a long moment, took a sip of coffee, then seemed to reach a decision. "I'm going to share something with you that I've only ever told my wife."

Oh god. "Okay," Ilya said.

"When I was playing my second season, in Detroit, I had a thing with one of my teammates. It doesn't matter who, and I'm not going to tell you, but we got drunk and fooled around one night during a road trip and then we . . . kept doing it a bit. For a few months."

Ilya didn't say a word.

Wiebe grimaced. "I'm not telling this right. The truth was, I'd been half in love with him before we first hooked up—before I'd even thought that was a possibility—and after that first night, I fell the rest of the way. I was nuts about him. But he was . . . he said he didn't feel that way about me."

"He was scared," Ilya said.

"Maybe. Or maybe he truly only wanted a bit of release on the road. We never hooked up at home. But I thought he might have returned the feelings more than he'd let on." Wiebe waved a hand. "Anyway. It all fell apart when I told him I loved him. He, uh, didn't take it well. I ended up being sent down to the

AHL for a while after that, and then he was traded in the summer. Haven't spoken to him since."

Ilya didn't know what to say. He'd been the first one to say "I love you" in his and Shane's relationship. What if Shane hadn't said it back? What if he'd been horrified?

"Sorry that happened to you," Ilya said.

Wiebe just nodded. "Now I look back and I think, maybe he saved me a whole mountain of trouble. If we'd been a real couple, trying to hide, I can imagine how hard that would have been." He gave a small smile. "So that's a long-winded way of saying I have your back. That I understand."

Ilya's lips curved up. "This team is very gay."

Wiebe laughed. "Technically, I'm bisexual. To be clear, I love my wife. I'm not hiding anything."

Ilya's smile grew. "Bisexual! Great. Yes, me too."

"I figured, what with your long and impressive history with the ladies."

"That is over. It has been only Shane for a long time."

"I'm glad you have each other. It's not going to sit right with a lot of people, but I'll be talking to the team about my feelings on it at a meeting before we get on the plane. Like I said, I can't do much, but I'll do what I can." He stood. "Thanks for the coffee. I should get going, but I'm sorry you aren't coming with us."

Ilya stood too. "Me too. Thank you for coming here. It has helped."

Then Wiebe embraced him in a hug, and slapped his back for good measure. "Stay strong, Captain. We'll be needing you in the playoffs."

"Keep winning," Ilya instructed.

Wiebe stepped back, smiling wide. "With this team? Easy."

# CHAPTER THIRTY-THREE

Walking into the Montreal Voyageurs locker room at the practice facility was the hardest thing Shane had ever forced himself to do.

For a long moment, he stood, frozen, just inside the door while everyone in the room—the men he loved like brothers—stared at him with obvious disgust. He felt sick. Or like his heart might explode. The only friendly face in the room was Hayden, whose expression seemed mostly apologetic.

"Hi," Shane tried.

No one made a sound, except J.J., who snorted and turned away.

Shit.

Shane walked to his stall, trying to look normal. Still Shane Hollander. Still the captain of this team. Still the same guy as the last time they'd seen him. He removed his coat and hung it on the hook inside his stall, hoping, optimistically, that he might be able to change into his gear and get on the ice without much fuss.

"Hollander," a voice barked behind him. Shane turned and saw Coach Theriault in the doorway. "Come with me."

Shane kept his head down as he left the room and followed his coach down the hallway to his office. Coach pointed to one of the chairs in front of his desk, and Shane sat.

"Was it a joke?" Coach asked. His voice was cold and serious. Shane knew saying yes right now was the only answer the man would accept.

"No," Shane said.

Coach's jaw clenched. He looked at the ceiling and sucked his teeth, clearly furious.

"How long?" he asked.

Again, Shane knew the only possibly acceptable answer would be "this was the first time."

"Years," Shane said, and didn't elaborate.

Coach inhaled sharply. "Go home. I will talk to management and we'll decide what to do with you."

"Am I . . . benched?"

"Yes, you're fucking benched, Hollander!" Coach roared. "What did you think would happen?"

Shane's whole body went rigid. He wanted to scream back in his coach's face. He also wanted to disappear.

Coach sighed. "This order comes directly from Crowell. You and *Rozanov*." He said the name like it was a particularly vulgar slur. "Until this gets dealt with, you're both sitting."

"Dealt with?"

"And don't even think about posting anything online about this. No statements. You're in enough trouble already."

"But—"

"Go home," Coach said again.

Realizing that arguing would be pointless right now, Shane left quickly. He considered leaving his coat in the locker room, but it had his car keys in the pocket.

Everyone stared at him when he walked back into the locker room. No one even tried to hide it.

Shane spread his arms wide. "Okay. Now you know. It's been going on for years and it's never stopped me from contributing to this team." He deliberately used the word *contributing*; a massive understatement. "We won the fucking cup last year."

"It's fucked up," someone said. Shane turned. It was Comeau.

"You think I don't know that?" Shane said. "That's why I've been hiding it for so long."

"Not from everyone," J.J. said angrily.

Shane took a step toward him, "J.J., I—"

"Don't want to hear it," J.J. said. "Is Coach sending you home?"

"Yeah, but—"

"Then fuck off and go home."

There were murmurs of agreement throughout the room. Shane's eyes prickled with tears. He'd expected this, but he'd also . . . hoped for better from this group of guys that he loved so much.

"Hey," said Hayden, standing up. "I know that everyone is fucking weirded out right now, but try to remember who the fuck this is. Shane is our fucking captain. Our leader."

"He's a fucking liar," J.J. said.

"He's our fucking *friend*," Hayden said sharply. "So maybe everyone feels weird right now or, like, totally grossed out. I get it. It's Rozanov."

"Okay, thanks, Hayden," Shane said.

"But that weirdness goes away, and then you're going to have to live with how shitty you were to Shane when he needed his fucking boys the most. So think about that."

There was some muttering that didn't exactly sound like agreement.

"It's okay," Shane said. "I'm leaving. If anyone wants to talk to me, you have my number." He locked eyes with J.J. "You know where I live."

J.J. looked at the floor, but then he nodded, once.

Shane left.

It was after ten o'clock at night when Ilya's phone finally lit up with a text from Shane: I ate a Snickers bar.

Ilya sent him a FaceTime request right away.

"Are your parents still there?" Ilya asked as soon as Shane's exhausted face appeared.

"Yeah," Shane sighed. "They went to bed, I think. I dunno. I'm in my room. I've been pretty antisocial."

Shane's hair was tied in a messy bun, and he was wearing his glasses. Ilya wanted to hold him so badly it hurt. "Did the chocolate make you feel better?"

"No," Shane grumbled. "Maybe. It was really fucking delicious, even though it was old. I think it was one you bought me a long time ago." He sighed. "You gonna gloat about it?"

Ilya didn't feel victorious. He knew eating candy was basically hitting rock bottom for Shane. "No."

"Why not? Isn't this what you want? *Fucking relax, Hollander*," he said in a terrible impression of Ilya. "Right?"

"Sweetheart," Ilya said gently.

Shane sighed. "Sorry. How's Anya?"

"Asleep," Ilya said, glancing at her bed in front of the fireplace. He'd used his fireplace more in the two weeks since getting a dog than he had in all the time he'd lived here before.

"What did your team say?"

"I only talked to Wiebe," Ilya said. "But he was good. Sympathetic." He'd already decided to keep what Wiebe had shared with him to himself. Wiebe didn't know Shane.

"Really? Theriault was fucking furious."

"Because he's a prick."

Shane winced. Ilya knew it was hard for him to hear a bad word spoken about his asshole coach. "He's just, y'know, old-school."

"Old-school," Ilya scoffed. "A fancy way of saying he is a prick."

"It works."

"My coach is not a prick and we are on fire," Ilya pointed out.

"Can't argue that. They're gonna be hurting without you, though." Shane shook his head. "It's such bullshit. We should be playing."

For a long moment, they just stared miserably at each other, wishing there was someone to blame besides themselves.

"What do you think the fans are saying?" Shane asked.

"I don't know. Have you looked online?"

"Of course not."

"No. Me neither. But some people have texted me. Harris. Troy. Wyatt. Max. Svetlana called me. That was nice."

"Yeah?" Shane said. "Max texted me too. And Rose. I guess she was right about needing a plan B. Whatever that would have been."

The truth was, plan A, B, or any other letter would be the same: they'd do whatever the league told them to do. Because they were professional hockey players and wanted to continue to be professional hockey players.

"We will see what Farah's statement says."

Shane ran a hand through his hair, knocking half of it out of its bun. "Coach told me not to post anything."

Anger flared in Ilya's chest. "He's not *my* coach."

"I know. And for what it's worth, I hate that he said that."

"Good," Ilya said. Then, "I can drive back there tomorrow. My team is on the road, so. No reason to stay."

"Yeah? God, I'd love that. I need you."

"I will leave first thing tomorrow. After I walk Anya."

Shane smiled at that. "I'm glad you got a dog."

Ilya grinned back. "Me too! She is so good! I will send you more pictures."

"Awesome." Shane grimaced. "I feel like shit."

"Try another Snickers bar."

"I shouldn't have eaten that. Or maybe I should have been eating them all along. Fuck, what am I even doing with this diet?"

"Trying to live forever, I thought."

"With you? No thank you."

"Eat what you want. If that is only healthy things, is fine. If you want treats, is also fine. It is your life, Hollander. Not the NHL's. Not the Montreal Voyageurs'."

"You sure about that?"

"I think we are both going to have to decide about that soon."

Ilya woke up to two emails the next morning. One was from Farah, and included the statement she'd written for them. The second was from the offices of Commissioner Crowell, informing Shane and Ilya that he would be at the Montreal branch of the NHL's offices tomorrow, and that he wanted to meet with both of them there.

*Fuck.*

Ilya went back to Farah's email and read the statement. The first paragraph plainly described the events as they had happened: a video had been circulated, it had unintentionally shown Ilya and Shane in an intimate moment, that Hayden hadn't realized what could be seen in the background when he'd sent it.

The second paragraph was more interesting.

> Although having the decision to disclose our relationship made for us isn't ideal, we would like to announce, officially, that we are in a committed, romantic relationship, and have been for several years. We wish we could have told you in our own way, but we don't hold this unfortunate accident against Hayden.

It was good, Ilya thought. To the point, and made it clear that they weren't blaming anyone (except fucking *Brad*, but anyway).

> We know that our relationship will be difficult for a lot of people to accept and understand. We have never let our personal relationship interfere with our competitiveness on the ice, and we believe our career achievements show that very clearly. We've always kept personal and professional separate, and we hope our teams, our fans, and the league can do the same.

Nice. Better than what he would have written himself, which probably would have been along the lines of, *We're in love and fuck you.*

A text from Shane popped up as soon as Ilya finished reading Farah's statement: Meeting with Crowell. Fuck.

**ILYA:**
Will be ok.

**SHANE:**
You sure about that?

**ILYA:**
Should Farah be there?

**SHANE:**

Probably but . . . I kind of want it to be just us? Is that stupid?

Ilya understood what Shane was saying. If things went sideways, they could involve Farah later. But this was about more than hockey, or their careers. This was personal, and Ilya, like Shane, wanted to fight this battle themselves if they could.

**ILYA:**

Not stupid.

**SHANE:**

I'll tell Farah about the meeting, but explain what we want to do.

**ILYA:**

Ok.

**SHANE:**

When are you getting here?

Ilya was keen to see Shane, but before he got on the road, Anya needed her walk.

**ILYA:**

Soon.

Ilya considered, as he walked around the slushy sidewalks of his neighborhood, that he should probably book another appointment with Galina. It had been a couple of weeks, and he didn't want to get lazy about it. He certainly had something to talk about now.

Oddly, he'd been feeling relatively peaceful since they'd been outed. Shane, he knew, was an absolute wreck, but Ilya was ready to face whatever happened next. Even though what was going to happen next was a meeting with Crowell. He should be nervous about that, but he was more curious than anything.

Curious, and ready to fight.

Ilya passed his neighbors' house—the one where Willa and Andrew lived—and stopped dead in his tracks. There was a large hand-drawn sign attached to the tree near the end of their driveway: *We love you, Ilya!*

Underneath the sign was a little shelf that held two Funko Pop figures: one of Ilya, and one of Shane.

Ilya fumbled for the phone he was glad he'd decided to shove in his coat pocket before leaving. He turned it on, took a photo, and sent it to Shane.

**SHANE:**

Oh wow. Is that your neighbors' house?

**ILYA:**

Yes. We are not so alone, I think.

# CHAPTER THIRTY-FOUR

"Are your parents still here?" Ilya asked as soon as he'd finished kissing Shane hello.

"No, I told them they could go home. I loved having them here, but I, um . . ."

"Want to be railed by your boyfriend?"

Shane's eyes darkened. "Fuck yes."

Their mouths crashed back together. Ilya gripped Shane's hair, still mostly wet from the shower he'd obviously just taken. He smelled like seaweed shampoo and sport bodywash and tasted like toothpaste. Ilya wanted to devour him.

"Make me forget everything," Shane murmured. "Just want to feel you." He started walking backward toward the living room, clutching Ilya's coat, pulling him closer.

Ilya broke the kiss to check on Anya. She'd found one of her toys on the living room floor and was chomping happily on it in her dog bed.

Ilya removed his coat and sneakers, leaving them in a pile by the door. "This way," he said, and took Shane's hand.

"The hell?" Shane said when he realized Ilya had led him to his trophy room.

Ilya just smiled at him.

"No way," Shane said. "Weird."

"Is it?" Ilya asked, trailing a finger along Shane's jaw. "I thought you need a reminder, before our meeting tomorrow."

"Reminder of what?" Shane said faintly as he tipped his head to the side and closed his eyes.

Ilya kissed just under his jaw, then in front of his ear. "Of who the fuck you are."

Shane gasped and grabbed a fistful of Ilya's T-shirt, as if to steady himself. "Yes," he whispered. "Remind me."

Ilya hauled him over to a leather armchair in the middle of the room. It was facing a wall of glass shelves that held miniature versions of Shane's three Stanley Cups, and of all the individual trophies he'd won during his career. Other shelves displayed various game pucks that were mounted and labeled with their achievements. There were also frames displaying his Team Canada jerseys from the World Juniors and the Olympics. On a smaller, lower shelf, boxes displayed his Stanley Cup rings and his gold and silver medals.

"Look at all of this," Ilya said as he bent Shane over the chair with a firm hand between his shoulder blades. "You almost need two rooms."

Shane didn't say anything as he braced himself on the sturdy arms of the chair with both hands, but his breathing had sped up. Ilya yanked Shane's gym shorts and underwear down together and let them pool at his feet. He slid his T-shirt up his back until it bunched across his shoulders and left it there.

Ilya bent over him, putting his weight on Shane's back for a moment. He brushed his lips against Shane's ear and said, "Stay there."

Then he straightened and headed for the door.

"Where the fuck are you going?"

"To get lube," Ilya said easily. "You know how sex works by now, yes?"

"Hurry up, then," Shane said bitchily.

Ilya, of course, took his time. He headed up to the bedroom, grabbed a bottle of lube and a clean hand towel, then, after a moment's consideration, went back to the nightstand and retrieved the vibrating cock ring he'd given Shane for his birthday last year.

He went back downstairs but didn't return to the trophy room right away. He checked on Anya, found her asleep in her bed, then went to the kitchen to pour himself a glass of water. He drank it slowly, trying to ignore how badly he wanted to race back to that room.

But that wasn't the game they were playing. He'd leave Shane in that room, naked and bent over a chair and surrounded by his proudest moments, because it was what Shane needed.

Finally, Ilya sauntered back into the trophy room. Shane hadn't moved a muscle. Ilya had to fight to control his breathing, to not give away how exquisitely Shane was destroying him with his obedience.

"Fucking finally," Shane snarled. "Did you go to the store or something?"

"No," Ilya said. He rubbed some lube on the silicone cock ring, keeping it out of Shane's sight. Then he loosened the toggle to expand the ring and reached around Shane's body to find his—of course—rigid cock.

"Oh shit," Shane said when he realized what Ilya was doing.

"Would be easier to do this if you were soft. But you never are, so."

"I am sometimes," Shane argued.

"Not when I am around." Ilya went to one knee beside him so he could get a better view of what he was doing. Once he got the ring in place, he tightened the toggle behind Shane's balls.

"Fuck," Shane breathed.

Ilya cradled his cock in one hand, gently rubbing a thumb along one prominent vein. "How does this feel?"

"Like my heart is in my dick. Like *everything* is in my fucking dick."

"Mm," Ilya hummed. He slid his thumb over the angry red head of Shane's cock, and pushed into the slit.

Shane's body jerked, and he sucked in a breath. "Jesus."

"Which is your favorite?" Ilya asked conversationally as he continued to rub the head of Shane's cock. "Of all of these trophies?"

"Rookie of the Year," Shane said quickly, and smugly.

Ilya huffed. "Fucker." He flicked Shane's dick, making him yelp, and then moan.

Ilya grabbed the lube and stood. He slicked his fingers then, without any further warning, pressed his thumb to Shane's hole.

"Oh fuck," Shane whimpered. He stepped back, stretching his arms until they were almost as straight as they could go, so he could bend forward more and lift his ass.

Ilya palmed one muscular cheek appreciatively with his free hand. "Is this for me?"

"I swear to god, Rozanov . . ."

Ilya chuckled, then got to work. It only took a few minutes before Shane was loose and ready for him, but Ilya dragged it out anyway. He stroked Shane's prostate and enjoyed the moans it shook out of him. He loved the way Shane was already rocking back against him, so eager.

Ilya reached around and turned on the vibrator, then went back to working Shane's prostate.

"Fuck," Shane panted. "Fuck, fuck, *fuck*!"

"Problem?"

Shane's back rose and fell in angry waves. "It's just," he gritted out, "a lot."

Ilya hummed sympathetically and added a third finger.

"Something you want to ask for?" he asked when he noticed the tremors in Shane's arms and legs.

"Fuck . . . fuck me."

"With what?" Ilya kneaded Shane's ass with one hand as he slid his fingers in as far as he could, then pulled them out completely.

This seemed to make Shane lose what was left of his patience. "Your *stupid dick*."

Ilya laughed, then quickly got himself undressed. He stood directly behind Shane, where it would be hard for Shane to see him without straining his neck. He bit back the moan of relief he wanted to let out when he finally freed his aching cock.

He lubed himself up while Shane took slow breaths and clenched his fingers against the leather chair arms. When Ilya brushed the head of his cock against Shane's hole, Shane raised his ass up in encouragement. They both let out loud moans of relief when Ilya began to slowly sink inside.

"Fuck yes," Shane panted. "Finally."

Shane was so tight, so perfect and hot, and the vibrations from the ring that was rumbling behind Shane's balls felt incredible on Ilya's cock. Ilya had to pause a moment, once he was fully inside, just to breathe and settle himself.

"Come *on*," Shane complained.

Ilya chuckled and carefully began to move. "Such a slut for it," he said after a couple of slow thrusts. "Is it me that made you so horny, or is it the room?"

"What," Shane gritted out, "are you talking about?"

"Are you all turned on thinking about all of your . . ." He adjusted his angle and gave Shane two quick, hard thrusts. "Many. Accomplishments."

"It's you. It's only you," Shane gasped.

Ilya loved it when Shane got like this, when he was flying too high to be annoyed or embarrassed. "Do you want to know a secret?" He bent over Shane so he could speak directly in his ear. "I feel like I am fucking a king right now."

"Ilya—"

He grabbed a handful of Shane's hair and tugged his head back. "Do you know how powerful this feels, fucking a king in his throne room?"

"Fu—fucking hell, Rozanov."

Ilya wrapped an arm around Shane's chest and hauled him up, as easily as if Shane were a doll and not a two-hundred-pound man. He held him close, Shane's back pressed against Ilya's chest, as Ilya pounded into him.

"You are Shane fucking Hollander," Ilya growled. "If you ever forget that, I will drag you back in here and fuck you until you remember."

"We—we'll share a trophy room someday," Shane stammered.

Ilya smiled. "Yes. A fucking empire."

Shane tilted his head back against Ilya's shoulder. "A dynasty," he breathed. "Oh, fuck, Ilya. I love you."

Ilya growled, and impulsively sank his teeth into Shane's shoulder. Shane cried out, then clenched around Ilya's cock as his orgasm rocked through him. His come splattered the chair, which Ilya knew would bother Shane as soon as he came down from his high.

Ilya didn't give a shit about the chair. He jackhammered into Shane, never wanting to stop. He swore in Russian, told Shane he was perfect in Russian, then came hard inside him.

Finally, he fell forward, resting his forehead on Shane's back as they both got their breathing under control. He realized that Shane must have turned off the vibrator while Ilya had been out of his mind.

"Holy shit," Ilya finally wheezed.

"That got weird," Shane said.

Ilya laughed, which made Shane laugh. Ilya kissed him between his shoulder blades, then carefully pulled out.

"I think I ruined the chair," Shane said, sooner even than Ilya had expected.

"It is another trophy now," Ilya said.

"Gross."

"There is a towel here," Ilya offered.

"Nah. I have some leather wipes I can use."

Ilya smiled. "Of course you do."

# CHAPTER THIRTY-FIVE

"There are few things in life that I absolutely can't stand," Roger Crowell said. His voice was deceptively calm, and Ilya didn't miss the danger in it. "One thing I hate is surprises. Another is disloyalty. And another is *liars*."

*And homosexuals*, Ilya added in his head.

"But the thing I hate most," Crowell continued, "is being embarrassed. And I especially hate it when the *league* is embarrassed."

"That does sound bad," Ilya said mildly.

Crowell shot him a warning look, and when Ilya turned to Shane, he saw a similar expression on his face.

"You can imagine," Crowell said, "how I feel about you two right now."

This time, Ilya was smart enough to keep his mouth shut. He could feel the tension radiating off Shane beside him. Ilya would behave. For Shane.

Crowell leaned forward, both elbows on the large table between them. "Your *actions* have put me in a very difficult situation. On the one hand, your behavior is completely unacceptable and absolutely cannot be allowed. On the other, you're two of the biggest stars in the league, and the playoffs are about to start."

"Can't be allowed?" Shane asked quietly.

Crowell's eyes narrowed. "I would think that part would be obvious. But I guess it wasn't, because there's a video flying around the internet of you two *making out*."

"It was a mistake," Shane said.

"You're fucking right it was a mistake!" Crowell yelled.

"I meant," Shane said, surprisingly steadily, "the video wasn't supposed to show that. We didn't know."

"Well, it did," Crowell barked. "And I had to fly to Montreal to deal with it. You think I have time for this?" He took a breath and said, more calmly, "We need to get things back to normal as soon as possible. I don't want a media circus around this thing."

"We don't either," Shane said.

Crowell nodded. "The league has prepared a statement." He opened a folder that was on the table in front of him and produced two sheets of paper. He handed one to each of them.

Ilya steeled himself, and began to read.

> For nearly eleven seasons, Shane Hollander and Ilya Rozanov have been elite players in the NHL. Their skill and performance on the ice demonstrates a rare level of talent that thrills hockey fans everywhere. Earlier this week, a video was circulated on social media that depicted Mr. Hollander and Mr. Rozanov in an intimate embrace. After being questioned by the league's commissioner, Roger Crowell, both players have confirmed that the incident was a prank they were pulling on their mutual friend, Hayden Pike. Both men regret their actions and the confusion it may have caused. They will return to their teams before their next scheduled games.

It was an easy out. Ilya knew this statement wouldn't fool everyone, but he suspected enough hockey fans would believe this lie. Pranks in hockey were normal, falling in love with your rival wasn't. This was something the hockey world—even other NHL players—could understand.

Shane was still reading. He hadn't brought his glasses with him and was squinting at the page. Ilya didn't *want* to hide anymore, but the playoffs were about to start and he couldn't honestly blame Shane if he chose this easy cover-up, just to make the drama die down for a while. Ilya would fucking hate it, but he'd agree to it, if it was what Shane chose.

Finally, Shane's head came up, and Ilya held his breath.

"But this isn't true," Shane said.

"It doesn't matter," Crowell said.

"It fucking *does* matter! It wasn't a prank. We're together. We're—we're getting married this summer."

Crowell's eyebrows shot up in obvious surprise, but he quickly composed himself. "That," he said coldly, "is not happening. Not if you want to remain in this league."

"Really?" Ilya asked. He wanted to flip the fucking table. "You are going to kick us out?"

"We'll sue the shit out of the league," Shane said, which honestly shocked Ilya.

For a long moment, Crowell said nothing. Then he said, "You're right. You could sue. But do you think any team would sign you after that? Either way, you'd be done."

Shane sucked in a breath. Ilya trembled with rage. They'd both given this league—this game—so much.

"We release the statement," Crowell said. "Most hockey fans will believe it because they'll *want* to believe it. There's no scandal, you boys get to keep playing for as long as you want, and we all move on. And, obviously, you don't get fucking married this summer."

Ilya's jaw was clenched so hard his teeth hurt. He was close to quitting the NHL on the spot. Instead he breathed through his nose and tried to figure out his next words.

Shane came up with some first. "Fuck this. Here's a plan: we do whatever we want this summer and then we come back and have all-star seasons *again* next year. We're not a couple of naïve rookies you can intimidate. You think we don't know what we're worth to this league?"

"What you *were* worth," Crowell said. "You're destroying your own brands with this shit."

"No," Ilya said. "We are making them stronger."

Crowell leaned over the table, fury flashing dangerously in his eyes. "I am offering the only option that will save both of your careers and the reputation of this league. If you post your own statement and start flaunting your . . . *relationship* . . . then you will obliterate your legacies. You'll be jokes. Choose carefully."

For a long, tense moment, there was only the sound of three men breathing angrily.

Then Shane stood and said, "I choose him. Come on, Ilya."

They both grabbed their coats from the backs of their chairs and left. Crowell was yelling something after them as they left the room, but Ilya didn't care. He put on his coat, took Shane's hand, and walked purposely toward the elevators. He was so full of love and adrenaline that he felt like he might explode. Once the elevator doors closed behind them, Shane said, "Sorry if I steamrolled that—"

Ilya didn't let him finish his sentence. He crowded Shane against the mirrored wall and kissed him ferociously. He sank his fingers into Shane's stupid hair and just devoured him, putting everything he felt into it. Because there was choosing Ilya over hockey, and then there was looking Crowell dead in the eye and basically telling him to go fuck himself. He never would have asked that of Shane, but Shane had done it anyway. Hadn't even hesitated.

The elevator dinged, ending their kiss. Ilya stepped back and admired how wrecked Shane looked, with his hair and coat disheveled and his lips swollen and pink. Those lips curved into a smile as the elevator doors opened.

"So," Shane said as they walked across the lobby to the exit, "you're not mad, then?"

"Not at you. I'm fucking furious at Crowell."

"Yeah," Shane said. "Well. I recorded the meeting. So."

Ilya's mouth dropped open. "Holy shit, Hollander. Good job."

"It was Mom's idea. Just in case we need it. But I think we're both going to be playing soon." They walked out into the chilly late-morning sunshine. It was late March, and Montreal was finally starting to thaw, but it would be a while before winter could be declared over.

They walked one block toward where they'd parked, then Shane stopped and glanced back over his shoulder.

"What?" Ilya asked.

"You know what? There's a place nearby that makes the best chicken parmesan. I've always wanted to take you."

Ilya's heart bounced happily at how fearless Shane was being. How sure he was about him. About them. He smiled and said, "If Hayden does not mind watching Anya for a bit longer."

Shane smiled back. "I'll check to make sure, but he was pretty excited about doing us a favor, so we should probably take advantage of that while we can."

They both started walking toward the restaurant. "Hayden is a good guy," Ilya said.

Shane nudged him. "Are you gonna tell him that?"

"Maybe. Someday." He reached for Shane's hand and they

walked, fingers tangled together, down a busy street in downtown Montreal with their heads held high.

"What about this one?" Ilya asked, and showed his phone screen to Shane.

Shane wrinkled his nose at it. "I look weird in that one."

"Yes. But I look very good."

Shane lightly punched his chest, which was easy to do because his head was resting on it. They were both naked, tangled up in bed together, and trying to find the perfect set of photos to pair with the statement for their mutual Instagram post. Shane was being, Ilya thought, overly fussy about it.

"This one," Shane suggested, and showed Ilya his phone. It showed a photo Yuna had taken of them together in their coach tracksuits on the first day of their first charity camp.

"Good. Okay," Ilya agreed. "Very respectable."

"Maybe that's enough," Shane mused. "We have four."

"One more," Ilya said, and stretched his hand holding the phone out above them.

"No way," Shane said, squirming away.

Ilya pulled him closer with an arm around Shane's shoulders. "In case people still don't believe we are together."

"No!" Shane squawked.

"For me, then," Ilya said, and kissed the top of Shane's head.

Shane relaxed against him. "Fine."

Ilya snapped a few quick photos, then lowered his phone to look at them.

"Oh," Shane said quietly. "Look at us."

They both looked so fucking in love it was disgusting. "I am keeping these ones," Ilya said firmly.

"I guess we don't have to delete those kinds of photos anymore," Shane said. "Within reason, I mean. I don't want anything graphic getting out there."

"Good thing I didn't take a photo ten minutes ago, then."

Shane's cheeks turned as pink as Ilya had hoped they would. "I think your hands were busy."

Ilya rolled on top of Shane, pinning him on his back. "They could be busy again."

Shane grinned up at him, all flushed skin and freckles and bright eyes. Ilya wanted to, like, crawl inside him somehow.

"We need to finish the post. And then you have a dog to pick up and a hockey team to get back to."

Ilya did miss Anya, so he flopped back on the mattress and got to work assembling the Instagram post.

"You have all four photos? The ones I texted you?" Shane asked.

"Yes, yes."

"And you're not including the one you just took?"

Ilya only huffed in response. He copied and pasted Farah's statement, made sure all four photos were lined up, and hovered his thumb over the post button.

"Ready?" he asked.

Shane blew out a breath. "Yeah. Let's do it."

They posted it.

Shane got a call from his coach shortly after Ilya left, gruffly letting him know that he was to be at practice tomorrow morning. It was a relief, and Shane was definitely looking forward to getting back on the ice, but he was nervous about facing his teammates again.

He still hadn't heard from J.J.

He tried to push it out of his mind by filling the rest of his day with exercise, meditation, and rest. He wasn't particularly successful at any of those things, especially rest. His body hummed with energy. He felt excited and terrified and a million other things.

He waited two hours after the post went up to check the replies. There were already over fifty thousand likes, and way more comments than he could read. A quick scroll showed that they weren't all positive, but a lot of them were. *Most* of them were.

Maybe things really would be okay.

His doorbell rang just before ten o'clock at night, while Shane was sitting on his bed texting Ilya and Rose separately, and checking the Instagram replies for the fifth time that day. The security camera app on his phone showed J.J. standing on his doorstep.

Shane bolted down the stairs and yanked the door open.

"Hi," he said.

J.J. was scowling, clearly still angry. But he was there.

Shane stepped back and J.J. silently entered the house. They stood in Shane's front hallway, staring at each other, for several tense moments. Then J.J. said, in French, "You didn't tell me."

"I'm sorry."

"Why the fuck didn't you tell me? You let me keep trying to find you dates, you—"

"To be fair," Shane interrupted, "I kept telling you to stop doing that."

"You fucking lied to me. After the Centaurs plane thing I said all that shit about you having one-sided feelings for Rozanov and you lied to me."

"I—"

"You could have told me. You told Hayden!"

"He . . . guessed."

"I felt sorry for you! I thought you were carrying a broken heart around but the whole time you've been *fucking Ilya Rozanov*!"

Anger shot through Shane. He stepped toward J.J., which meant he had to tip his head back to see his face. "Ilya is my *boyfriend*. I love him, and I have for years. Don't make it sound like . . . less."

"Oh, shit, I'm sorry," J.J. said sarcastically. "Obviously I should have known about your epic love affair with Ilya fucking Rozanov because you've told me so much about it! You're one of my best friends, Shane. What the fuck?"

"Maybe," Shane said tersely, "I thought you wouldn't exactly be supportive."

"Of what? Sneaking around with your fucking rival?"

Shane tipped a hand toward J.J. "See?"

J.J. turned his back to him, the rage obvious in the rise and fall of his shoulders. Shane folded his arms, and waited.

"Look," J.J. finally said, in English. "I don't think this is okay. It's fucked up that you're dating the captain of the team we're probably going to be facing in the playoffs."

Shane immediately got angry. He couldn't help it; he'd had enough of people being grossed out by his relationship for one day. "Thanks for your fucking input. You think maybe that's exactly why I didn't tell you?"

"How did Hayden react at first? Thrilled for you, was he?"

Shane's mouth dropped open. He tried to think of a defense, but in the end he just closed his mouth again.

J.J. huffed. "That's what I thought."

"Look. The less people who knew, the better. It's nothing personal."

"It fucking feels personal."

"God, would you stop? I've been hiding this thing for eleven fucking years. It sucked, okay? I'm sorry if your feelings are hurt, but come on, man."

Somewhere in the middle of Shane's outburst, J.J. had gone very still. He looked like he'd seen a ghost. "Eleven years?" he said quietly.

"Um," Shane said, "give or take."

J.J. walked to the staircase that led to the second floor and sat down hard on the third step. "Eleven fucking years. The entire time I've known you."

A lump formed in Shane's throat. "We haven't been, like, *a couple* that whole time."

J.J.'s shoulders slumped. "Fucking hell, Hollander. Who *are* you?"

Shane took a chance, and sat next to him on the step. It was . . . cozy. "I'm your friend. And your teammate. And I fell in love with the most complicated person I could possibly fall in love with."

"Ilya fucking Rozanov." J.J. shook his head. "Jesus, Shane. Why?"

"Because . . ." Shane didn't even know where to start. Finally he just said, "He makes me happy. I know it doesn't make sense, but he's it for me. We're getting married."

J.J.'s head whipped around to face him, eyes wide. *"Married?"*

"Uh, yeah," Shane said nervously. "So, y'know. Watch for an invitation."

"Fuck, Hollander. This is a lot."

Shane nudged him. "I'm the same friend you've always had. And I'll still be the same when I'm Ilya's husband. I swear I'm normal."

A long, tense silence fell between them. Then J.J. sighed and said, "No one who's never heard of Cardi B is normal."

Shane barked out a surprised laugh. "Fuck off. I'd heard the *name*, I just didn't know any of his songs."

"*Her*, you fucking dipshit."

They leaned against each other and laughed, and it felt like things might be okay between them.

"I don't want to be mad at you, Hollander."

"I know. But you can be." Shane smiled. "Until tomorrow. Then we've gotta play hockey."

J.J. smiled back. "Deal."

# CHAPTER THIRTY-SIX

*April*

"The king is back!" Bood yelled as soon as Ilya entered the Centaurs locker room.

Everyone in the room clapped and whooped in excitement. Ilya felt himself blushing a bit.

"Thank you," he said, meaning it. Shane had told him a bit about his own team's reception of him earlier that morning, and it had been a lot more wary and awkward than this, which made the warm welcome back even more touching.

It felt so fucking good to be on the ice again. Sometimes he thought he was getting tired of this game, but being kept away from it for a week had made him realize how much he still loved it. Needed it.

"All right," Coach yelled after he'd given everyone time to warm up. "Gather 'round."

Everyone grouped around him at center ice, most taking a knee. Ilya stood at the back with Wyatt and Bood.

"What's happening next week, Dykstra?" Coach asked.

Evan smiled. "Playoffs, Coach!"

"That's right. Who here has been to the Stanley Cup playoffs before?"

An alarmingly small number of the guys raised their hands, including Ilya and Wyatt.

"To be honest," Wyatt said, "I was mostly *watching* the playoffs, in Toronto."

Coach waved a hand. "It doesn't matter that we don't have the playoff experience that most teams have. Some people will say that experience is the most important thing, but I think it's heart. I think it has more to do with working together than it does with following a few leaders. I believe in this group. These past few months we've shown everyone how well this team works together."

There were stick taps and murmurs of agreement.

"Bood," Coach said, "what was the attendance at our last home game?"

Bood grinned. "Full house, Coach."

"Who was the player of the week last week?"

"Wyatt fucking Hayes," said Dykstra.

"Because we've got the best goalie in the league," Coach confirmed.

"Aw, thanks," said Wyatt.

"We're going to be playing Montreal in the first round, and that's going to be tough, no question. They're the defending champions, and the number one ranked team in the league at the moment."

*And,* Ilya added in his head, *everyone is going to be gossiping about the two captains, which is going to be a huge distraction.*

"We've beaten them before, and we can do it again," Coach said. "Roz, you're back on the line with Bood and Barrett. Let's get to work."

The coaches worked them hard all practice, and the whole team was exhausted by the time they were allowed to return to the locker room.

As he was getting undressed, Ilya decided to clear the air. There'd be enough going on over the next few weeks without having an elephant in the room to deal with.

"I want to say something," he announced.

The room was dead silent.

"You read the post, probably, about me and Shane." He glanced around the room, and saw a few nods. "So. Yes. We are together."

There was a long, weird silence, and Bood broke it by saying, "Figures."

Ilya raised his eyebrows at him and waited.

Bood smiled. "You stealing the fucking spotlight. Barrett comes out, announces his relationship with Harris, and then Roz says 'hold my beer.'"

"Yeah, Ilya," Troy said with a grin. "What the fuck?"

The room erupted with laughter, and Ilya's heart swelled. He loved this team.

After more playful ribbing, everyone got back to the business of getting changed and showered. As Ilya was pulling on his sweatshirt, Wyatt approached him.

"Is that what the ring's about, then?" He pointed at Ilya's chest.

"You noticed?"

"I'm a goalie." Wyatt pointed to his own eyes. "I notice everything."

"You are perceptive," Ilya said, trying out a word he'd recently learned.

"It's my superpower. I didn't want to ask, but now it seems kind of obvious that it's from Hollander."

"It is. We are engaged." Ilya was still getting used to saying those words aloud. To believing them.

"Then Shane Hollander is a lucky man."

Ilya was in danger of crying, so he wrapped Wyatt in a hug to hide his face. "Thank you," he said.

"No problem." Wyatt patted him on the back. "Just try not to make your wedding day the same as Harris and Troy's, okay? I don't want to have to do a lot of running around that day."

Ilya laughed, and then sniffed. "Okay, Hazy."

Shane couldn't ever remember being so nervous at the start of the playoffs before. Not even as a rookie. He shuffled his skates anxiously as the national anthem was sung, trying not to stare directly at the back of Ilya's jersey, fifty feet in front of him.

Holy shit. This was happening.

The Montreal crowd was deafening but couldn't drown out the blood pounding in Shane's ears. He needed to pull himself together because, yes, it felt weird standing on the ice with Ilya when everyone *knew*. And, yes, most of his teammates had been less than friendly since Shane had returned from his suspension, but the team had silently made a pact *not to talk about it*, which should have been a relief but actually made Shane feel awful.

Ilya's team had accepted him back with open arms. They'd talked about his relationship with Shane—joked about it, even. Shane felt like he was playing an unending version of that board game, Operation, and the slightest mistake—anything less than perfection—would get him zapped. It was exhausting, and it was pressure he didn't need on top of the usual playoffs expectations of the Montreal fans.

Finally, it was time for the puck to drop. Shane was clinging to the hope that he'd start to feel normal once the actual game started. Except, of course, the opening face-off was between him and Ilya.

They both bent at the waist over the face-off spot, and for a moment, their gazes locked.

"Good luck," Shane said. It was all he dared to say right now, with everyone watching.

Ilya's lips quirked up in his usual crooked, cocky smile, and then the puck dropped.

Ilya won the face-off.

Fucking hell, playoff games were intense. Ilya had almost forgotten.

The game was going . . . okay. Troy Barrett had opened the scoring early for Ottawa, which had been exciting, but Montreal had answered quickly. And then added a second goal.

But 2–1 was a respectable start to the third period. Better, Ilya thought, than anyone had expected Ottawa to fare against Montreal.

During a break in play, Ilya checked in with his goalie. "You good, Hazy?" he called out over the screeching vocals of AC/DC's "Thunderstruck."

"Yep," Hazy said cheerfully. "Hey, do you like this song?"

Ilya's brow furrowed. Was this seriously what Wyatt was thinking about right now? "Is okay."

"I always thought it had all this buildup and then falls kind of flat, but I dunno. Anyway, score a goal, okay?"

Neither Ilya nor Shane had scored yet. Ilya had noticed that Shane had been a bit off the whole game. Not handling the puck as cleanly as he usually did, not getting the scoring chances he was known for.

Ilya wanted to ask Shane how he was doing. He wanted to hold him, but they'd agreed not to see each other off the ice during this playoff series. Because, despite everything else between them, they were two NHL stars who both wanted to win the Stanley Cup, and neither was about to let their fiancé stand in the way. Ilya wasn't sure it was a sound strategy. After a week of being apart from Shane, he wanted to tear his own skin off.

So there was more than one incentive to end this series quickly, even though that meant one of them would lose.

As they bent for the face-off at the beginning of the third, Ilya noticed a glint of gold, on Shane's neck.

"You have a chain now?" Ilya asked quietly.

"Yeah," Shane said. "And a ring."

Ilya smiled, and totally lost the face-off.

Ilya stared at the photo of Shane's ring, nestled between his muscular, shower-damp pecs, for nearly the entire bus ride from the arena to the hotel. Shane had sent it from the locker room, presumably, which was bold and also super hot. It took some of the sting of losing 2–1 away.

He waited until he was safely in his hotel room before he texted Shane back: **Can I see that ring again?**

A couple of minutes later, a FaceTime request from Shane appeared on his phone.

"Hey," Shane said. He was shirtless, the ring on full display. His hair was tied back and he was wearing his glasses, a lethal combination. "Sorry about the game."

Ilya huffed. "No you are not. When did you start wearing the ring?"

"This morning."

His heart flopped over. "Did anyone say anything?"

"No. I don't think anyone wants to talk about it." Shane sighed. "Tonight was the first time I hated playing against you. I may have even hated playing hockey altogether."

"Was weird," Ilya conceded, "but you love hockey."

"You guys played a great game."

"Not as great as your team."

"It's only the first game. We're not cocky." Shane grimaced. "Well, some of the guys are cocky."

"Good," Ilya said. "We like to be underestimated."

"Big word," Shane said with a cute little smile.

"Hockey word. One of the first ones I learned in Boston."

"Montreal and Boston were both terrible teams when we joined them. I forget that, sometimes."

Ilya smiled. "Do I need to fuck you in your trophy room again until you remember?"

Shane's cheeks darkened. "I wish."

"Do not forget," Ilya said seriously, "what that team owes you."

Shane chewed his lip and nodded. Ilya knew what the expression on his face meant. "Do you need help to relax before bed?"

Shane nodded again. "Please."

Ilya rummaged through his suitcase with one hand until he found his folding tripod. "Get started. I will join you in a minute."

Ottawa shut the Montreal crowd up by winning the second game, then both teams headed to Ottawa for games three and four. Ottawa made their home crowd roar by winning game three, then Montreal won the fourth game, tying the series at two wins apiece. They went back to Montreal, and the Voyageurs absolutely trounced the Centaurs 6–1 and put them on the ropes. Ottawa had to win the next game, back home in Ottawa, or they were out.

The Ottawa arena was packed for game six. It had been sold out for most of the past three months, but that night Ilya thought the noise rivaled the crowd back in Montreal. The

Centaurs charged out onto the ice to an earsplitting roar from their hometown fans.

"Does the noise scare you?" Shane asked as they got ready for the puck drop. "I know you're not used to it."

Ilya snorted. "This is nothing. Wait until I score."

"Oh yeah? When's that happening?"

Ilya bent over the circle. "Right now."

He won the face-off, knocking the puck back to Dykstra and immediately getting himself in formation with Troy and Bood like they'd practiced. He watched as Troy dodged Hayden and took the pass from Dykstra. Ilya made sure he was exactly where he needed to be when Troy sent the puck over to him, and as soon as it hit his blade, Ilya took off.

J.J. was in front of him, which was definitely a challenge, but Ilya was ready for him. He passed the puck back to Bood, moved quickly to the side of the net, and waited for Bood's shot. Ilya was there for the deflection, and directed the puck over Drapeau's outstretched pad, making it 1–0 Ottawa less than thirty seconds into the game.

Troy slammed into Ilya against the glass, his mouth stretched in a wide smile. "Let's fucking go! Hell yes."

Ilya hugged him as Bood pressed up against both of them. "Now this is fucking fun," Bood yelled.

Ilya grinned at the crowd, a sea of red Centaurs jerseys. "Let's keep going."

Montreal didn't make it easy for them, but Ottawa ended up winning the game 4–3, and Ottawa, in their first playoffs appearance in over a decade, had taken the series all the way to game seven. Against the number one team in the league and the defending Stanley Cup champions.

"Eat shit, everyone!" Bood yelled in the locker room after the game. "Easy sweep for Montreal my ass. We just fucked up everybody's playoff pools."

Everyone in the room was in a great mood, Ilya included, but playing a game seven against his boyfriend was going to be intense, to say the least.

Game fucking seven.

Shane usually lived for this, but tonight he was a mess as he waited in the locker room for the game to start. Coach was barking at them, and Shane was barely listening. He was deep in his own head, trying to settle his nerves.

*I wonder how Ilya is feeling.*

He quickly shoved that thought away. It wasn't useful right now.

One of them was about to win, and the other was about to lose. Shane knew their relationship would withstand it; they'd been rivals their entire careers, there was no reason to start being petty now. But even so, this series felt bigger than anything they had faced each other in previously.

The Montreal crowd went wild, as always, as their team entered the arena. The starting lineups were announced, and Shane took his place on the blue line for the anthem. He focused on the three most recent Stanley Cup banners hanging from the rafters, and not on Ilya's number 81 jersey across from him.

"We got this, baby," J.J. said as they waited for the anthem to start.

Shane steeled his expression, nodded, and said, "Let's get it."

The game was a battle, and then it went to fucking overtime. Because of course it did. Everyone on both teams was exhausted, but desperate to win. And now there was less than five minutes left of the first overtime period and Shane was dreading a second one. He bent to take the face-off against Ilya in the Ottawa zone.

"This is fun," Ilya said conversationally. "I forgot how it feels, to have such high stakes."

"It will be less fun when I score in a few seconds."

Ilya smiled around his mouth guard, then won the face-off.

Shane didn't let Ottawa keep the puck for long. He stole it from Zane Boodram, then glanced around quickly for someone to give it to before he got rocked by Troy Barrett. He spotted J.J. and sent the puck back to him to give Montreal some breathing space.

Shane managed to dodge Troy's hit at the same moment he watched Ilya intercept his pass to J.J.

*Fuck!*

Ilya took off, and Shane darted after him. Within seconds they were over the center line, completely alone, and Shane was in a good position to cleanly poke the puck away from him. He was just about to do that, when instead he stumbled forward and went crashing to the ice in a frustrated heap.

He was helpless to do anything but watch Ilya carry the puck to the net, and bury it between Drapeau's pads.

*Fuck, fuck, fuck!*

Shane couldn't believe it. Montreal's hopes for a repeat Stanley Cup win—their hopes for eliminating fucking *Ottawa*—had just been crushed. Because Shane had *tripped*.

He'd be lucky if he wasn't tarred and feathered right here in the arena.

He watched miserably, on one knee, as the Ottawa bench spilled onto the ice and piled on top of Ilya in celebration. Eventually he felt a hand on his shoulder, and he knew without looking that it was Hayden.

"It's over, buddy," Hayden said. "Come line up for the handshakes."

Shane forced himself to his feet, and skated over to where

his teammates had gathered in a devastated cluster, waiting for Ottawa to stop celebrating. It could be a long wait.

"Good game," Shane said to Drapeau, who looked stunned behind his mask. "It wasn't your fault."

Drapeau fixed his intense goalie eyes on Shane's face and said, coldly, "I know."

He skated away, leaving Shane feeling confused and upset. Obviously Shane could have stopped Ilya if he hadn't fucking tripped, but it was unlike Drapeau to be a fucking ass about it.

They lined up for the handshakes. Shane's brain was still whirling with shame and confusion and disappointment and anger. He shook the hands of several Centaurs in a blur, then realized that each of them were saying nice things to him.

He first noticed it with Troy Barrett. The other man gripped Shane's hand firmly, then pulled him in for a quick, brotherly hug. "I'll see you at the camps this summer, okay?"

"You will?" This was the first Shane had heard of it.

"Yeah." Troy pulled back and smiled, his vivid blue eyes twinkling with the thrill of victory. "Bood too, I think. We're excited about it." He released Shane's hand. "I hope we can be friends, y'know?"

Somehow Shane had completely forgotten that Troy was gay, despite his very public coming-out a few weeks ago, and the fact that Ilya had talked endlessly about what a great couple he and Harris were. "Definitely," Shane said.

Troy patted his arm one more time, then moved on. Shane shook a few more hands and received more nice words. Then he was face-to-face with Ilya.

Shane didn't know what to do. He wanted to wrap his arms around Ilya and breathe him in. Tell him he was proud of him. He was also so angry he could barely look at Ilya's gleeful face right now.

Except Ilya didn't look gleeful; he looked concerned, and maybe just as unsure of what to do as Shane was.

Shane knew there were about a million photos being taken of them right now. Professional photographers on the ice, thousands of fans taking photos with their phones, and people at home making gifs that would live on the internet forever. He knew, but all he saw in that moment was Ilya's wary expression.

Finally, Shane stuck out his hand, and Ilya shook it. It wasn't nearly enough.

"You guys earned it," Shane said. "That was a fucking incredible series. I'm excited for you." He wasn't lying. Mostly he was disappointed that he couldn't be a part of it.

"I thought you had me," Ilya said.

"I did. Must have caught an edge or something. Fucking embarrassing." Shane sighed. "Are you flying back tonight?"

"Yes. And to New York tomorrow."

"Oh." Shane was about to suggest that he drive to Ottawa tonight and meet Ilya at home later.

Ilya must have seen it in his eyes. "Get some rest tonight."

Shane wanted to argue that he needed Ilya more than he needed sleep. Or food. Or oxygen. But in truth he knew he'd crash hard in about half an hour, completely drained after this emotional series.

He nodded and said, "Kick Scott Hunter's ass, okay?"

Ilya smiled, cocky and sexy. "I can't wait."

The handshake line ended with Wyatt, who pulled Shane in for a hug. "Always a pleasure watching you play, Hollander. I'll see you in July."

"You too, Wyatt. Good luck in New York."

"Oh shit, we've gotta win another one of these?"

Shane laughed and patted Wyatt's massive chest protector. "I'll be rooting for you."

It wasn't until Shane was back in the locker room that he started to notice that it wasn't just Drapeau who seemed upset with him.

"I can't believe I fucking tripped," Shane said to J.J. as they were tossing their jerseys in the laundry bin.

"Did you?"

Shane tensed. "What's that mean?"

J.J. stared at him for a few seconds, then shook his head. "I don't know, Hollander. Just . . . *fuck*, tell me it was a mistake."

*"What?"* Shane couldn't fucking believe this. "You think I fell on purpose? That I *let* Ilya score?"

Comeau stood from where he'd been slumped in his stall. "I know what I saw. What everyone saw. It didn't look like an accident."

"Well, it *was*. What the fuck?" Everyone in the room was staring at him now. Shane turned to face as many of his teammates as he could. "You guys don't actually think I fell on purpose, do you?"

There was mostly silence, with some muttering in both French and English. Finally, J.J. blew out a breath and said, "No, I don't think that."

Suddenly, Hayden was at Shane's side. "Of course we don't fucking think that. Come on, guys. Shane would never betray his team."

But Hayden and J.J. seemed to be the only ones who were sure of that.

"Fuck this," Shane muttered, and began to angrily remove the rest of his gear. These were the guys who were supposed to have his back. They'd won a cup together last year and fought like hell all season for another one. Some of these men had played with Shane for over ten seasons. It made him sick that they were so quick to believe him to be a traitor.

Shane's parents were waiting for him outside the locker

room by the time he'd gotten showered and changed. He didn't even bother saying goodbye to his teammates. If any of them wanted to apologize, they had his number.

"If you want to stay longer," Mom said, "we can head to the house without you."

"No. I want to get out of here. Now." He walked quickly down the hall toward the underground parking, leaving his parents scrambling to catch up. He was being rude, he knew, but he felt like he wouldn't be able to breathe until he was out of the fucking arena.

When he got to his car, he leaned back against it and stared up at the ugly ceiling of the garage. His eyes burned with furious tears. "They think I fell on purpose," he said.

*"What?"* Mom said. "Who said that? I want names."

Shane shook his head. "I've given this team everything and . . ." His face crumpled.

Dad wrapped his arms around him. "I'm sorry, Shane. It's been a rough couple of weeks for you."

Shane sniffed. "It can only get better, right?" He glanced over Dad's shoulder to see Mom frowning at her phone. "Oh god. What now?"

Mom forced her lips into the least convincing smile Shane had ever seen. "Nothing important. Let's go home."

"You were checking Twitter, weren't you? What's everyone saying?"

Mom slipped her phone into her pocket. "Like I said. Nothing important."

# CHAPTER THIRTY-SEVEN

The next morning, Ilya was disgusted to see that hockey media was full of opinion pieces that wondered aloud if Shane had intentionally let Ilya score.

"This is insulting to me as well," Ilya complained on the phone to Shane. "They think I can't beat you unless we cheat?"

"You wouldn't have beaten me if I hadn't tripped," Shane pointed out for no reason at all.

"Shane," Ilya sighed. "Not now. And of course I would have."

"I'm so fucking angry," Shane said. "I don't deserve this."

Ilya was glad to hear him say it. "You're a free agent now. Get the fuck out of there. Go somewhere that will appreciate you."

Shane snorted. "Like where? Ottawa?"

Ilya held his breath. Because of course, yes. Ottawa.

"I mean, I couldn't, could I?" Shane said.

"This is why you have an agent. Find out."

"They don't have the salary cap space for me. Not with you and Troy and Wyatt. And didn't Bood get a big raise last season? Haas will be looking for more in a couple of years."

"How much money do you need?" Ilya asked.

"I don't know. I just want what I'm worth, y'know?"

"Of course. But consider maybe your very wealthy husband."

Shane sputtered out a laugh. "I guess that's true." He was silent a moment. "Is there room for me on that roster, though?"

"We need depth at center. And having both Ilya Rozanov and Shane Hollander would be *very* deep."

"Jesus, we could win Ottawa a cup."

"Hey!" Ilya complained. "I am trying to do that right now!"

"Sorry. I didn't mean to—I completely believe in you."

"Hm."

"Anyway, this is a lot. I'm just angry right now and it's making me want to do drastic things. I'll calm down soon."

Ilya was sure he would, which was why he was trying not to get his hopes up about Shane joining him on the Centaurs. Shane loved Montreal, and it would take a lot more than a few stupid editorial pieces and angry tweets to make him leave.

"I have to get going. Plane leaves soon."

"Okay," Shane said. "Good luck. I'll be watching. And call me. And send me pics. And, fuck, I really miss you."

"I miss you too. Come to Ottawa. I'll get tickets for you and your parents for games three and four."

Shane seemed to brighten at that. "Yeah? I could stay with them, so I don't distract you or anything."

"We can talk about it in a few days."

"All right. Hey, um. No one on your team thinks I tripped on purpose, right?"

Ilya huffed. "No one with a brain thinks that."

The first two games were in New York, and Ottawa lost both of them. Then Ottawa won the third game, in Ottawa. All three Hollanders had been in the audience for that one, which had been exciting for Ilya. He'd never had so many people he loved at one of his games before.

The following afternoon, on the day between games, Ilya and Shane were watching tennis together on Ilya's couch. Or at least that's how it started. Within half an hour Shane was sprawled out and panting while Ilya tortured him with the slowest, laziest blowjob ever.

"D-did you forget how to do this or something?" Shane gasped.

Ilya paused from gently tonguing just below the head of Shane's cock and smiled. "Are you in a hurry? Playoff game to get ready for?"

Shane's mouth dropped open. "Oh *fuck you*."

Ilya laughed while Shane hit him repeatedly with a throw pillow. That devolved into wrestling, then kissing.

And that's when Ilya's phone alerted him that someone was at his front gate. He grabbed his phone off the coffee table and checked the security camera. Then he barked out a surprised laugh.

"What?" Shane asked.

"Is Scott Hunter."

*"Here?"* Shane scrambled off the couch, tucking his still-hard dick into his sweatpants.

"Yes." Ilya hit the button to open the gate.

"Why? What does he want? Fuck . . . I've gotta . . . I need a few minutes."

Shane jogged to the stairs, then up into the bedroom. Ilya, meanwhile, calmly adjusted himself, straightened his shirt, and walked to the front door. He glanced toward Anya's bed to make sure she wasn't going to make a run for the door, but she was still fast asleep after the long walk they'd taken her on that morning.

He opened the door just as Scott reached his front steps. "Hunter. You are at my house."

Scott looked a little bewildered, as if he hadn't realized this would be Ilya's house or something. His perfect fucking face glanced around like he'd been dropped there by aliens. "Yeah, I um. I got the address from Wyatt. He had to make sure my intentions were noble first."

Ilya really wasn't sure what the *intentions* were of the rival team captain—the man whose team the Centaurs were currently in the middle of a playoffs series against—standing on his doorstep. "You could have texted."

"You seem to enjoy showing up at things unannounced. Maybe I wanted to see what it was like."

Ilya smiled at that. "Come in."

And then Scott Hunter was in Ilya's house.

Shane had returned to the living room, still a little rumpled but mostly presentable. "Hi, Scott."

Scott nodded at him. "Shane. Good. I was hoping you'd be here too."

"He usually is," Ilya said, a bit smugly and for no real reason. Something about Hunter always made him feel territorial and juvenile.

And god, it felt good to finally be able to let people know that Shane Hollander was *his*. He knew that Scott was happily married and not looking at Shane in that way any more than he was looking at *Ilya* in that way, but still. Ilya was proud of himself for landing such an impressive boyfriend.

"Oh, were you guys watching the Madrid Open?" Scott asked, glancing at the TV.

"Uh, yeah," Shane said.

"Kind of," Ilya added.

Scott sat in an armchair, perched on the edge of the cushion. "I know it's awkward because we're in the middle of a playoff series, but I wanted to talk to you guys about . . . you know." He waved a hand between Ilya and Shane.

"Uh-oh," Ilya said. "Are we getting a lecture from Dad?"

Scott looked at Shane. "Is it possible for him to not be an asshole for five seconds?"

"No," Shane said. He sat on the couch, facing Scott. "So what did you want to talk about, exactly?"

"Well, first of all, I'm sorry you guys got outed that way. That's awful."

"It wasn't great," Shane agreed.

"Ruined our plan to kiss on television," Ilya said dryly.

Scott narrowed his eyes at him, then directed his next words to Shane. "When I heard about what happened, I felt sick, honestly. Being outed was my biggest fear for years. That decision shouldn't have been taken from you."

Ilya joined Shane on the couch. "Is that the only reason you felt sick?"

Scott gave him a wary smile. "I was pretty shocked. Not gonna lie."

"If you are here to tell us our relationship is okay or not okay, we don't care," Ilya said bluntly.

"Jesus, Ilya," Shane muttered.

"I'm not," Scott assured Ilya. "I have no idea how this thing with you has even been working, but you guys obviously have it figured out. It's definitely never interfered with your hockey."

Ilya understood what that meant: Scott didn't believe Shane had tripped on purpose. He lowered his defenses and said, "Thank you for saying so."

"How'd Crowell react to your relationship?"

Ilya snorted. Shane said, "You can probably guess. I think if he thought he could get away with it, we'd both be out of the league."

Scott's expression turned dangerous, the way it often did on the ice. "I think he felt the same way about me when I came out."

"And Troy Barrett," Ilya added. "Troy got an email after that was like . . . what is the word? Nice but sounds angry?"

"Passive-aggressive," Shane said.

"Yes. Okay. That."

"Crowell's a dinosaur," Scott said. "He's standing in the way of progress, which is part of why I wanted to talk to you. Carter Vaughan and I are trying to start a group of NHL players." He paused. "No. Of *hockey* players—I've already reached out to Max Riley and Leah Campbell—who are interested in fighting back against toxic hockey culture. Not just homophobia, but all of it: racism, sexism, rape culture, transphobia, toxic masculinity. I know that sounds kind of huge and impossible, but it has to start somewhere."

"Like a club?" Ilya asked. "Of nice hockey players?"

"Basically," Scott said. "I thought when I came out that would make a difference for other queer hockey players."

"I think it did," Shane said. He glanced at Ilya. "It did for us, anyway."

Oh god. That was embarrassing. But it was true; Ilya probably wouldn't have taken a chance on trying to be with Shane if Scott hadn't kissed his boyfriend on television after winning the Stanley Cup.

"Yeah?" Scott asked, sounding surprised and maybe a bit touched. "That's nice to hear. But when I heard Troy's story, it made me realize that queer NHL players still didn't feel safe coming out. And that's just *one* problem with hockey culture." He sighed. "Sometimes it all seems so broken I don't know if it can be fixed. But I want to try."

"So," Shane said slowly, "like, if someone in hockey says or does something awful, we would speak as a united front against it? Is that what you're thinking?"

Scott's eyes flashing with excitement. "Exactly! Right now

it's scary, speaking out, when you're just one person. But if we have an organized group who can release statements, it's a lot less scary. It's powerful." He leaned forward. "I have over fifty hockey players interested in joining already. I think we can really do this."

Ilya was impressed. This was actually a really good idea. "I'm in."

"Me too," Shane said. "A hundred percent. I know J.J. and Hayden would be into it too."

"My coach might join as well," Ilya said thoughtfully. "He is a very good guy."

"Yeah? That would be great. I'd love to get some people from that side of the bench." He smiled. "Sorry I kind of jumped right into my pitch. I mostly came here to tell you that, y'know, I've got your back. And congratulations, I guess."

"You can congratulate us after we are married," Ilya couldn't resist saying.

Scott's eyebrows shot up. "And when will that be?"

"July," Shane said, even though they hadn't officially decided. He glanced at Ilya. "Makes sense, right? Maybe the week before camps start?"

"Sure," Ilya said easily. "Whenever."

Scott blew out a breath. "Jesus. This is really weird. Sorry."

"Why?" Ilya asked. "Because we are both men?"

"What?" Scott sputtered. "No! Because . . . you know what? Fuck you, Rozanov."

Ilya laughed, then stood and extended his hand to Scott. "You are a good guy, Hunter." When Scott took his hand, Ilya pulled Scott to his feet and, without really thinking about it, wrapped him in a hug. Scott let out a surprised-sounding "Oh," when his enormous body collided with Ilya's.

"Well," Shane said. "There's something I never thought I'd see."

Scott laughed and stepped out of the embrace. "Funny. I said the exact same thing when I saw you guys kissing in that video."

"I want to be friends," Ilya said simply. The truth was, he'd always had a lot of respect for Scott, and there was no reason to pretend otherwise. Being honest felt great. He'd have to tell Galina about it.

"Me too," Scott said. Then he grinned and added, "After this series ends, of course."

Ilya smiled back. "I will be busy in the semifinals after that."

"Dream on, Rozanov."

In the end, New York won the series against Ottawa four games to one, knocking Ottawa out of the playoffs. The Centaurs and their fans were disappointed, but optimistic about the team's future.

On the plane home from New York, immediately after the game, Ilya felt himself start to spiral. He was frustrated about the loss, but it was more than that. He wanted to fucking disappear. He didn't want his teammates to look at him, he didn't want to talk to anyone. He was exhausted and he couldn't remember what it felt like to not be exhausted.

It was a tiny bit devastating to learn that none of the changes he'd made in his life—therapy, winning, getting a dog, coming out to friends and teammates about his sexuality *and* his relationship with Shane, getting engaged—had fixed him. Even with so much to be happy about, he was almost hoping for the plane to crash for real this time.

No. Of course he didn't want that. He just needed to get home to his own bed, and stay there forever.

"Hey," said a voice, and Ilya turned away from the window to see Troy leaning on the empty seat between Ilya and the aisle. "Can I sit for a minute?"

"Yes. Sure."

"You sticking around Ottawa this summer? Besides the camp in Montreal, I mean?"

Ilya almost told Troy about the wedding plans, but didn't feel like sharing that right now. Instead, he said, "Usually we go to Shane's cottage. Is on a lake, maybe two hours from Ottawa."

"That sounds nice."

"What about you? Ottawa? Home to Vancouver?"

Troy wrinkled his nose. "Definitely not Vancouver. I'm going to look for a house outside Ottawa. Somewhere Chiron can run around."

Ilya raised his eyebrows. "You are going to live with Harris, then?"

Troy's cheeks pinked. "Yeah. I know it's super fucking soon, but yeah."

Ilya smiled. "Is Harris. Why wait? He is perfect for you."

"He really is." Troy's face shifted into a dreamy expression that he quickly shook off. "So anyway, if Anya needs someone to play with, me and Harris are around all summer."

God, it was nice to finally have friends who knew about Shane. "Thank you," Ilya said sincerely. "Maybe you guys could come to the cottage for a visit. It is very nice. And, like, huge."

Troy smiled. "That sounds cool."

He left shortly after, and Ilya felt a bit lighter for a few minutes. He wished he knew how to make the good feelings last.

It was nearly two in the morning by the time Ilya pulled into his driveway, but Shane was waiting right inside the front door, Anya barking happily at his feet.

"She's missed you," Shane said. "But she's surprisingly easy to take care of, y'know?"

"Because she is the best." Ilya bent to scratch her head. His hand was trembling for some reason. "I missed you too, sweet girl. I am done traveling for a long time now."

He stood to meet Shane, who was studying his face with obvious concern.

"What?" Ilya asked.

Shane opened his arms. "Come here."

Ilya's face crumpled before he was in his embrace. He sobbed against Shane's shoulder, not even knowing why. Shane held him and stroked his hair and shushed his apologies.

When he'd finished crying, Ilya felt empty and so fucking tired. Shane took him up to bed. Anya followed.

"No," Shane said firmly when Anya jumped on the bed. He pointed to her dog bed in the corner. "She kept trying to sleep with me. I think she hates me because I won't let her."

"Is good, probably," Ilya sighed. "I am too soft with her."

Shane rested a hand on Ilya's cheek. "You're soft with everyone you love."

Ilya's lips curved up. "Don't tell anyone."

They both got undressed, freshened up, and got into bed. Shane gently kissed Ilya's cheeks and forehead, and finally the corner of his mouth. "I missed you so much," he whispered.

"Yes. Me too."

They gazed at each other, a few inches apart on the bed.

"I like seeing the playoff beard again," Shane said, stroking his fingers over the thick hair that now covered the lower half of Ilya's face. "Been a while."

"Should I leave it?"

"Maybe for a bit. It's sexy."

Ilya closed his eyes and enjoyed the soothing brushes of Shane's fingertips. "Shane," he said quietly after a couple of minutes. "If we are getting married—"

"If? Of course we are."

Ilya swallowed. "You need to know, then."

"Know what?"

Ilya opened his eyes. "I am not okay."

"With what?"

"I am . . . maybe like my mother. Depressed. Sometimes. And it is not fixed. It might not be something to fix."

Shane looked surprised, but he covered it quickly. "Okay."

"You cannot blame yourself, if it . . . gets bad."

Shane propped himself up on an elbow. "Ilya. Are you saying you think about, like—"

"No. Not really. I don't know. I feel like I *could* think about it. Okay?"

Shane blinked a few times. "Okay," he whispered.

"The therapy helps, and we have talked about maybe trying some medication. And how that might be hard at first, with side effects. Is hard to find the right pills, the right amount. I need a doctor for the pills, though. I think I will talk to Terry—he is the team doctor."

"You think he'd be okay with prescribing antidepressants?" Shane asked.

"Yes. Of course."

"I think our team doctor would be weird about it."

"Then your team doctor is bad."

"Yeah," Shane sighed. "Maybe."

He stroked Ilya's hair, and Ilya's eyelids began to droop.

"I hate that you feel like that sometimes, Ilya," Shane said softly. "I hate that you have to fight yourself. But you're never going to scare me off, okay? And I'm never giving up on you, or on us. So whatever you need, I'm right here."

"What if there is nothing you can do?" Ilya asked in a small, scared voice. "What if you can't help?"

Shane's features shifted into his Hockey Captain face—determined and fearless. "Then I'll be standing by until I can."

He kissed Ilya's forehead. "I'm marrying you, Ilya. I want to have kids with you. I want to be your date when we're inducted into the Hall of Fame. I love you so much."

They kissed, and Shane said, "What do you need right now?"

"Sleep," Ilya answered honestly. "In the morning, probably coffee." He grinned impishly. "And maybe five or six blowjobs."

Shane smiled so wide his eyes crinkled. "Blowjobs aren't a cure for depression, Ilya."

"Are you a doctor now?"

Shane laughed and kissed him again. "Go to sleep, idiot."

# CHAPTER THIRTY-EIGHT

*May*

Shane turned thirty in May, with very little fanfare. He celebrated at the cottage, with his parents, Ilya, and Anya. His dad barbecued hamburgers, and Shane ate two of them, washed them down with beer, and finished it all off with a big slice of chocolate cake. He'd decided he was done with fighting the future, and with trying to be perfect. He'd been an outstanding hockey player his whole life while also eating the occasional cheeseburger, and he could keep on doing that.

He was also, he'd decided, done with being a Montreal Voyageur. J.J. had apologized for even suggesting that Shane had tripped on purpose, but none of his other teammates—or his coaches—had. The media in Montreal had been vicious to Shane, and he didn't think he could ever feel good about representing that team again.

Now, a week after Shane's birthday, he and Ilya were just waiting until July, when the free-agent season started, to see what would happen. Shane had told Farah that Ottawa was his first choice. She hadn't been surprised at all. Whether he ended up in Ottawa or somewhere else, whoever signed him would have to accept that they were signing Ilya Rozanov's husband.

They'd sent out wedding invitations. It was short notice, but it wouldn't be big and they'd hold it in Ilya's backyard in July, a week before their charity camps started. Whoever happened to be in Ottawa could come. No pressure.

At the end of the summer, they were taking a honeymoon to Spain, because neither of them had been there and because, when Shane had worked up the nerve to ask him for vacation suggestions, Scott Hunter had enthusiastically rattled off a bunch of places there that were "gay as hell." It would be another giant step outside of Shane's comfort zone, but he was ready for it.

And he knew Ilya would be effortlessly spectacular in Ibiza.

Shane found Ilya in the hammock behind the cottage, gently rocking as the sun set spectacularly over the lake. It was, Shane was pretty sure, what photographers called "the golden hour." Ilya was bathed in warm light, making his skin glow and picking out every bronze strand in his mop of curls. The playoff beard had been shaved down to his usual lazy stubble, and the ring and crucifix around his neck glinted against his bare chest. Shane wished he'd had his own phone on him so he could take a picture. No one had the right to look that perfect.

"Comfy?" Shane asked.

Ilya smiled sleepily at him. "Very."

Shane hugged himself and rubbed his bare arms. "It's getting cold, though."

"Mm." Ilya reached out his hand, and Shane took it.

"You never use this hammock," Shane said.

"Yes, well." Ilya didn't finish his sentence, and Shane supposed he didn't need to.

"I made tacos."

"Oh yes?" Ilya sat up, and then gracefully extracted himself from the hammock in a way that seemed impossible to Shane. Whenever Shane had used the hammock, he'd basically dumped himself onto the lawn, sprawled out on his belly. "Where is Anya?"

"Asleep after that epic walk." They held hands as they walked back up to the house. "Want to watch the game tonight?" The final round of the playoffs was starting that night, between New York and Colorado.

"Not really," Ilya said.

Shane smiled. "Me neither."

"Do you know what I want to do?"

"Is it filthy?"

"No. I want to make a video."

"That sounds filthy."

Ilya laughed and tugged Shane closer, bumping their shoulders together. "For Instagram. I want to post about us." He stopped walking and pulled out his phone. He tapped it a few times, then held it at arm's length in front of him.

"Oh," Shane said. "Now?"

"Yes." Then, after a second's pause, Ilya cheerfully said, "Hello! I am Ilya, and this is my boyfriend, Shane. Say hello, Shane."

"Um. Hi."

"Shane, when are we getting married?"

"July."

Ilya made an exaggerated surprised face. "July!"

Shane could see his own goofy, lovesick grin on Ilya's phone screen. They hadn't officially announced their engagement yet. "Still can't believe it, huh?"

"We are getting married. And then we are going to keep playing hockey, break more records, and win more cups. Yes, Shane?"

"Hell yes."

"See you in October, hockey fans," Ilya said. Then he kissed Shane loudly on the cheek, and ended the video.

They watched it back together, and Shane had to admit they both looked pretty good, what with the perfect golden light. Also, they looked giddy with how in love they were. "I think Crowell is really going to like that video," he said dryly.

"Fuck Crowell. I am posting it now."

Shane still felt a twist of terror at the idea of angering the commissioner, but he quickly squashed it. They weren't going to hide anymore. Not from anyone, and not for anyone. "God, I hope someone signs me."

Ilya snorted. "Of course they will."

"What if—"

"Shane," Ilya said seriously. "Do we have to drive back to your trophy room in Montreal?"

Shane blushed. "No."

"Or maybe you watch a YouTube video of your best goals while I blow you?"

Heat flooded Shane's stomach. "I mean. It wouldn't hurt to try."

# CHAPTER THIRTY-NINE

*July*

"What do you think?" Shane asked.

Ilya couldn't think. He didn't have a thought in his head because he was full to bursting with happiness. It was a week before their wedding, and Shane was standing in front of him in an Ottawa Centaurs jersey and ball cap. He knew that Shane had gone to the team offices to sign the contract today, but seeing him now, wearing the uniform, in Ilya's house, was overwhelming.

"You make that stupid logo look so good," Ilya said.

"It *is* stupid, right? It's not just me?"

"No. We all think so. Come here." Ilya wrapped him in a tight hug. "I cannot believe this. Is too much. I am too happy."

Shane laughed against him. "Me too." He pushed away. "God, I can't *wait* to play with you! I know we're both centers, but I'll bet we'll be on the power play together. This is going to be so awesome!"

"And," Ilya added, "no more hiding."

"No more hiding. Everyone I met in management was so

great. Oh! Harris was there too. It was nice to finally meet him. I guess he's getting promoted to Senior Director of . . . something. Communications?"

"Good. He deserves it."

"The owners actually booked us a table at some fancy restaurant downtown tonight."

"With them?"

"No. Just the two of us. They said it was a welcome-to-the-team thing, but also . . ." Shane's cheeks flushed. "They said it was an early wedding present. Can you believe it?"

"Yes." Ilya had known the owners—three siblings from an old money Ottawa family—for years, and they'd always been decent to him.

"I was stunned. I barely remembered to thank them."

"Maybe I should have gone with you after all." They'd decided that Shane would go alone to sign the contract, just so the press about it wasn't all about them.

It probably would be anyway.

"So, dinner tonight?"

Ilya smiled. "A date. Yes. Can you wear that jersey?"

Shane laughed. "No."

"Can I take you to bed now, then? And you wear only that jersey?"

Shane leaned in and kissed him. "Is this a hazing thing?"

"Yes. I do it to everyone."

"Shut up."

"Troy was incredible."

Shane shoved him with both hands. "You're the worst. Come ravage me."

Ilya grinned and chased him up the stairs.

Ilya ran a hand over his cheek as he examined himself in the mirror. It felt weird, being so clean-shaven, but he'd thought it would look sloppy to leave stubble on his face. He wanted to look perfect.

It was his wedding day, after all.

"Sheesh," said a voice behind him. Ilya turned and saw David standing in the door of Ilya's bedroom. "I was going to offer to help you with your tie or something, but you clearly don't need my assistance."

Ilya smiled at him, then pulled his own cuff links out. He held out the round gold and mother of pearl studs to Shane's father. "You can help me put these in."

David chuckled as he stepped forward and took the cuff links. "I appreciate you trying to make me feel useful."

"Shane doesn't need help?"

"Yuna's got him," David said, which they both understood meant Shane had all the help he needed.

Ilya held out his left wrist and David held it carefully in one hand. A surge of jumbled emotions rose in Ilya as he watched him carefully thread the cuff link through the crisp white material of Ilya's dress shirt. There was no way Ilya's father would have been there, even if he had still been alive—and Ilya wouldn't have wanted him to be—but having David here, helping him get ready, was nice. More than nice.

"We could only have one child," David said quietly. "We thought about adopting, but we decided in the end to just focus on making Shane the best person we could. I think we did an okay job of it."

Ilya smiled at the understatement.

"We couldn't be prouder of the man he's become," David continued. "I don't have any Stanley Cup rings, but I have Shane."

Ilya swallowed. "I'll take care of him."

David smiled up at him. "I know." He finished the first cuff, then took Ilya's right hand and got to work on that cuff link.

"What I'm trying to say, and Yuna's always been the better speaker, is I've always felt so lucky to have a son as wonderful as Shane that I never expected to be blessed with a second one."

David's hands, and Ilya's shirt cuff, turned blurry. Ilya blinked rapidly, refusing to cry before the wedding even started. David glanced up from his work, and Ilya could see the tears in his eyes too.

"It's not fair that you don't have your family here on your wedding day," David said, "and I'm not trying to overstep, but—"

That was all Ilya let him get out before he engulfed David in a tight hug. "My family is here," he said simply, and with surprising steadiness.

It seemed impossible that anything in Ilya's life was real; that he was about to marry *Shane Hollander*. In front of *people*. That they would be teammates next season. That Ilya was about to officially become a part of Shane's family, and that he and Shane might start their own someday. It was too staggering to think about, so instead he hugged Shane's father and tried not to cry.

After a long moment, they released each other, and David took a step back. He sniffed once, then said, "Well. You look good."

Ilya wiped hastily at his eyes. "Usually, yes."

David shuffled a bit awkwardly, probably unused to wearing his emotions so plainly, and glanced out the window. "Anya's keeping the Pike kids busy in the yard."

"Good. And thank you. For helping me with my shirt. And for . . ." Ilya couldn't possibly put into words how grateful he was for Yuna and David's support, and the easy love they had for their son, and seemingly also for him. For raising Shane to be the man that he was, and for believing Ilya was good enough for him. He finished by saying, "Everything."

David nodded. "Thank you for making Shane so happy. You're good for each other."

Ilya smiled. "Yes. It is time for the world to see how good."

"Holy shit," Shane said.

He'd pulled back the curtain in the guest room he'd gotten dressed in, and could not believe how many people were in Ilya's backyard.

*Our backyard*, he reminded himself. They lived together now.

"Are you surprised?" Yuna asked as she fussed with his boutonniere. "You're both very popular."

"I haven't felt very popular lately."

"Well, you are. Deal with it." She stood back and gasped. "You're so handsome!"

"Yeah? I look okay?" Shane turned to examine himself in the mirror. He was wearing a light gray suit, not a tux, with a pale blue tie, and he was sweating already. He'd gotten his hair trimmed, but it was still fairly long, and he was wearing it down.

"You look like Kit Harington," Mom assured him. "If Kit couldn't grow a beard."

Shane huffed. "Thanks, Mom. Is Dad helping Ilya get ready?"

"Yes, but you know that's just an excuse for the two of them to hang out."

Shane smiled at that. He wished Ilya could have had family here today, but he was glad he'd grown so close to Shane's own father.

"Well," Mom said, beaming at him, "we should probably get down there. Do you have the ring?"

Shane patted his pocket. "Yep."

"And your ringer is turned off?"

"I'm leaving the phone in the house. But yes."

Mom peeked out the window again. "Oh! Ilya's out there."

Shane tried to go to the window, but Yuna stopped him. "You'll see him at the ceremony! It's bad luck to see him before then."

"Mom. I saw him this morning. We woke up together, had breakfast." He left out the third thing they'd done.

"Just indulge me. My only child is getting married! I'm allowed to be nuts."

Shane smiled and hugged her a bit awkwardly because they were both trying to avoid crushing the flowers that were pinned to their chests. "You are seriously the best mom in the world."

"Well," she said, with a slight tremble in her voice. "You made it easy."

They walked downstairs together, then through the living room that was, as of a few weeks ago, full of framed photos of Ilya and Shane together. Shane still felt the urge to hide them in drawers, but he loved seeing them. Loved knowing there was nothing to hide anymore.

When he stepped through the back door, he was stunned all over again by the crowd. There had to be close to a hundred people crammed on the lawn between the house and the river.

He spotted Hayden and Jackie and their kids. Farah and her husband were chatting with Leah and Max. Wyatt Hayes and his wife were laughing with Ryan and Fabian. Troy and Harris were talking to Ilya's coach—Shane's coach now—and a woman who was probably Coach Wiebe's wife. Rose waved to Shane from across the lawn where she was talking to Ilya's friend Svetlana, who Shane had met for the first time yesterday when the three of them had lunch together. There was a small cluster of Centaurs players who were surreptitiously staring at Rose. There were, in fact, a *lot* of Centaurs players.

The only Montreal player there, besides Hayden, was J.J., and Shane felt a little choked up just seeing him. Their friendship was back on solid ground, but it still meant a lot to Shane for J.J. to be here.

Then, Shane found Ilya in the crowd, talking to Zane Boodram. He looked incredible, of course, in his burgundy suit. Anya was at his feet, freshly groomed and wearing a burgundy bow on her head.

Shane wasn't sure if he was allowed to approach Ilya. This whole thing was very loose; there weren't even chairs.

Ilya turned, and their gazes met. Ilya gave him one of his easy, sexy smiles, and Shane felt like his body was turning to stone.

*We're getting married.*

There was a gentle tap on his elbow, and he turned to see the justice of the peace they'd hired to perform the ceremony. "Ready?" she asked with a warm smile.

Shane glanced at Ilya again and mouthed, *Now?*

Ilya nodded.

Shane exhaled. "Yeah. Ready."

"Do you have the ring?" Shane whispered as they stood across from each other, in front of everyone.

Ilya barely stopped himself from rolling his eyes. "Why? Is it important?"

Shane glowered at him, and the justice of the peace—Nancy—got things started.

She said a bunch of words that were probably very nice, but Ilya was only focused on Shane. He looked so handsome and so happy. It was hard to believe this was the same person Ilya had tried to ignore in a Saskatchewan arena parking lot thirteen years ago.

Except the freckles were the same. The dark, intelligent eyes and long black lashes. The adorable little nose, and the soft, enticing lips. Those were all the same.

The way Ilya's heart went fucking bananas when he looked at him was the same.

"Ilya?" Nancy said gently.

"Hm? Sorry." He heard laughter all around him, and he smiled sheepishly.

"You can take out the ring now."

Right. Yes. Wedding.

He removed the ring from his coat pocket and waited for instruction. They didn't write their own vows because, well, neither of them was particularly eloquent.

"Please repeat after me," Nancy said. "I call upon these persons here present . . ."

Ilya repeated the words, somewhat clumsily. Was his accent worse than usual? He sounded ridiculous.

"To witness that I, Ilya Rozanov . . ."

Oh, good. She remembered not to use their middle names. Ilya didn't want any part of his father here today. He repeated the words.

"Do take you, Shane Hollander, to be my lawful wedded husband."

Okay, maybe they should have written their own vows. These were bleak. Completely stiff and devoid of emotion. Who would ever feel anything from these bland vows?

Ilya's voice cracked before he even got to Shane's name. Which made Shane's whole face scrunch up in an effort, Ilya guessed, to keep himself from crying.

"I'm sorry," Ilya whispered.

Shane just shook his head, lips tight. With some effort, he got through his turn to repeat the vows. Then Nancy gave them some more words to say as they exchanged rings.

"With this ring, I shall love, honor, and cherish you. And this ring is the symbol of my love," Shane said.

"Gross," Ilya muttered, which made Shane snort and start laughing. Which made everybody else laugh.

Shane slipped the newly resized ring onto Ilya's finger, and Ilya smiled goofily at him.

Nancy said some dull stuff that ended with "do hereby pronounce you, Shane and Ilya, to be married. You may celebrate your marriage with a kiss."

Oh hell yes. Ilya grabbed Shane, dipped him, and planted one on him. Everyone cheered.

Shane looked dazed after the kiss, but Ilya held their joined hands in the air and said, "We are married!"

Ilya had no idea where they were supposed to go now. There wasn't an aisle or anything, and this was their house.

"Um," Nancy said quietly, "you still have to sign some paperwork."

"Oh, right," Shane said. "Inside, then?"

"Yes," Ilya agreed. At least now they had a destination. To the crowd he said, "We have to sign some things, but we will be back to party!"

More cheering. Evan Dykstra called out, "You need a DJ?"

Ilya pointed to him. "No."

They walked quickly toward the house, hands held tight, as their friends cheered all around them.

"This was not the real wedding," Ilya assured Ruby as they both enjoyed some cake. "The real one was the one you did. This was just for show."

Ruby smiled at him, then nudged her sister Jade. "I *told* you."

Evening was closing in, and someone had turned on the strings of lights that Yuna had insisted on draping in rows across the backyard. It looked very nice. Magical.

Ilya's neighbor's kids, Willa and Andrew, approached and pulled Ruby and Jade away to play some game that seemed to involve a lot of running.

"So," said a voice behind Ilya. He glanced up from where he was sitting on the grass and saw Hayden. "You stole my best friend."

"Yes. But you outed us in a FanMail video, so maybe we are even."

"Look, I'm really fucking sorry about that. I—"

Ilya laughed, and stood up. "I am kidding."

"Oh. Well, I'm happy for you guys," Hayden said glumly. "And I get why Shane left Montreal. But I'm going to miss having him around."

"You should sign with Ottawa. Your contract is probably cheap, yes?"

Hayden shook his head. "You're a hard guy to like, Rozanov."

"That is not what Shane thinks."

"What doesn't Shane think?" asked Shane, sneaking up behind Ilya.

"Nothing," Ilya said, smiling like the love-struck fool he was at his brand-new husband.

"So . . ." Shane said nervously. "Mom has it in her head that we need to, like, dance. In front of everyone."

"Oh?"

"Honestly, I hadn't even thought about it, but I guess that's a wedding thing, right?"

Hayden looked gobsmacked. "Yeah, it's a fucking wedding thing, you moron. Did you guys not even pick a song?"

"Shane does not know any songs," Ilya said.

Shane was apparently too nervous to acknowledge Ilya's quip. "So, like, do we just get whoever is in charge of the music to play a song and we, like, slow dance in the middle of the lawn? I don't really know how to dance."

"Come on," Ilya said, and extended his hand.

It turned out that Harris had taken over the music duties and had his phone connected to Ilya's wireless speakers, which someone had brought outside.

"Harris," Ilya called from the middle of the yard. "Play something romantic."

"You're letting *me* choose?" Harris sounded terrified.

"Just put on whatever. Is fine." Ilya glanced at Shane's anxious face. "Something short."

Ilya held out his hand to Shane.

"Oh, are *you* leading?" Shane asked.

"Yes. Because you can't dance."

Shane huffed and took his hand, then placed his other hand on Ilya's back as the opening vocals of Rihanna's "Diamonds" started playing.

"This sounds like a weird choice," Shane said.

"No," Ilya said softly. "Is perfect."

They danced—well, rotated—under the lights and surrounded by everyone they loved as Rihanna sang lyrics that, secretly, had always made Ilya think of Shane.

"Oh," Shane said, halfway through the song. "I've heard this before."

Ilya laughed. "I love you so much it sucks."

Shane beamed at him. "That's too bad, because this is as good as it's going to get."

"No," Ilya said fondly. "I don't think it is."

# EPILOGUE

*October*

"You know," Shane said. "The last time I was at an Ottawa Centaurs home opener, I was twelve years old."

Ilya smiled at him. He hadn't been able to stop smiling since he'd woken up that morning, and Shane had been just as giddy. They'd kissed each other awake, then took Anya for a jog. They made a big breakfast together and ate it on the back deck because it had been a beautiful, sunny day. Shane had reminded Ilya to take his pill with breakfast—unnecessary, because Ilya had an alert set on his phone to remind him, but still very sweet. They'd had lunch with David and Yuna because Shane had insisted that was an important opening night ritual.

They'd driven together to the arena, stopping at the end of Willa and Andrew's driveway to get a pep talk and to read their sign. This time it had said *Shane Hollander + Ilya Rozanov* = and then what had looked like a crude drawing of the Stanley Cup.

It had been a perfect day. Ilya was looking forward to ten more years of them.

"You look good," Ilya said now. "Even with that stupid logo."

Shane glanced down at his jersey. "It's growing on me."

"Liar."

"Stop flirting and get in order," Bood said with a smile. "Shane, you're supposed to be way up there, between Luca and Tanner."

"Yes," Ilya said solemnly. "The back of the line is for *captains*."

Shane glanced again at his own jersey, this time to the empty space on his left chest. "Right. Not used to not having that C."

"Get used to it," Ilya said, tapping his own C. "This stays right here."

Shane gave him a mocking salute, then made his way up the line.

"Fucking prima donna," Bood teased.

"Who the fuck does he think he is, right?"

"He's coming for that C."

Ilya smiled. "I know."

He heard Shane's name being called, then the roar of a packed house cheering for the hometown superstar they could finally claim as their own.

"Shit. He's already more popular than us," Bood said.

"More popular than *you*, maybe."

A few minutes later, Ilya rocketed out onto the ice and completed the circle at center ice. Shane stood directly across from him, smiling wide. Ilya smiled back.

"Time to finally get one of those banners, I think," Bood said over the cheering and the pounding music. "For real this time."

They absolutely would. Ilya had never been so sure of anything.

"Let's fucking get it."

*Don't miss the highly anticipated seventh book in* New York Times *bestselling author Rachel Reid's Game Changers series—*Unrivaled*!*

# RELATIONSHIP TIMELINE

**2008**

Shane and Ilya face-off for the first time, knowing they've finally met their match

**2009**

Shane goes to Montreal, Ilya to Boston, and their story starts here

> Will you disappoint them, **Hollander**?
>
> – ILYA ROZANOV

**2010**

Shane and Ilya's rookie season makes headlines, leading to sparks both on and off the ice & What happens in the locker room, stays in the locker room ☺

**2011**

The year Shane and Ilya became Jane and Lily

**2013**

Rookie season may be over, but Shane and Ilya aren't

> They hadn't even **kissed**
>
> – SHANE HOLLANDER

**2014**

Ilya brings home the Stanley Cup, and wins something else too

**2016**

Ilya's feelings bubble up like ginger ale and Shane melts into Rose Landry

**2017**

Yuna gives her stamp of approval

> Stupid Canadian **wolf bird**
>
> – ILYA ROZANOV

**2019**

Ilya and Shane commit to each other, even in secret

**2020**

Ruby and Jade's wedding dress rehearsal

**2021**

Hayden!!! (oh no) & Shane and Ilya finally shining bright like diamonds

# ACKNOWLEDGMENTS

Huge thanks to everyone who read, reviewed, and recommended *Heated Rivalry*. I am overwhelmed by how much love the book received, and I really appreciate it.

Thank you to everyone who wrote to me to let me know you loved Ilya and Shane. To everyone who made fan art. To everyone who noticed tiny details in the book that I didn't expect anyone to notice and completely made my day. To everyone in my hockey-watching Discord group, and everyone in my author support groups. To the Russian speakers who helped me with Russian phrasing. To my agent, Deidre Knight, who made this sequel happen. To everyone at Carina Press for always being so easy to work with. To my amazing editor, Mackenzie Walton, for making this book better.

And finally to my husband, Matt, and my kids, Mitchell and Trevor, who could not be more supportive and I really appreciate their patience.